MW00575758

4

Control

Manna Francis

CASPERIAN
BOOKS

The author wishes to dedicate this book to her cats, and cats everywhere, for being so self-ish and beautiful, and giving so much pleasure.

CONTROL. Copyright © 2009 by Manna Francis. All rights reserved. No part of this book may be used or reproduced in any manner whatsoever without written permission except in the case of brief quotations embodied in critical articles or reviews. For information, ad-dress Casperian Books, PO Box 161026, Sacramento, CA 95816-1026.

www.casperianbooks.com

Back cover image by Orit "Shin" Heifets
Front cover image by Ceredwyn Ealanta (www.gothbunny.net)

ISBN-10: 1-934081-11-6
ISBN-13: 978-1-934081-11-2

Table of Contents

Control 5
Wait for It..92
Caged..114
Unaccustomed As I Am 125
Helen...129
Shopping, No Fucking 141
Losing It..146
Coming from America 166

Control

Chapter One

❖

Sara stared at the cracks in the ceiling and tried to stay awake. Even though the pain medication made her drowsy, she didn't want to sleep. First thing in the morning she'd had the most horrible nightmare. She'd woken up and then thrown up, and then, fortunately not long afterwards, her mother had arrived and stayed until lunchtime. Calming her mother down had helped keep her calm.

Now she was on her own again, for the afternoon. Not for very long. There would be friends arriving once work was over. Her sister was coming for the evening. All she had to do was stay awake and think about something else and she'd be fine.

Someone knocked at the door. "Come in," she said.

She expected another medic, wanting to ask her another lot of questions. To her surprise, it was Toreth, only partially visible behind an enormous bunch of white flowers. He stopped inside the doorway and stared at her, clearly appalled. "Sara? Jesus fucking Christ. You look like you've been answering questions over at Justice."

"Great. Thanks for that." She edged up on the pillows and tried to smile without stretching her lips. "It looks worse than it is, honest. I'm only in bed because I was knocked out for a while; I'm not supposed to go wandering around unsupervised, in case I fall over and sue the hospital."

He came over and put the flowers down on the bed. Getting a closer look at them, she couldn't help laughing, even though it hurt her ribs. "They're lilies."

"What?"

"The flowers." She stroked the thick, velvety petals. "Lilies are for funerals." Maybe it wasn't so funny, at that.

"Are they? Damn." He grinned, looking almost sheepish. "Sorry."

"It doesn't matter—they're lovely. I'll get someone to put them in some water. It's really nice of you to come," she added as she rang for a nurse.

He shrugged. "There's the safety meeting this afternoon, which is going to win

7

awards for boredom. And since my admin didn't turn up for work and her desk is a mess, I couldn't find the crap for it, anyway."

Her desk was nothing of the kind, and besides, she'd transferred the files to him yesterday. Only yesterday. "Memo me."

"I'll let you off."

He sat down by the bed, looking her over more assessingly. She'd explained most of it to him that morning when she'd called work, and she felt relieved that she wouldn't have to go through it all again. That was the bad thing about visitors, medical or otherwise.

"What happened to your hand?" he asked when the nurse had come and gone.

He had an unerring eye for the worst injuries. She looked down at the bandaging, feeling strangely reluctant to tell him. "It's fine. It's, well...he gave me a ring. I don't know if you noticed it? Antique. Nice. It belonged to his grandmother or something. Or that's what he told me." As she continued talking, the words came more easily. "He said that while I was wearing it, I was his. Yeah, I know, how moronic was I to think that was sweet. Possessive fucking maniac. That's what set him off. Said he'd seen me looking at someone else. I told him he didn't own me and he could stick his money if he thought he could buy me."

She rubbed her temple, wincing as she caught a bruise. "Christ, I must have had my brain switched off." Out of the corner of her eye, she noticed Toreth fidgeting slightly in his chair. Really, she knew better than to expect him to sit patiently through too much of this kind of stuff. But it was an unexpected relief to say it all to someone who would sit and almost listen, and not get hysterical or feel obliged to comment. "Anyway. When he stopped...before he left, he took it back. The ring. Only it was rather a tight fit and some bits of my finger went with it. They're doing something to it tomorrow. An operation. But don't worry, it's fine, honestly." Anger bubbled up suddenly—anger with herself for saying that, because it wasn't fine at all, none of it was. "I'm sorry," she said, as she started to cry.

He handed tissues over from the box by the bed and waited until she was done, silent and wonderfully unembarrassed.

"Stupid. I was so stupid," she said eventually, staring at the crumpled tissues in her hand. "I should've seen it. Bastard didn't like him."

Toreth sighed. "Sara, that fucking cat hates everyone in the world except you."

"And Daedra told me what he was like. I thought she was just being a bit off because when I met him at first he was still with her sister. He seemed so...it's all my own stupid bloody fault. I was an idiot. I—"

"Did you call Justice?" he asked, interrupting.

"No." She sniffed, and sighed. "I thought about it. Mum wanted me to. But there's no point. His dad's some important corporate. Lots of friends, lots of money. They'd investigate and there'd be no case. You know how it works."

He nodded. "Who is he?"

She hesitated, understanding what he was offering with the question. Asking her permission, maybe, because it would be dangerous, and it might only make things worse. Maybe she shouldn't...

Then the memory of her terror came back, very nearly sharp enough to make her sick again. The bruises didn't matter. It was the helplessness—nothing she could have done then, and nothing she could do now. The sound of him laughing at her as she slid into unconsciousness, her last clear thought being the certainty that he would kill her before she came around. Laughing because he knew no one could touch him. Because his money *could* buy her, one way or another. Because if he wanted to hurt her again, there was nothing she could do to stop it.

"Jonny. Jon Kemp. He's a student. I don't know where he lives." She cursed her stupidity again, silently, because she should have known. Normal, safe people didn't hide things like that. "Daedra might know."

He nodded again. "He hit you?"

What the hell did he *think* had happened? "I didn't walk into a door twenty times."

"No," he said levelly. "I mean, that's all he did?"

"Oh." She swallowed down the rising nausea. "Yes. Nothing else."

"Right." He stood up. "I have to get back to work. I'll see you tomorrow."

Warrick was on his way out of his office when reception called to say that Toreth wanted to see him. He checked his watch, sighed, and told them to send him up. He sat on the edge of the desk, tapping his fingers impatiently, until the door opened.

"You're lucky you caught me. I've got a meeting with—" The sentence died out as he registered Toreth's expression. "Grim" didn't do it justice. "What's wrong?"

"Nothing." Toreth closed the door. "Except that I need you to do me a favor, and not ask me what it's about." Anger, but not directed at him. It was focused elsewhere and under tight control.

Warrick considered briefly. He had the feeling that if he asked, Toreth would tell him. On balance, though, he decided that Toreth deserved at least that much trust from him. "All right, I'll do my best. No guarantees."

"I need an address for a Jon Kemp. He's a student at the university, probably history or art, possibly lives somewhere in the new development north of campus. Rich corporate father."

A trivial question, if it hadn't been for his tone of voice. "You can't find this out at I&I because...?"

Toreth frowned, but answered anyway. "Because then there'll be a record of

9

the inquiry and I don't want to be connected to him. And, if you can, I'd like to know if there's any internal video security wherever he lives, and if he lives alone."

Warrick felt his eyebrows go up before he could keep the surprise from showing. Toreth started to say something, but he cut him off. "Give me ten minutes."

Toreth stood behind him, humming tunelessly and irritatingly, while he ran the searches. Warrick didn't think it was worth asking him to shut up. "There you go," he said eventually. "Small house on the edge of the development. Do you want me to write the address down?"

"I'll remember it."

"No other occupants listed, for what that's worth. And according to the insurance details, there's no video inside. Odd, considering how expensive it is."

"Probably doesn't want Daddy finding out the kind of thing he gets up to." Flat and cold.

Curiosity kicked in again, but he'd said he wouldn't ask, so he wouldn't. "Anything else?"

"No. And you—"

"Never looked at the files. Never even heard the name."

"Right." He paused in the doorway on the way out. "I might not come round tonight, after all. It depends. But I'd like to be there, if it's possible."

Warrick nodded, understanding the oblique request. "No problem. Thanks for letting me know."

Even though he was late, Warrick stayed at his desk for a minute, looking at the closed door and wondering. It would be nice to know what Toreth was up to, beyond the obvious conclusion of it being illegal and very likely dangerous. Then he carefully erased the records of his inquiries and went off to his meeting.

As dusk fell, a patch of rather prickly bushes provided Toreth with an uncomfortable changing room on the northern edge of the university campus. The under-the-counter Justice uniform had cost him a large favor at the I&I stores. He'd added a pair of thin leather gloves to the outfit. They weren't a normal part of the uniform, but they wouldn't be too conspicuous. He folded his own clothes into the bag he'd brought the uniform in and hid it under a pile of leaves. It should be safe enough until he got back—this shouldn't take long.

The pleasant and obviously expensive development was within easy walking distance of the university, but still nicely insulated from the less salubrious areas where most students lived. Tall terraced houses, some split into flats, surrounded courtyards with areas of well-tended grass and even parking spaces for private vehicles; just the right sort of place to look for a spoiled corporate brat who thought he could get away with a little assault and battery.

A spoiled corporate brat who'd find out that he'd picked the wrong fucking woman this time.

He activated the comm at the address provided by Warrick, and offered a highly unofficial Justice ID to be scanned and authenticated. The first risk was that Jonny would tell him to come back tomorrow, when he would have a lawyer ready for him. Toreth hoped he was too arrogant to be frightened by some Justice nobody. He wouldn't want his father to hear what he'd been doing if he could help it. Not good for the corporate image, even if they would be able to bury it.

Now it all depended on whether Jonny was alone. To Toreth's relief, it was Jonny who appeared on the screen. Or at least the man matched Daedra's description of wavy dark hair, olive complexion, and dark, long-lashed eyes. Attractive, Toreth would have said under other circumstances. If he answered his own door, that was promising. Keeping his face in shadow, Toreth said, "Officer Pat Vardon, Justice Department. I'd like to speak to Jon Kemp, please."

"Come in, Officer," Jonny said, and unlocked the door. The fine edge of contempt he gave the title made Toreth grit his teeth.

Once inside, Toreth closed the door, slid home the security chain, and waited in the hall until Jonny appeared on the stairs. "This way, Officer."

On the way upstairs, Toreth assessed his target. Tall, well built. He made a couple of modifications to the plan, but he still felt confident he could handle him without too much trouble. Jonny led him into a living room—small but expensively furnished, Toreth noted on an automatic sweep—and still they'd met no one and heard no sounds from elsewhere in the house.

"What can I do for you?" Jonny asked, without offering him a seat.

"A complaint of assault has been made by a young woman, sir, against your good self," Toreth said in his best Justice Department manner.

"Oh?" Not fear. Not guilt. Just insolent questioning and something very close to amusement. Jonny rubbed the back of his right hand absently, and Toreth could see the bruises on his knuckles, faint but unmistakable. He decided not to bother with the rest of the questions, except for the important one.

"Are you alone in the house at the moment?" Toreth asked.

Surprise slid into suspicion on Jonny's face even as he said, "Yes. Why?"

On that, Toreth moved, quickly and confidently. After a struggle almost too brief to qualify as one, Toreth held him pinned easily against a wall. They were much the same height and weight, but training and technique won out, just as he'd expected they would.

"This is your lucky day," Toreth said conversationally, as Jonny swore and twisted futilely. "You hurt a friend of mine. So I'm going to hurt you. But because I asked her a question and she said 'yes,' I'm not going to kill you. Do you feel lucky yet?"

He didn't seem to.

Once Jonny had tired himself out somewhat with fighting, Toreth hit him—not hard, but strategically. Then he let him drop, so that he landed heavily, sobbing for breath. Toreth smiled at the sound. "Oh, we're only just getting started."

Jonny began swearing at him again, weakly. Toreth switched it off. It didn't matter, any more than it mattered when prisoners did it at work, except as a measure of how much progress he was making. He gave himself five minutes. Long enough to do what he wanted to, not so long that someone was likely to come along and interrupt them. From hereon in, the plan was simple—maximum pain and minimum damage. No marks at all, ideally.

As time went by and the swearing faded out into breathless whimpers, he had to expend less effort in keeping physical control, and so could devote more concentration to stretching the limits of nonbruising violence. Striking with impersonal efficiency, he found the old lessons coming back easily. Drugs and direct nerve induction were better tools, but the physical contact had a certain satisfaction. Especially here. Especially with this cowardly fuck who'd hurt Sara. He felt his temper slipping, caught it, and carried on.

Finally, he checked his watch. Time up. He moved back, leaving Jonny crumpled on the floor by the wall, and gave him a few minutes to recover.

"Get up."

Unsurprisingly, there was no response, so Toreth pulled him to his feet and slammed him against the wall, then took a couple of steps back. Jonny stayed leaning on the wall, wiping tears of pain from his cheeks. When the bastard was breathing more easily, Toreth said, "I want the ring."

He looked up, caught a breath. "What?"

"You heard me. You took a ring back from my friend. I want it."

Jonny shook his head, dazed and sullen. "It was—it was my great-grandmother's engagement ring."

As if it made any fucking difference. "She'd be proud of you. Get it." Toreth took a step towards him. *"Get it."*

"All *right*." A more pleasing edge of panic. "It's in there."

"Well, go on."

Jonny tried to stand up straighter and stopped, still leaning heavily against the wall. "I can't," he whined. "Please. It's on the dressing table."

Toreth weighed the situation up, deciding not to take the risk. If he left Jonny alone, he'd take the chance to call for help if he could. Rich corporate kids were trained what to do in situations like this—he'd even trained a few himself. He grabbed Jonny's arm, and hauled him upright despite his anguished protest. "My heart bleeds. Move."

Once in the bedroom, the box was easy to spot. Toreth opened it and checked the contents, keeping one eye on the other man. Empty. He'd been half expecting that. "One last fucking chance, or I take the rest of the debt out of you."

12

Jonny hesitated for a couple of seconds, some of his former manner creeping back already and sorely testing Toreth's resolve over his time limit. "It's in the drawer," he said reluctantly.

Remembering his training, obviously: cooperate and keep calm. Pity. "Then you'd better open it slowly and not do anything I don't like the look of. No, don't put your hand inside. Good. Now step away. Sit down on the bed."

There was only one likely box, and Toreth took it and checked the contents. Finally. He closed the drawer. "I'm leaving, now." It was an anticlimax, unexpectedly dissatisfying, because Jonny was still sitting, watching him with a competing mixture of fear and hatred. Not unconscious and bleeding. He wasn't going to come around alone in a dark flat and have to crawl across the floor to call for help because some pathetic, obsessive, jealous—

Stick to the plan, he told himself firmly.

"You're thinking about the comm. Before you call anyone, you might want to see if there's any significant evidence that I laid a finger on you. And then you might also want to think what you'll say about *why* I was here. Talk, and what you did to my friend comes out, too. Even at Justice we'll have to do something about her complaint then."

That should have been it but, as he started to walk away, Jonny struggled to his feet, took a couple of steps across the room towards him, and found his tongue again. "Don't think you're going to get away with this."

Toreth stopped dead, turned back slowly. "What the hell did you say?" he asked quietly.

"You won't get away with it. Don't you know who my father is?" All anger now, and barely shaken arrogance. "I'm going to have you crucified. You and your stupid whore. She was *mine* and—"

Rage and reflexes took over. Seven steps to close the distance, a couple of seconds to brush his resistance aside, and then Toreth had him down on the bed, knee on his chest and left hand around his throat.

He had a moment of clarity to savor the utter shock in Jonny's eyes, although it was only a moment. Then plans and time frames and subtlety all flashed over into white-hot fury, and he hit Jonny and kept on hitting. Not with a great deal of strategy this time, but with significantly more enjoyment. The crunch of knuckles against flesh and bone jarred through him, hot as fucking, and even the dimly felt pain in his knuckles only fed back into the rage. It wasn't until he finally registered that all resistance to his assault had ceased that the haze cleared and he could make himself stop.

Panting, he assessed the results. Jonny lay on the bed, barely conscious and bleeding enough to satisfy any comparisons, a halo of blood spatters around his head speckling the pale duvet. So much for the "no marks" resolution, but the injuries seemed to be mostly cosmetic. That was something, at least.

13

Fuck.

Fuck Jonny for being so stupid, and fuck himself for losing control. He knew better and he'd been trained better. He took a few deep breaths. Damage limitation was needed, and quickly, or he would be seriously screwed. Stay in charge; make it look planned.

Jonny moaned and coughed, saving Toreth the trouble of slapping him back to full consciousness. He waited until his eyes opened and focused on him. Then he dug his fingers into Jonny's throat again and the man gulped desperately for air, gagging on the blood trickling into his throat from his broken nose.

Toreth leaned down and put every ounce of menace he could summon into his voice. "Listen to me very, *very* carefully. If you tell *anyone* what happened here, I'll fucking kill you. You can run and hide wherever the hell you like; it won't make any fucking difference. Say one word, and I'll know about it. And then I'll find you." He shook Jonny for emphasis. "*This* was just a taster. One word, to anyone, and by the time I'm finished with you, you'll be begging me to let you die. Is that one hundred fucking percent clear? Well? *Well?*"

Deeply satisfying as the expression of absolute terror was, Toreth realized that if he wanted an answer he would have to loosen his hold enough to let Jonny speak.

"Yes," he croaked.

"Good. You'll keep your mouth shut, and you'll stay the fuck away from my friend. If you even fucking *look* at her, I'll be back. She's nothing to do with you. You don't own her. You never did. *Understand?*"

Without his noticing, his grip had tightened again. Jonny nodded wordlessly, struggling for breath. "Are you sure?" Toreth forced his fingers to relax. "You don't look very sure to me. I'd hate you to forget this in the morning."

"No... no. Yes. I'm sure. Please."

The little shit was crying properly now, which went a tiny way towards making up for having to watch Sara do the same thing at the hospital. Toreth held him down for a while longer, as he sniveled and choked out pleas and promises. A shame Sara wasn't here to watch. Finally, he let go and stood up. "Anything else you wanted to say before I go?"

Jonny shook his head minutely, frozen in place on the bed. Toreth knew the look well: not daring to believe it could really be over, that he might live.

"Good plan." He paused in the doorway, checked that the ring was still in his pocket, and smiled with no humor whatsoever. "Don't forget, now."

He let himself out of the house without hearing any movement from the bedroom, and walked out of the development without meeting anyone. Still miraculously unobserved, he made it back to where he'd left his clothes and changed. The gloves were ruined, and he'd have to get the uniform cleaned before he returned it.

Standing in the pleasantly cool night air, he considered what to do next. It had

14

been a stupid lapse of self-control but, despite fucking up his original plan, he felt reasonably sure that Jonny wouldn't report this to Justice, or anyone else who mattered. There was more than an outside chance, though, that word of the too-visible damage would get back to his father anyway. Unfortunately, there was nothing he could do about that now. Time enough to worry when, or if, it happened.

Even though it was a long way to his flat, he wouldn't risk catching a taxi from near here, not now. Warrick's place was much closer. His right hand had begun to hurt like fucking hell, so he picked up his bag left-handed and started across the campus.

Warrick changed his dinner plans and casseroled something that would keep in the oven until needed. Then he filled an hour or so creating the alibi Toreth had obliquely asked him for, making up edits for the building entrance and flat surveillance records, which would prove to the absolute satisfaction of anyone who might be curious that Toreth had been there all evening. Once prepared, they would only take a few minutes to finish and install in the building's security system.

After that, he spent ten minutes on unnecessary tidying around the flat, until he began to annoy himself and instead went back into the office to do some work. That was the wonderful thing about coding; it could take his mind off anything. It absorbed him sufficiently that he didn't really feel the time pass. Even so, he hit the button to open the door to the building before Toreth had time to take his finger off the comm.

He let Toreth into the flat and closed the door without comment.

"Have you got any ice?" Toreth asked. He didn't look in a significantly better frame of mind than he had at SimTech.

"What do you—" Then Warrick caught sight of his hand. No cuts he could see, but badly bruised and starting to swell. "Come into the kitchen."

Toreth helped himself to a drink while Warrick crushed ice cubes and wrapped them in a plastic bag. Then he handed the ice pack over and dropped a couple of whole cubes into Toreth's drink.

"Are you hungry?" He tried to sound unconcerned, keeping his impatience to know what had happened out of his voice.

"No." Toreth pressed the ice onto his hand and hissed through his teeth. "Fuck, that smarts."

"Would you like painkillers to go with your alcohol?"

"Yes."

"I'll see what I've got."

All he had were standard over-the-counter tablets, but Toreth accepted them and professed gratitude. Warrick sat in silence and watched him drinking and slowly unwinding from whatever it was that he'd done. In an abstract sense, he was aware that seeing Toreth like this should probably scare him, or at least worry him. Dilly would've had fifteen kinds of fits. He wasn't frightened, though, and all the worry he had was for the man in front of him. He must remember to find out the times for the security tape.

Eventually, Toreth spoke, startling him. "I trashed your gloves. The ones you gave me for the New Year before last. Sorry."

"It doesn't matter." Doing what to whom? "It'll give me something to buy for your birthday. You're a hard man to choose presents for."

Toreth didn't smile. "I don't think I said thanks for the information."

"Any time."

Toreth nodded. Then after a short silence he cleared his throat and said, "Warrick?"

"Mm?"

He swirled the watery remains of his drink and then drained the glass. "Warrick, I wouldn't...that is, I'd never..."

Warrick couldn't remember ever hearing him sound so uncertain. "You'd never what?" he prompted after a while.

"I—" Toreth shook his head. "Nothing. It's not important." Putting down his glass, he looked across the table, focusing on him at last. "Did you say something about food?"

Warrick smiled, relieved. "Yes, I did."

He'd ask about it later. Or tomorrow. Or maybe not at all.

Sara was trying to eat a breakfast of unappetizing hospital porridge when Toreth called in to see her on his way in to work. She hadn't slept very well, not entirely because of the bruises, and she'd been hoping he'd come.

"You look much better," he said, closing the door behind him.

"Liar." She noticed he had an elastic bandage covering his right hand.

He followed her gaze. "Sprained it at the gym." Sitting down by the bed, he offered her a small box. "Souvenir."

She took it, opened it, and when she saw what was inside she dropped the box on the bed as if it had burned her. The ring fell out and Toreth caught it as it slid towards the floor.

"I don't want it," she said, sickness tightening her throat again.

"Then smash it. Or throw it down a drain. Or sell it and go on holiday. Up to you." He held it out again, and she took it reluctantly.

"I think I'm going off antique jewelry," she said, trying to keep her voice steady. "New only, from now on." She turned the ring over in her hand. "He gave it to Daedra's sister as well, you know. Daedra told me when she came round yesterday after work. She said you, er, hadn't spoken to her."

"She wasn't very helpful," he agreed.

"Mmm. He must have been royally pissed off when he lost it."

"Royally," he said with great satisfaction.

It probably wasn't a good idea to talk about it too much, here, but she had to ask. "Was he ... sorry?"

"Oh, yes. Yes, he was. Very, *very* fucking sorry."

"*Good.*" She'd worried during the long night that this thing he'd done for her might not make her feel any better after all. But it had. "Thanks," she added after a moment.

"Nothing to thank me for," he said, then stood up. "I've got to get to work. I'll be back later. I'll bring you some transcripts to keep you busy."

She heard him whistling as he went off down the corridor and smiled, ignoring the twinge in her lip. Christ, he really couldn't carry a tune in a bucket.

Sara lay back and closed her eyes, the ring still in her hand. She'd smash it, probably, although it seemed a waste. She wouldn't like to own anything she bought with money from it. Maybe she could sell it, though, if she blew the money on something silly. She hadn't held a really good party for a while, with fizzy wine and decent bought-in stuff for nibbles.

She'd think of an excuse. The cat's birthday would do. She could invite all her work friends, and people from her building, and her sister and the childhood friends they still kept in touch with, and the assorted other acquaintances such as Cele, Warrick, and Dillian. The flat was far too small, but maybe she could talk her neighbor into opening the connecting door again and letting it spill through. She'd paid him for the damage from the last time.

She was still planning when she fell asleep.

Chapter Two

❖

As the sun began to edge into the room, Warrick looked out of his living room window, searching the street below. Plenty of strolling Saturday-afternoon pedestrians, but not the one he wanted to see. Toreth was late. As an event, it rated in improbability somewhere around night following day and water flowing downhill. It wasn't even as if he was so consistently late that it was easy to plan around him. Anywhere between five minutes and an hour was perfectly likely. Occasionally, he was even early. That usually meant he wanted to fuck, though, and then they would be late, anyway. To his annoyance, he caught himself smiling, spoiling the bad mood he'd rather been enjoying. Pity Toreth hadn't been early today.

For peace of mind, if they were required to be anywhere on time, Warrick had taken to giving himself fifteen minutes lead on the real time they needed to leave by, and then simply leaving without him if necessary. He was on the verge of doing precisely that when the comm chimed.

A call from Toreth's flat, which meant there was no chance of his getting here on time now. What would the excuse be this time? Something mildly creative, no doubt, since it was a Saturday. On a weekday it was usually work, because Toreth knew he wouldn't want details. To his surprise, though, he heard Sara's voice, cutting in halfway through a sentence. "—hell are you? Come on, answer, come on, come on—"

"Sara?"

"Oh, thank Christ," she said, managing to sound relieved and panicky at the same time. "Is Toreth there?"

It couldn't be about anything else, of course. Their main topic of mutual concern. "No. He's late. He was supposed to be here a quarter of an hour ago. What's wrong?"

"Fuck. Fuck, fuck, fuck. When did you hear from him last?"

"Yesterday, after lunch, I think. To confirm about this afternoon. Sara, what's wrong?"

18

"I was hoping...he's disappeared."

"What the hell do you mean, 'disappeared'?"

She hesitated. "Don't go anywhere," she said finally. "I'm on my way over."

Handcuffed to the wall in near darkness, Toreth had plenty of time to reflect on what an idiot he'd been.

He'd been surprised when the door to the flat had opened. Warrick and Sara knew the code, but both of them usually called up rather than let themselves in. Stupidly, he hadn't thought what that might mean, other than to assume he'd made a mistake. Hadn't he arranged to meet Sara at the bar? So he'd called out, "In here," and sat there, waiting for them. Making it easy.

Nondescript dark suits—that was the first thing he'd noticed about them. They could have been some obscure branch of Int-Sec, or Justice getting above themselves, but they didn't show any ID. They piled through the door and across the room to him while he was still getting out of the chair. He hadn't had a real chance against four of them, all decently trained. He made a mess, though, and broke a few glasses, which was what he'd wanted to do. The struggle came to an abrupt end when one of them caught his right wrist, twisting it up and back until he felt the bones grinding, and he'd yelled out, from the surprise as much as the pain.

One of the men, dark-haired and cold-eyed, had stepped around in front of him, straightening his suit as he did so. "My instructions are to bring you in alive *if* possible. So don't fuck me around. Cooperate, and you'll get out of this alive. Understand?"

It wasn't entirely convincing, but Toreth had nodded. Possibly dead later was better odds than definitely dead now.

"Cuff him, bring him along."

Once they left the building, he had decided to try to run for it anyway, because that would probably be his only chance. As the door opened onto the street, and he saw the black car parked immediately outside, he felt a cold pressure on his neck. Unconsciousness had followed so quickly that he didn't remember hearing the hiss of the injector.

Stupid. He'd been so fucking stupid. He heard Sara's voice in his head, saying the same thing to him at the hospital. *My own stupid bloody fault.*

He shifted against the wall, trying to find a position that would allow him to relax a few muscles. Chained as he was, facing the wall and with his hands at head height, there weren't many options. His legs, back, arms, and shoulders were all on a sliding scale somewhere between aching and agony.

When they'd cuffed him to the wall, he'd been coming around, fuzzy with the aftereffects of whatever they'd given him. It hadn't been too bad at first, but he'd known how it would go. Known in a professional, abstract sense—he'd never had it done to him before.

He wondered how the hell Warrick could do this for fun. Except, of course, that he didn't. He did it for half an hour, an hour, so high on the game that it couldn't hurt him anyway. Then he got fucked hard against the wall, and afterwards he went to bed. That was fun. Not hour upon hour of the pain getting worse, long past the point when that had seemed impossible.

Putting up a fight in his flat no longer seemed like such a brilliant idea. His wrist hurt like fuck—broken, or nastily sprained, the handcuff biting into the swollen flesh. When he'd made the mistake of trying to take some of the strain off his shoulders onto the cuffs, he'd nearly blacked out. Despite the pain, he flexed his fingers from time to time, checking for feeling. Plenty of that, which he supposed was a good thing. He'd never fancied gangrene.

Apart from his wrist, he didn't seem to be in terribly bad shape. Beating him up while he was unconscious would have been a waste of time, after all. They'd taken his jacket and shirt off while he was out, but he didn't feel cold. The air in the room was warm and still—stuffy, in fact. The dim light from around the door revealed no hint of a window, but he'd yelled a few times anyway, the sound dying quickly against the walls. No sound of machinery or traffic, no voices. Underground, would be his bet.

Now they were waiting. Stopping him sleeping, lowering his resistance. Effective, and requiring minimal use of valuable personnel. Someone had read the manual.

This place definitely wasn't an I&I cell, because the doors there didn't let in light. At first, he'd guessed Internal Investigations, because Justice would never dare pull anything like this and one or two of the things he'd done could justify a disappearance. As time had crawled by, he'd begun to let himself hope that it wasn't Internal. If it were, surely someone would've come to speak to him by now, or he would be dead. It wasn't as if he was short of alternate candidates. He'd made enough personal enemies over his career, Jonny Kemp—and possibly the rich father Sara had mentioned—being only the most recent.

With the possibility of Internal Investigations receding, he allowed himself a touch of optimism. This wouldn't go down as one of his better weekends, but he might get out of the other end of it alive. Whatever the hell they were going to do to him instead of killing him, he wished that they'd get on and do it. Toreth twisted around, trying to rest his hip and shoulder against the wall without putting too much pressure on his wrist. Still agonizingly uncomfortable, but in a new and interesting way. He leaned his head against the wall and closed his eyes.

Now. You can come back any time now. Whenever you're ready.

Eventually, he drifted into a haze of pain and exhaustion, time passing slowly.

Warrick filled the time until Sara arrived with futile calls, which in all probability she had already made: to I&I, to Toreth's flat, to his personal comm—which was dead, to coin an unfortunate phrase—and, more pessimistically, to various hospitals. Nothing.

He'd always known something like this would happen eventually. Toreth would fuck the wrong person and an outraged husband or wife would come after him. Or, worse, would send someone professional after him. Ironic that it should be now, when he'd been screwing around less than usual. Or at least he'd been keeping it quieter, which was almost as welcome and probably more likely.

When Sara arrived at the flat she looked as distraught as she had sounded. Her face was mottled with bruises a few days old, and she had one finger encased in a protective plastic sheath. "Have you heard from him?" she asked as soon as he closed the door.

"Nothing, no."

"Oh, Christ, this is all my fault." She looked to be on the verge of tears, which wouldn't help either of them.

Taking her arm gently, he led her down the hall. "Come through to the kitchen. Can I get you something to drink?"

"No, I'm fine. I . . . " She sat down in a chair and wiped her eyes angrily with her good hand. "It's all my fault," she repeated.

Despite her refusal, he poured her a glass of his cooking brandy and pressed it into her hand. She took a sip automatically.

"All right." He sat down opposite her. "Start at the beginning."

She gestured to her face. "Boyfriend."

"Jon Kemp?" he said, and she stared, glass halfway to her lips. "I found the address for him. But he didn't tell me why he wanted it. I think I can guess, though."

She nodded. "I didn't ask him to do it, Warrick. I wouldn't have. But I didn't tell him not to, either."

Even though his first thought had been to blame her, he said, "From the temper he was in when I saw him, I don't think it would've made any difference, whatever you'd said."

"He's done something like it before, though. I mean, he didn't say anything first, not that time, but I guessed afterwards what he'd done and I didn't say anything. I knew what he was going to do to Jonny. And I know how crazy Jonny is. I should've—"

"Sara, this isn't going to help him. Tell me what happened, please."

"Okay." She had another mouthful of the drink. "We were supposed to go out last night. Work thing. He went home to change and then he never made it to the bar. I didn't think much about it because I assumed he'd met someone and—" She paused. "Well, you know."

"Yes, I know." All too well.

"Then he was supposed to be at work today. He asked me to come in, specially,

21

to tidy up one of the cases; he wouldn't have forgotten about it. He never showed up. I waited until lunchtime because I had plenty to do, and I thought he'd call in eventually—he always calls, wherever he's ended up—but he didn't."

To his surprise, he found his hands clenching, her panic communicating itself to him. Considering that he'd rarely seen her so much as ruffled, that wasn't surprising.

"I tried to get hold of him," she continued, "but his personal comm isn't connecting. So I called his flat, no answer. And then I went round. I don't know why."

To look for a body, Warrick thought.

"He wasn't there. But there was a mess. Broken glass, stuff knocked over. That's when I started to get really worried."

"Blood?"

She stared at him for a moment, then shook her head. "No. No blood."

That was something. Not much, but something.

"It has to be Jonny," she continued. "Him or his wonderful corporate bloody father. It's my fault. Jesus, he could be dead and all because I—"

"No, he won't be." Warrick uncurled his hands, laid them flat on his thighs to stop them from shaking. "What did he do to this Jon Kemp?"

She sniffed hard, composing herself. "Beat him up. He didn't say in so many words, but I think he...lost control. He made a mess of him—more than he meant to. Enough that I had the feeling he was worried about Jonny's father finding out from the medic or someone like that."

"But he didn't kill him. Then he'll be all right."

"How can you be so bloody *calm* about it?" she exploded.

Briefly, he was tempted to tell her the truth, but it wouldn't help the situation. "Think it through. Toreth's a para-investigator. Senior para-investigator." This once, that was something he was unreservedly glad about. "He's not someone a corporate can have vanish. However rich his father is, he won't be able to buy off Int-Sec over something like that. So they'll take him somewhere, rough him up a little—" a lot, it would be a lot, "—do their best to frighten him, and then they'll let him go. Killing him would be stupid."

"So where is he? They took him last night. If that's all it was, where *is* he?"

That was the gaping hole in the explanation. "I don't know. But they won't kill him," he said, trying to sound reassuring for both of them.

She shook her head. "His father mightn't. But Jonny...you don't know him. *I* didn't. He's a maniac—you should've heard what he said to Toreth. He threatened him, right to his face. He thinks no one can touch him. He might kill Toreth and not think about the consequences until there's an armed squad kicking in his door."

He didn't want to believe her, especially not when he'd almost managed to convince himself otherwise. However, she was the one who knew Jon Kemp. Sitting still was suddenly impossible. Pacing worked better, and thinking about what he could *do*. "Very well," he said. "There was a struggle at the flat, so they've taken him somewhere, alive. Not to the address I gave him, though, because that would be too easy to find. You don't know anywhere else? Damn. Have you told I&I?"

"No. If I tell them..." She shrugged.

"Everything comes out and he'd be sacked at best. Sacked is better than dead, though." He looked at her, read what she didn't dare say because of how it would sound. "But it wouldn't just be sacked and it wouldn't just be him—it would be you as well."

She nodded. "Not just me, either. You found him the address. We'd all be screwed."

He hadn't thought of that, and he dismissed it now. "If we can't think of something else, though, I&I is all we have to fall back on."

"Of course." She looked hurt that he'd even suggested she wouldn't agree, but he didn't have attention to spare to apologize.

"Do you know any other houses Jon Kemp might have access to? Most probably somewhere not too far away."

"No. I didn't even know where he lived. But I can call Daedra Kincaidy. She might know something."

While she made the call, he broke off pacing long enough to make tea. He'd had a coffee just before she arrived, but the ritual helped to calm him. Stick to the practical; don't speculate on what might be happening. What might already have happened, making all this frantic hunting for leads useless.

Toreth didn't notice the lights come up slowly, or the door open.

"Good afternoon, 'Officer.'" The mocking voice pulled him back to alertness. He turned around, ignoring the pain in his wrist. Doubts about who had sent the men were banished when he saw Jonny standing in the open doorway. He was twisting a thick leather strap between his hands—which cleared up any other questions Toreth had about the planned program—and grinning like the arrogant little shit he was. The bruises Toreth had given him were still vivid, though, and satisfyingly worse than Sara's.

Jonny closed the door and strolled over, stopping a couple of meters away— out of kicking range. "Did you *really* think you were going to get away with it, Para-investigator Toreth? That I couldn't find out who you were?"

No, I just didn't think you'd be stupid enough to try anything, he thought, but he kept his mouth shut. He might as well make an effort to be sensible to start with. With Jonny's native talent for pushing his buttons, it wouldn't last long.

"You're going to pay for everything you did, a hundred times over. Unfortunately, I have a prior engagement this evening, so I'm afraid you'll have to stand here," he smiled, "all night. Again. I hope you don't mind. Tomorrow will be worth waiting for,

I assure you. And then, when I'm finished, I'm going to kill you. Slowly and painfully."

Toreth blinked. It hadn't occurred to him until now that Jonny would seriously consider killing him. But, Christ, he *meant* it. Sara was right—he was a maniac. She hadn't mentioned that he got his overrehearsed dialogue from bad films, though, not that that made him any less dangerous.

"Not so cocky now, are you?" Jonny continued.

"Why don't you uncuff me and say that again?" he suggested, his resolve slipping already.

Jonny took a couple of steps to the side, where he'd have a clearer view of Toreth's face. "No, I don't think so. Not while I can think of things to do with you there. Maybe later. When *I'm* listening to *you* begging for death. You can do that on your knees."

This time Toreth tried to keep his expression neutral, give no reaction.

Flexing the strap in his hands, Jonny stepped closer. "Was that stupid bitch worth dying for? I hope you got a fuck out of your white knight act, because you won't be having her again." Toreth kicked out, sooner than he'd meant to, and missed. Jonny stepped back smartly, laughing again. "Behave yourself, or I'll get someone in here to break your legs."

It was the tone as much as the threat that chilled him: happy anticipation, a child with a new toy.

Jonny smiled. "Well, are you going to behave?"

Toreth's first impulse was to spit in his face and tell him to go fuck himself. On the other hand, he had the strong impression that once he'd given the order, Jonny would go through with it whatever Toreth said. And then leave him here all night. Toreth couldn't begin to imagine how much that would hurt, if the shock didn't kill him.

"Well?"

"Yes," Toreth said, through gritted teeth.

"Yes, what?"

"Yes, I'll behave." If he wanted any more than that, he wasn't getting it.

Fortunately—or unfortunately—Jonny didn't seem to be willing to wait any longer to get on to the main event. He stepped closer, still watching Toreth's face, daring him to move, then lifted the strap and brought it down hard.

The smack across Toreth's shoulder sounded loud and, Christ, it hurt. It had been telegraphed enough to give Toreth plenty of time to set his jaw, but he couldn't stop the gasp of pain.

Jonny smiled, eyes bright and mad as a fucking mink, and did it again.

Again.

And over and over again.

When Sara came back, Warrick didn't need to ask what the answer was. "Damn. All right, I'm tapped out. Your turn."

She poured herself a cup of tea, slowly stirred in milk and sugar. "I think you're right. He's still alive. Because they took him on Friday—they weren't to know he was supposed to be at work today. They'd have until Monday to...do whatever."

"Sounds reasonable."

"Reasonable." She looked at him briefly, and shook her head. "Anyway, if they needed that long, they won't be giving him a kicking and throwing him into an alley somewhere. They—I don't know why I keep saying 'they.' It's Jonny, it has to be. Not his father." She trailed off, and the only sound in the flat was the spoon clinking gently against the cup as she kept stirring mechanically.

"Yes?"

"There's only one thing I can think of to try. It's a bit of a risk, though." She looked up. "For you."

"Anything," he said simply. "If there's any chance at all it will work."

"Call his father. Let him know what Jonny's done. If Jonny...if he kills him, then it'll cause a hell of a mess, like you said. Bad for the corporation."

He considered the idea. "Will he believe it?"

"I don't know. I never met him. I never met any of his family."

If Kemp knew nothing about Toreth's disappearance, then the idea was a sound one. If he was behind it himself, then it could place both of them in as much danger as Toreth. However, on balance, it seemed like the best idea so far. "I agree—it has to be worth a try."

Jonny had more self-control than Toreth would have credited him with, pacing himself, spacing the blows, waiting between strikes for the first burning shock of pain to fade. He must have done this before, and he was enjoying doing it now. If he screened out his own harsh breathing, Toreth could hear Jonny panting, only partly from the exertion, if he was any judge.

Nice hobby the bastard had.

Professional admiration worked as a distraction for only so long. Eventually the pain from the strap began to drown out the pain of aching muscles. Of everything, in fact, except his wrist, repeatedly jolted by the blows.

Jonny might stop if he asked him to, if he begged hard enough, because that was what he wanted to hear. It was tempting, although Toreth knew he'd only switch to something else afterwards, once he'd enjoyed his first victory. Surrender would start the familiar pattern: breaking, moving on, breaking, moving on. Still, against his will, the words formed.

No. He was fucked if he was playing that game.

Toreth took a couple of breaths to steady his voice, not caring any more what was the sensible thing to say, just wanting to find something which would stop it without humiliating himself. "Getting off on it yet?" he asked.

Jonny paused, strap raised. "What?"

Toreth dropped his gaze to Jonny's crotch, looked up again slowly. "I said, 'getting off on it yet?'" He managed an unpleasant smile. "If you wanted a date, you should've asked. You like to take it, right?"

Jonny's eyes went blank with rage, and he dropped the strap, clenching his fist.

It was a reaction, anyway. Toreth took the punches, counting four of them, then let his head fall forwards. He'd seen enough prisoners passed out to allow him to fake it convincingly. But to make it look right he had to hang from the cuffs, and even taking as much weight as he could on his left arm, he nearly didn't have to pretend.

Jonny stopped at once, shook his shoulder, and gave him a couple of open-handed blows to the face. Then, close enough that Toreth could feel his breath, he reached past him, took his right wrist, and squeezed.

Razor-edged claws of pain ripped at his self-control. Toreth somehow kept his muscles loose, didn't make any more noise than an unconscious man might.

Fucking, fucking *hell*. I'm out, you moron. You knocked me out. For Christ's sake, stop it and go away.

Swearing, Jonny kicked the strap across the floor and stamped out of the room. After a few seconds, the lights went out again. Once five minutes had passed with no sign of his return, Toreth let himself take his weight on his legs, without shifting position too much, and bit back a moan of relief. Wary of the possibility of a low-light camera, he kept his head hanging forwards. Not the most comfortable position, out of the range of extremely uncomfortable positions available to him. For the moment, though, it felt pretty fucking good. He wondered how long he'd been here now. Jonny had said "good afternoon." Unless he was smart enough to be screwing with Toreth's sense of time, that meant it was probably Saturday.

Eighteen hours at least, and Sara would've missed him by now. Lucky that they'd had to work today. Jonny must have been hoping for a clear run up until Monday when he'd...what? Let him go? If he'd come to his senses by then. Kill him, if he hadn't. Toreth knew which one he was betting on. He could only hope that the people working for Jonny, whoever they were, weren't as fucking demented as he was and that someone would put a stop to this.

Sara would have missed him. Most likely she'd tell Warrick, and they would be doing something about it. Even though he couldn't imagine what, the idea was strangely comforting.

Sara had been making yet more calls in the living room, so as not to disturb Warrick. Going back into the study, she put down the comm earpiece and looked at her nails. She'd chewed almost all the varnish off. It had taken her ages to apply it properly, too, with her finger in the stupid sheath.

"Have you got through to Kemp yet?" she asked.

"Yes." Warrick didn't look up from the computer. "I found his personal comm in the end."

"And?"

"I told him I was missing one senior para-investigator, and that it wouldn't be long before I&I missed him, too."

"Did he believe you?"

"Not at first. Possibly not at the end, either." He sounded impossibly calm. "But in his position, I wouldn't risk not checking, even if I didn't believe. Did you get anywhere?"

"No. Daedra couldn't find anything. She called her sister, and *she* managed to track down another couple of Johnny's exes. None of them knew a fucking thing about him except that they never wanted to see him again."

"Right," he said, obviously not listening beyond hearing the negative.

"She said she'll keep trying and she'll call if she gets anything. Her sister's going to get hold of some friends at the university who probably won't know anything, but it's the only thing she can think of. They might at least be able to give her the names of some of his friends. If the bastard has any."

"Good."

Sara took a deep breath. She appreciated that he was doing his best to help Toreth, and she appreciated that it wasn't useful to panic, but it would be nice to have someone there who acted as if they cared. She had a sudden urge to throw something heavy at him, but she knew she was really angry with herself. It was all her fault. She'd let Toreth do it and maybe she couldn't have stopped him, but that didn't matter. Her stupid mistake had started it. If she'd listened to Daedra—if she'd listened to *herself* when Jonny had started acting like a creep...

"What next?" she asked.

"I'm going to keep looking. There might be something out there, something to let us track him down."

He didn't sound convinced, and she didn't blame him. There was no reason to think they would be able to find their lost needle in the haystack of New London if Jonny's father couldn't or wouldn't. But anything was better than simply sitting and waiting.

"Give me something else to do," she said.

Now he looked at her. That was the way to get his attention—make a noise like a useful tool.

"Ah, all right." He pointed to the screen on the other desk. "I'll send some records over there. I assume you know how to do the searches."

She sat down and waited while the screen filled, nibbling the last patch of Metallic Midnight Blue from her thumbnail.

Toreth had given up faking unconsciousness when the pain from the position he was in became too much to bear. To his surprise, Jonny hadn't returned immediately. Not that he was complaining. In the dark, he couldn't tell for certain, but he felt bruised from neck to waist, with a few stray hits on his legs which felt as if they'd bruised even through his trousers.

He'd tried it before, but he couldn't help another tug on the cuffs. He hooked the fingers of his left hand around the bolt in the wall and twisted. Nothing. Whoever had put the thing in had done a good job. He pulled harder, until finally his hand slipped and his right wrist slammed into the wall, driving the edge of the cuff into the abused flesh.

"Jesus fucking *Christ*. Fuck, fuck, fuck—"

He bit the words off and waited, breathing hard, for the door to open.

After a minute with no response to the noise, he let himself relax again. Ha. Relax—there was a joke. He concentrated, cataloging his body, trying to find something that didn't ache. His eyelids felt pretty good. His tongue, although he was thirsty as hell. And no one had kicked him in the bollocks yet, although no doubt Jonny would get around to it eventually. There was a cheerful thought.

Another few hours of this, twelve at the most, and Toreth knew he wouldn't be able to stand unaided. After that his chances of getting out on his own were zero.

When the lights came up again, he'd completely lost track of time. For a disorienting moment, he imagined he'd been there all night and it must be Sunday. Surely it couldn't have been that long?

The door opened and Jonny entered, with the dark-haired man who'd spoken to Toreth at his flat. He was speaking to Jonny now, urgently. Toreth caught the tail end of the sentence. "—but no one saw us. No one."

Jonny looked more like he had after their first meeting: flushed and wide-eyed.

"Get him out of here, Chris. Get rid of him." Jonny was obviously trying to keep his voice low, but the high, panicked whisper carried perfectly.

"Sir?" Toreth recognized that tone of voice: an underling's disagreement phrased as a request for clarification.

"You know what I mean. Get *rid* of him."

The man addressed as Chris nodded, still looking reluctant. He waited by the door; Jonny crossed the room to stand in front of Toreth, making a poor stab at composure.

"You're in luck. Change of plan. I have to go somewhere, so you get to die today instead of tomorrow." He smiled, a shadow of his normal arrogant smirk. "Do you feel lucky yet?"

Toreth looked at him with open contempt. He didn't believe a word of it. The gutless fuck was running scared of something. An unlikely surge of optimism pushed the pain back.

"When I&I gets hold of you, you little shit," Toreth said clearly, projecting to Chris and anyone beyond the open door, "it's going to take a fuck sight more than a rich daddy and a handful of hired muscle to help you. Looking forward to the re-education, are you?"

Jonny stood for a moment, his eyes sliding away from Toreth's, and then he turned to Chris. "Do it. Kill him," he said, leaving no room for misinterpretation. Then he hurried out of the room, without another glance at Toreth.

Chris spoke to someone outside, then stood in silence, chewing his bottom lip and staring at the floor.

"What's going on?" Toreth asked without much hope of an answer. He didn't need to ask, anyway, not for the general outline. "I hope you realize that if you kill me, you're stepping into deep shit. I&I doesn't appreciate losing employees."

Chris looked up, actually seeing him for a moment.

"Didn't your boss mention?" Toreth said. "I'm a para-investigator."

"Shut the fuck up," Chris said after a moment. "Or you'll be a dead para-investigator, sooner rather than later."

Toreth shut up. There was nothing more he could say, anyway. He hoped a sense of self-preservation would do the rest for him.

If it was going to, it didn't do it straight away. The three other men who'd collected him from his flat came into the room, looking professionally stoic. Chris gestured to him. "Bring him along," Chris said without enthusiasm, already turning to leave the room.

Perhaps something in his tone made them hesitate. No one moved, and he stopped and glared at them. "Are you fucking deaf? You're not getting paid to stand around—get him to the car. I won't be long. I'm going to discuss bonuses."

Warrick checked his watch. Two minutes later than when he'd last looked. Every minute that passed was a tiny decrease in the odds of seeing Toreth again. Warrick used to know the statistics for corporate kidnap victims by heart, before he'd decided that it was pointless to worry about it.

"I was going to have a party," Sara said, unexpectedly.

Warrick looked up from the computer, startled. She sat at the other desk, staring blankly at the screen where Jon Kemp's credit and purchase records lay open, illegally accessed.

"What?"

"The ring Toreth took back—I told you about it earlier. I was going to sell it and have a party."

"You still can."

She didn't reply, because she didn't need to. Not if he's dead, was what she meant.

"He's going to be fine." Every time he said it to her, he believed it a little less. He wished that she'd go away, back to her own flat, so that he wouldn't feel obliged to keep pretending. Or at least leave him alone in the study for a while. Seeing her there, though, stricken with guilt, he couldn't say it.

His stomach rumbled, reminding him of missed lunch, and he thought of a way to kill two birds with one stone. "Why don't you get us something to eat?" he suggested. "Take a break from the screen. Make sandwiches. Or there's fresh soup in the fridge."

"I'm not hungry."

"Well, I am."

She hesitated. "What would you like?"

"Banana sandwiches. With plenty of black pepper." Coding food. Comfort food.

She wrinkled her nose. "God, that sounds revolting."

"I like them."

"Okay. Maybe I'll try one as well."

He smiled, knowing it wasn't going to look very convincing. "You'll love them, I promise."

After she left, he turned back to the screen, where the computer was running searches of Kemp's properties, looking for some link to Jonny, for somewhere he may have taken Toreth. An illusion of action, nothing more than killing time.

Amazing how many metaphors used that word, when he thought about it.

Toreth sat in the car in a daze, sick with the relief of being able to lower his arms at last. They'd blindfolded him and recuffed his hands behind his back, and his wrist was still settling slowly back down from agony to manageable pain, but at that exact moment, he didn't care about any of it. It was almost worth the prospect of being shot if he could relax his shoulders until then. The abused muscles ached viciously, but at least it was a different kind of hurt.

The door opened and closed as someone got in. Chris, at a guess. Toreth wondered how the bonus negotiations had gone. He hoped Jonny had told Chris where to stick it, but he very much doubted that he had. Judging from Jonny's expression in the cell, he'd probably pay anything to get rid of Toreth.

A voice from the front of the car asked, "Where are we taking him?"

"The usual place," Chris said. Toreth's hopes rose slightly, because he didn't sound happy. Maybe the bonus wouldn't be big enough after all. "Tell the car to take a long way round."

"What do you—"

"Oh, for God's sake. A long way. *Any* way."

Toreth was tempted to say something. In the end, he decided against making Chris any more annoyed than he already clearly was.

Sara ate her sandwiches in the sitting room, watching the setting sun finger-paint the sky in dabs of neon pinks and reds. Pollution in the atmosphere, as her dad always said when there was a particularly beautiful sunset. Lights were starting to come up across New London. This time yesterday she had been in the bar, laughing at one of Kel's stories, only sparing a minute or two to wonder where Toreth was and who he was fucking. Knowing she'd get all the details at work in the morning. If she'd checked last night, instead of today...

All her fault. Her mistakes, all along the way.

Warrick wasn't in the study. She found him in the kitchen, brewing yet another pot of tea. The water was starting to boil, and he stood, apparently watching the steam wisping from the kettle.

"We should've heard by now," she said.

He didn't answer.

"I thought it was going to work," she said bleakly. "I really did."

"It still might."

"We would've heard. It'll be dark soon." She didn't know why that mattered, but it did.

He looked around briefly. The effort it cost him to keep his voice level showed in his set expression. "Sara, there is no reason to expect to hear anything. A call to us is a connection. An admission. Dangerous. All we can expect is that he turns up or he doesn't."

She knew all that. It wasn't why she'd come to look for him. She'd wanted to ask him something since she'd first thought of it, a couple of hours ago. She hadn't asked then because she already knew the answer. "What if Jonny finds out we called Kemp?"

"Then there's a chance that he'll kill Toreth." No hesitation—he'd obviously thought about it as well. "Perhaps even if he hadn't planned to do it before."

She stared at him, speechless, hating him for not lying to her.

"That was always the risk." He paused, then added, "It was still a good idea. *Is* a good idea. It isn't time to write it off yet."

31

She couldn't tell if he meant it, or if he was merely being kind. It didn't matter, anyway. It had been her idea and so, if it went wrong, her fault yet again.

The water was boiling hard now, and the click of the kettle switching off sounded loud. "We have to call I&I." Sara didn't know why she was asking permission. She should just make the damn call, whatever he said. He'd been the one who had wanted to do it in the first place. "If they start a full-scale search, they can get Justice to help."

Warrick looked up from pouring water into the teapot. "If we do, he's finished. We won't be able to stop everything coming out."

"The sun's setting." The feeling came again that this was important. The last chance.

"Give it another hour. Half an hour."

Then she lost it. "I don't know why you're so keen he keeps his bloody job! You hate it, anyway. I'd have thought you'd be *pleased* if they threw him out."

He turned quickly, slopping tea from the pot onto the floor. "Then you don't—"

Then, before she could register the emotion—anger? fear?—it was gone. Taking a cloth from the sink, he wiped up the tea. "Do whatever you think best," he said coldly, and went back into the study.

She watched him go, thought about the comm.

She'd give it an hour.

The long way around hadn't felt very long. All the time he'd hoped for Jonny to call and tell them to let him go, or for Chris to have a spontaneous attack of intelligence. Neither had happened.

Now he stood on a muddy bank, listening to the river nearby. That's where he'd end up, when they'd done with him. He could also hear a low, muttered discussion, not unlike the ripple of the water. An argument. He knew that he ought to try to listen, to work out what was going wrong and how he could use it. He ought to, but it was taking all his concentration to keep control of the knowledge that, whatever the trouble was, he was probably going to die here. Even if I&I hunted Jon Kemp and all his hired thugs down and nailed them to the wall over it, it wouldn't do him one fucking bit of good because his funeral would be long over. If anyone ever found his body.

Dead and gone and he'd never... well, he'd never done a lot of things. Precious little point thinking about all that crap now, and it still might not come to that if he could keep his head.

Concentrate.

He tried to map out his surroundings: river to one side, voices in front and behind, the ground slippery underfoot. The air had a cool, evening feel against his

32

bare skin and a warmth on his right side suggested sunlight. Stink of tidal river in the air. Death and decay.

Chris's voice rose behind him, silencing the others. Sounding worried. "Yes, sir. Yes, I'm listening."

Long pauses between the phrases—he was speaking over a comm. "Yes, I do appreciate that. Thank you, sir." Now he sounded relieved, and there was an answering murmur from the others around him. Relief that they weren't going to have to take the risk of killing him?

"I didn't—no, sir. No. Yes, I can do that, sir, absolutely. I understand. Of course. Thank you, sir."

Then footsteps approached, squelching up behind him. "Kneel," Chris ordered.

No way. No way in hell. "Fuck off."

He felt a light touch on his thigh, then sudden, searing pain. Muscles spasmed, pitching him full length. More pain stabbed up his arm as he reflexively tried to bring his hands around to break his fall. As it was, the soft ground cushioned the impact, but left his mouth and nose full of filthy mud. Lifting his head, he coughed and spat. Shock stick, he thought. Not a high setting, so there wouldn't be any permanent damage. Then he realized how little that mattered. He struggled to his knees, despite the residual spasming in his leg, but he couldn't manage to stand. Bastards.

"Fuck you," he said distinctly, hoping there was an open comm of some kind, so that Jonny could hear him. "Fuck you, you spineless cunt. I should have done the world a fucking favor and killed you when I had the chance."

Then he closed his eyes tight behind the blindfold, feeling the grit in his mouth and the handcuff digging into his throbbing wrist. Cold mud clung to his chest, making him shiver. It couldn't take long. Now the order had been confirmed, they wouldn't stay out here in the open, wherever here was, for longer than they had to.

Time stretched out, filled with the sound of the waiting water. Please, let them finish him before they threw him in. He'd always loathed the idea of drowning— been terrified by it. Nightmares, since forever, of fighting the need to inhale. Feeling the pressure of water against his face, then pouring down his throat, flooding his lungs. In the sim he'd never been able to breathe underwater, even though Sara said it was piss easy, and now he felt himself starting to gag at the thought of it. Not with his hands bound. Hands bound and his life bleeding away into the cold water as—

Focus. Focus on at least not acting like the worthless piece of shit who'd put him here. He swallowed the sickness and the fear and clenched his fists, distracting himself with pain.

Time passing, and the river.

Then Toreth heard vehicles approaching and his tenuous hold on dignified

33

resignation vanished. Friend or foe? He tensed, listening desperately, ready to run or fight.

He heard nothing around him to suggest that the arrivals were unexpected. A firm, blunt pressure between his shoulder blades and a sharp "Keep still!" put an end to any idea of resistance. Whether gun or shock stick, it wasn't something he wanted fired into his spine. Pathetic, really, that he could still cling to the slimmest hope that it wouldn't happen anyway.

The vehicles drew up nearby—two of them. Doors opened and closed. Jonny come to witness his execution in person? Low voices, then silence. His whole awareness shrank down to the hard contact against his back. Soon. The pressure shifted slightly. Now. Christ, it would be soon, it would be now, it was—

Hands under his armpits hauled him upright, steadied him. A few steps sideways and they pushed him against what felt like a car and held him efficiently as the cuffs were removed. The relief from the pressure on his wrist was instantaneous, despite the agonizing protest of strained muscles as he moved his arms. Then he was turned and the blindfold pulled away, leaving him squinting into the sun setting beyond the river. Shapes became visible through the orange and gold, more men than the four who had brought him here. Too many, too close for escape, even if he'd been in any condition to try it.

Without a word, one of the newcomers handed him a towel. It was damp and, most bizarrely of all, faintly scented. Something floral. He took it numbly in his good hand. What the *hell* was going on?

There was nothing else to do, so he cleaned the mud from his face, wiped the worst from his chest and trousers, and then handed the towel back. He was tempted to say thanks, but considering the reason he'd needed the towel in the first place, it seemed inappropriate to say the least.

Next came a fresh shirt, again offered silently. He put it on, struggling against the painful clumsiness of his arms and shoulders. His fingers left smudges on the white fabric as he buttoned it awkwardly, left-handed.

A smartly dressed slender woman—management, not muscle—opened the rear door of the large dark blue car. Its minimalist sharp lines made it look brand-new and expensively corporate, and Toreth wondered if that was good news or very, very bad. "Get in, please," the woman said.

Still unsure as to exactly why he wasn't dead, but not feeling like pressing the point, Toreth did as he was told.

Inside the car were two large men with the look of extremely professional bodyguards. Opposite them sat an older man, dark-haired—maybe dyed—and with dark eyes which assessed Toreth with sharp, arrogant intelligence. His suit must've cost more than Toreth's yearly salary. Then the man smiled, showing perfect, even teeth. "My name is Gil Kemp. Please, sit down."

Chris or one of his sidekicks—one without a death wish—must have tipped the man off about what Jonny was up to. Toreth sat, opposite Jonny Kemp's father and between the watchful guards. Moving slowly seemed to be a sensible idea, as well as all he could manage.

When he had settled into the seat—wonderfully comfortable despite his bruised back—Kemp continued. "I apologize unreservedly for your unfortunate treatment, Val. I assure you that I had nothing to do with it. I make it a rule never to interfere with Int-Sec employees."

"I didn't think it was anything to do with you, sir." He didn't think he'd return the use of the personal name. No point going out of his way to sabotage the unexpected reversal of fortune.

"I also ask you to pass my regrets along to...your friend." Kemp's voice soured. "My son is a coward and a bully, amongst other of his less attractive qualities. However, he is also my only son and as such I am obliged to do the best I can by him."

Not so promising. "Does this mean you're going to make an exception to your rule?"

The expensive smile gleamed again. "No. I merely wish to secure an assurance that Jon has nothing further to fear from you. May I tell him that the matter is closed?"

Tempting to say yes. Tempting, in fact, to say whatever the hell it took to get out of here. He could feel the pressure between his shoulders, the choking fear. The river still flowed by, only yards away.

As steadily as he could, Toreth said, "You can tell him that if he lays one finger on her again, I'll be back to do exactly what I said I'd do."

Silence stretched out for what felt like minutes, with Kemp's expression unreadable, then he nodded. "You have my word that your friend will be perfectly safe," he said, in a voice so hard that Toreth believed him instantly.

He let out the breath he'd been holding to steady his voice. "Then if I never see him again, it will be too fucking soon."

"More than acceptable. Thank you for your forbearance."

"It's..." It's my pleasure? Hardly. "It's over. As far as I'm concerned."

Kemp nodded to one of the bodyguards. Toreth expected him to open the door, but instead the guard touched a panel and the car began to move, over the rough ground and then onto a smooth, paved road. Leaving the river behind.

Through the window, Toreth caught a last glimpse of water, darkened by the tinted glass, as it disappeared behind a building. He still didn't recognize where they were, but he allowed himself to relax a tiny fraction. The sliding hiss of a panel opening jerked his attention back to the interior of the car. It took him a moment to register the open drinks cabinet, tiny but well stocked.

"Would you like something?" Kemp offered.

After looking longingly at the range of bottles, Toreth said, "Just water,

35

thanks." He'd forgotten for a while how thirsty he was, and his mouth still tasted of the dirty river mud. He accepted the glass and drank slowly, gauging the reaction of his stomach. Throwing the water straight back up onto the expensive upholstery wouldn't create the best impression.

"Now," Kemp said, "we can get to the real reason I wished to speak to you in person."

The *real* reason? Automatically, Toreth glanced at the bodyguards, but they appeared to be as relaxed as people in that line of work ever were. "Which is?"

"I wish to offer you a job."

There wasn't any way he could have misheard, but he still didn't believe it. "A...job?"

"Indeed. My businesses employ a number of former para-investigators, in various capacities. I would like you to join them. The precise terms of the position and remuneration can be worked out later with my representatives, but I can assure you they will be generous."

Too stunned for a considered response, he said, "Why the hell do you want to give *me* a job?"

Kemp seemed amused rather than annoyed. "You have qualities that I value highly in my employees. Loyalty. Courage. Intelligence. A willingness to take risks for people who are important to you. Your encounter with my son, while I may deplore your actions, demonstrated those qualities amply."

Toreth was becoming convinced that Kemp's disapproval was purely formal. "I fucked up," he said evenly. "I lost my temper."

"Considering the circumstances, I won't hold it against you." Kemp smiled thinly. "Your security file suggests that was a singular lapse."

Had everyone seen the fucking thing except him? He was going to have to ask Warrick for a copy, and damn the risk of letting slip to someone that he'd read it.

"Do you have an answer for me?" Kemp enquired.

He stalled with a mouthful of water, then said, "I'll have to think about it."

Kemp frowned. He obviously had the same problem as his son about not getting what he wanted. "May I ask why?"

"I try not to make important decisions when I've just had the shit kicked out of me."

"Then I suggest you sleep on the question and give me your answer tomorrow."

The conversation was clearly supposed to be over, but Toreth asked, "Where are we going?"

Kemp frowned, irritated. "When I was informed of your whereabouts, or rather, informed that your whereabouts might be a matter for concern, I was also provided with an address to which you should be returned."

"Warrick," he said without thinking, then cursed himself.

Kemp merely nodded. "One of my subsidiaries has a speculative investment in Dr. Warrick's corporation." He smiled at Toreth's expression. "That was not intended to influence your decision in any way, neither as a recommendation nor a threat. It merely made him a more credible source for information I did not want to hear about Jon." Kemp sighed, his voice becoming quieter. "I ought to be used to it, by now. Sometimes I wonder if he is punishing me for something that I've done. Or failed to do. I used to hope that I would find out what it was, so that I could make amends. But now..."

Toreth kept his mouth shut. People like Kemp didn't expect comments when they decided to share their personal problems with the furniture. All Toreth wanted was to get out of here in one piece, or at least in as few pieces as possible. He flexed his right wrist as carefully as he could. Sprain, he was sure.

Kemp sighed again, then turned away to look out of the tinted window, further discussion now very definitely closed.

Warrick hadn't spoken to Sara since he'd so nearly lost control in the kitchen. He'd stayed in the study, running increasingly unlikely searches, more for something to do than because of any lingering hope. They'd had only one chance, and it didn't look as if it had worked out. He should have let Sara call I&I. Eventually, admitting defeat, he shut off the system and went to look for her.

He found her in the living room, sitting with a clock in her lap, staring out of the window. There was no trace of the day left in the sky. "Did you call?"

She shook her head. "Fifty-six minutes."

"Sara, I'm sorry."

"Forget it. I'm sorry I yelled at you."

"I think, under the circumstances, you're entitled." He took the clock from her, being careful not to jar her injured hand, and set it back in its place. "Do you want to call, or shall I?"

"I'll do it."

Before she could pick up her comm, the door to the flat opened. They both froze, looking at each other, Sara with her hand still outstretched. Then, as they started for the hallway, he thought, it could be Dillian.

As the car pulled up, Toreth still didn't truly believe they would let him go. Even as he walked away, he found his shoulders tensing, hurting the strained muscles, waiting for the shot. Stupid, because the middle of a corporate residential district would be an insane place to carry out a killing.

Then he was inside the building, inside the lift, outside the door to Warrick's flat, desperately racking his brain for the entry code. He should have knocked, but he didn't think of it. Then the door opened and he was safe. He was still trying to lock the door behind him, left-handed, when he heard footsteps and turned to find Sara flying down the hall towards him. He lifted his injured arm out of the way just in time to catch her up with the good one. She buried her face against his chest.

"Oh, Christ, I was so worried," she said, her voice muffled in his new shirt. She looked up at him, without letting go, and bit her lip when she saw the marks on his face. "Are you hurt?"

Looked like he'd been right when he guessed she'd miss him at work. "I'm fine. Some bruises. Nothing fatal."

He looked over her shoulder to find Warrick standing just out of arm's reach, smiling slightly, although at which one of them he wasn't sure. Then Sara squeezed too tightly and he winced. She released him hurriedly. "I'm sorry," she said. "Come sit down. Jesus, look at your wrist."

"It's okay." He let her lead him towards the living room anyway, because he did feel like sitting down. While it was still voluntary.

"What happened?" Warrick asked on the way down the hall.

He considered the options, then smiled. "I had a job interview."

They both stopped and stared at him.

"A what?" Warrick inquired after a moment.

Toreth grinned. "Get me a drink and I'll tell you all about it."

Even the edited version took a while. As he talked, Sara demonstrated how well she'd been paying attention on the admins' first aid course, and disinfected and bandaged his wrist. He'd have preferred she left it alone, but she looked to be enjoying herself, and it had to be done sometime. Warrick contributed tea and a couple of painkillers, then sat on the chair opposite, listening intently.

As he neared the end of the account, he began to wish he hadn't mentioned the job offer. It had been too tempting a line not to use. Now, however, it occurred to him that Warrick would probably like him to take it. A nice, safe corporate job he wouldn't have to remember not to talk about. But he couldn't, and he couldn't explain why.

Not that he particularly cared about Warrick's opinion, but, as the last dregs of adrenaline drained from his system, he found that he couldn't face an argument, or silent disapproval, or any other fucking thing which wasn't closely connected to food, a shower, and sleep.

He sketched out the scene by the river, glossing over the details. Better not to think about it. "And then the cavalry arrived, thanks to you."

Warrick waved the credit aside. "It was all Sara's idea. I merely made the call and put on my best corporate act. Which obviously worked."

"More or less. He's a sponsor, you know."

Warrick nodded. "Indirectly. But I didn't know that until after I'd spoken to him. He was extremely unwilling to believe me at first, but that at least gave me some confidence that he knew nothing about it before I called. After we'd contacted him, we had nothing else to do."

"Except keep trying to find you," Sara put in. "And I am just going to forget how many files I looked at illegally while I was doing it. I hoped Kemp would call to let us know you were all right, but of course he didn't. The first thing we knew was when you opened the door." He thought for a moment she was going to hug him again, but she just tucked her legs up under her and grinned. "Anyway, what the hell did you mean about an interview?"

"Kemp asked me to work for him," he said lightly.

Her mouth fell open. "He what? Seriously? He offered you a *job*? After what you did?"

"No, because of what I did." She looked at him blankly, and he shrugged. "I didn't get it either. But yeah, he was serious."

"Are you going to accept it?" she asked, suddenly subdued.

"No." Don't leave an opening. Never qualify a refusal.

"Good. Unless you could get me a job as well." She brightened. "Do you think you could? You'd still need an admin, I should think. What did he want you—"

"I'm *not* taking it." He hadn't meant it to sound quite so forceful, but she shut her mouth abruptly.

To his surprise, he found himself wanting to tell her why. Ridiculous, because she wouldn't—couldn't—understand. When he looked away from Sara, he found Warrick watching him, frowning slightly.

Sara stood up. "I should get home."

"You don't have to," Warrick said without looking at her.

"No. I need to get back and...feed the cat." She looked between them. "Or something." On the way out, she stopped behind Toreth and, after a moment, he felt her hand on his shoulder. "See you on Monday."

He touched her hand and nodded. "See you."

"She thinks it was all her fault," Warrick commented, when the outer door had closed behind her.

"It wasn't."

A second's pause. "I was merely telling you what *she* thought."

"Well, don't. It's none of your business." He wished straight away that he hadn't said it, because whether it was or not, it was something else he couldn't bear to argue about right now.

He sat up, too quickly, and the room tilted and blurred, a buzzing in his ears drowning out Warrick's voice. When he could focus again he found Warrick looking at him with guarded concern.

"I'm fine," he snapped.

"When did you last eat?" Warrick asked the practical question in a neutral tone.

39

"I don't remember. Yesterday. If yesterday was Friday?" He found he wasn't sure.

Warrick stood up and carefully straightened the cushions on the sofa.

"Yes, it was. Why don't you go and get cleaned up and I'll make some food?"

The shower helped more than he'd thought it would. It was an indescribable relief to be free of the filthy clothes—and the clean shirt—and wash away the sweat and mud and then to stand under the soothing warm water, letting his mind go blank. As he dried himself, very carefully, he admired the rest of the bruises in the mirror. No swimming until they'd faded.

Swimming made him think of the river again and, before he could draw in a breath, the nausea swept over him like a tide. He leaned over the sink until his stomach stopped heaving; there was nothing much to throw up, anyway.

By the time he'd brushed his teeth and borrowed a clean, soft dressing gown from Warrick's wardrobe, he felt halfway human again. Or he would, with about forty-eight hours' sleep.

In the kitchen he found Warrick standing by the counter, slicing something with unnecessary violence. He apparently hadn't heard Toreth come in, and walking up behind him unannounced didn't seem like a good idea. "Warrick?"

He started, but not enough to lose any fingers. "Feeling any better?" he asked.

"Yes." He bundled his clothes into the washing machine, with the exception of the shirt. They'd be dry in the morning and the only reminders he'd have left would be the impressive collection of bruises. Even they would be gone before too long. It was over, just as he'd told Kemp.

The shirt he stuffed into the recycling.

As the washer started up, Warrick spoke without turning around. "I didn't mean to sound as if I blamed Sara for what happened. I don't. While we were waiting, she told me what he did to her. So I quite understand why you did what you did."

"Forget it. It doesn't matter."

He sat down at the table and watched Warrick work. "Possessive fucking maniac," Sara had called Jonny. He found the words poised again. I wouldn't hurt you. I'd never do to you what he did to Sara.

Who would he have been trying to reassure? He could hurt Warrick, he knew damn well he could. In the past he nearly had. He'd wanted to—but he'd only wanted to. Jonny had wanted to and done it. That was the difference. He could stay in control.

Except when he hadn't been able to. Toreth flexed his right hand, and even with all the other aches and bruises, his knuckles still hurt. What if one day Warrick pushed him that hard? Would he be able to step back?

Even if he'd been sure the denial was true, he couldn't make himself say it aloud. Warrick had more than enough of him already; he wasn't giving any more away.

Warrick finished doing whatever he was doing, and wiped the knife blade carefully. Then he laid it down and turned around, squaring his shoulders. Toreth expected him to say something else about Jonny or Sara. Instead he asked, "Why aren't you going to take the job?"

The question surprised him, because Warrick hadn't pursued it earlier. "Not everyone wants to work for corporates," he said after a moment.

"That's not the reason."

"You don't want to hear it."

"I do. That's why I asked. However, if you mean that you don't want to tell me, that's fine. I won't mention it again."

He could have let it go. When Warrick said something like that, he meant it. Instead, following his earlier impulse, he said tentatively, "I missed some of the detail out. Some of the more colorful parts."

Warrick nodded. "I rather thought that might be it. That's why I didn't ask when Sara was here. What happened?"

"By the river, before Kemp turned up, they...made me kneel." He rubbed his thigh. "With a shock stick, and *that* hurt like fuck to start with but then, after that, they held a gun against my back. Until Kemp arrived. Which took...I thought—I was absolutely fucking sure—that they were going to kill me."

Hungry water lapping at the bank, the river waiting for him. He felt sick again, and light-headed. Warrick said nothing, but his face was tight with anger.

"I've never been so fucking frightened in my life," Toreth continued, when he could. "I didn't...I've had people shoot at me, I've been stabbed, but I've never had time to think about it like that. Kemp did it. He was the one who told them to do it."

"Bastard," Warrick said softly. Then, "How can you be sure?"

The question didn't offend. Warrick wasn't disbelieving, simply asking. He hadn't even considered the point before, the certainty was so strong. He thought it through, going back over the events. "Chris—the one with gun. The way he talked over the comm. He didn't talk to Jonny like that. It was much too respectful."

"Why the hell did he do it?"

"Fuck knows. To scare me off from his precious son. Test his potential employee. Because he gets a kick out of that sort of thing—maybe it runs in the family. He tried to make it sound as if Jonny was responsible for everything, but he wasn't. Not for that."

Warrick nodded. "Kemp doesn't sound like someone you ought to be working for."

"Understatement of the fucking century." And that was all he wanted to say. All he could say, and he couldn't believe he'd said anything at all.

Warrick cleared his throat. "I thought—"

Whatever it was, he didn't want to hear it. "I'm going home," he said, levering himself to his feet despite protesting muscles. "I need to get some sleep. I'll call tomorrow."

Warrick ignored him. "I thought you were dead," he said, his voice still quiet. "Or rather, not precisely that, but I thought that there was a significant possibility that you were."

Then he stopped. That was, apparently, everything.

Oddly, that was almost the last thing Toreth had expected him to say. "I'm sorry," he said reflexively. He knew he ought to add something else, but he couldn't come up with anything, not with Warrick looking at him with such uncharacteristic, uncomfortable openness. Toreth finally persuaded his fingers to release the back of the chair. "I'm going. I'll—"

Warrick moved towards him, a hesitant approach that petered out halfway. He stood perfectly still for a moment, then smiled, very slightly. "Do you want to fuck?"

Toreth blinked. "Do I want to fuck?" he repeated stupidly, while his brain tried to catch up with a second quite unexpected comment. Why, he wondered, couldn't Warrick hold conversations in the same way as other people?

Warrick shook his head, the smile slipping away. "No, probably not. But I don't know how else—" He lifted his hand, then let it drop. "Don't go. Please. Stay, and come to bed with me."

To his surprise, Toreth found his exhausted, aching body responding. Wanting the contact, the closeness, if nothing more. Wanting not to wake up the next day hurting and alone. Wanting Warrick, too much, as usual. He thought again about leaving, but he didn't have the energy. Or, he realized belatedly, the clothes. He nodded. "Okay, I'll stay. I'm starving, anyway." Formal excuse, however unconvincing.

Warrick smiled again, properly this time. "I'll finish the food first, then." He closed the rest of the distance, moving with confidence this time. "It won't take long."

The food or the embrace? Toreth didn't really care. He shut his eyes, leaning into Warrick, surrendering—just for now—and ignoring the complaints from his bruises. It helped that he was too damn tired to care about whatever wasn't being said. Eventually Warrick pulled back and kissed him once, lightly. "Sit down. I'll be five minutes."

Good idea. He sat, resting his head on his left arm and considered falling asleep right there. He could hear Warrick, by the hob, and after a minute or so, he smelled bacon frying. Maybe he could stay awake for that.

As he waited, despite his best efforts to think of something else, his mind wandered back to the river. Then, strangely, on to Sara in the hospital, telling him about the ring. Did he feel any different for having told Warrick about the mock execution? In the end, he decided that he wasn't sure—he had no idea how he would have felt if he hadn't. He didn't possess a basis for comparison for the last twenty-four hours.

He'd think about it again later. Much later. In the morning, when everything was back to normal and he would be back in control.

Chapter Three

❖

Fragmented images. Hands tied behind his back. The instructors' experienced hands pushing him down, forcing his head under the water. The world blurring above him. Losing the fight not to panic, not to struggle. Dull, distant laughter and cold, cold water in his mouth, in his throat, as he screamed—

Then a vicious, disconnected pain, and Toreth woke, gulping air. For a moment, he still didn't know where he was. Then it came back, in bits and pieces: where he had been and where he was now.

Warrick's flat. Warrick's bed. His injured wrist had slipped over the edge of the mattress, hitting the bedside table.

Rolling onto his back, he groaned quietly. Every muscle ached and the bruises on his upper body added an extra level of hurt. It was every single time in his life that he'd overdone it at the gym added together and then magnified tenfold. He also had a sick headache, which felt like dehydration. Wonderful—a morning after without the night before. Painkillers. He wanted lots and lots of painkillers. And water. And breakfast. And then another night's sleep.

He straightened his legs and groaned again. Warrick turned over beside him, and he felt warm fingers curl gently around his shoulder. "It's all right. You're safe. I'm here," Warrick mumbled, sounding more than half asleep.

"What the hell are you talking about?"

"Mm?" After a few seconds, Warrick propped himself up on his elbows. "Sorry. You were . . . you kept waking up."

Water in his mouth, in his throat, flooding his lungs.

Old dream. Done it before. Boring. "I don't remember."

"I'm not surprised—you never woke up for long. And you were absolutely spark out, in between."

Warrick was clearly being tactful. How much had he been able to work out? "Sorry if I kept you awake. I should've gone home."

Warrick shook his head. "If it had bothered me too much I would've gone to sleep in the spare room." Then he rolled away, out of the bed. "Stay there for now, anyway. I'll be right back."

Toreth thought about sitting up, but in the end he decided that flat on his back was the least painful place he could be. Sunday today, which meant that technically he could lie here and do nothing except wait for Monday. That seemed like a very attractive option, apart from for the fact that he was ravenous. With any luck, Warrick had gone to get breakfast.

In fact, the first delivery was water, a couple of tablets, a cup of coffee, and a spray can. Warrick set the tray down, then picked up the can and read the label while Toreth washed down the painkillers. "What's that?" Toreth asked.

"Prescription-strength analgesic spray."

"What the hell are you doing with a can of that?"

"Comes in handy sometimes." He shook the can half a dozen times, then stripped the sheet down to Toreth's hips. His eyes narrowed as he surveyed the bruising from the strap.

"Is that safe to use with the tablets?" Toreth asked.

"According to the label, yes. Put your hand over your eyes."

The nozzle hissed as Warrick swept the can back and forth, slowly down from shoulders to stomach. The mist settled, burning cold, then hot and almost painful. Then the sensation faded into a faint tingling, which eventually died away completely, taking the pain of the bruising with it.

"Mmh. That feels fucking fantastic."

Warrick laughed. "I'll have to remember that." Toreth opened his eyes to find Warrick looking at his watch. "Turn over."

Warrick repeated the procedure, and this time even the brief burning was a pleasure. He stretched warily, his numbed skin feeling peculiar against the sheets. All that was left were deep muscle aches and the throbbing in his wrist, which the painkillers were already blunting. Absence of pain wasn't something he'd appreciated enough in the past.

"Do you want breakfast in here, or in the kitchen?" Warrick asked.

"Give me a minute, I'll be along."

Actually, it took more like ten. For one thing, what had felt good lying down wasn't as wonderful when he stood up and started moving around. He found his clothes folded on a chair and, for a moment, he wondered where his shirt was. Against his will the riverbank came back into sharp focus, making his shoulders twitch at the memory of the gun.

They made me kneel.

Why the hell had he told Warrick about it? Some unbelievably stupid reason, obviously, which he couldn't now recall. Any minute now, he would have to go into the kitchen and sit and eat breakfast, knowing that Warrick knew.

I've never been so fucking frightened in my life.

Had he really said that? Reluctantly, he searched his memory of Warrick's face, his reaction to the words. He could find nothing he'd been afraid of remembering. No pity, no contempt—only anger and outrage. Warrick had been angry again, just now, looking at the bruises, which was . . . nice of him, Toreth supposed. Either that, or Warrick was pissed off because he was too fucked to be fuckable.

As he brushed his hair, he decided to forget it. It could be so much worse. He hadn't mentioned the river, and that was something. He could live with it—with himself—knowing that secret at least was safe. Stick to worrying about the important things in life. Breakfast, coffee, that sort of thing.

In the kitchen, Toreth sat at the table, helped himself to coffee, and watched Warrick cooking—pancakes, which somehow didn't surprise him. Even aching and tired as he was, he found it a mild turn-on. Something to do with the skill and concentration, maybe; he liked to watch anything being done well. Plus, for reasons he'd never bothered to explore, pancakes had coincided with some spectacularly good after-breakfast fucks. Not today, though. Not unless the painkillers had a lot more kick left in them.

"How are you feeling?" Warrick asked when the stack of pancakes reached a respectable height.

"Much better, thanks. Top marks to the spray."

"Take the can with you when you go, if you like."

"I might just do that."

"Right. Ready." Warrick set down the plates and sat down. The table already held coffee, fresh juice, breads, butter, and conserves—everything for a perfect lazy breakfast. A nice relaxing way to spend a Sunday morning, if he hadn't felt as though he'd been trampled in a riot.

Fortunately, pancakes were easy to deal with one-handed. After they'd eaten in silence for a while, Warrick asked, "Are you still planning to turn down the job?"

"Yes. Why? Changed your mind about it being the right thing to do?"

"Good God, no. I was merely wondering about Kemp."

"What about him?"

"How he's going to react to your refusal."

He didn't want to think about Kemp, even though he probably ought to. "I told him it was over. I don't see it makes any difference to that."

"But will he agree?"

"God, I hope so." He rubbed his wrist gingerly. "I'm really not in the fucking mood to do that again."

"Mm." He had, Toreth noted, started the toast thing again. What was coming next? When the slice had been buttered to satisfactory evenness, Warrick bit the corner off and asked, "What are you going to do if he decides otherwise?"

"I don't know." He hesitated, hating the sound of that. "Taking on corporates of his class one-on-one is punching a long way above my weight. There's nothing I *can* do, that I can see, except to do to him what he did to me. Only I'd finish the fucking job."

Warrick put the toast down. "No."

The firmness caught Toreth by surprise. Before he could say anything, Warrick continued, "You wouldn't get away with it. And this isn't worth getting killed over."

That was the problem. It nearly was, or it was beginning to feel that way. The humiliation burned in a slow, lasting fire. Nothing he could do, and he hated helplessness more than just about anything else. His life taken out of his control. Anger welled up and threatened to breach the dam.

"Untouchable bastard corporate *wankers.*" He smacked his left palm on the table, because Warrick wouldn't appreciate it if he threw his cup across the room. "Someone should shoot the fucking lot of them."

Warrick steadied his own cup. "Rubbish. No one's untouchable. To pick a random example of a bastard corporate wanker, I'm not."

"I didn't mean you," he said before he could stop himself. Oh, well done. Just what he needed—to give Warrick more ammunition.

Warrick smiled, looking delighted to have drawn a response. "Of course not. But there are always ways. Personal ways or business ways, depending on what you want to achieve. I know where I'm vulnerable."

He counted points off on his fingers as he talked. "Dilly, and family in general. Friends, some of whom are also colleagues. You. That's on the personal side. Professionally, SimTech has its own set of skeletons in its cupboard—we make sure they never rattle, that's all. Disgruntled employees are always a danger, even though we make an effort to treat people well." He paused briefly. "And then there's the old business with the investigation. Plenty of approaches, if you think about it."

Toreth considered the idea. He was used to looking at those situations from the other side, sifting through the debris of corporate unpleasantness when it escaped into the open. It hadn't occurred to him to try to play that game himself.

"Kemp will have his own weaknesses," Warrick continued. "Far more than I do, I would say, because he's so much more successful."

"Richer, anyway," Toreth said absently, still thinking about the list Warrick had given.

Warrick smiled. "Thank you. Yes. Richer, anyway. But if he thinks he's safe, he's sadly misguided. We'll be able to think of something to correct the misapprehension."

"We." Warrick's casual inclusion of himself in the enterprise almost slipped past him. "It's nothing to do with you. Whatever he says about the job, I'll sort it out myself."

Warrick looked at him, then shrugged. "I'm not planning to go round to Kemp's office and punch him on your behalf, if that's what you're worried about."

"I'm serious, Warrick. I want you to stay out of this. Is that clear?"

"Perfectly. Would you like anything else to eat?"

"I—yes. Couple more pancakes, if there are any going."

"Just let me get the pan hot."

Topic closed. Opening it again would be the first step on the slippery slope down to a serious discussion of things he had no desire to talk about. After which Warrick would do whatever the hell he wanted to, anyway.

Once he had poured in the batter, Warrick said, "To change the subject very slightly, what are you going to do about your flat? Specifically, about the security system."

"I hadn't thought about it."

"Well, if I might make a suggestion, you could consider replacing it with one which actually provides some measure of security."

Toreth shrugged. "I've never needed it before. It's not like there's anything much valuable there."

"Mm. I could send someone round, if you don't mind—a company that does some security consultation for SimTech. They're very good. They did here."

"Expensive?"

"Not excessively. Consider it an early birthday present. Or you can pay me back, if you prefer. Later. However, I think it would be a good idea to have it fitted now."

I thought I was the one who bought the chains. "I don't need—"

With miraculous timing, the door to the flat opened. They both froze, Warrick with a pancake half-lifted, until Dillian's voice called, "Keir? Are you ready? Sorry I'm late."

Warrick flipped the pancake and did the remaining two quickly. "Oh, damn. Burned." He raised his voice. "We're in here."

"We? Oh." Toreth heard her voice change as she came down the corridor. "Good morning, Toreth, I—"

As she came into the room she stopped dead.

He didn't bother to look around. She'd obviously seen the bruises—they were a little difficult to miss. "Morning, Dillian. I have to be going, I'm afraid. I've got things to do."

"I'll send someone round, shall I?" Warrick asked, as Toreth stood up.

Taking the opportunity offered by Dillian's presence, when he wouldn't argue. Still, on the other hand, pride was a poor substitute for being alive. "Okay."

Warrick nodded. "Do you want to borrow a shirt?"

"Yeah, thanks."

48

To Warrick's relief, Dillian didn't say anything until the outer door of the flat closed. Then she asked, "Keir, what happened?"

"Would you like a pancake?" He should have remembered that she was coming around. At least then Toreth could have had a shirt on. "And there's coffee, if you want some. Or we can get going."

She sat down. "You can stop that right now. I'm not going anywhere until you tell me."

"It's a long story."

"I have plenty of time. Is he all right?"

The genuine concern in her voice surprised him. "Yes. What you could see is more or less all the damage there is."

"Good. There's no need to look at me like that. I may not like him very much, but I don't want to see him hurt. And I don't want to see *you* hurt, either."

"It's absolutely nothing to do with me." He offered her a cup. "He was beaten up by someone who didn't even know I existed."

She took the coffee, looking skeptical. "That didn't look like the result of a bar fight to me. Who was it? Outraged husband?"

"Something like that."

"You are the worst liar in the world, you know that? Tell me."

He knew that she wouldn't let it drop until he'd told her something. "All right. But you have to promise me that you will keep this an absolute secret. Don't even tell anyone else involved that you know about it. Not Toreth, not Sara, not anyone at all."

She stared at him. "Now you're scaring me. Yes, all right, I promise."

He gave her the condensed version of the condensed version, missing out the whole scene by the river. When he'd finished, she didn't look any happier.

"I can't believe you helped him."

"I didn't know why he wanted the name."

She sighed. "It wouldn't have made the blindest bit of difference, though, would it? You'd have done it for him anyway."

"Probably, yes."

"Oh, God. What were you *thinking*, Keir? What if this boyfriend of Sara's had gone to Justice? What if it had all come out? And how did you get hold of the name, anyway?"

He ignored the last question. "He didn't go to Justice then, he can't now. There's nothing to worry about."

"Nothing to *worry* about?"

"Not about me. I'm not involved." Yet. The unspoken qualifier sounded so loud to him that he was surprised when she didn't pick up on it.

"But you told this Kemp your name when you called him, didn't you?"

"Yes."

49

"Oh!" She threw her hands up. "How can you be so, so—"

"Calm? Look, he has no idea that I had anything—"

"No, you idiot. How can you be so *stupid*? God, now I'm sorry that I felt sorry for him. I wish they'd broken every bloody bone in his body, twice over, for dragging you into this."

He could feel his patience beginning to stretch thin. He tried to keep his voice level, because she was only worried for him. "Dilly, drop it. It happened, and it's over now."

"Really?" She dragged the word out, disbelievingly. "What if Kemp doesn't think so?"

Sometimes he wished she wasn't so astute. "Then Toreth's in serious trouble, which should make you happy."

"No. No it doesn't, because it would make you very unhappy." She sat back in her chair with a sigh. "God, but that man is *aggravating*. Do you remember when I worried about you spending too much time in the sim? I take it all back."

As usual, he couldn't manage to stay angry with her. He reached across the table and took her hand. "Everything will be fine." He squeezed her fingers gently for emphasis. "You caught the tail end of it. Nothing more is going to happen, I promise."

She smiled wryly. "Don't make promises you can't keep. Just tell me that you'll try to stay out of it."

He nodded, grateful that she'd said "try."

"And all the rest," she said after a moment. "All the usual."

"I know. I will be." Another squeeze, then he let go of her hand and checked his watch. "Do you want to go? We'll only miss twenty minutes or so."

"No. I'm not really in the mood for music any more. I think I'll do some shopping, and then I'll go home and fret for a while."

Relief that he hadn't had to cancel the day out himself cheered him slightly. "If it makes you happy, dearest Dilly darling."

She made a face. "You know, sometimes you almost deserve him."

When she had finally gone—after extracting more promises that he would take care—he set about finishing his breakfast. Dilly's arrival had been a mixed blessing. At least he'd managed to get Toreth to agree, however reluctantly, to the new security system. He'd anticipated a much tougher fight over that, and he'd better sort it out as soon as possible, before Toreth changed his mind.

He wasn't in the least surprised that Toreth had left. The only real surprises were that he'd stayed as long as he had, and that he'd said what he had last night.

Thinking it over now that he was alone, he felt incredibly . . . well, "flattered" might be an acceptable approximation. Pleased that Toreth had trusted him enough to tell him what had happened—even though he was very probably regretting it now—and then to stay afterwards, although he knew that neither of them would mention it again. It had been a display of trust by Toreth that a couple of years ago Warrick would have found impossible to imagine.

Give it another ten years and they'd be living together.

While he ate, he amused himself by exploring the full horror of the concept. Then, when he'd finished, he made another pot of coffee and took it into the study. Time to start finding out about Gil Kemp.

When he checked his comm back at his flat, Toreth found Kemp's job offer waiting for him. Quick work—it made him wonder how often the situation arose for Kemp. Curiosity prompted him to see what he was turning down.

Sitting down—wincing as his back hit the chair—he paged through the details, impressed despite himself. "Generous" was a more than adequate description, starting with an undertaking to buy out any remaining training obligation to the Administration. Not an excessive amount in his case, after so long, but still a consideration. Plenty of corporate offers didn't include that, or translated it into a loan to be deducted from salary, although with the size of the salary on offer that wouldn't have been much of a deterrent.

Accommodation was included in the package and reasonable latitude as to location, plus the option to appoint his own assistant. Had Kemp been thinking of Sara? The idea of working for Kemp hadn't seemed to bother her at all. Or had she just not thought it through then? Maybe he'd ask her tomorrow.

Toreth paused. Was he sliding towards thinking about accepting the offer? Generous terms, indeed. For a moment, he deliberately directed his mind back to the river.

Doesn't sound like someone you ought to be working for, Warrick had said, and he'd definitely had the right idea about that, although hopefully he was wrong about Kemp's likely reaction to a refusal. Toreth spent a while drafting a polite negative, then sent it to the reply address given on the offer. Kemp probably wouldn't see it until Monday, if ever.

That was it. It was over.

To his surprise, it wasn't even lunchtime before Warrick's pet security company turned up. As he'd expected, they were highly professional and efficient but, in such a small flat, it was impossible for them to work around him without disturbing him. In the end he asked for an estimate of how long it would take and went out to enjoy the first real sunshine of the summer. Or at least to try to do so.

He walked to the perimeter of the Int-Sec complex, scanned his ID at one of the unmanned staff entrances, and headed for the landscaped gardens around the small lake. Being a Sunday, it was quiet, although a few Int-Sec employees had brought their families along to this lower security zone to picnic in the sun. Perk of a good Administration job. Toreth lowered himself carefully to lie on the grass, watched the clouds passing, and thought about corporates.

Theirs wasn't a world he lived in, but it was one he understood well. Beating the crap out of a partner was something any senior corporate of middle ranking or higher could expect to get away with, as long as they picked the right victim, preferably someone poor and unprotected.

Everything was relative. Jon Kemp was the son of a major corporate, but not influential himself. Sara worked for a powerful division, but had a low-status job within it. Toreth himself was a more important figure than Sara—too important to consider simply disposing of, as Gil Kemp had clearly understood. Set against Gil Kemp, though, Toreth's personal influence was no more significant than Sara's.

He couldn't banish the uneasy feeling that it wasn't over. Warrick's doubts, clearly demonstrated in his insistence on the new security for the flat, and Toreth's own instincts agreed on that point. As a rule, he didn't trust instinct. In this case, though, he could spot a control freak at a hundred meters—not difficult, because "control freak" and "senior corporate" were practically synonymous. By not playing the game, by refusing the gilded cage, he'd probably upset Kemp a great deal more than he had by assaulting his son.

A loud splash wrenched him away from the depressing ruminations. He sat up too quickly, heart pounding, to find a small shoe bobbing in the center of a widening ring on the lake and a child being soundly scolded by its mother.

He looked at the dark water, ripples smoothing out in the gentle breeze, and wondered why the hell he'd come here instead of another part of the grounds. But moving somewhere else, now, would be an admission of defeat. Looking at his watch, he decided to head back home, via some food shopping. He didn't fancy going around to Warrick's for a few days, so he ought to get something in.

On the way out, the scanner rejected his ID three times before it let him through. A glitch in the system, nothing more, and common enough. Still, it didn't improve his mood.

The security firm estimated well. When he returned, they were finishing up, and the woman in charge, who styled herself as a personal security consultant, walked him through the system. He couldn't deny that it made him feel safer. It would be easier to come through the wall than the new door, and the upgraded alarm system encompassed all the windows, as well as sensors in every room.

The personal security consultant told him that the invoice was already settled, but she gave him a copy without protest when he asked. Briefed by Warrick, no doubt. The total made his eyes water, and he decided to let Warrick pay it, if he really wanted to.

52

Chapter Four

Toreth nearly didn't go in to work on Monday. He hadn't slept well, and his wrist ached nastily. Although the bruises and general muscle pains were a little better, he still required handfuls of painkillers before he made it out of bed. In the end, though, hanging around at home with nothing to do but hurt seemed less attractive than hurting slightly more while being busy.

As he prepared to leave the flat, Kemp called him. Not even half past eight.

"What can I do for you?" Toreth asked, knowing the answer.

"I have a note here saying that you declined my offer." Kemp's voice wasn't a bad approximation of friendly, but it had an edge of anger.

"Yes. Thanks for the thought, and I appreciated the package, but I'm happy where I am."

"That's a shame. I was looking forward to having you working for us. May I ask why?"

I don't work for fucking psychos. "Personal reasons."

"I see. A pity. But I have a number of friends at Int-Sec, and even a few at I&I. If there is anything I can do for you in the future, as recompense for your unfortunate experience, I hope you'll remember my influence there." Now the edge in his voice was definitely a threat.

"Thanks. I will."

"Excellent. I shall keep my eye on your doubtless successful career. Goodbye."

❖ ❖ ❖

That afternoon, Toreth sat at his desk and looked at his sixth coffee of the day, cooling in front of him. It was always a bad sign when Sara provided drinks unprompted, particularly in these quantities. It meant that one of them was seriously out of sorts. Since it wasn't him, there had to be something wrong with her.

He knew what it was. He'd known before Warrick had said it in the flat—she blamed herself for what had happened to him. Annoying, but probably inevitable, Sara being who she was. As inevitable as the fact that he'd have to talk to her about it, although he wasn't sure what to say.

No time like the present to find out. He tapped the comm. "Sara, could you come in here for a moment, please?"

The "please" probably threw her, because it took a few seconds for her to say, "I'll be a minute."

"Now, please." Before he changed his mind.

She took so long that he was about to go and drag her in. Then the door opened and she stepped through, stopping just over the threshold. "Yes?"

"Sit down."

"I'm busy."

"And I'm your boss. So sit."

Reluctantly, she perched on the edge of the desk.

That would have to do. "Have you got something to say?"

She hesitated, biting her lip.

"No? That must be a first." He pushed his chair back, put his feet up on the desk, and looked at his watch. "I've only got an hour before I'm due in a very boring meeting, and I've got better things to do with it than sit here and wait. But I will."

"I'm sorry." She met his eyes briefly, then looked down at her hands. "I know you don't want to hear it. But it's my fault that you got hurt, and I'm so fucking sorry."

"Oh? Well, that explains it then."

She looked up, puzzled. "What?"

"How they got the code into my flat."

Her eyes went wide. "I've never told anyone! Why would you even think I— oh. That's not fair. You know what I mean."

"Yes, I do. And that's bollocks, too. If you want to blame someone, try Jonny. That's who I'm blaming. And his fucking father."

"His father?" She frowned. "Why?"

Oh, hell. Careless and stupid. He'd have to cut back on the painkillers. "Nothing serious. He made some threats he can't back up, to try to keep me quiet."

Now she looked alarmed. "Threats? But I thought he offered you a job?" Something of his manner from Saturday night must have filtered back, because she shut her mouth abruptly.

Toreth sighed. "There's nothing to worry about, I promise." I hope. "It wasn't your fault." Weak, and not surprisingly ineffective.

"Yes, it was. If I hadn't been so stupid as to get mixed up with Jon in the first place, you wouldn't have had to do anything."

"*Had* to? Right, of course. You held a gun—" Fucking, fucking hell. "You held a gun on me and forced me to go over and beat the shit out of him. Because it would never have occurred to me to do it on my own, would it? Seeing as the bastard richly deserved it and I *wanted* to do it. Anyway, it's just a few bruises and a bit of a sprain. Forget it, and we can get back to work."

She looked down again. Impasse. This wasn't getting them anywhere. He should have put more thought into it to start with—now he was stuck for a line of attack and that always looked bad. Luckily, as he was considering telling her to go, she gave him an opening. "I should have told you not to—"

"You could have told me anything you liked. I'd still have done it."

She glanced up. "You know . . . that's what Warrick said."

Thank you, Warrick. "Well, he's not just a great fuck."

"God, he must be thrilled with me."

"Not that it's any of his business what I do for my friends, but he thinks it was the only thing to do."

"Really? He said that?"

It seemed like a reasonable interpretation of Warrick's position to Toreth. Or at least plausible. "Of course, really. Ask him yourself if you like. Look, if me and Warrick both say that I'm stupid enough to have done it on my own, whatever the fuck you said about it, can we agree that it wasn't your fault?"

Small shrug. "I suppose so."

Well, that was a slight improvement. "Anyway, I didn't say thanks properly, did I?"

She looked at him blankly. "For what?"

"Getting me out of there. I mean, it was your idea, wasn't it? Calling Kemp? I'd have been far more fucked up if he hadn't arrived when he did." Dead in the river, in fact. "So, thanks."

"No. I mean, um, I was only trying to—"

"So we can call it quits. Right?"

Another shrug. "All right."

"Then are you going to stop this guilt crap? It's pissing me off, and I'm getting caffeine shakes."

She smiled wanly. "Sorry."

Progress, at last. Time to get things back to normal. "Right, that's it—final warning. If I hear you say sorry one more time, I'll spank you."

"You'll what?" Her smile turned into something almost worthy of the name. "You wouldn't dare."

He took his feet off the desk and sat up. "Try me."

"That's harassment, you know. Even admins have rights." She slid off the desk, jolting it and spilling his cold coffee. "Oops. Sorry."

He let her beat him to the door, then went back to his chair. He meant to get back to work, but instead he found himself thinking about Kemp. The conversation this morning had been worrying. Kemp didn't strike him as the kind of man who made empty threats. If he said he had friends at I&I, he probably had. Which meant that Toreth's career prospects had sharply nosedived.

Worst of all, he wouldn't be able to fight it. A call here, a word dropped there—invisible, immune to retaliation or even discovery. He'd seen it happen to others, watching as their lives unraveled. People who'd played the game, fucked up, and lost. Stupid or careless enough to have pissed off someone bigger than they could handle.

Not him. He wasn't helpless. He couldn't be. If Kemp wasn't willing to let it go, Toreth wouldn't be the one who sat around waiting for the next move. He needed something on Kemp, some pre-emptive defense he could use to persuade the corporate that it would be easier to leave him alone. Or, better, something to shaft the bastard good and hard. To take him down and pay him back for what he'd done, although that was too much to hope for.

He had an idea of where to start, too.

Finding Chris's full name was easy. Toreth had a good memory for faces and it took him less than an hour to put a profile together and come up with the address. A search for Chris had none of the risks associated with putting Kemp's name through the I&I systems.

Chris, last name Harper, had a very uninteresting record of a few minor Justice-level offenses. The rest of his file was equally dull: married; privately rented registered living address in an insalubrious part of the city; personal contract with no name supplied, which was legal enough if a little unusual; no known political affiliation, which wasn't a surprise. Standard-issue corporate muscle, except without a corporate job.

Closing the file, Toreth smiled. It would make a welcome change to deal with someone he didn't have to treat with kid gloves. Still, it would be easier and safer with some help.

Toreth decided to go looking in person, rather than use the comm. Chevril's office was empty, but Toreth found his fellow senior in the coffee room, staring at the newly installed coffee machine with an air of baffled irritation.

"Do you know how this bloody thing works? I'd only just got the hang of the old one when they changed the damn thing. Kel's off and if I don't get a coffee soon, I'm going to kill the next prisoner I work on."

The coffee rooms were theoretically not under surveillance, but it wasn't a theory Toreth had ever wanted to test over anything serious. "Come out for lunch, and I'll buy you one."

Chevril tended to regard unprovoked offers like that as possible chat-up lines, in which he was extremely uninterested. His expression of guarded suspicion prompted Toreth to add, "I need a favor."

After a moment, Chevril shrugged. "Okay. I was thinking about going out anyway, since it's so nice."

Like yesterday, the day was bright and summery. It was pleasant to get out of the office, even if Toreth's muscles weren't yet keen on prolonged exercise. At least the aches slowed him down a little—Chevril, barely touching one meter sixty and so thirty centimeters shorter than Toreth, was normally hard work to keep in step with.

As they walked through the Int-Sec grounds towards one of the commercial complexes on the periphery, Toreth explained what had happened, as nonspecifically as he could manage, leaving out the names and as many details as possible. Chevril—who was fond of Sara—reacted just as he'd expected. "So that's what happened to her. Kel didn't know. I hope you broke his bloody neck."

"I probably should have."

When he reached the end of the account, glossing over the river with what was becoming practiced ease, Chevril shook his head. "Jesus, if there was ever a candidate for re-education. You were bloody lucky—but then you always are, aren't you? Alive, and a nice corporate job offer. Some people."

"I didn't take it."

Chevril stopped dead and looked up at him. "You what? You turned him down?"

"That's what I said."

"Why, for fuck's sake?"

He couldn't tell him the real reason, so he settled for the general one that had kept him at I&I for so long. "I'm not selling myself to a corporate."

"You mean he's not offering enough?"

"He's offering plenty. I mean I'm not doing it, whatever he offers."

"So what was the deal?"

Toreth had to admit he'd been hoping Chevril would ask. "More or less twice what I'm on now. Housing paid for on top of that, training debt cleared."

"More or less...Christ al-bloody-mighty." Chevril's face screwed up in what looked like genuine pain. "If I turned that down, Elena would rip my heart out and casserole it."

"I don't fancy the idea of being someone's property, and that's what a personal contract makes you."

This was one of Chevril's favorite arguments, and this time he had the added outrage of a genuine opportunity being refused right in front of him. "Bollocks does it. Besides, even if it did, it's no different to where you are now. The Administration owns your soul and Tillotson gets the rest of you."

57

"That's not the same as belonging to some*one*. Tillotson works for I&I, just like us. He has a bigger office, that's all."

"Right. Of course. So you're staying principled and poor." Chevril shook his head. "You're completely bloody mad. Or am I missing the whole point, and he pays for everything these days?"

Stupidly, Toreth didn't realize what Chevril meant until he added, "The bloke with the corporate car and the expensive suits. The suspect you weren't—" he grimaced slightly, "fucking all the way through that dead-end corporate murder."

Although he knew Chevril was only saying it to get a rise, he couldn't help responding, not with the new alarm system in his flat. "You can fuck right off. No, he doesn't. And he was never a suspect."

"If you say so." Chevril grinned, leaving it unclear which part he was referring to. "But anyway, apart from making me puke with envy, is there a point to any of this? What's the favor?"

"I've got a nuts-on-the-chopping-block feeling about the father. I don't think he's willing to have me running around out here, where he can't control me, knowing what I know. I want to find something to give me some leverage if he won't back off."

Chevril shook his head firmly. "Not through me, you bloody well don't. I'm not running any searches on corporate higher-ups, if that's what you want to ask."

"No. But there's someone who might know some things. I want to have a nice little unofficial word with him, but I don't want to go on my own."

Chevril, who despite his pan-European-competition-standard whinging was good at his job, thought for a few seconds, then asked, "Bloke who picked you up?"

"That's him."

Chevril considered for a moment longer. "As long as you remember that you owe me for it. When? Tonight?"

"Tomorrow morning. I don't want to risk missing him and having to go back."

"Okay. You know," he added after a moment, "you could solve the whole thing if you'd take the bloody job. You'd make *me* feel better, anyway."

When he'd woken up for the second time that night, gasping for air, Toreth gave up on the idea of even trying to sleep. Instead he got up and kicked through the pile of washing until he found something to wear. The air felt cool against his damp skin, which made a good excuse for the shivering.

His wrist ached, as did the muscles in his shoulders, so he detoured to the bathroom for painkillers. Once in the living room, after switching on the heating, he poured himself a drink, sat down, and thought about drowning. Thinking it through sometimes stopped him dreaming about it later. Sometimes.

Or sometimes he worked himself up to near hysterics, and couldn't go to bed at all until he was drunk enough to pass out instead of fall asleep. Worth a try, though, because he knew that otherwise he *would* have the dream again, and he needed some sleep. Tomorrow he had things to do and he had to be sharp enough to get them done without screwing up.

So. A couple of mouthfuls he didn't even taste, and then back to his first year of training. They'd known, of course. It would have been in his psych file—accident on a family holiday, no permanent physical consequences, but...that's why they'd picked him out first, hoping he'd put on a good show to scare the rest of them. Well, that part had worked out.

The dream was everything he remembered; it was more than possible that he was remembering the dream and the real thing had been nothing like that. The rest of it he'd heard from Chevril afterwards: panic stations and emergency resuscitation and finally, reluctantly, a call to the medical unit. The instructors had been shitting themselves, at least according to Chevril. Killing recruits must generate a ton of paperwork.

The next day, though, when he'd discharged himself over the protests of the medic and turned up for training, the chief instructor had merely looked him up and down and said, "Can't you hold your fucking breath?"

"No, sir. Sorry, sir."

He'd won back whatever reputation he'd lost from his performance when Internal Investigations arrived.

He'd told them it had been an accident, a practical joke that got out of hand. No, sorry, he couldn't remember who'd been involved. It had been dark; they'd all been drinking. The investigators had looked profoundly unconvinced, but they'd finally gone away, leaving him with a confidential contact number in case he changed his mind. After about ten seconds' thought he'd decided that he'd rather have a career, and had deleted it.

That had pretty much been that. Why it still bothered him was a mystery; in fact, most of the time it didn't. The idea of being underwater made him uneasy, even in the sim, but he went swimming at the gym and enjoyed it. Or maybe enjoyed the mastery over what he was...what he disliked. Some psych rubbish like that, anyway.

It never, really, went away, though. Months would go past and then he'd get a run of dreams. Sometimes there was no reason he could think of for it. Occasionally he knew what kicked them off.

Once, he'd been over at Justice and he'd stood by and watched them breaking all the rules of due process to do to a prisoner what had been done to him. Screaming nightmares every night for a fortnight, after that one. The prisoner had talked, though. Jesus, who wouldn't?

This time, the river. Worse, because he'd had his hands tied again. Just the thought, and his heart started to race.

No big deal. It had happened, he'd survived, and he hadn't even got his feet wet so there was no reason for feeling like this. It would stop soon, because it always did in the end, and things would go back to normal. In a few weeks, he'd have forgotten all about it.

This was the first time for a couple of years, and beyond the unpleasantness of the dreams themselves, it annoyed him that he couldn't see Warrick. Bad enough that he'd spent the one night at Warrick's flat—those nightmares could be written off to exhaustion and the aftereffects of a day that would be an excuse for anyone to sleep badly. He could go around to fuck, but Warrick would want him to stay, and he knew he'd be tempted to say yes, in case being there meant he wouldn't—

If he did, though, if Warrick was there and heard it, again, then he'd know. That was intolerable. He'd stay away until the nightmares stopped.

Still, there was no harm in thinking about Warrick, because he made a pretty good distraction from anything. He'd sleep better once he'd come—he always did. Toreth lay down on his back on the sofa, finding it surprisingly comfortable now the painkillers and alcohol had kicked in, and started flicking through his mental database of Warrick fantasies. Some time ago he'd noticed that the majority of his fantasies involved Warrick nowadays. It had worried him briefly, and then he'd decided not to think about it.

His right wrist hurt too much, so he placed his drink on the arm of the sofa above him and used his left. Ambidextrous, for all the important things—who had he said that to? He closed his eyes, and pulled a memory to the front of his mind. Familiar and comforting. Warrick fucking him, moving against him, slow and deliciously deep inside him; Warrick's mouth pressed against his neck as he breathed faster...

The glass was still balanced above him when the light through the window woke him in the morning.

Insalubrious turned out to be something to which Chris's neighborhood could only aspire. Toreth couldn't recall ever coming to the area before, which was distinctly more of a Justice place than I&I. Ugly high-rise housing blocks, which looked like early second generation, built to replace even less substantial accommodation thrown up after clearance of the contaminated ruins of the old city.

Chris's building was slightly above average. At least there was a security lock on the door, and a guard in the entranceway—old and deaf, but not too deaf to understand that their visit was one best not remembered or commented on. A glance over his desk showed that the security cameras in the entrance were at least partly functional. He and Chevril were on record, which put a limit on the amount of pressure they could apply, down here or with Chris.

They took the stairs, and by the time they reached the eleventh floor they had to stop in the corridor for Chevril to get his breath back. Toreth leaned on the wall—wincing as the bruises protested—and watched the other senior panting, hands braced on his thighs. After a while Toreth said, "You ought to get to the gym more often."

"That's what Elena keeps telling me." He straightened. "Ah, bloody hell. We should've used the bloody lift."

"Somewhere like this? Even if it worked, I don't fancy being in an enclosed space with an emergency stop."

Chevril looked up and down the empty corridor, his breathing still heavy. "Do you really think someone would try something?"

"Probably not. But I don't want to end up having to explain to Justice what we were doing here, in uniform but without an investigation in progress, after we had to call for assistance."

"Fair point. Okay, let's get on with it and get out."

They walked down the corridor, which was fortunately blessed with a logical numbering system. Toreth stopped and checked his hand screen. "This is the one."

Chevril nodded. "Shall I? If he recognizes you, he might do something stupid. I'm not getting shot when I'm not properly on duty. Plays hell with the pension."

"Go ahead."

The comm proved to be broken, so Chevril settled for thumping the door. It took nearly a minute to get a response, before the door opened a crack.

Through the space Toreth could just see a woman's face—pale in a frame of short, blonde hair—and, lower down, a child, dark-eyed and with skin the color of milky coffee.

Chevril held up his ID, but the uniform had already registered. Her eyes went wide with fear, and she started to close the door. Chev put his foot in the way. "Don't be stupid."

Reluctantly, she let them in. From an unobstructed viewpoint, she proved to be somewhere in her late twenties and fairly attractive, in a pinched way. She was also pregnant—not heavily, but enough to show and to make her ineligible for various methods of interrogation. The little girl moved around behind her, shy in front of the strangers.

Toreth nodded to Chevril, who stepped back, letting him take over. "We want to speak to Chris Harper. Is he in?"

"No." He was preparing to cut his way through the ritual denials, but her expression had changed to one of surprise and, oddly, relief. "He's gone out—just to the shop. He'll be back."

"We'll wait."

She showed them through to the tiny living room. An effort had been made to decorate the room, but spreading damp darkened one wall, the cheap wallpaper mottled with black patches. Fresh air from the wide-open window failed to eradicate the smell of mold.

Toreth stood by the door, in case Chris was in another room waiting for a chance to run. The woman offered them a drink, which they refused, and then perched on the edge of a chair, her arms around the girl.

"You're sure he'll be back?" Chevril asked.

"Yes, of course. A few minutes at the most. I thought you might be him. We've been having trouble with the door. We've complained to the building agent, but he won't do anything about it."

Whatever the reason for her earlier change of mind, she was still nervous as a cat. He let her keep talking, while he waited by the door.

Nervous or not, her estimate had been good. After six minutes, Toreth heard the front door open. He stepped away, out of line of sight from the hallway, and put his finger to his lips. She nodded. The child beside her called out, "Daddy!"

After a few seconds the living room door opened and Chris stepped through, balancing full shopping bags. "I'm here, 'gator. I—" Then he saw Toreth and stopped dead. "Oh, *fuck.*"

Reflexively, the woman put her hands over the girl's ears. "Chris?"

He dropped the bags onto a chair and went to stand beside her, touching her shoulder but looking at Toreth and Chevril.

Toreth smiled, pleasant and calm, keeping the coldness for his voice. "I'd like a word with you."

"Dina, I need some privacy here." Chris's eyes didn't leave Toreth's face, pleading with him. "Take Allie, go downstairs to Manak's. I'll come and get you when we're done."

Toreth shook his head. "No. Chev, stay in here and keep them company."

Out of the corner of his eye, Toreth could see Chevril grinning. He kept his own face expressionless, but it was an effort. Chris had just handed them whatever they wanted from him on a plate.

Dina looked between them. "Chris?" she asked again.

Chris glared at Toreth, then nodded. "It's all right. Everything's going to be fine."

Reluctantly, he obeyed Toreth's gesture to leave the room. Out in the hallway, Toreth pointed to a door at random. "What's that?"

"Bedroom."

Perfect. "That'll do."

The bedroom was better than he'd hoped. Reminders of—what had her name been? Dina?—everywhere, and best of all, a cot in the corner. Exactly what he wanted to keep Chris's mind focused on cooperation.

"Sit on the bed. Good. Now, you're going to answer some questions for me. There's no need to make this official. If I like the answers, we'll go away and you can tell Dina everything *is* fine. Understand?"

"Yes. I understand." The anger showed only in his eyes, not his voice. "What do you want?"

"I want to know about your employer."

"About Jon Kemp?" He'd expected more resistance, but Chris seemed almost relieved. "That would be my *former* employer. Sure. What do you want to know?"

"And also about his father."

That produced slightly more of a reaction, a brief hesitation—a man deciding what was safe to say. "I don't know anything about him. Except that after he told me that Jon wouldn't be paying me any more, he offered to pick up my contract."

Sacked, then immediately reemployed. Obviously Kemp wanted Chris where he could keep an eye on him, at least for a while. "Did you accept?"

"Did I *accept*?" Chris laughed. "Of course I did. You don't turn people like him down, especially not when they make it pretty clear that it's an order, not an offer."

"Well, at least it's a job."

"Except that the tight bastard cut the rate and won't pay me everything Jon owed me and I don't feel like pushing it with him. So I owe money to the ... well, to lots of people, and I'm up shit creek."

One of Warrick's listed vulnerabilities—a disgruntled employee. "That's what you get for working in arrears. What are you doing for him?"

He grimaced. "I'm supposed to be keeping an eye on Jon. You won't be surprised to hear Kemp's sacked the previous watchers. So I'm back doing my favorite job, for less money."

"Music to my ears. So what's Jonny been doing since I saw him?"

"I don't know." Chris held his hand up. "I really don't know. He's been with Kemp senior since Saturday evening, back at the family mansion. I think after the last fuckup, Kemp's planning to keep him locked in his room for a while. About the only thing I've done is collect Jon's gear from the campus house. Not that I care if Kemp wants to pay me to do nothing."

Well, even Jonny probably had the sense to stay out of trouble for a while. "I want to know everything Jon Kemp's been up to that his father wouldn't want people to find out about."

Chris shrugged, temporizing. "Well ... I didn't work for him for that long. Ten months. He promised me a corporate contract after three—then he said no deal. I was planning to leave as soon as I could find something else."

"Bad timing," Toreth said without sympathy.

"No shit. You probably noticed that he's got a screw loose. Not one fucking screw tightened, in fact. But he paid well, and that's why I stayed. All we had to do was clear up after him and make sure his father never heard anything he wouldn't like."

"So tell me what happened in ten months."

"Not much. I dealt with suppliers and prostitutes, I took him to some very dodgy clubs and stopped people beating him up in them, I paid off a couple of women who'd pissed him off, and I had a word with another one who took it into her head to get in touch with Justice about him."

Toreth wondered if one of those three was Daedra's sister. It didn't matter, though. There was nothing there he could use—none of that would come as a surprise to Kemp. "Anything else?"

"Well..." The word dragged out with a promising show of reluctance.

"What?"

"We dumped a body for him. Woman. We cleaned her up and dropped her in the river."

At the usual place, no doubt. A good choice, because by the time she was found, if she was found, connecting her to Jon Kemp would be hell's own job. Toreth had a brief but absolutely clear image of Chris and his friends, of the body being lowered in. Of Sara's face, sliding under the water. He might never have found out what had happened to her. Anger tightened his shoulders, sending twinges down his back, but losing his temper again over might-have-beens wasn't productive. "Who was she? How did she die?"

"I got rid of the body, I didn't check her DNA and do an autopsy."

"Funny. What *do* you know?"

"She was a prostitute, and she tried to blackmail him over something. I don't know what about if it wasn't the obvious—pick any fucking thing, he could have done it."

Useless, no-account victim. He pursued it anyway, because it was all he had so far. "Why was he worried about her?"

"I don't think he was—I expect she just said the wrong thing and he lost his temper. Easily done, with him. Or he got carried away once he started on her. Mind you, he did mention that she had Almond's number. That's who she was threatening to call."

"Who?"

"Almond. I don't know his first name—the bloke who does the same thing for Kemp senior that I did for his son. Worked for Kemp forever, according to Jon. And he scares the shit out of Jon too, so hearing Almond's name might've been enough to tip him over."

Interesting. "Corporate or private?"

He shrugged. Toreth looked at his watch. All taking too long, and he wanted to finish and get going. He took a single step towards Chris, who looked up from his contemplation of the floor. "Hey! I don't know. Would you prefer me to lie about it? If you want me to guess, I'll say no. Almond's private, for private messes."

"Does Kemp make much of a mess?"

"I should think so." Chris raised his eyebrows. "I mean, with the way his son behaves? The man can't be normal."

Not a bad point. "No. I didn't think much of his sense of humor, for one thing."

Chris glanced towards the door. For the first time, Toreth noted. Impressive discipline, under the circumstances. "Listen, that was Kemp's idea," Chris said, voice low. "You understand? It... oh, fuck." Toreth knew what was coming. "I was just doing my job. It wasn't anything personal. You understand?"

Pleading. Looking at the door again, one step away from breaking down. Don't hurt them—if you want to hurt someone, hurt me.

Toreth didn't particularly want to hear it. He didn't feel a pressing need to settle any score with Chris, at least not pressing enough to want to complicate things any further. Besides, he might need him later, and he'd be far more useful grateful and no more humiliated than he had been.

He was about to wrap things up, when he found himself sidetracked by the automatic, professional pursuit of something unusual in his witnesses' behavior. A suspicion strengthened by something missing from Chris's file. "If I asked for it, you could show me a valid conception license, couldn't you?"

Chris stared at him for a long moment, then nodded jerkily. "Sure. Yes. Of course."

Toreth pulled out his comm earpiece. "Thirty seconds makes that an official inquiry to the Department of Population."

"No!" He started to rise, only relaxing when Toreth put the comm away. "All right. No. We don't have one." Which neatly explained Chris's surprising willingness to talk about Kemp, as well as Dina's reaction in the hallway.

"Tell me about it."

Chris stared back, sullen and frightened, until Toreth reached for his pocket again. "*All right.* Allie isn't my daughter—you probably guessed that. Dina had a partner, not for long. Allie was still a baby when we got together. And don't get me wrong, she's a lovely kid. But—" He shrugged. "I wanted—*we* wanted—a child together. But the DoP won't give us a license. We applied, we did it all legally. Christ, we even appealed it when they turned us down, with the best representative we could afford, which wasn't saying much. But the system's not fair." His voice rose, making justifications he must know wouldn't do any good. "We're not doing anything wrong. I don't have any kids. I've never even applied to the DoP before. I've got a right to—"

Bored, Toreth cut him off. This wasn't what he was interested in. "You have a right to make the application, not to have it granted. How are you working it? Implant failures?"

Chris shook his head. "The DoP doesn't accept double implant failure these days. Even if it's true, they'll force a termination. We're buying a fake pregnancy for... a woman we know. She'll call the baby hers and then we'll adopt him. We can get a license for that."

"It'll get picked up at the hospital, when they do the genetics."

"There's a... it's all taken care of."

"Expensive?"

Chris nodded. "Very."

It would be. The reproduction control laws allowed no latitude. When everyone in the Administration was obliged to have a free and extremely reliable contraceptive implant, unlicensed pregnancies were almost always both deliberate and criminal. So bribes alone would cost a fortune: corrupt doctors to be paid off, other staff at the hospital and test lab, probably someone at the Department of Population. Someone like Chris would never be able to afford them on his own, and for an organized scheme to repay the time and expense, it would have to be big. In all probability, Chris and his wife would be one of dozens. Even hundreds.

Toreth never understood why people did such fucking stupid things, simply out of some atavistic urge to breed. Still, if he couldn't find anything on Kemp, he'd take this as compensation. If he could dig up enough names, it would make a nice little case—conspiracy, corruption, violation of numerous population control laws.

He sat down on the bed next to Chris. "You don't need me to tell you how much shit you're in, but I will anyway. Reproduction without a valid license is a Justice matter. If I call it in now, they'll send someone round to arrest both of you, and that will be it. No mitigation, no right of appeal—automatic processing."

He paused for a moment to let that sink in, then continued. "It starts with enforced termination and sterilization, and it doesn't improve much after that. Reeducation for both of you, and when they're done, you won't be seeing each other again. Or Allie. At her age she'll probably end up in Administration care until she's fifteen, then she's out on the streets. Do you understand all that?"

Chris nodded, staring straight ahead, hands clenched in the bedspread.

"Now, here's the alternative. I can make it an I&I case, *if* you can tell me who else is involved. If you give me enough information to work it up into something I like the look of, I can have you classified as a privileged informant. That means money and resettlement, somewhere nicer than this. And I can get the pregnancy legitimized."

Now Chris looked at him. He licked his lips and said, "Really?"

"Yes, really."

Toreth watched as Chris thought it over. Whatever his character flaws, impulsiveness wasn't foremost among them. After a while he said, "Does my name get tied to it?"

There was no point lying. "Possibly. If there's anyone involved who can afford expensive lawyers, they might be able to force a disclosure of evidence. Or, well—" he shrugged.

Chris nodded. He'd know that all it took was a source in the right department, and I&I wasn't immune to that. "So what about protection? For Dina and Allie. Fuck—for me too, once Kemp hears about it."

"Why the hell would Kemp care?"

"He likes his employees to stay on the straight and narrow. And—" Chris hesitated, then the tension in his shoulders relaxed suddenly as he made up his mind. "Because he's behind it. He runs the scheme."

Briefly, the bed seemed to tilt under him, like a bad room transition in the sim. It went way beyond "too good to be true." So far beyond, in fact, that Toreth wondered if he'd hallucinated the statement. "*Runs* it? Kemp senior?"

Chris nodded.

"How the fuck do you know?"

He should've guessed the answer. "Jonny told me."

"So how did he know?"

"No idea. But . . . well, after I'd been working for him for a couple of months, I told him I needed a corporate contract. It might've helped with the DoP. He said he couldn't do that, but he knew a different way round it. He said he'd fix it up."

"Are you sure it was Kemp behind it?"

"Yeah. Jonny took me up to Kemp at some kind of black-tie family event and he—" Chris shrugged. "He just asked him about it, right out. Kemp was pretty fucked off, I can tell you. But the next week Almond, the man I mentioned before, came round to the flat to explain to us how it worked. He said—"

"Wait a minute—Kemp knows that you know he's involved?"

"I . . . yes, he does. Or he knows Jonny told me he was."

Why was it that every fucking thing he heard made the situation more complicated? Toreth thought about the security cameras and the guard on the main desk. Not promising. If Gil Kemp got word that he and Chevril had been here, things were going to go very badly indeed. Bad for him and a great deal worse for Chris.

"Is there a way out of here that isn't covered by the cameras?"

"Yes. Out the back—that's the way I came in." He grimaced. "We owe a month's rent, so I'm avoiding the agent. Why?"

"Because you need to get out of here, quickly and quietly. I'll find somewhere for you, temporarily."

"Dina and—"

"Yes. All three of you. Pack whatever you need, enough for a few days. Go down to the back and we'll be waiting for you." He hesitated. "No. Wait until we leave, go out the back and come in again through the front. Make sure the guard sees you. Then pack and come down. You know why I'm saying all this, don't you?"

Chris nodded. "Kemp. So he doesn't know I talked to you."

"Right. So you weren't planning to do anything fucking stupid, were you? Like run?"

"No." His gaze slipped away, very briefly.

"Not good enough. Listen to me. If you run, it becomes a question of who finds you first—Kemp or me. It might not feel like it, but with me you have rights. I can only do what the law lets me. Now, that's a lot of very unpleasant things, but it's nothing compared to what Kemp can do, if he feels like it. How old's Allie?"

Chris frowned at him, confused by the sudden question, then said, "Seven."

"Which is below the age of criminal responsibility. Whatever you've done, I can't touch her. Kemp can do whatever he wants. No waiver, he just needs to find someone willing to do it for him. Think about that."

It took another few seconds before Chris nodded. "Okay. Yes. I'll do what you said."

"Good. Don't explain anything to Dina—you can do that when we get you somewhere safe."

"She won't panic. She isn't like that."

Toreth sighed. "Just do what you're fucking told. Get in practice for later."

At the reception desk, Toreth and Chevril stopped to inquire, slowly and loudly, whether Chris had arrived after they had, and then to impress how important it was that he didn't hear they'd been there.

As the car drove around to the back of the building, he explained the plan to Chevril.

"Why my flat?" Chevril asked, once the car had parked in the least conspicuous spot they could find.

"Because they know exactly where I live. And I'm not risking a division safe house—Kemp told me he had lots of friends. Maybe he does, maybe he doesn't, but I'd rather not take the chance of him finding out we have Chris. We need to get some solid evidence on him."

"I'm not putting Ellie in danger. What if another load of his bloody heavies turn up?"

"They won't. Kemp isn't as fucking stupid as his son. Chris is all the link we have to him at the moment—Kemp'll go for him and leave us alone."

"Remind me again why I'm doing this?"

Toreth grinned. "Bonuses and commendations? Don't you want to be famous?"

Chevril rolled his eyes. "No, I want a nice, cushy job exactly like the one you turned down. I wonder if stitching up a major corporate player is going to help my chances?"

"Don't fuck around, Chev. Can I use the flat?"

"Of course you can." Chevril sighed. "But don't say I didn't warn you if it all blows up in your bloody face. Our bloody faces."

Rather to Toreth's surprise, Chris came out of the rear of the building only a few minutes after they parked the car. He looked frightened but in control, as did

Dina. She didn't say anything for the duration of the journey, keeping her eyes fixed on the floor of the car. Toreth's spirits rose slightly—hysterical witnesses were near the top of his list of dislikes about his job.

At their destination, they stopped the car only long enough to get people out and into the building. Chevril agreed, somewhat reluctantly, to take the car and check for any signs that they'd been followed. Once inside, Toreth felt safe enough. Although, unlike his own place, the majority of tenants weren't Int-Sec employees, the place was solidly respectable middle-ranking Administration. The security covered all the entrances and corridors.

Chevril's wife Elena welcomed them with her usual imperturbable calm. The abrupt appearance of Toreth and a fugitive witness complete with family seemed to cause her no more surprise than if it had been her husband at the door. Once inside, Toreth explained what they needed, and Elena smiled, nodded, and said it would be perfectly all right. "Thanks, Elena," Toreth said, as she took Dina and the child through to show them the guest room.

"My pleasure. Help yourself to something to drink. You know where everything is."

As he turned towards the kitchen, Toreth noticed Chris watching Elena walk away, his mouth slightly open. She tended to have that effect on men—hell, she certainly did on him, even after knowing her for fifteen years. Her long, black hair hung down her back in an immaculate curtain, swaying as she walked. Dina, pretty enough in her own way, looked drab beside her, as well as suddenly tiny.

When Chris tore his gaze away, Toreth raised an eyebrow. Chris frowned, defensive. "I was only thinking..."

"What?"

"She's tall."

Tall, dark, and mind-meltingly gorgeous. "One-eighty, in bare feet."

Chris shook his head. "And she's married to—"

"Chevril. Yeah. Which, incidentally, is none of your fucking business, except for being grateful to have somewhere to stay."

Chris smiled sourly. "Grateful. Right." Then his expression changed as he caught sight of Toreth's face. "I am! I am. It's just not what I was planning to do with my day."

Toreth nodded. "Remember—any time you want to get rid of me, I can call Justice and they can take over."

Chris closed his eyes briefly. "Don't—please, don't say that to Dina. She isn't thinking about it at the moment, and I don't want her to start."

"Behave yourself and it won't be a problem." Toreth led him into the kitchen. "I'll make some coffee, and then we can go through everything you know about Kemp and his operation. Starting with names."

Chris shook his head. "I don't know any. Honestly, I don't. Almond, that's all, and I only know that because Jon told me. None of the medics we met used names."

"Fair enough, then we'll start with descriptions..."

They were still talking when Chevril reappeared. "I didn't see anyone, which means they aren't there, or they're very good. Probably the latter, knowing my luck. How's things?"

"Fine. Did you keep the car?"

"Yes. It's round the back." Chevril looked at his watch. "Are we going to have time?"

"Should do—they're very quick. Take over here for a minute, while I get everything set up."

He went out into the hall to call Sara. When she answered, she sounded upset. "Toreth? Where are you?"

"Somewhere."

"I was worried."

Daylight dawned. "No need. I'm fine. I've got caught up in something, though. Is there anything I absolutely have to be there for this afternoon?"

"Let me look." Normal, unruffled Sara again. "Nothing that I can't postpone or delegate for you."

"Good. I need you to do some things for me. First, I need a privileged informant application submitting. Chris Harper—his file is already pulled in my name. It needs to go into the system *now* and, this is the important bit, it's got to be processed before this evening."

"That's no problem."

"Great. Second thing: connected to that, file an IIP, joint for Chevril and me. Conspiracy by someone to commit something corrupt—as vague as you can make it."

"Okay."

"It's got to include an authorization for the use of outside agencies for gathering evidence."

"Oh."

"Yeah." He could imagine her face as she imagined Tillotson's. "Can you do it?"

"How expensive will it be?"

"Low thousands if it all goes wrong. Less if it doesn't."

"Um...is it an emergency?"

Toreth considered. If everything came off, it wouldn't matter whether it was or not. But if things fouled up, this was where Internal Investigations would start taking them to pieces. It had to be by the book. "Could be—depends what happens, and when."

"Fine. I'll say it is, and I'll put it through this afternoon. You're in luck—it's Tuesday."

For a moment, the comment puzzled him. Then he remembered: Tuesday was Tillotson's long lunch day. Fucking his mistress was the popular assumption, although Toreth found it hard to believe—both that Tillotson had one in the first place, and that he'd take time off work for her if he had.

"Is that all?" Sara asked.

"No. One more thing—get someone on my team to start some *very* discreet inquiries as to where Jon Kemp's got to. Probably his father's place, but I want to be sure. I don't want him brought in, I just need to know where he is. It's more important that no one hears about it than that we find him—ask B-C to do it. That's all. I'll be in touch."

As he was looking for the second number he needed, someone spoke behind him. "Para-investigator?"

It was Dina, without her daughter or Chris, and looking even more scared than she had at home.

"What can I do for you?" Toreth asked.

"Chris says . . . that if he helps you, you're going to sort things out with the Department of Population." She put one hand on her stomach. "Is that true?"

Chris hadn't kept his mouth shut after all. "Yes."

She looked up at him, her eyes searching his face. After a few seconds, she nodded. "Will you put that in writing for me?"

Taken aback, he hesitated.

"I'm sorry," Dina said, not sounding anything of the sort. "It's not that I don't trust you, but promises like that sometimes get forgotten. If you got taken off the case, I mean, or . . . something like that."

"I understand." She had guts, that was for sure. Not many people would face down an I&I uniform, especially when it was plain she understood how much shit she was in. "In writing—of course. Now?"

"Yes, please. If it wouldn't be too much trouble."

"No trouble at all. Go through to the living room, and I'll be there in a few minutes. I've got one more call I have to make."

Toreth felt confident that if Kemp was going to try something, it would be done tonight, because it was only worth the risk if it happened in time to stop Chris from talking to them. Chevril's flat was closer to Chris's place than was I&I, so they both waited there. They took turns monitoring the emergency comms networks for anything that might show Kemp's men had moved. They'd need to get there quickly if they heard anything.

Besides, it gave him an excuse to stay awake. The dream—the river—lurked in the back of his mind, barely held at bay, waiting for sleep to release it. Sitting in the living room with Elena made a perfect distraction.

Without any discussion, Elena seemed to have decided to stay awake with them. He watched her, admiring her hair, as she told him something about her family. He vaguely remembered they didn't like Chev and had cut her off without a cent when she married him, or something like that. They were old corporate money, anyway. Chevril hated them with uncharacteristic passion, and was willing to explain why at stunningly tedious length if Elena wasn't around. Toreth wasn't sure what she thought—about her family or anything much.

She had a distant, veiled quality: she flirted gently, took everything in with quiet attention, and hid her feelings with a slight smile that, in function if not appearance, reminded him of Warrick. Toreth used to call her Enigma, and that had made her smile too, impenetrable as ever.

Sara, less charitably, said she was probably stoned all the time, because you'd have to be to marry Chevril for love.

All that said, Elena wasn't entirely impenetrable, at least literally. He'd fucked her, once, but afterwards he'd been able to read her no better than before and her attitude towards him hadn't changed in the slightest. He wondered sometimes if Chevril knew about it. He was always keen enough to keep the two of them apart, but that could easily be on general principles, since—

A question caught his attention. "Don mentioned that you're seeing someone?"

He blinked, surprised both by the inquiry and by the idea that Chevril would have said anything about it to her. "Yeah."

She smiled. "And?"

"And, well...that's it."

"How long has it been going on?"

"A couple of years, I suppose. Although it's not really 'going on' at all. It's a casual thing." That was, he reflected, sounding increasingly—and uncomfortably—improbable.

"Does the casual thing have a name?" Although her smile hadn't changed, there was a definite note of teasing in her voice.

"Warrick. Keir Warrick. He works at the university."

"Don said he owned a corporation?"

Now that was the kind of thing Chevril *would* mention. "SimTech. They develop virtual reality tech."

"That must be very interesting."

Away from Warrick and onto the topic of the sim, he felt more secure. "Yeah, it is. Fantastic, actually. Most mind-blowing thing I've ever seen in my life. It's...

well, it's hard to explain what it's like. Very, very real, mostly. I could try to get you some time in it, if you'd—"

"Toreth!" Chevril's voice, from the kitchen.

"Yeah?"

Chevril appeared in the doorway, grinning. "Fire at Harper's flat. Going up a bloody treat, if you believe the fire service comms. Come on."

By the time they arrived, the fire service had beaten them to it, and they had the blaze well under control. The flat, however, was gutted, and it would have made an unhealthy place to leave a valuable witness.

Toreth tracked down the lead fireman in the team. After taking his name and rank, he said, "I need a favor."

The man considered Toreth's uniform, then nodded stiffly. "Sir?"

"This flat is part of an investigation in progress. When you get in there, the place will be empty—it'd be helpful for me if there was a rumor you found three bodies. Man, woman, and child. It's what the neighbors'll be expecting in any case."

The man nodded again, looked relieved—probably that he wouldn't be spending the night extracting charred corpses from the ruins.

Once the flat had cooled sufficiently, they went inside. Even to Toreth's relatively inexperienced eye, it was obvious what had happened—a charred hole, halfway up the door, marked the start of the fire. Just inside, Toreth kicked something under the layer of fire suppressant foam. He retrieved it, burning his fingers slightly as he did so. It turned out to be the twisted remains of a small gas canister.

"To start the fire?" Chevril suggested.

"Or narcotics, if they wanted to make sure of them. They might as well, since they didn't bother making it look like an accident. We ought to know soon enough, anyway." He dropped the canister, and it disappeared under the foam. "Something for forensics to get excited about."

Warrick's security company had been as good as their word—the discreet box concealed in a cupboard in the kitchen had survived the fire unscathed, and the equipment inside was undamaged. Rather than watch the recording there, he took everything with him. No point in giving Kemp's men a chance to wonder what had taken them so long in the flat.

Back at Chevril's flat, they woke Chris and gave him the bad news. He was predictably upset but Toreth lacked the time or patience to care. "The division will pay for the damage in the resettlement. Put in as big a claim as you like, I'll sign it. Now watch the fucking recording."

It took only a few seconds of viewing before Chris nodded. "That's him. Almond."

All he needed, and enough for tonight, or what was left of it. A glance at his watch showed it to be after three in the morning. Rather than go home, Toreth went to I&I. He prepared warrants, firmed up the IIP so that Tillotson wouldn't quibble over it too much, and left a list of things for Sara to do in the morning. Eventually, he fell asleep at his desk as dawn started to lighten the courtyard outside his window.

Chapter Five

❖

If Toreth had a nightmare then he was too exhausted to remember it, or for it to wake him up. It was Sara who woke him, at ten o'clock, with a cup of coffee and a plate of bacon sandwiches. When he sat up, his back and shoulders screamed protest at the uncomfortable night.

"Anything new?" he asked, wishing for painkillers but settling for caffeine.

"Chevril told me what's going on," she said reproachfully.

"I didn't want to make it at all official until I had a link in to Kemp." Not much of an excuse, he reflected, since he'd told her any number of highly unofficial things in the past.

She didn't comment on it. Instead she broke off a crisped piece of meat from the edge of a sandwich and nibbled it. "Do you think you're going to get him?" she asked.

He blinked at her blearily, surprised by the question. Sara was a superb admin, but she rarely displayed any interest in the outcome of particular cases. No reason why she should. Of course, this was more personal than usual. "I hope so. Nowhere near enough evidence yet, but if Almond can give us names...maybe. Probably, even."

She smiled. "Good. No more important corporate father."

Ah. "What about Jon Kemp? Any sign of him?"

"Not yet." She licked her thumb and finger carefully. "Toreth, I don't want to be stupid about this, but if he—"

"I'm not bringing him in. I want to know where he is, that's all. Nothing's going to come out."

"Yes, of course. I'm sorry."

"Are you? Consider yourself spanked." He put the coffee down and picked up a sandwich—doing everything one-handed was growing tiresome. "Where are we up to with Almond?"

"Um...the ident system coughed up a full name—Jack Almond. I've pulled his security file for you. Chevril's sent some of his team out looking for him—says he's got a few spare he can use without having to put a request in to Tillotson for any from the pool. There's an address in the system, but Sedanioni called in to say that it's empty, and looks to have been that way for a while. She's talking to the neighbors, just in case, and then starting on a list of places Harper suggested."

"Great." Toreth swapped back to coffee and considered options. Not a lot he could do until Almond was found, except... "Call Warrick and ask him to meet me at my flat, if he can. If not, let me know. I'm going there now, anyway—I need a shower."

Not wanting to waste time, he took a taxi home, although the sun was shining again and the day promised to be beautiful. Maybe it was a good omen for things to come.

Back in the flat, the first thing Toreth did was find the painkillers. Then, after showering and changing, he tidied up a little. Normally he didn't bother but it seemed like the least he could do, since he was about to ask Warrick for a rather more significant favor than finding Jon Kemp's address. By the time Warrick arrived, the place looked almost respectable; judging by his raised eyebrows, he clearly noticed. But after sniffing the air, his only comment was, "Coffee?"

"Yeah—the nice stuff you left behind. What do you think of the new door?"

"Very impressive."

"I'm fucked if I ever forget the code. The old one opened if you kicked the right place. Have you got access?"

Warrick shook his head, smiling. "I only sent them round to fit it. I didn't ask them for the code."

Of course, he wouldn't have, but the compulsion to check had been... compulsive.

To his relief, Toreth could remember the instructions given by the security consultant, so didn't embarrass himself by setting off the alarm while trying to open the authorization program. Leaving Warrick to introduce himself to the system, Toreth went to fetch the coffee.

He'd already washed the mugs, to save himself from Warrick's usual pained expression. Toreth poured some milk into a mismatched jug that had come with the flat, and even found a packet of biscuits at the back of a cupboard. He didn't remember buying them, but they seemed edible enough so he piled a handful on a plate and set them on the coffee table. He surveyed the results. Pretty hospitable, if he did say so himself.

Once they were settled on the sofa, Warrick asked, "Well?"

"It's Kemp. Gil Kemp. I went looking for a bit of leverage, something to keep him at bay, and I found something a lot better than that. He's running an operation to bypass population control laws, probably on a large scale."

He enjoyed surprising Warrick—it happened so rarely. Warrick stared at him, mug halfway to his mouth, before he blinked and put the mug down on the table. "Kemp? Are you sure?"

"Yes."

"Why on earth would he?"

"Money is my guess. At least the sample of one I have so far is being squeezed for everything he can afford. If it's idealism, it's very lucrative."

"Good God." Warrick narrowed his eyes thoughtfully. "I suppose . . . it might make a certain amount of sense."

"Oh?"

"Yes. I've, ah, been doing some checking into his finances myself. Like you, I considered the desirability of leverage. I have the SimTech legal department hunting for loopholes in the sponsorship contract, to shut down our deal with his corporation. I thought they might need some help—they're very good, but distressingly honest, for lawyers."

Toreth frowned. "Why?"

"Probably something to do with our hiring policies. I ought to speak to Personnel." Warrick's face didn't show even a flicker of the evasion the answer certainly was.

"Not that—why are you canceling the sponsorship?"

Warrick picked up his mug again, leaned back on the sofa, and took a sip of coffee. "After due consideration, I decided to take what happened to you personally. I don't appreciate having my . . . having you assaulted and threatened. It annoyed me. SimTech doesn't need his money—or any money—that badly."

Warrick's lawyers weren't the only ones whose honesty was disturbing. Toreth decided to drop it, and also not to mention that he'd asked—ordered—Warrick to leave Kemp alone.

"So what did you find out?" Toreth asked.

"Primarily that there is something of a repetition of history in progress. Gil Kemp fell out with his own father, James Kemp. It was a long time ago now, but the conclusion was that they parted company extremely acrimoniously, and he went to start training as a medic."

"Jesus. Some fucking bedside manner he'd have."

Warrick nodded. "Quite. However, he never qualified. In some way no one I spoke to was clear about, he became involved in the running of a small private hospital. The enterprise was extremely successful and the hospital expanded. That became the foundation of the current Kemp Incorporated. He and his father were never reconciled, but I understand that by the time Kemp senior died, Gil Kemp had forced him to surrender control of several of his companies—and the rest was left to him in the will."

Toreth raised his eyebrows. "How old was James Kemp when he died?"

"Probably not old enough. Lots of talk of corporate sabotage at the time, or so I was told, but no one was ever charged." Warrick half smiled. "You know how it goes. I doubt anyone pressed the investigation—James Kemp was, by all accounts, as charming as his son and grandson. But if you want to suggest that Gil Kemp was involved, I'd advise very good lawyers before you even let the thought cross your mind."

"Happy fucking family. So you think the illegal conception money might have been the basis of it all?"

"It's more than possible. What have you found out about it?"

Toreth outlined the progress of the investigation so far. He finished with a problem. "I can't find Jon Kemp, though, which is good and bad. It'd be helpful if he'd confirm what I got from Harper, but this whole thing could get complicated if my visit to his flat comes out. If we find enough evidence to move on Kemp, we won't need Jonny-boy, anyway."

"Ah, now there I can help. He's in a high-level private re-education center. Booked in first thing on Monday morning."

It was Toreth's turn to stare. "A what?"

"Well, it's not how they describe themselves in the brochure, but that's what they are. Expensive, exclusive, but they're still going to work his mind over so thoroughly that by the time they've finished he probably won't even remember who you are, never mind what he did to you. Or to anyone else."

"So Kemp's written him off?"

"So it would seem. You must've been the last straw. Kemp's probably hoping to make sure he doesn't cause any more embarrassment in the future."

Or any more than he would cause by merely existing. Kemp's corporation would never accept his son as a successor now, not after a visit to any kind of re-education center, however carefully euphemized. "How did you find out? Have you got his personal comm?"

Warrick shook his head, slightly sheepish. "Nothing so impressive, I'm afraid. I heard it at a business lunch yesterday, from one of the other sponsors. As you can imagine, it's news that's making the rounds in bastard corporate wanker circles."

It dawned on Toreth that Warrick was never going to let that comment go. Ignoring him seemed like the only hope of nipping it in the bud. "Right, well, that makes it easier. Concentrate on Kemp. Have you got his security file?"

"He has expensive friends. It's the blandest piece of rubbish I've seen since I read Marcus Toth's."

"Christ, I'd forgotten all about that." Toreth laughed. "Seems like years ago."

Warrick grinned in response. "It was. But I remember Marcus *very* well. However, the point is that it's probably safe to assume the old file held some interesting tidbits, if he went to so much trouble to have it hidden. There may be copies in the system somewhere, although you are no doubt better placed than I to find them."

"Once we're moving in on Kemp, I'll get Sara onto it—I don't want him to hear that we're coming. If you happened to come across a copy..."

Warrick nodded. "Anything else?"

"The second problem is money. If he's still running the scheme, there have to be fucking huge sums of euros washing around. Whether they go into Kemp Incorporated or straight to him, there must be a trail somewhere. Once he's arrested I can get Corporate Fraud digging, but it would help if I could tell them where to look. He'll shut everything down fast, if he gets half a chance."

"As I said, I've been looking into his finances, so that will give me somewhere to start. I can't promise anything, but I'll do my best."

"Thanks." Warrick's instant, unquestioning cooperation was a wonderful relief after the tiring politics of trying to get things done at I&I. "I wouldn't ask if—"

"I'm happy to help. If I wasn't, I would say so."

"Just be careful."

Warrick smiled again. "Do you know, that's exactly what Dilly said once she'd given up all hope of making me promise not to do anything stupid."

Well, Dillian wouldn't be very happy if she ever found out about *this*. Breakfast in Warrick's flat seemed like weeks ago now, rather than...how many days? Only three, which was still far too fucking long. He put his drink down. "Let's think about it later."

Warrick caught the change in mood at once. "Don't you need me to get started on Kemp's files?"

"Yes, but half an hour won't make any difference."

On the way into the bedroom, Toreth paused, looking at the chains on the wall. He hadn't taken them down because...because he would have known why he was doing it. While he hesitated, Warrick brushed past him and went over to them. Wrapping the chains around his hands he let them take his weight, hanging still, head bowed.

Toreth watched him, and although he didn't want to play that game right now, his pulse picked up speed. An automatic response to the curved back and strained breathing caught him up, rubbing away the pain-filled hours in handcuffs. The recent memories had a light hold, compared to the months—no, years—of enjoying this. Watching Warrick. Wanting him. Wanting him so fucking much, sometimes it—

With a sigh, Warrick stood up and crossed the room again, examining the pressure marks from the links imprinted on his palms. When he looked up, his eyes were bright. "Beautiful," he said after a moment.

Toreth wasn't sure whether he meant the chains, the marks, or, rather less plausibly, himself. Before he could ask, Warrick smiled and said, "But not today."

"You don't have to..." What? Worry about it? Worry about me? Consider my fucking feelings?

Warrick shook his head. "That's not it. I'm thinking about too many other things. Thinking kills it. Some other time."

Was there anything Kemp hadn't managed to spoil? Glittering arrest prospect or not, right now he felt tired of the whole bloody mess. "Christ. How did this all turn into such a fuckup?"

"Forget it. We'll fix it." Brisk and dismissive, and this time Toreth didn't—couldn't—protest the plural. "Now, are we going to stand here all morning, or are you going to fuck me?"

Put like that, it wasn't a difficult choice.

Back at I&I, there was no news, so Toreth dealt with the rest of his cases—things which had piled up over the last couple of days. It was afternoon by the time Sedanioni finally called in to say that they had found Jack Almond. While she brought him in, Toreth considered whether to ask Justice for a priority waiver. Better not to waste the time. To start with, he'd see what he could get from a level one.

As far as Almond was concerned, Chris and his family were dead, and as long as Toreth didn't actually lie to confirm that, the misapprehension would be very useful indeed.

In the interrogation room, Almond watched the recording from Chris's flat, and Toreth watched him. As time went on, the confidence drained out of Almond, leaving him pale and sweating.

The footage from inside showed the method of attack clearly—a hole through the door, the gas canister falling into the hall, hissing, then a long pause before the liquid splashed in after it. It was beautifully complimented by the camera view in the hallway, where Almond's face was eminently clear for most of the time, and he was obviously the one giving the orders. As the flames licked up, and the safety systems failed to engage, Toreth froze the picture on the screen.

"The Justice Sentencing System takes a dim view of people gassing flats they know contain seven-year-old kids and then pouring flammables in afterwards. It looks very, very premeditated."

"I didn't mean to kill them," Almond said mechanically. "It was supposed to be a warning."

Toreth laughed. "Really? So who was going to get them out of bed? Who was going to wake them up?" He leaned across the desk. "Who disabled the fucking fire suppressant system?"

The man shook his head.

"Oh, wait, no need for you to tell me. I have something here about that, too."

The pictures from the security station camera tap were not quite as clear, but

Almond's face was visible for several seconds, as was which system he was tampering with.

"Lucky we caught that—someone seems to have wiped the official security logs. We talked to the guard, but he'd been called away to a false alarm in one of the flats. Didn't you trust him enough to pay him off? Can't say I blame you, because he was bloody useless when we spoke to him."

"I didn't..." Almond sighed. "All right. What do you want?"

"Much better. I want to know where the orders came from."

Almond's eyes flicked back to the tableau of flame, but he didn't say anything.

"With the evidence I've got, I can apply for a damage waiver without any problem. You will tell me, in the end. You know that—you know what's going to happen. Do we really have to go through it?"

Toreth held his breath, waiting for the reply. Arson without bodies wouldn't get him the kind of waiver he needed to break Almond quickly, and every delay increased the risk of Kemp getting away.

Finally, Almond nodded. "Gil Kemp sent us." He looked up, the decision to surrender restoring some of his composure. "Before I say anything else, I want protection. I want a guarantee of a light sentence. And I want it all in writing and signed by my Justice rep."

"It's yours."

It took him an hour to get the authorization through. Back in the interrogation room, he took Almond quickly over the details of his mission to Chris's flat. Nothing much, and it was all Almond's word against Kemp's—worthless, really. In any case, it was only a lead-in for his real interest. Something to hold over Almond if he changed his mind.

"And now I want to know about Gil Kemp's involvement with the laundering of illegal conceptions."

It was one of the moments of his job that Toreth really enjoyed—something to look back on in his retirement. Almond stared at him, his mouth open, pure disbelief suffusing his face. Then he rallied and said, "I don't know *anything* about—"

"Shut up. Check the wording on your precious guarantee. You answer any questions I have, to the best of your ability, or the whole thing is void. I know you're involved." He smiled. "I have a witness."

"You—" He stared again, then said, "Harper isn't dead?"

"Very much alive and, like you, he's realized that his only fucking chance is to come very clean indeed. Neither of you means anything to me. If this doesn't turn into a serious case, I'm going to throw both of you to Justice, and for all I care they can bury you deep. You know what kind of sentences they hand down for conspiracy to evade population control laws. Kemp won't do anything for you, not once he hears how you tried to sell him out. I'm offering you the same deal I gave Harper—immunity and privileged informant status."

If Almond had seemed cooperative before, it was nothing compared to his eagerness to help now. "What do you want to know?"

"I need names. As high up as you know, and most importantly, I want people who can confirm that Kemp's involved. People who've spoken to him about it, who've told him how things are going. People who've taken orders from him."

"The people I deal with are Doctor Corella Foley—she runs the hospital end of things—and Rajvir Rungren. He works for the DoP. No one else—Kemp likes to keep everyone separate. They'll be able to give you more."

"Has Kemp ever spoken to them about the scam, in person? Think about that very carefully."

Almond gave it at least the appearance of thought, before he nodded.

"Do you introduce the clients to the medics personally?"

He shook his head. "I don't meet any of them—that's all handled by agents who don't know my name or Mr. Kemp's."

"So why Harper?"

"Mr. Kemp asked me to deal with him."

Because he already knew Kemp was involved, so it was safer to keep him away from the agents. Toreth wondered why they hadn't just killed Chris—he bet the same thought had crossed Almond's mind. "Have you got any details of clients, though?" Toreth asked. "Names and addresses?"

He nodded. "Some of them—people who still owe money. I don't know about the old names, but it's still hundreds of arrangements."

"What about the money?"

Almond shook his head. "It goes into a few accounts, and that's the last I see of it."

Not much, but something—at least it might help Warrick with his attempts to track the profits. "Give me the numbers."

That secured, he went outside and called Parsons in to finish getting the information from Almond. The names of the rest of Kemp's breeding customers would be helpful for the case, but not vital, not when there was bigger game in prospect now. Justice could sweep up the debris later, and with hundreds of names, at least, the DoP medical division would be putting in for a lot of overtime.

With Almond's enthusiastic confession as evidence, Justice was disconcertingly cooperative about the arrest warrants and damage waivers. Although Toreth had kept Kemp's name out of the picture so far, someone over there had clearly scented a big case in the pipeline. He wondered if they would be so keen once they realized exactly how high the stakes were.

The best thing about ostensibly respectable criminals was that it was easy to find them. By seven o'clock that evening, Chevril had brought in both Foley and Rungren. Toreth assessed their catch on the holding cell monitors. Both had come without making too much of a fuss, so if they worked quickly, they could get the information they needed before the arrests became common knowledge.

These two could give him Kemp—they had the status to be believed, and probably the documentary evidence to prove it. There would be no deals here, though. They were both major players in the scam, and they would go down with Kemp.

He flipped Chevril for the prisoners and lost, so he ended up with Rungren. When they'd been brought in, Foley had been all but confessing on the spot, and Chev always preferred to take the easy route. As it was, Toreth had barely finished explaining the damage waiver to his prisoner when Chevril called him out to say that Foley had handed over Kemp's name, without any prompting, along with a list of other names on the medical end of the operation.

"Get their files, and run the pictures past Harper, see if he can give us a hit on the medics he dealt with," Toreth said to Chevril. "That'll be enough to push the waivers up a level or two."

Chevril didn't look much happier. "And what about Kemp?"

"Let me worry about him."

"I wish I could."

Chevril was fretting over nothing, Toreth thought as he walked down the corridor to the assigned interrogation room. One more independent confirming statement and they could pull Kemp in, and there would be nothing his lawyers could do to stop them, no matter how expensive. With any luck, Rungren wouldn't prove much harder to break than Foley.

It quickly became apparent that luck wasn't going to do the trick in this case.

After two hours, Toreth stopped to consider his approach. The prisoner sat in the interrogation chair, only a short step from incoherence, his dark head hanging forwards, and still he wouldn't give up the names. Toreth had a very good instinct for this sort of thing, and he knew it would take an inconveniently long time to break this one. Rungren knew full well the consequences of confessing, and like many of the inexperienced prisoners that passed through I&I, he still held on to the delusion that not talking was a serious option.

If Kemp had time to wipe out all his connections to the operation before they could issue an arrest warrant—or worse, had time to run—it would be infuriating. With the rest of the organization there for the taking, he and Chev would still have a case, and a good one, but for once that wasn't what Toreth wanted. He wanted the bastard to feel the gun against his back and know there was no way out. To know this was the end.

Dismissing the thought, Toreth decided to move on to a different drug family. He knew he was pushing too hard, because he desperately needed the result, but it was worth the small risk. The needle slipped easily into an already impressively punctured vein.

As Toreth dropped the needle into the clinical recycling, he heard a choking gasp. A quick glance confirmed his worst fears. "Oh, fuck—he's fitting." Toreth hit the medical comm frequency. "Team to D503. Priority."

Then he automatically went into the emergency procedures, training carrying him past the brief panic. The guards helped him get the convulsing body onto the gurney. The three of them held Rungren down and by the time the medical team arrived to take charge, the fits had nearly stopped.

As the medics began to work, Toreth sat down at the table, feeling more than a little shaky, his wrist aching fiercely from the effort to restrain Rungren.

This wasn't the kind of prisoner whose loss could be chalked up to bad luck and let go with a quick investigation by another senior. Section-head-level Administration employees didn't die without a good reason, and Internal Investigations could come down on him like a ton of bricks. There would be a full-blown inquiry and the DoP would push it every step of the way. Worse, if Rungren died without confirming his guilt, the link into the DoP would be cut off.

There'd been nothing in the prisoner's medical file to suggest the possibility of an adverse reaction to a perfectly ordinary drug. Damn Central Medical Services and their fucking awful record keeping, but he'd be the one who'd get the blame.

One of the medics approached and Toreth looked up with his best professional face firmly in place. "Well?"

The man shook his head. "Fifty-fifty is the best I can give you, and I doubt he'll be talking if he does pull through."

Damn, damn, and double damn.

"Is he conscious?" he asked, hoping desperately.

"For now. Not for very long." The medic's eyes narrowed. "If we don't take him down soon, he'll die for sure."

"I'll take responsibility." Toreth moved over to the table and started selecting more drugs.

The man followed him over. "And he'll die a hell of a lot faster if you put that shit into him."

"I'll take responsibility," Toreth repeated clearly. "That'll be on record. Now get out and let me work."

"All right. It's your funeral." The medics cleared the room, keen to disassociate themselves from the looming failure.

After a minute or two, the mix of stimulants and more exotic drugs did their work, and Rungren focused weakly on his face.

"Listen to me." Toreth spoke quietly. "Can you hear me? You're dying."

His eyes widened. Yes, he could hear.

"You don't want to die, I know. But if you won't help me, there's no point in my doing anything for you. Give me the names, and I'll get help for you."

He shook his head, but Toreth could taste the fear coming from the prisoner in waves. If he only had time, he'd give it up.

"We've already got names from someone else in the scam. All I need from you is confirmation of the people you took orders from and who else in the department knew about it. It's much too late for silence to do you any good."

He spared a glance for the monitors around the gurney. Fuck, this was cutting things fine. "Give me the names." He touched the prisoner's hand lightly, adding the emphasis of physical contact to his words. "Give me the names and you can live."

Finally, confused and alone and so very afraid, Rungren did.

Kemp was the first one.

More prompting persuaded him to go through the list a second time, omitting a few of the names and giving a few more. A third run through was all Toreth got before the monitors flatlined, but that matched well with the first two.

Toreth sat down in the chair again, feeling almost as shaky as before. Then he smiled. Oh, yes. Success. Fucking success. The prisoner's death meant less now— unfortunate, and there'd be an inquiry, but the DoP would bury it now the corruption there was confirmed. They'd be eager to help and get it all over with as quickly as possible.

Without a glance at the motionless body he had to thank for this happy prospect, Toreth went off, whistling, to submit a warrant for Kemp's arrest.

Fifteen minutes later, he was still in Tillotson's office, and no longer feeling like whistling. "I should have been kept informed." Tillotson was twitching with anger, intensifying his already startling resemblance to a ferret.

"I'm sorry. There wasn't time."

"Don't give me that. You have a duty to inform me of a new investigation in progress."

"The report was submitted." Toreth tried for innocent surprise. "On Tuesday, I think."

Tillotson looked down at his screen for a moment. "Yes...well. For a suspect as important and politically sensitive as Gil Kemp, I should have been informed in person."

Memo me, as Sara would say. "I'm very sorry, sir—I've been busy. And now I need that warrant."

"No."

85

"I've got three independent interrogations giving Kemp's name. That's enough."

"One of which is from a senior and now extremely dead DoP official." Tillotson's nose twitched again.

"All inside the waiver. The drug reaction wasn't my fault. The interrogations are signed off and ready to submit to Justice."

"It's not good enough. Sudden accusations out of thin air. You're trying to tell me that Gil Kemp has been at the center of this conspiracy for years—decades—and no one has noticed before now?"

Toreth struggled for patience. "We have the names of a network of people, medical and DoP. It all ties in."

"Then pull them in and question them. Show me some more evidence."

"If we do that, Kemp will have time to cut loose. By tomorrow morning, he'll have found out about the arrests we've made so far, if he hasn't already. He could even try to run for it. If he gets out of the Administration, we'll never bring him back, not with the kind of protection he'll be able to buy."

Tillotson leaned back in his chair. "Well, from the perspective of enforcing the law, does that really matter?"

When was the last time you gave a fuck about that? "Sir?"

"If Kemp does evade prosecution, it won't make that much difference to the outcome for us. The operation will be destroyed, we'll have the rest of those involved."

All without running the risk of arresting someone with powerful friends. "Except that you can bet there'll be no money to be found when Corporate Fraud finally start digging. The section won't get its cut of confiscated funds."

For a moment, he thought he'd got Tillotson. The visible struggle between fear and budgetary greed made an interesting spectacle. Eventually, though, the section head said, "No. You're reading too much into what you have. Show me something to back up the size of the operation, or the timescale you're suggesting, and I'll consider it."

Someone knocked on the door, loudly enough to make the point that the matter was urgent.

"Yes?" Tillotson called irritably.

Sara entered immediately, clutching a hand screen. Toreth tried to read her expression and failed. She had her admin mask firmly in place, which meant the news was either very good, or very bad indeed.

"What do you want?" Tillotson asked.

"I'm terribly sorry to interrupt, sir." She turned to Toreth. "Para, I have the file you asked me to find and I thought you'd want to see it now."

Toreth stared at her blankly. Taking a step sideways, so that he blocked Tillotson's view of her, Sara mouthed, "Kemp's file. From Warrick."

Thank fuck. He took the screen and scanned it quickly—she'd left it set to the relevant page. Despite the urgency, he read it three times, to make quite sure, then passed it to Tillotson. "There you are—there's the history you wanted. Kemp was questioned six times over suspected illegal births at the hospitals he ran, but never with enough evidence to interrogate."

"I see . . ." Tillotson read the entries, clearly hoping for a reason to disregard them. "The most recent was thirty years ago."

"History's in the past. That's one of its defining features."

Tillotson looked up sharply. "Why is there nothing since?"

"Because after that he got rich enough to stop the skeletons rattling. If there were any suspicions, I expect that people were too gutless to follow them up." Than earned him another blistering glare, which he ignored. "Will you authorize the warrant, sir?"

Tillotson looked down at the file again, then nodded. "You'd better be right about it, that's all. If it's a setup, if it's corporate dirty tricks and we've been pushed into carrying out someone's private vendetta for them, we're going to end up with a lot of explaining to do. No—*I'll* be doing the explaining. *You'll* be unemployed, if you're lucky."

Before Toreth set off for Kemp's house, he went outside the I&I building and called Warrick on his personal comm. "Thanks for the file. You saved my fucking neck."

"My pleasure. I was filling in time while I did the other searches. It's harder to lose a file than people think. Archives are wonderful things."

"Do you have anything for the other thing?"

"A little. Starting from the accounts you gave me, the trail *looks* to stop with . . . the man in question personally, not his corporation. Something else that you'll like— there may well be other streams of euros flowing into the same system, from else- where in the Administration. All apparently originating in places where the corporation has interests in medical centers."

All his New Years and birthdays come at once. "Are you sure?"

"Some of it's guesswork. I have beginnings and an end, but I can't yet confirm some of the steps in middle. Give me a little more time, and I will."

"No, that's good enough." Perfect, in fact. "Send it all to Sara. It'll be logged as anonymous information and passed on to Corporate Fraud. They'll do all the confirming necessary. And—"

"Yes?"

How to make sure Warrick knew this was serious? "Stop looking right now. I mean it. However clever you think you can be, I don't want to risk you . . . it could blow the whole case if you get caught. Stop looking, and make damn sure Corporate Fraud aren't going to find any trace of you in there."

"Of course. I understand."

Toreth hoped that he did.

For once in his life, Toreth lost a bet with himself over Justice bureaucracy. They called Tillotson back three times to confirm that he really wanted to arrest Gil Kemp—*that* Gil Kemp, as in Kemp Incorporated?—but after that they processed the warrant and sent it back without another murmur. Tillotson brought it along to him in person, coming into his office and glancing around as though he'd always been vaguely curious as to how the peasants lived. The last time Toreth could remember him being there was during the Selman case.

"Here you are." Tillotson transferred the warrant to Toreth's hand screen, then stood looking at the screen for a moment before he shook his head. "I'm trusting you over this, Toreth, so don't disappoint me. I pulled a lot of strings to get it done quickly. If you go down over it, I go with you." Then he left, before Toreth could think of anything to say.

Following Tillotson out of the office, Toreth found Sara staring after the section head.

"What the hell was he doing here?" she asked.

"Wishing me luck."

She looked around. "You mean...?"

"Yes. It's on. Call Chev and tell him to get moving."

Chevril took most of their temporarily joint investigation teams to start making arrests of names from the hospital and the DoP. Toreth didn't care about them—tomorrow he would, but just now only Kemp mattered.

By the time Toreth was ready to go, there were fifteen people in the group. Most were systems techs, there to confiscate computer equipment in the house and start the search for evidence. He also took along a couple of investigators and four I&I security guards, more for the look of the thing than because he seriously expected any trouble.

He included a rep from Justice, because he wanted to make very sure that things went smoothly and there were no loopholes in the arrest for Kemp to squirm through later. The rep who arrived in response to his request was so young that Toreth wondered if she had in fact finished her training. She introduced herself as Marielle Chin. A sacrificial lamb, he decided, in case the arrest went wrong—

once Justice realized the case was good, she'd be replaced by someone more senior, to take the kudos. Toreth didn't bother to tell her that—let her have her moment. At least she was keen to help, and sufficiently overawed by the prospect of the big-name arrest that she wouldn't be a nuisance.

The guards at the gate of Kemp's mansion actually argued with them on the way in. They'd probably never had I&I there before, or even thought it would be possible. Once they had been convinced, Toreth took one along with him, to point the way to Kemp's room.

Inside the building, Toreth barely noticed the décor, although he could see Chin beside him, staring, open-mouthed. Obviously, she hadn't been along on many high-level corporate arrests. Not that there *were* that many. Corporate fucking privilege. Sometimes he could understand why the resisters whined about it so much.

Kemp was still asleep when they knocked on his bedroom door. When he opened it and saw Toreth, his first reaction was blank amazement. Then his face flushed with anger. "What do you want?"

That was something Toreth hadn't thought of, or rather had forgotten. If Kemp said anything about their past history, now, in front of the Justice rep, it could be very awkward indeed. Even a complete neophyte would notice some things.

He moved Chin aside and offered the electronic copy of the warrant to Kemp—Toreth's name was at the top of the screen, which covered at least one potential danger. Kemp took it and glanced at it, and the flush deepened. "*Arrested.* Para-investigator Toreth, whatever you—"

"Read the warrant in full, please."

Kemp glanced at the group, then did as he was told. Toreth could tell when the man reached the initial charges, because he went quite still. He glanced up at Toreth, murder in his eyes, then returned to the screen. He read it through once, then again more slowly. Finally he said, "I shall need to dress."

Tempting as it was to drag him out of the house in his pajamas, there were professional considerations. Everything needed to be very much by the book. Toreth sent a guard into the bedroom with Kemp, to make sure he didn't use the comm, and went to wait in the hall. By the time Kemp came downstairs, immaculately dressed, he had regained some of his composure, although he still looked angry. Stopping at the foot of the sweeping staircase he beckoned to Toreth, separating him out from the rest of the group.

When Toreth came over, Kemp asked, "What do you want?"

Meaning, what do I need to offer to make you go away? "I explained that already. You are under arrest. You're welcome to inspect the authorized copy of the warrant again, if you wish."

The fury returned to Kemp's face. "You're going to be very sorry you did this."

Toreth carried on as if he hadn't spoken. "The charges will be explained fully once you have been processed into custody. Broadly, you will answer questions on—"

"I don't have to talk to you about anything," Kemp said. The absolute confidence in his voice was breathtaking, and strongly reminiscent of Jonny.

Toreth smiled, very slightly. "I'm afraid that you do. And you will, I can promise you that. Eventually."

Kemp started another protest, but it died on his lips as the full meaning of Toreth's words sank in. Like father, like son, the arrogance fled and his face paled to a sickly gray—a color not so very far from that of tidal mud. On the third try, Kemp managed to speak. "I demand to speak to my lawyers."

Too, too perfect. "You can ask your Justice rep over there to arrange it, in the morning. Representative Chin. I'm sure she will be delighted to help." Toreth turned to the watching guards. "Cuff him, take him to the car."

Toreth stepped back and looked on impassively, somehow keeping a grip on the huge fucking grin he could feel struggling to escape. Deplorably unprofessional as it was, he couldn't help hoping that Kemp would resist in interrogation. For a long, long time.

It was nearly three in the morning again by the time they finished the paperwork. With all the forms submitted and the prisoners locked down, the frantic pace of the last couple of days had finally come to an end. It was a relief and anticlimax in one. Now it was simply a question of extracting confessions and passing the prisoners on to Justice. Then sitting back to enjoy the plaudits while Corporate Fraud did the hard work of chasing euros across Europe.

With success secured, Chevril seemed to have finally decided that they'd done the right thing, and had developed a frankly unnerving cheerfulness. Their teams were tired, but equally happy. There were even unconfirmed rumors that Tillotson had been seen down in interrogation, gathering reflected glory. Toreth had his doubts, but he supposed it was possible. If Chevril had stopped complaining, he'd believe anything.

As the others dispersed, Toreth found himself at a sudden loose end. Nothing to do until the morning, which meant...home and sleep. Sara was the last to leave, hovering in the doorway for an unnecessarily protracted goodbye. She had quite obviously been worrying about him. That annoyed him, but not as much as the fact that she must have been able to tell that something was wrong. He didn't want to go home. Tired as he was, he didn't want to sleep. But there was no need, nor excuse, to do anything else.

He made it as far as the shiny new door to his flat before he changed his mind. Without letting himself think it through, he caught a taxi to Warrick's. Outside, he hesitated over the comm. There was no reason, this time, to wake Warrick up at such an unsociable hour. It would be far more considerate simply to let himself in and go to sleep.

Inside, without switching on the light, he reset the security by touch and went down the darkened hall to the bedroom. As quietly as he could, he stripped and slipped into bed beside Warrick. By the time he'd settled down, the room was still silent except for Warrick's breathing and Toreth found himself wondering whether he really wanted him not to wake up. It had to be better, surely, for Warrick to realize he was here now, than for him to find out when Toreth woke him up in a couple of hours with his stupid, pathetic, bloody dream and—

Warrick rolled over, bumped into him, and muttered something unintelligible. After a few seconds he lifted his head and said, "Toreth?"

"Good guess."

"Mm. Everything went all right?"

"Fine. I'll tell you about it in the morning."

"Oh, good." He lay down again, his cheek against Toreth's shoulder, and sighed. "I'll look forward to it."

That seemed to be that. It was less than half a minute before Warrick's breathing slowed back into sleep. Toreth wondered if Warrick would even remember the conversation in the morning. It didn't matter—he felt better, now that his presence had registered. There was only the prospect of the nightmares to come to keep him awake.

Somehow, now that he was here, Toreth found that he didn't care. He was still vaguely wondering about that when he slipped into a dreamless sleep.

Wait for It

❖

Day One

Toreth licked his way down Warrick's side, down to his hip, then back up, keeping half an eye on the sliver of sunlight creeping across the wall. When it touched the head of the bed, it would be time to get up and go to the gym. Their Saturday morning routine.

They'd missed the usual Friday night bondage fuck, because Warrick had been at some incredibly important SimTech dinner meeting. Toreth had spent the evening reading pharmaceutical journals he'd been putting off for weeks, and enjoying the idea of Warrick at a table full of clients. Warrick trying to concentrate on business, but occasionally distracted by the idea of him. Warrick smart and formal and in absolute control versus Warrick kneeling in chains, naked, and flawlessly submissive.

Warrick moaned and grabbed Toreth's hair, pushing his mouth towards his nipple. Toreth licked, teasing, and grinned. He pressed the flat of his hand on Warrick's cock, feeling the hardness, judging the flex of his hips and the startled, urgent intake of breath above him.

Fridays were still their main night, even though they played on other nights, too. For one thing, it allowed the bruises time to calm down by Monday. Warrick had a definite edge right now—an eagerness that he wouldn't usually have on a Saturday. Probably meant Warrick had come home from the dinner and spent a while thinking about him, but not done anything about it. Toreth read prisoners in interrogation, he read casual fucks, but it felt odd, if he stopped to think about it, that he knew Warrick's reactions in bed so well he could tell whether or not he'd had a wank the night before. He didn't give it much thought now, because the idea triggered another one.

Toreth shook his head free of Warrick's hand, then put his own hand on Warrick's chest, pressing until Warrick lay still. "Stay there," Toreth said. "I'll be back."

He twisted around, finding the bedside table and scrabbling through the cupboard, hunting by touch. Plastic and glass rattled, and then a rain of soft thumps signaled the departure of most of the contents onto the floor.

"Fuck." Toreth rolled over and peered over the edge of the bed, wondering if anything had spilled on the pale carpet. Bottles everywhere, fortunately closed, but none were the one he wanted. He edged further over, then further still, feeling the blood rush to his head. Finally he found what he wanted—unscented massage oil, which had rolled under the bed.

When he hauled himself back up, Warrick was grinning broadly. "Nice view," he said.

Toreth went to kneel astride Warrick's thighs. "Glad you enjoyed it. See what you think of this."

He dribbled oil over Warrick's cock and his own, then took Warrick's hands and oiled them, too. Then he looked up and lost track of the plan, distracted by Warrick's dark eyes. Warrick was watching him with a combination of curiosity and hungry excitement that temporarily cleared Toreth's mind of all plans.

Finally, he focused on Warrick's parted lips, and that at least prompted movement. He tightened the lid on the oil, then leaned down, took his weight on his elbows and kissed Warrick. Then he kept kissing him until he realized that not only had he forgotten the plan, he'd forgotten to breathe as well.

Toreth lifted his head, feeling a little dizzy. Warrick shifted below him, rubbing rhythmically, prompting a reflex response in Toreth's hips. "Mmh," Warrick said. "So far, I like it."

"What? Oh, yeah. I mean, no, that's not it." He lifted his hips a little and guided one of Warrick's hands down. "Put your hands round both—*fuck* yes."

All his senses focused down to the individual prints of Warrick's fingers, to the hard length of Warrick's cock held tight against his own. Quick learner, he thought vaguely as he dipped down for another kiss. Then Warrick stroked his hands down around their cocks and they thrust up together, simultaneously breaking the kiss to gasp for air.

"Mmh," Warrick said. "Do you think...more oil?"

It wasn't necessary, but it certainly wouldn't hurt. "Okay."

The cool flood of oil ended the conversation for a good fifteen minutes—a very good fifteen minutes. Then Warrick, who had been breathing hard but otherwise keeping unusually quiet, suddenly yelped, his hands tightening around them. Toreth felt the rush of warmth as he came, gasping, eyes wide.

Warrick relaxed and his hands stilled, and Toreth managed to hold still, too. "Oh," Warrick said, sounding surprised. When Toreth, unable to help himself, thrust again, Warrick hissed and added, "Stop a moment. Too sensitive."

"Do something." Toreth didn't really like sounding that desperate but he couldn't help it. "Sooner the better."

"Kiss me," Warrick said, and as Toreth did, he felt Warrick change his grip, releasing his own cock and wrapping his hands tightly around Toreth's and oh, *fuck* that was good. He thrust hard and fast, reveling in the heat and Warrick's hands shifting, squeezing just exactly, perfectly right, because he knew what Toreth wanted without having to ask because he knew *him,* he knew—

Then he lost the thought, arching back, his eyes squeezing tight closed as he came—feeling, not thinking, for endless delicious seconds.

Awareness expanded slowly to include his other senses. Taste first, a faint tang of blood where he'd somehow bitten his cheek. Then the sound of panting breaths, then light, sunlight on the wall. He lowered his head and relaxed his shoulders a little. Oh, yes. Even the evidence analysis system at its fussiest would have to call this a statistically significant result.

He guessed Warrick had a similar opinion of the experiment. He was looking up through half-lidded eyes, his fingers laced together on his chest. "Good?" Toreth asked.

"Makes a mess." Warrick lifted his hands then folded them again, keeping them away from the bed.

"Yeah, but it's all on us. Saves the sheets."

Warrick's smile widened. "Actually, I was going to change them today, anyway."

"Big fucking surprise."

Toreth gave in to the complaints of his neck and rested his forehead on the pillow, turning to breathe against Warrick's neck, drinking in the tang of his hot skin. Usually it turned him on unbearably. In his current haze it stirred different feelings, warming and relaxing him, urging sleep. Pity he couldn't stay—even taking his weight on his elbows he must be crushing Warrick. He'd move, just as soon as he found the energy.

Somehow the brief rest stretched out. After a few minutes, Warrick shifted, his hair tickling Toreth's face. "What inspired that, then?" Warrick asked.

"Honestly?" Toreth lifted his head and rubbed the side of his nose with the heel of his hand.

After a moment, Warrick nodded.

"Well, I did it with a fuck on, um, Monday night. His idea. He was dead keen. It's not my favorite thing—I've done it before a couple of times."

"And because you didn't enjoy it with him, you thought you'd do it with me?" Warrick sounded curious rather than pissed off. And also a little breathless.

"Yeah, well—" Toreth slid down beside him to take the weight off, careless of the state of the sheets. "I wondered if it would feel the same."

"And?"

"It was a fuck of a lot more fun with you. Weird, huh?"

"Sex very often is. I thought it was…very involving." Warrick's hand smoothed absently over Toreth's chest. "Actually, I was concentrating so much on

94

the technique and your reactions that I didn't notice how close I was, which made a very pleasant change. One problem with working in the sim is that, outside the game, I'm always very aware of what's going on."

Toreth propped himself up on his side, feeling warm, well fucked, and generous. "What would you like to do with the rest of the weekend? Anything you fancy. How about a scene tomorrow, since we missed yesterday?"

Warrick smiled, eyes bright. "That sounds like an even better idea than your last one. Do you have anything in mind?"

"Plenty. I've had some incredibly dull meetings lately. But is there anything you'd like?"

"I'm sure I'll love anything you have planned."

Toreth felt enjoyably flattered by the confidence. "Okay. No requests at all?"

After a moment, Warrick glanced across the room towards the cabinet.

Toreth shook his head. "Try again."

"You said anything I fancied." Warrick's voice held an edge of pleading so arousing it almost hurt. "It's been a month."

"It's been three weeks."

Warrick looked away.

Do it anyway, said the part of Toreth's mind that didn't care about long-term nerve damage, or Dillian, or Justice. Do him in the cabinet because it's mind-blowing and he'll beg for it. It was the part of his mind that seemed to be wired directly into his cock. As its previous brilliant ideas had included fucking Carnac and—long before that and immediately prior to Toreth's hasty transfer to General Criminal—fucking the wife of the head of the Political Crimes section, he had learned to resist some of its suggestions. Probably not enough of them, but still . . .

"Ah, fuck." He took Warrick's oily right wrist in his hand, rubbing his thumb firmly over the pulse point. There were no visible bruises but Warrick's fingers twitched, his arm pulling away. Toreth let him go. "Six weeks. That's the rule. You know why."

"Yes." Warrick closed his eyes for a moment, then said, "Yes, I do know why. Sorry. Use the manacles instead, then. The first pair you bought."

He should have guessed—Warrick's favorite toy after the cabinet. "Don't you ever get bored with them?"

"Never. In fact, it's better every time."

Toreth moved against him, enjoying the slide of thoroughly oiled skin, and kissed Warrick's jaw. "Yeah?"

"Mm. It's a cumulative effect. Every time there's another memory for them to bring back." Warrick settled back, looking at the ceiling, eyes narrowed. "Last time you chained me, I was standing by the wall. The time before that, you made me kneel and ask for them. Over and over. Oh, and before that, it was my hands behind my back, and at the end you fucked my mouth—we hadn't done that for

95

more than a month." He swallowed, and Toreth nipped his throat. "Mmh. That time was..."

Silence. "It was what?" Toreth breathed into his ear.

"I'm not sure if you'd want to hear it."

Twined on the bed, soaked in the heat of skin and the smell of sweat and sex, nothing could spoil the moment. "Tell me."

"It was perfect. There was just you and what you wanted from me. I like it when you hurt me—God, so much—but sometimes it's even better if I can get there without it. Purer. I remember I was so lost in it..."

Toreth remembered it too: Warrick's wet, open lips and the moan he had made as Toreth pulled back. Toreth had been panting, one hand on the wall for support, still buzzing from his orgasm. Most clearly, he remembered Warrick's eyes, dark, glazed with desire, stunned with the intensity of the encounter.

Then he'd knelt and taken hold of Warrick's cock, and whispered, "Move. Do it." Letting Warrick fuck his hand, struggling in the confines of the chains. Toreth had buried his face in Warrick's neck, holding him close while he sank his teeth into Warrick's shoulder and listened to him gasp and whimper and finally scream.

Coming back to the present, Toreth realized that Warrick lay still, his breathing quiet and distant. Toreth lifted his head and looked down at him. Warrick was frowning thoughtfully. "Mmh," Warrick said.

"Well?"

"I'm thinking about what I want. I think..." Warrick smiled suddenly. "Go home today—don't stay the night. Come back on Sunday, but don't let me know the exact time."

Toreth grinned. He liked the sound of this already. "And when I come round?"

Warrick was breathing quickly now, and his cock twitched once, then again, before it accepted the laws of nature and gave up. "When you come round, bring the gear."

"What, exactly? The manacles, and what else?"

"The—no. Surprise me."

Because the edge of uncertainty was part of the game. "Okay. And then?"

Warrick said nothing. Toreth ran his thumb over Warrick's lips, then kissed him. "And then," he repeated, breathing the question into Warrick's ear.

"Ah—make me wait. Make me wait for it."

"How long?"

He expected, "As long as you want," but instead Warrick closed his eyes again and said, "As long as you can stand it."

Toreth smiled slowly. He liked a challenge.

Day Two

On Sunday morning, Warrick risked a foray out for fresh food; it was highly unlikely that Toreth would turn up so early. Then he made a barley broth which would benefit from cooling and reheating to bring out the flavor: something hot and savory for later on in the evening, after a hopefully exhausting session.

In the afternoon, he tried to stick to tasks that could easily be interrupted. This meant no intensive coding, not that he could have concentrated on it. It left him, for once, with nothing at all to do. In fact, he spent ten minutes trying to remember the last time that had happened and failed. Not that he was bored—anticipation was taking care of that—but it felt peculiar. In the end he decided to listen to music. He had a ridiculously long list of unlistened-to presents and purchases that had accumulated over the past months. It *was* nice to have a free afternoon, he thought as he lay on the sofa and closed his eyes. Hopefully not free for too much longer, but enjoyable in itself.

Dinnertime came and brought with it the first stirrings of dismay. Was Toreth planning to take "as long as you can stand it" far too literally? Warrick couldn't call and ask without destroying the setup. On the other hand, it would be just like Toreth to wait until Warrick was convinced he was staying away, then show up.

Or he hoped it was.

Eventually, he had a bowlful of the broth with fresh bread, and put the rest in the fridge.

Midnight. One o'clock. Two.

Finally, Warrick conceded that Toreth wasn't coming, and went to bed, virtually vibrating with sexual tension.

Day Six

The project estimate on the screen in front of Warrick was for the cold weather training programs, but every time he read the word "snow," he thought of Toreth on skis, lips reddened by the wind, squinting into the snow glare. Under all the layers he'd be hot, freshly sweaty from the exercise.

Against that, the estimate stood no chance. With a vividness that matched the sim, Warrick could picture stripping Toreth, peeling back the layers to reach the smooth, salty skin. He'd steam in the cold air—and complain like hell, of course, but that would be in the real world. In his mind, Warrick could have him however he liked. Tasting him, kneeling in front of him in the crunching snow, taking Toreth's cock in his mouth to taste a subtly different saltiness...

He shook his head, finally managing to dislodge the image. Changing to another estimate wouldn't help; he'd already tried that. After four days with no word at all from Toreth, everything reminded him of Toreth in general and sex in particular. He shifted in the chair and sternly informed his body that it would simply have to wait. It had had three years to get used to sex with Toreth—shouldn't it have at least little contempt bred by the familiarity?

The answer seemed to be no.

It might, he decided, improve his patience if he had some idea of when the hell he'd see Toreth again.

Toreth's personal comm still wasn't taking Warrick's calls. His home comm was set for messages. Warrick stared thoughtfully at the blank screen. He'd assumed the absence was due to the game they'd started, but it was always possible there was a more sinister explanation. In the past Warrick had missed the warning signs of Toreth's intermittent retreats. If this was one, it would be better to uncover the source of the problem before things got out of hand.

He set the comm to sound only, because his face would certainly give too much away to her sharp eyes.

"General Criminal, Para-investigator Toreth's admin speaking."

"It's Warrick. How are you?"

"Oh *hello*," Sara said cheerfully. "I'm great. Never better, really. I wondered when you'd call."

She certainly didn't sound as if Toreth was in a bad mood. "How's Toreth?"

"Fine. Out of the building on a case. I'm afraid I can't tell you what it is, but we're all on overtime right now which should tell you something, considering how tight they are about authorizing it."

She was far too good an admin for him to tell whether or not it was a lie. "He left a message for you," she added. "He hasn't forgotten, but it'll probably be Sunday now, or maybe next Friday. Does that make sense?"

Damn. Damn, damn, damn. "Did he mention anything at all about tomorrow?"

"You mean your—hang on." There was a long pause. "Sorry, B-C wanted me. Regular Friday, right? He said to let you know he'll be too busy and to say sorry."

Warrick said goodbye, canceled the connection, kicked a perfectly innocent waste bin across the floor, and sat back in his chair, breathing heavily.

Sunday. Sunday, if he were lucky, Friday if he wasn't. Three whole days at best; a week would probably kill him.

He turned his attention back to the screen and stared at it for a minute without reading a single word. Not possible, he decided, and called up the program for the sim bookings. What he needed was a nice relaxing hour or so in the sim, buried in someone's trial, where he could forget about Toreth. Trials were always full, but what was the point of being a director if he couldn't kick people out of his own creation?

To his surprise, a trial currently in progress still required volunteers. When he read the protocol, the reason became clear. It was run by Wenzel Aldren, one of the senior physiologists, who always had trouble filling his slots. This particular test was part of a series investigating the latest sim sickness suppressant systems. Or, in other words, you lay in the sim until Wenzel succeeded in making you feel so sick you had to disconnect. Even the most dedicated volunteers balked at that.

As Warrick reached the sim suite, a young man he recognized but couldn't put a name to stumbled out into the corridor. One of the new students, Warrick thought, and looking distinctly pale.

The student leaned on the door that had closed behind him and stood for a few seconds, breathing deeply. Then he looked up and saw Warrick. "You're not going in there?" he asked.

"Actually, yes."

"Then you're bloody mad. Last time I volunteer for that bastard." The man blinked at him, frowning as if trying to identify him, then seemed to give up. "Good luck."

It still surprised Warrick every time it happened, although it had been a while since SimTech grew too large for him to remember immediately everyone who worked there, and for everyone who worked there to know him. The student must be new, but even so, it was both disturbing and a pleasing sign of the growth of the corporation. Less than a year to the start of production, if everything went well. The idea, as usual, set off faint butterflies in his stomach, flapping with an equal degree of excitement and apprehension.

Inside the room, the unoccupied couch showed signs of a hasty departure. Wenzel lay in the other couch.

When Warrick announced his presence over the sim comm, there was a brief pause, then Wenzel slid his arm out of the wrist strap and lifted his visor. He looked predictably delighted to see Warrick—predictable because he always looked pleased to see anyone. His broad, friendly face belied his ruthlessness in pushing the limits of his subjects' endurance. "I got through my quota of volunteers already," he said, then grinned. "Weak stomachs, no sim experience. You're just what I need."

And vice versa. "I like to keep in touch with the practical work."

Wenzel nodded. "But I've only just put out a message for emergency help. Did you spot the empty slots already? Can't slip anything past you."

"That's what being a director's about. What do you need?" No need to mention that he was only here in search of distraction from acute sexual fixation.

"I'm stress-testing the latest motion-induced nausea antagonist algorithms."

That should do it nicely.

❖ ❖ ❖

In the sim, the entrance room opened onto a simple outdoor scene with a clear blue sky over a lawn. Wenzel's sim body stood behind a large virtual screen.

"Just stand in the middle of the grass. We're doing average ten second switches from free-fall simulation to full gravity from a random direction. You'll be held in place during the switches, but—" his smile broadened, "—I've thrown in changes in the room's perceived orientation, out of phase with the gravity changes."

If this didn't quash the intrusive fantasies, nothing would. "No wonder that student looked green round the gills."

Wenzel appeared delighted. "Whether the new or old algorithms are in place is randomized too, I'm afraid, so I can't tell you whether it'll be horrendous or just plain awful. Let me know when you can't take any more—the longer you can last, the better."

Warrick smiled, competitive urges roused. "What's the best so far?"

"Twelve minutes." Wenzel checked the screen. "That was Stephen Laine."

One of the more experienced room coders who led the low-gravity-training sim team. Well, that gave him a target. "I'm ready."

At first, it wasn't too bad. He'd spent so long in the sim under such varied conditions that his body had a certain tolerance for the abuse of physical reality. In fact, he recalled as the sky snapped to below his feet, he'd spent a day at a theme park on a SimTech outing last year and been distinctly underwhelmed by the rides.

After what he thought was a few minutes, the constant lurching began to take its toll. It was the room inversion, he decided, concentrating on analyzing the experimental design. Nothing distressed the inner ear like apparent sudden changes in the surroundings with no corresponding change in gravity.

Not, however, as badly as he would expect. The sim had certainly made progress since the days when standing up from a chair made half the users ill. Hopefully that meant the new anti-nausea systems were feeding just the right signals into just the right places to counter the feelings. Sim sickness was still the biggest object blocking the smooth road to production. They had an array of pharmaceutical remedies tested and approved, but a sim-based alternative would be far more saleable. Wenzel had been optimistic the last time Warrick had spoken to him that the new system would do the trick.

"Is it—" His stomach lurched as the gravity snapped on at forty-five degrees to visual vertical. Two seconds after that, the room turned ninety degrees. "It is all right if I close my eyes?"

"Rather you didn't."

He blanked his mind, reaching for calm. This was all an illusion. His body lay still on a couch, and there was absolutely no reason at all for him to want to vomit.

100

All psychosomatic. To feel really ill, he'd have to tense his stomach muscles and the sim would be making sure he didn't. His inner ear would just have to cope. Persuasion and slow breathing kept him going for longer than he'd expected. Either the test protocol wasn't as bad as Wenzel thought, or the new algorithms were very good indeed. Then the sickness intensified sharply, as though some kind of barrier had been breached.

"Now," he gasped, eyes closing involuntarily. "Stop, please." The words and the urgent tone suddenly and vividly reminded him of Toreth, driving a spike of arousal through the nausea. So much for the distraction plan.

The world had stopped flipping and Warrick opened his eyes. Wenzel still stood by the screen, smiling, studying the result. Warrick waited, taking back control of his body sufficiently to stop his virtual legs shaking. He wondered how he would feel outside the sim. Like hell, he suspected. While he was in the sim, however bad he felt the direct nerve controls would stop him from actually vomiting. Once out, he was on his own. "How did I do?" he asked Wenzel.

"Fifteen minutes." He sounded impressed. "Which will stand as a record because the protocol has a fifteen minute max."

"Were the new algorithms running?"

"Don't know. I can't tell until I break the codes after the analysis."

Warrick nodded approvingly. All nicely controlled.

"If they were running," Wenzel continued, "they'd have cut out as the program stopped. Did it feel different right at the end?"

"I won't spoil your blinding by telling you. Let me know the results."

Wenzel nodded, then looked down at the screen. "I will say I like the look of the test so far. Two very clear clusters of results. I think we've cracked it, or at least taken a big step in the right direction. I have another victim waiting, so if you could..."

When he lifted the visor and the sim winked out, Warrick discovered a junior programmer waiting nervously by the door—Goldie Cheesman. He tried to smile encouragingly at her, but unfortunately it took a whole minute before he could manage to stagger off the couch and back to his office.

Day Seven

The wooden wall of the sauna pressed smoothly against his back, the air rich with wet heat and eucalyptus. Nothing touched his front yet, but through half-closed eyes he could see Toreth standing only half a meter away. Standing and simply looking at him. "What?" Warrick asked.

"Incredible." Toreth moved suddenly, bracing his hands on the wall on either side of Warrick's head. "You look fucking incredible." Then slowly, so slowly, he dipped his head down. So very slowly that when his mouth touched Warrick's—

The timer beeped and Warrick opened his eyes. His lips tingled slightly. On the screen, the letters slowly came into focus, words joining up until it all made sense again and the last of the fantasy had cleared from his mind.

Over the years it had become a rule to allow himself the occasional five minutes' indulgence at work, and no more. Long enough to allow an examination of a scenario, but not long enough to drive himself completely insane with frustration. At least, not often. From time to time he hit upon a particularly compelling situation; a few times he'd even called Toreth to describe the idea before the edge wore off.

Each time Toreth had laughed and told him that thinking about it wasn't his job. Then months later, when Warrick had forgotten about it, he'd find himself in the middle of the scenario. Always better than he'd imagined, too, improved and polished by Toreth's attention to detail and genius for interpersonal cruelty. This week might have set something of a record for twisting suggested scenarios into something new and unbearably absorbing.

He made himself a cup of chamomile tea and was trying to think calming thoughts when the comm chimed—his direct personal line. By the time he'd set the cup down, his palms were damp and his breathing unsteady. Toreth?

He hoped the disappointment didn't show on his face when Cele appeared on the screen. She was at her studio, a medium-large canvas out of focus in the background. "Keir! Sorry to bother you at work." She didn't sound at all sorry. "I've just finished a piece."

Concentrate, he told himself sternly. "For anyone I know?"

"Actually, no. It's not a commission—to be honest, I just couldn't resist the subject even though I have my time booked for what feels like the rest of my life. Anyway, I thought you might want to see it. Hang on."

She moved out of the way, and the comm refocused on the painting.

Faded blue shutters hung folded back against a whitewashed exterior wall, framing an open window. A male nude sat sideways on the deep windowsill, pinkish early-morning sunlight glowing on his golden hair and warming the color of the worn stone flags at the foot of the canvas. The man leaned against the edge of the window frame, one leg bent up, foot resting on the sill, the other leg out of sight in the room. Forearm resting on his knee, his hand dangled, relaxed and casual. His face was turned away from the viewer, looking back into the shadowed room behind him, but Warrick didn't need to see it. The smooth, clean lines and easy physical confidence were unmistakable, and so very much what he didn't need to see right now that he almost laughed.

"Toreth," he said.

"Ha! I *told* him you'd know who it was." Cele sounded delighted. "I did it from photographs, because he won't sit long enough to get anywhere, not even for unlimited alcohol and the dirtiest jokes I know. He made a flying visit Wednesday afternoon to let me recheck the pose and put in the finishing touches."

"He didn't say anything about it." Toreth had been modeling at the studio on Wednesday? So much for being tied to I&I. Although if he'd only been at Cele's for a few minutes . . .

"Hardly worthwhile—there wasn't much to mention. He spent more time getting in and out of his clothes than he did on the job. I hope he's got more stamina than that in bed." Cele reappeared in the screen. "What do you think?"

He kept his face deadpan. "Oh, definitely a lot more."

Cele chuckled. "About the picture."

"It's beautiful. Subject and execution." With Toreth's body out of sight again, Warrick realized he wanted the painting, or rather, how badly he wanted it. Cele had said it wasn't a commission, so ownership was possible. He'd just have to make sure that she agreed to a high enough price this time. "What are you going to do with it?"

"It's promised to a gallery for a show called 'Summer in Autumn.' Made me feel less guilty about the self-indulgence. After that I'm not sure. The exhibition finishes around New Year, I think." She grinned. "I wonder if you know anyone who might like it as a present?"

"I think I know someone who'd like to buy it."

Cele shook her head firmly. "Uh-uh. It's not for sale."

He contemplated arguing, but after all these years, he told himself, he ought to have learned to accept generosity gracefully. It was hardly Cele's fault that her gifts had become so valuable. "Then, yes, I know someone who'd love it."

The picture would look beautiful in Warrick's living room, and he wondered if Cele had picked the faded blue of the shutters for that reason. Toreth would be delighted by the chance to look at his favorite subject.

"How about a drink tonight?" Cele asked. "I feel like celebrating."

"Shall I come round to the studio?"

"No. I'm sick of the sight of the place, and you'd only put your fingers on the painting before it's properly dry. We could have dinner if you're not busy. Oh, except that I know Friday's usually—" she winked, "—you-know-what with you-know-who."

"Not tonight." Warrick tried to keep his voice casual. "He's busy with a case."

"You don't say?" Cele smirked, and Warrick wondered if his frustration was that obvious. "Shall I call Dilly as well, see if she's free?"

"I'm afraid she's in Kiel."

"Oh? Nobody ever tells me anything. Or maybe I forgot. Why's she there?"

"Talking to deep-water engineering people, I think. Last-minute rush. They want to offer her a few weeks of troubleshooting for some project that's having problems."

"Sounds gripping. Just us, then. Eight o'clock suit you? I had a recommendation for a new place at the Varsity Complex."

As he climbed out of the SimTech car, Warrick mused that the Varsity—bars, hotels, shops, and all the usual trimmings of a leisure complex—wasn't the best place to visit in his current mood. He and Toreth had spent some very enjoyable evenings there. On the other hand, since Toreth was otherwise engaged, he should take whatever distraction was available, and Cele was invariably excellent company.

Cele had chosen the bar to meet up in, but she hadn't arrived when Warrick reached it. Not surprising, given her usual timekeeping. He checked the name of the bar again, just to be sure, then bought them both a drink and sat down at a vacant small table for two.

He scanned the bar idly. A little too loud and dark for his tastes, and surprisingly busy for the relatively early hour. Lots of corporates in working suits who obviously hadn't made it home yet. Many of them looked settled in, making groups and couples on the low chairs around the edges of the room.

He was, he realized, virtually the only man there alone. He caught the occasional glance in his direction, amusement and pity mingling. Of course: a single man plus two drinks equaled stood up. He checked his watch. Cele was already ten minutes late. He waited until he couldn't bear the feeling of self-consciousness, then he picked up both drinks and moved back to the bar.

At least there, he was one of a crowd. He squeezed past a blonde woman in a tight black dress and took an empty stool at the very end of the bar, beside a smartly suited man talking business to a much younger woman. She was making a halfhearted attempt to feign interest, which seemed to be good enough for her companion, who sounded to be something to do with software marketing.

Warrick listened to the conversation with half his attention, which was all it took to bore him, too. Should he call Cele? No doubt she'd be on her way. Beyond the couple, the woman in the black dress was hunting through a tiny, overflowing handbag, muttering under her breath. Someone called Ian would be in trouble if she ever found her comm.

He should call. If Cele were going to be a while, at least he could get rid of the second drink. He should have known better than to buy it, Warrick thought as he searched his inside jacket pocket for his own comm. The day Cele was on time—

Over the noise of the bar, a woman said angrily, "Watch what you're doing!"

Warrick turned, but the woman in the black dress wasn't talking to him. She had her back to him, her shoulders set angrily as she looked up at a blond man.

Toreth.

Instinctively, Warrick looked away, leaning on the bar, hand against his face. Occupied with a case was now definitely a lie. He glanced sideways, using the dull salesman as cover. The woman had stepped back from the bar, where one of the staff was mopping up a spilled drink. Toreth smiled at her apologetically, going from disinterest to full charm in an instant. "Terribly sorry about that. Please let me get you another."

"Oh. No, it's okay." Now she sounded flustered. She ducked her head slightly and her hand came up, hovered uncertainly, then tucked a few strands of her short-bobbed hair behind her ear. "No harm done."

"Glad to hear it." Toreth's smile warmed a few degrees. "I've seen you before, haven't I?"

"It's the first time I've been here."

"Oh? Somewhere else then." His confidence didn't waver. "I'm sure I remember you. You've cut your hair—it used to be much longer. It looks good like that."

Her posture relaxed. "Thanks."

Toreth stepped back a little and looked her up and down. A flush crept around her neck. "Did I spill anything on you?" he asked.

"I—" The woman ran her hand over the front of her dress. "Yes, a bit."

"My name's Marc. I'll give you my number. Get in touch when you've had it cleaned, and I'll pay for it."

Warrick studied Toreth more closely as he transferred his details. Not really interested in her, he decided. Maybe she was too obviously willing.

He felt oddly triumphant when Toreth's smile cooled and he turned away to hand his credit card to the barman. As he waited, Warrick saw the woman's shoulders tense once or twice. Then, after Toreth picked up two drinks and walked away, she muttered, "Why the hell didn't you *say* something?"

The question so perfectly mirrored Warrick's own thoughts that he almost said, "I don't know."

His next thought was that he'd somehow—impossibly—been mistaken. It couldn't have been Toreth. But when he turned to watch the man cross the room, there was no more doubt than there had been when he saw the picture. Every movement was Toreth, his body unmistakable.

Should he follow him? Warrick had almost decided yes, when he saw Toreth stop next to a corner booth occupied by a dark-haired man and place the drinks on the table. Toreth squeezed onto the bench and immediately took his comm earpiece out of his pocket. Warrick watched, trying not to stare too openly; the other man was a little taller than Toreth and almost as heavily built, and Warrick didn't like the idea of inadvertently starting a fight.

After a brief conversation Toreth put the earpiece away, then returned to his companion.

The last of Warrick's shock vanished, flushed away by anger. Bastard. Out on the prowl and lying about it, which was the irritating part. Irrationally irritating, at that. Warrick knew perfectly well that Toreth slept around. Toreth knew that he knew and also that he didn't like to hear about it. So "I'm out" or "I don't feel like coming round tonight" adequately covered the whole situation. Or, indeed, "I'm busy at work." They'd fixed on this long ago as the best compromise that didn't involve a visit to a re-education center for a fundamental reconstruction of Toreth's libido.

Tonight, however, the lie infuriated Warrick and, while he surreptitiously studied the pair, he tried to work out why. One casual partner more or less was nothing, and although it always annoyed him to meet them, it didn't usually rankle this badly. It was the previous Saturday that made the difference, he realized suddenly. They had set a game in progress; they had made an agreement that Toreth would wait, and Toreth had broken it.

After a minute or two, Warrick shook his head. He had no intention of waiting here until Toreth took his conquest elsewhere. That was, if he didn't simply conclude business here in the toilets. He should go home and try to forget about the experience. Unless—oh, God. Cele was due any minute. Putting up with Toreth's idiosyncrasies was one thing, having his behavior witnessed by a friend was another.

Warrick paused, hand in his pocket. Cele. Cele had arranged the meeting. Cele, who had seen Toreth recently. Not that he imagined for a moment that Cele would knowingly participate in a scheme to humiliate him, but Toreth certainly wouldn't be above setting her up too, if the idea amused him.

Or... or this *was* the game, still, and Toreth had no intention of leaving with the stranger. A pick-up scenario, which was something that Cele would help arrange with great enthusiasm.

Then Toreth turned his head and looked across the bar, straight at him. He held Warrick's startled gaze for a few seconds, then smiled vaguely, as if to a stranger who'd made eye contact, before he looked away.

Warrick was still trying to decide what he believed, when his comm chimed. "It's me," Cele said when he answered it.

"Is there a problem?"

"Yes. I'm afraid I can't make it. Something's come up. Are you there already?" Before he could answer, she carried on. "Of course you are. Mr. Punctual. Now you see the advantages of being late. If you were me, you'd still be at home and you'd have saved yourself a trip."

Added to Toreth's call a few minutes ago, this went beyond the realms of coincidence. However, asking Cele would ruin the game. "Don't worry about it. We'll get together some other time."

As he pocketed the comm, a group vacated a small table, and Warrick moved quickly to claim it. This gave a better view: Toreth's face clearly visible, but the other man's back towards Warrick. Now he could watch as obviously as he liked. It shouldn't take long to decide what kind of game Toreth was playing, and whether Warrick wanted to take part.

Toreth's reactions were perfect, and highly promising. It apparently took him a few minutes to notice Warrick watching, and then a few minutes more of casual glances in Warrick's direction to decide what to do about it. Then he spent another couple in close conversation with his well-built companion before they both stood up. The man clapped Toreth on the shoulder and left the bar without a single glance in Warrick's direction. Toreth watched him go, then picked up his drink and strolled over.

Warrick watched him approach, wondering what to say. Better to let Toreth have the opening line.

Toreth leaned on the fluted black pillar by the table, and his white shirt tightened over his stomach. He looked down at Warrick, direct and utterly self-possessed, and said, "I saw you looking at me. Did you want something?"

Warrick paused to catch his breath, then said, "You reminded me of someone."

"Yeah? Who?"

"I'm not sure." He edged around the semicircle of bench. "Join me, and maybe it'll come back."

Toreth sat down, then held his hand out, awkward in the close space. "I'm Marc."

"Keir Warrick." There was a short pause, then he said, "Can I ask you a question?"

"Go ahead."

"I was at the bar when you went to buy a drink."

Toreth nodded. "I noticed you."

Noticed, not saw. "The woman you spoke to—had you really seen her before?"

"No."

"So how did you know she'd had her hair cut?"

"Easy. Did you see her duck her head, and the way her hand came up? She was used to having long hair, to having to push it out of the way. That kind of habit doesn't last longer than a few weeks once the props change." He smiled slowly, eyes fixed on Warrick. "You can tell a lot from body language. What people want, what they're going to do...everything they don't want you to know."

It gave Warrick a delightful feeling of déjà vu to sit in a bar and be seduced by Toreth. Or rather, not quite Toreth. There was no one thing that Warrick could point to and say was different, but as they made wary-but-interested strangers' conversation, it was surprisingly easy to remember to call him Marc.

After an utterly fictitious and frighteningly plausible description of his job with a private security consultancy firm, Toreth asked, "You married?"

"No," Warrick said, then couldn't resist adding, "I have a partner. A male partner."

107

Toreth's eyes narrowed briefly, then he said, "What's he like?"

Warrick considered a string of flattering epithets before he settled on "Jealous."

This time, Toreth's expression didn't flicker. "Yeah? So you'd never—?"

"Be unfaithful?" The ghost of Girardin hovered nearby. Warrick shook his head firmly. "Never."

Toreth smiled, approving and anticipatory. "Let me get you another drink, Keir."

Warrick had meant to spin the evening out as long as he could—what he'd really wanted was to provoke Toreth into breaking his assumed role. For some reason, though, the impulse quickly faded. Perhaps it was the days of uncertainty. Perhaps it was the wonderful knowledge that he didn't have to wait until Sunday after all. Perhaps it was the sight of Toreth beside him, casual and relaxed and inexplicably different.

Whatever it was, only half an hour passed before they'd finished the drinks and Toreth stood up. "Would you like to go somewhere a bit quieter?" he asked.

"Love to." Warrick stood up, too quickly, and the blood rushed to his head, leaving him dizzy.

"Okay?" Toreth asked.

The feeling passed. "Yes, fine."

There was no discussion of where the quieter place might be. Toreth simply led the way to the main hotel lobby. The lift up started with a slight jolt, and Warrick lost his balance. Toreth seemed steady enough. He merely looked at Warrick sidelong and smiled. He was humming, which seemed oddly more tuneful than normal. A side effect of being Marc, perhaps.

As they stepped out of the lift door, the dizziness came again, and this time it didn't go away. He stumbled, and only Toreth's arm around his waist stopped him from a headlong fall.

"Thanks," Warrick mumbled. "Can't seem to . . . sorry."

They started down the corridor, and Marc—Toreth—didn't let go of him. Warrick shook his head, trying to clear his vision. The colors and angles were all subtly wrong, out of true. There was something strange happening. Something very, very strange, but somehow he didn't care, or couldn't be bothered to worry, and wasn't it Toreth with him? Everything would be all right.

They halted, and then a door clicked opened and closed and only then did he realize he had his eyes shut and he forced them open.

Hotel room. A light brightened, then dimmed, and that made the world swim again. He clung to Marc, welcoming the anchor of his effortless strength. He low-

108

ered his heavy head, letting it rest on Marc's shoulder, giving in to the temptation to mouth the taut muscles through his shirt.

"Right, Keir." Marc took him by the chin, gently tilting his head back. Kiss, Warrick thought vaguely, and started to gather his strength to protest, because Toreth wouldn't want him to…no, this *was* Toreth and why the hell did everything feel so—

"Let's get you to bed," Marc said, and Warrick nodded gratefully. Sleep. Always better in the morning. Jen used to say that to them, kissing them goodnight.

Then, somehow, he was lying on the bed on his side, naked, head resting on his outflung arm. He tried to lift his head and couldn't, and the wrongness of that finally broke through and roused the first thrill of fear.

Marc stood by the bed, trousers already gone, stripping off his hypnotically white shirt, looking down at him intently.

"What…" Warrick licked his numb lips, his tongue thick and clumsy. "What is it? What did you do?"

Marc crouched down and smiled coldly. "Free tip for the future, if you ever get a chance to use it: you should be more careful about accepting drinks from strangers."

Shit. There'd been something in the drink, of course there had been—how could he have been so stupid?

Marc touched his face again, a whisper-soft brush across his cheek, then ran his hand down, over his chest, tracing a line from breastbone to navel to… Then the bed shifted and dipped, and Warrick wondered what was happening until he realized he'd closed his eyes again. Let them stay like that, he decided.

This time, the hand that took his chin wasn't gentle and when he tried to shake it off, it closed around his throat instead, finger and thumb curling up over his jaw. Before Warrick could protest, Marc's mouth sealed over his, forcing a kiss on him. Marc bore down, covering him with solid heat, pressing him into the bed with frightening strength, and God, he was naked and hard. They were both hard.

And Warrick couldn't fight. Couldn't fight because his body wouldn't listen, wouldn't move. It could only feel.

Helpless. Oh God, so helpless, chained without chains, and hyperaware of every touch. Marc's free hand left trails of fire on his skin, the touch burning long after his fingers had left. He felt every point of contact, every flex and press of the body grinding inexorably against him. Hot skin touched him everywhere, overwhelming his spinning senses. So good—wonderful—dangerous, and terrifying—and he reveled in it and tried to fight because he couldn't remember who it was or where they were or whether this was wrong.

The kiss ended, and when Marc's mouth returned, it brushed over his cheek, around to his ear. Soft, teasing mouth, but the grip on Warrick's throat didn't relent. "Keep still," Marc whispered, "and quiet, and just maybe I'll let you live."

That was it—that was enough. Warrick bucked up, gasping, choking back the cry as he came.

Keep still. Keep quiet. Quiet he could manage—still was hopeless, no chance of that as he shivered and panted, clinging to the muscled back until his hands were suddenly empty. When had Marc moved?

When he forced his eyes open, he found Marc kneeling over him. "I know you can hear me." Marc's eyes narrowed and he moved to lay his fingers over Warrick's right nipple. Not quite a pinch. "Can't you?" When Warrick said nothing, Marc tightened his fingers. "Can't you, Keir?"

He pinched again, harder, until Warrick managed to croak, "Yes."

"Good. Because I want you to know that we're not finished yet."

Marc rolled him over, arranging him on the bed, spreading his legs. Opening him. Half his mind screamed stop, half begged for Marc to touch him, and neither impulse mattered because Warrick could do nothing but be done to. Do nothing but be taken. Do nothing but accept the cock pressing into him, the slow, deep strokes—the hand pulling his head around—the mouth taking whatever Marc wanted.

He lost track of time, forgot that he supposed to fight. It felt too good and whoever the hell it was—Toreth, Marc—all he wanted was to stay here forever and be theirs. The slow pace tortured him. He was hard again, aching, tensing his muscles against the weird paralysis that magnified the tiny movements he managed. Nerves fired back pleasure with every minute rub of skin, every touch of the sheets.

He squirmed on the bed—all the movement he could make, but more than he expected—and Marc gasped and stilled. Warrick moved again, lifting his hips, flexing around the cock pinning him to the bed, and this time Marc groaned.

"Jesus *Christ*, Warrick." For a moment it was Toreth above him, then his voice changed. "I warned you to do what you're told, Keir. Keep still."

The rough voice brought back the memory of the game they'd played to get here. Warrick managed to marshal his lips and tongue to produce an approximation of "Shan't, you bastard." Then he set about resisting in earnest.

Toreth's arms shook with the strain of not surrendering to the urge to thrust. He bit his lip and thought about yearly budget appraisals with Tillotson until the arousal dampened down.

The drug had begun to wear off, and Warrick's struggles had become stronger and seriously exciting. Warrick still, helpless, and utterly in his power had been arousing enough. Warrick swearing and fighting him and failing was, was—

Toreth slowed again, the fuck reaching the point where if he slowed much more they'd simply be lying on the bed. It would be easier to keep control if Warrick would stop moving, but he hadn't and Toreth couldn't manage another coherent threat. Warrick twisted under him, and over his own harsh breathing Toreth heard him whispering, "No. Marc, please, no."

Shit. This was impossible. Toreth looked away from Warrick, from the sweat curling the hair at the nape of his neck, from the tendons tightening as he turned his head...

He slid into Warrick, pressing as close as he could, then began to rock firmly against him, pressing—hopefully—Warrick's cock down into the soft bedcover.

Warrick made a startled noise, muffled by the pillow, and Toreth tilted his head back and smiled. He concentrated on his breathing, keeping it deep but steady. Better. Like this, he had a chance of keeping control for a while longer. Or at least he would if Warrick would shut the fuck up. His helpless, pleading whimpers and moans sparked electricity down Toreth's spine. No longer struggling, Warrick moved with him, hands clenching desperately in the pillow, thrusting up against him and down into the bed, too good to bear.

Toreth, I don't doubt the accuracy of your assessments, but there is a cross-departmental limit of three percent for team raises, which—

Fuck, it wasn't working. "Stop," Toreth panted. One at a time, he grabbed Warrick's wrists and dug his fingers into the tendons, forcing Warrick to let go of the pillow, and Warrick moaned. Toreth pulled Warrick's hands to the side and pinned them. "Stop it, keep still, keep—"

Warrick's head came up, his back arching, and he came. If he screamed, Toreth didn't hear him because every last scrap of self-control was blown away by Warrick's body tightening around him.

As long as you can stand it—harder, faster, this was—*as long as you can stand it*—perfect, yes, so good; God—*as long as you can*—ah, God, Warrick—*as long as*—so close, soon, soon—

Toreth bit the nape of Warrick's neck, because it was the only way he could keep quiet, stop himself from telling Warrick how good it was, how much he'd wanted it—and then he was coming so hard that his eyes teared.

When Warrick woke, the clock by the bed said ten to ten, which didn't seem late enough. He rolled over, vaguely surprised when his body obeyed him. Toreth had gone. The sheets were a mess. He felt sick and lightheaded, which had to be the aftermath of whatever drug Toreth had slipped him. His wrists ached and he also felt to have a prize collection of bruises and bites on his neck and shoulders.

He felt wonderful. Warrick smiled and settled back into the pillow to relive the choice moments of the evening, imprinting them in his memory while they were fresh.

A few minutes later, Warrick noticed that his face ached, too. He was still smiling. He pressed his lips together, wiping the expression away, then rubbed his cheeks and sat up. The room swam briefly, then settled down. When he stood up, keeping a cautious hand on the bed head, his balance had returned.

His clothes lay in a pile on the floor, and it took him a moment to find his hand screen. Warrick called the security system at his flat, which told him Toreth hadn't gone there. Then, feeling only slightly guilty, he did the same to the system at Toreth's flat. Toreth had freely given him access to the system, and he knew Warrick well enough to guess what he could do with it.

Toreth was there, which brought the smile back again. Only twenty minutes there by taxi, and he could pick up something for them to eat on the way over.

Downstairs at reception, he discovered that Toreth had left him to pay the bill. Of course.

Warrick closed the flat door and went straight through to the living room.

Toreth was lounging on the sofa, screen on but muted. He watched Warrick set the box on the coffee table, then raised his eyebrows as Warrick came around the table. "Didn't Sara tell you I was busy tonight? I thought—"

Warrick placed his hand firmly in the center of Toreth's chest and pushed him back against the sofa. Then he kissed him until he felt he'd conveyed sufficient appreciation of the evening's entertainment, and until Toreth's heartbeat had picked up speed under his palm.

He broke the kiss and stood up. Toreth wiped his mouth, and smirked. "You brought pizza?" he asked. "Great, because I have beer."

Toreth reached up, grabbed Warrick's belt, and pulled him down to sit on the sofa. Then he leaned down over the side of the sofa, produced two cold beer bottles, already opened, and set them on the table.

"I thought you'd be round when you woke up, and the flush-out time on that stuff is pretty tightly defined. How do you feel?"

"I was a little dizzy when I woke up, and queasy, but it went away by the time I left the hotel."

"Good. Some people get a bitch of a headache from it." Toreth opened the pizza box and helped himself to a slice. He bit off the point of the triangle, then gasped, sucking air in through pursed lips. "Hot. *Fucking* hot." He grabbed a beer. "Pepperoni and garlic," he said when he'd dealt with the mouthful. "Just what I wanted. How did you guess?"

"I'm naturally lucky." After three years, it was hardly a staggering feat of deduction. Warrick picked up the remaining beer, set the bottle to his lips, then lowered it. He lifted it and raised his eyebrows.

Toreth laughed. "Nothing but beer, promise. Want to swap?"

Warrick shook his head and risked a swallow. He might as well take Toreth's word for it. For one thing, all the offer really meant was that if Toreth had dosed the beer, then he'd also taken an antidote to it. Setting the bottle on the table, Warrick took a slice from the heated box and, out of habit, wrapped it neatly in a napkin. At least this was Toreth's flat, where crumbs on the floor were merely part of the ecology.

"Who was the man in the bar?" Warrick asked after they'd eaten in silence for a while.

"Christofi. Political Crimes senior. Believe it or not, we were talking about work. He wanted to talk somewhere outside I&I and I thought he'd add a bit of color."

"He certainly did that—I nearly walked out."

"Really?" Toreth looked delighted. "Then you'd never have known what you'd missed."

"And that would have been a great pity," Warrick said fervently.

"Enjoy it?" Toreth asked.

"It was perfect."

"Not quite. It was supposed to happen this weekend, on Sunday."

"So why did you do it tonight?"

"Guess."

Warrick considered. The line was obvious, but Toreth would prefer him not to get it. "Because it's game night?"

Toreth shook his head, helping himself to more pizza. "Try again."

"Because it's the day Cele finished the picture?"

Another shake.

"Because bars are too quiet on Sundays?"

"Good point, but no." Toreth paused, the second slice of pizza sagging dangerously, the topping threatening to slide onto his lap. He looked at Warrick sidelong, then grinned again. "Because that was as long as I could stand it."

113

Caged

❖

The cool metal of the collar fastened around Warrick's throat, and he felt the tremor of excitement, uncontrollable, run through him as he waited for the click of the lock. Instead, the collar lifted away and Toreth said, "I'm bored."

Toreth had a wide variety of boredoms. Many of them translated into something along the lines of "I don't want to do that" or "This is too intimate" or "I need attention." This sounded, for once, like genuine boredom, which meant Warrick had a small chance to talk him out of it.

"What about me?" Warrick asked.

"What about you?" The bed shifted as Toreth moved away. "I'll fuck you later, how about that?"

"I would like to be fucked now."

"Jesus, you're insatiable, you know that? How old are you?"

"What?"

"How *old* are you?" He sounded to be over by the window now. "It's simple enough—take this year, subtract the year you were born in, adjust for the month. You're supposed to be good at that kind of thing."

"I'm thirty-six. Although I fail to see what that has to do with anything."

"Because at thirty-six you should be able to wait for a few hours for a fucking."

"The only reason I can't wait is because you make me want it so much."

There was a brief silence, then Toreth laughed. "Oh, no. You're not getting me like that."

"I thought it was worth a try. Very well. You can untie me."

Footsteps, and then the blindfold came off, leaving him blinking at the light. Toreth released him, lingering over the straps as if he hadn't entirely convinced himself it was a good idea.

Warrick sat up, rubbed his wrists where the leather had chafed, and looked down at himself. "I can't help but feel it's a pity to waste all that hard work."

"Okay, fine." Toreth slammed him backwards onto the bed, pinned him down, and sucked him off with a ruthless efficiency that wasn't as good as a morning of carefully orchestrated bondage, but still left him gasping for breath.

By the time he sat up for the second time, Toreth was already dressed. "Right, that was my good deed for the day," he said. "Come on."

Warrick got off the bed and started trying to track down his own clothes among the detritus on Toreth's bedroom floor. "Where are we going?"

"No idea. Where would you like to go?"

He refrained, with some effort, from pointing out that he'd been perfectly happy where he was. "Well, if I'm passing a Sunday on my own, my usual choices, outside the sim, are galleries—"

"Went to one once."

"Museums—"

"No."

"Concerts, if there are any on."

"Definitely not."

Warrick finished buttoning his shirt. "You're doing this to annoy me, aren't you?"

"No, I'm doing it because I'm bored." He grinned. "Anything else is a bonus."

"You have the shortest attention span of any man I've ever met. Or woman, come to that. How do you manage at work?"

Toreth looked surprised, not surprisingly given that work was a closed topic.

"I'm not asking for details, it was merely a general question about concentration."

"Work's different." He shrugged. "I concentrate all the bloody time at work. And I do a lot of boring crap conscientiously, because it's important that it gets done properly. When I'm not at work, I do things for fun."

"And fucking isn't fun?"

"Of course fucking's fun, usually, but not today."

Warrick finally located his second sock. "Something I did?" he asked, keeping his tone neutral.

"No. Nothing. You're...it was fine. I'm bored, that's all. I'm...I don't bloody know. I just fancied a change." He walked over to the doorway, a little too quickly, hesitated there, then turned. "Aren't you *ready* yet?"

That was as much as it took for Toreth to start getting uncomfortable. If Warrick pressed any more, the good mood would evaporate completely, and beyond that Toreth would leave. Luckily, Warrick knew the signs well enough by now that unpleasantness was usually avoided. "Yes, ready." Suddenly, he knew where to go. "I don't have the car; I'll call a taxi."

"Where are we going?"

"It's a surprise."

He was always flattered when Toreth was willing to accept something like that without question.

115

"The *zoo*?" Toreth asked as they got out of the taxi.

"Why not? It's a beautiful day. Besides, you've already rejected everything else in New London." A slight exaggeration, but Toreth didn't pick it up. "Don't you like zoos?"

"No idea—never been to one."

"Then it'll be a new experience." Not Toreth's favorite thing actually, but he tried to make it sound like a bonus. "I like it a great deal."

"Yeah? You never said."

"The topic never arose. This way."

The sun shone brightly and the zoo was clearly going to be busy, a crowd already forming outside the ornate gates. Primarily families, enjoying an inexpensive day out. Citizens making the most of the Administration-funded facility.

Warrick paused, caught by the memory of standing there himself, with Dilly, Tar, and Aunt Jen, when the gates had seemed a lot taller. The zoo had been one of Jen's favorite holiday diversions when the children were at home and her sister was at work. A promise of a trip there was worth at least a week of good behavior. Then, once they were inside, he'd fight with Dilly over what they went to see first, and Jen would make them take turns to—

Toreth coughed. "Are we going in, or not?"

Bypassing the main queues, Warrick scanned his ID at a smaller gate, and they were let through.

"How come you get in free?" Toreth asked.

"Funny family story that I won't bore you with. The punch line is that Dilly and I bought each other life membership one New Year, without knowing what the other was buying."

"Doesn't sound very funny."

"And that is precisely why I didn't tell you the rest."

Beyond the gates was a large paved area—a place for meetings and departures. Warrick stopped by the tall, fluted post bearing signs with white letters on black metal pointing down the radiating paths to the various sections. "What would you like to do first?" he asked.

It was an unfair question, in a way, since Toreth couldn't really be expected to know. To Warrick's astonishment, he said, "Do they have flamingos?"

"Er, yes. They're over this way, I think." He wondered all the way whether to ask, deciding in the end that Toreth would tell him if he wanted him to know. As it was, Toreth didn't say anything at all as they walked. However, he was whistling. Usually a good sign, if hard on the ears.

They reached the flamingo pool, next to a picnic and play area. Toreth picked his way through the already swarming children with the particular expression of

116

concentrated distaste he always wore in their presence. When he reached the edge, he stopped and leaned on the low wall, looking at the birds. Ignoring the noise, they had formed a tight group in the center of the shallow water, the majority asleep, balanced on one leg with their heads under their wings. Their pink plumage looked faded—something to do with diet, Warrick recalled.

"They're smaller than I was expecting," Toreth said as Warrick came up beside him.

Warrick couldn't tell if that pleased him or not. "Oh?"

"Yeah." After a moment he straightened up and brushed his hands off. "Okay. What do you want to see?"

Given Toreth's earlier declaration of boredom, Warrick decided to avoid the more scientific areas, like the research and breeding centers, and concentrate on less demanding entertainment. He picked the Reptile House, more or less at random, and they set off. On the way, Warrick looked mostly at Toreth, and Toreth split his attention between captives and spectators. At least he appeared to be enjoying something so far—the zoo was as good for people watching as for watching any other kind of animal.

After they'd toured around the Reptile House, where Toreth pronounced himself disappointed by the general torpor of the inhabitants, Toreth used his turn to choose their next goal to suggest a drink.

They sat at a small café, drinking coffee and watching other visitors passing. Before long, Toreth slipped into a near-constant stream of assessments of his chances of picking up one or another of them. Warrick considered being offended, but decided it was harmless enough when there was no chance of Toreth actually setting off in pursuit—although he tried not to express disbelief at any individual claim, just to be on the safe side.

However, when Toreth had offered a dead cert on a man in his late twenties escorting a woman and two children, he finally gave in and asked, "How the hell can you tell?"

"Practice." Toreth sipped his coffee. "Lots of practice."

"No, seriously. What is it about him, in particular, that made you pick him out?"

Toreth looked at him sharply, and the flash of jealousy made Warrick smile. "I'm not interested in *him*. Just in the theory."

"Okay. Come on, we need to get round in front of him again."

They finished the coffees, took a shortcut across a triangle of grass, and then waited by the tapirs for the family to reappear. Before they did, Toreth picked out another couple. "Now, look at these two here—he's never going to be interested. Straight as they come. Watch this. Watch him."

Toreth cut across their path at a diagonal, looking the opposite way, a little distracted, and almost-but-not-quite collided with the woman. There was a moment of confusion, smiled apologies, and Toreth carried on. Warrick watched obediently, not entirely sure what he was supposed to be seeing.

When he reached the far side of the wide path, Toreth stopped and leaned on the wall. Warrick was about to join him, but Toreth gestured for him to stay put. He realized why a moment later when he spotted the dead cert and his wife approaching. Toreth repeated the maneuver with them, ending up next to him again.

"Well?" Toreth asked.

"No, sorry."

"You didn't see any difference?" Toreth sounded genuinely surprised.

"Not really."

"Never mind. I'll find someone else, and you can try again."

"You could simply tell me."

"No, this is more fun—we're supposed to be looking at wildlife, aren't we? But it's a bit quiet here. Come on." Warrick followed along as Toreth searched for a more suitable hunting spot. It was, he reflected, an odd way to spend a Sunday—taking pickup tips from your something-like-a-partner.

After the next demonstration had proved equally fruitless, Toreth took pity on him and said, "You're probably looking at the wrong part. Watch them as I'm walking away."

Two more pairs of couples, and then he saw it. As Toreth made his charming apologies and departed, the dead certs watched him, the others watched their wives. It was almost disappointingly easy. "Is that it?" he said, when Toreth strolled back up to him.

Toreth laughed at his expression. "Yes, that's it. Basically it, anyway. It's all in how they look at other people. Mind you, that's the perfect setup to demonstrate it—under normal circumstances, it's harder to spot. But how long would it have taken you to notice on your own?"

"Probably never," he admitted. "Actually, it would've never even occurred to me to look."

"Good. Doesn't always work, anyway. And it only works exactly like that if the other half is around."

"So how do you tell if they aren't?"

Toreth laughed again. "As if I'm going to tell *you*. There you go, then, demo over. It's your turn to pick somewhere—try to choose something that moves, this time."

As the day progressed, the zoo filled up, and navigating the crowded paths became more of a chore. Finally, they retreated to the refreshments complex, built on the top of an artificial hill. There Warrick chose one of the more upmarket of the restaurants, and they had a very late lunch.

Afterwards, they took their beers out onto the terrace and sat in surprisingly comfortable wrought iron chairs, watching the crowds milling around below them.

In their enclosures, the animals seemed to be mostly asleep and unmoving in the heat. From up here, the blended voices of the visitors made an almost musical background. Children's voices, in the main. To Warrick the zoo had always been a childhood place, a family place, although he'd never say something like that to Toreth.

"What do you think of it, then?" Warrick asked.

Toreth shrugged. "It's okay. I wouldn't mind coming back, anyway. Especially when there aren't so many kids. Far too many, and far too bloody loud."

Thinking about the same thing, coming to such different conclusions. "I like kids."

"I know you do, Uncle Keir." Toreth stretched out in his chair and closed his eyes against the sun. "And you're welcome to the nasty little fuckers."

Since Toreth couldn't see him, Warrick allowed himself a smile. Toreth's reaction to children always amused him. There were so many topics that Warrick wouldn't normally dare raise with him, most of them to do with their relationship. Any suggestion that they would be together in the long term was risky. Offers of affection that weren't tied to fucking, expressing any kind of disapproval over his compulsive infidelity, even bringing food around to Toreth's flat too frequently— any of these and more could trigger a retreat. Then there were the standalone topics, such as Toreth's family, which were absolutely unmentionable.

Children, however, simply irritated him. Never, as far as Warrick could remember, had Toreth ever reacted badly to his expressing approval of them. He found it funny because the topic was, classically, a panic-inducing one for the commitment-phobic. His best guess was that it had never occurred to Toreth that "I like children" might in any way be connected to "I would like to have children of my own," with all the concomitant relationship implications. It had never seemed like a good idea to suggest the link to him.

He'd discussed the idea once with, of all people, Sara. She'd brought it up, the excuse being that her own mother was beginning to mention grandchildren excessively; in reality, she'd been fishing. She'd seemed to approve of his generally positive views on the subject, then worked briskly around to whether he, in the specific, wanted any.

He'd closed that avenue off with bland nothings, with which she hadn't bothered to hide her annoyance. Then, casual conversational distraction, he'd asked her what she thought Toreth would be like with children. Sara had given it long and serious thought, and then said, "I think he'd probably eat them."

He'd laughed, and that had been it. Because, really, it was so true that there was nothing else to say. Keeping Toreth around involved sacrifices, and this was one of them and by no means the largest.

It was very pleasant, sitting in the sun and doing nothing. Not something Warrick did often, with or without Toreth, and he decided they ought to do it again. Not necessarily the zoo, but they didn't spend much time together simply...being somewhere together.

It was something that would be better not discussed, but just quietly arranged. Maybe he'd even risk suggesting a holiday that wasn't disguised as a conference trip. A few days somewhere warm, with a beach; given his dislike of being underwater in the sim, Toreth probably wouldn't dive, but he might be induced to snorkel...

Warrick closed his eyes imagining Toreth's body, powdery with dried salt. Blond hair bleached a shade lighter by the sun. Blue eyes squinting against the dazzle from the sea, softening the hardness of his face. Tanning skin, with perhaps a touch of sunburn along his shoulders—just a little something to stroke soothing lotion over. He smiled at the picture, and his body's approving reaction to it. Maybe insatiable wasn't such a bad description at that. Better make it somewhere secluded enough for nude swimming. Fine, hot sand, which of course would be far more inconvenient than it was in the sim, but still—

A squeak of metal on stone caught his attention and, sure enough, when he looked around, he found that Toreth was watching him. "What're you smirking about?" Toreth asked.

Warrick sat up. "Guess."

He kept the scrutiny up for a few seconds longer, then grinned. "Well, of course—what else?"

They finished their beers, then had another round. After those had also gone down, Toreth looked at his watch. "Shall we go?"

"Why not? Except that..." Warrick hesitated. When he'd thought of the zoo, he'd had something specific in mind, but he wasn't sure he wanted to risk it spoiling the day. "I wanted to show you something before we do. She was new here the last time I came with Dilly, a few weeks ago, and I'm thinking of modeling one for the sim."

"What is it?"

"Just come and see. It won't take long," he added.

Toreth shrugged amiably. "If you like."

The enclosure had been newly renovated and the small path up to it started just beyond the flamingo pool. On that basis, it might be expected to be busy, but at the start of the path stood a board displaying, "NO CHILDREN," reinforced by a chronically bored attendant. He nodded them through and then returned to a comm conversation with what sounded to be a profoundly unhappy girlfriend.

They walked in silence between artificial rocks planted up with ferns. Then the path opened out, and Warrick hung back to let Toreth go first.

The cage wasn't small. Some of the space was an illusion created by painted walls and artfully arranged plants and stone, but there was plenty of open space, tall wooden frames with platforms, and a rugged fake cliff. Thick glass separated the enclosure from the viewing area, with a polite notice on the screen beside the glass, requesting visitors to stay back behind a makeshift tape barrier.

"Visitors" currently meant only them, for which Warrick was grateful. Other people would have spoiled the moment.

"There," he said, although there was no need. The solitary occupant was in plain view.

The panther paced across the front of the cage immediately behind the glass. Not the whole width—barely a third of it, in fact. She had worn a path in the grass, turning each time at precisely the same spot, moving with a tightly contained energy that he found painful to watch.

Prowling—that was the word traditionally linked to big cats. She should have prowled, but she didn't. Warrick had spent a long time in front of the cage when he'd been here with Dillian, trying to work out why the word felt so wrong, and eventually decided that prowling implies an interest in the world around. The panther showed no awareness of anything beyond her endless turn and return.

Unlike many of the other cages, there was no sense of being watched back. It was possible to map many things onto the flat, yellow eyes—restlessness, rage, boredom, despair, madness, a desperate determination never to surrender to stillness and death—but nothing that touched the viewer, nothing that connected to anything outside the animal's own mind.

She was in beautiful condition, coat glossy, muscles flowing under her skin as she moved and turned, moved and turned. That only made it worse, that such a healthy specimen could be so sick. The simile was obvious, and had occurred to him almost immediately he'd first seen her. He'd been thinking it over for a while when Dilly had turned to him and said in a low voice, "You know who it reminds me of, don't you?"

The remark had surprised him. These days Dilly never mentioned Toreth unless it was absolutely required. There had been no question as to who she meant, though. He'd nodded, and they'd left it at that.

Just as he'd done with Dilly, they stood and watched the panther in silence for a long time.

"Why's it doing that?" Toreth asked eventually.

"She came from somewhere where she was kept in a very small cage with insufficient stimulation. The repetitive behavior is called stereotyping. A stress-reducing response, or so I understand."

"So why is it *still* doing it?"

"Probably because she hasn't noticed yet that things have changed."

"God, no wonder they're extinct in the wild if they were all that stupid."

"It's not a question of intelligence. It was all she'd ever experienced, according to the exhibit entry." He offered his hand screen to Toreth, but he was still watching the panther. "She arrived at the other place as a young cub, and after that she was always kept alone in the same cage." Without meaning to, he switched into his lecture voice. "Normal brain and central nervous system development depends

121

on the proper kinds of environmental stimulation. When a stimulus is present, the developing nervous system reacts to it, learns from it and is shaped by it. There was nothing she wanted in the world around her, and no unpredictable events that required a reaction, so eventually she ceased to respond to it."

"Yeah, sounds vaguely familiar. I think it came up in a psychology course." Toreth glanced around. "How come you know so much about it?"

"I read a little of the field for some of the early sim work. We were interested in the possible side effects of feeding artificial stimuli into the brain."

When he stopped, Toreth prompted, "And?"

"And nothing. The consensus of available research was that any stimulus was equally well received, and that any small abnormalities created were quickly corrected by re-exposure to the normal world. Our initial results supported that and we dropped the project. A pity, because it's an interesting subject, but we had commercial considerations. I think one of the university groups at the AERC still works on it."

"So why aren't the new stimuli correcting *that*?" Toreth ducked under the tape and walked right up to the glass, following the panther along the cage.

"Her stereotyping is very deeply ingrained. Our work was with adults—the nervous system is developed by then, and changes are largely limited to relatively minor remodeling. The damage was done to her during early development, and was then heavily reinforced for a number of years."

"So it's going to be like this forever?" The panther turned and Toreth turned with her, perfectly in time and barely less graceful.

"They hope not. They've had other animals arrive in a similar condition, and most of them can be coaxed out of it eventually. Helped to learn new behaviors. It's likely to take a long time, though. Months at least. Perhaps years before she's anything like normal."

"Why's it staying just there?"

"I don't know for certain. Possibly she paced at the front of the old cage, where she could see the most, and so she's doing the same here. If you look, the track is where the light from out here is strongest. I don't imagine there's much choice involved in the activity—it's a reflex, that's all. A compulsion, rather."

Toreth stopped pacing and crouched down, palm pressed against the glass. The panther moved away from him, unheeding. "Poor fucking thing."

It was virtually the only time Warrick could remember him expressing sympathy for anything, animal or human.

Still crouched, Toreth turned away from the glass towards him, his eyes narrowing with suspicion. "Warrick, why did you want me to see it?"

"I thought you might be interested, that's all."

"No." He stood up. "No, that wasn't it, was it?"

"Yes, it was. Partly." He didn't carry on, waiting for Toreth to ask.

"Come here," Toreth said after a moment.

Warrick joined him beyond the barrier, without hesitation. Toreth took his arm, turned him to face the glass just a few inches away. The panther paced by, gaze fixed inwards, blind to the freedom around her.

Toreth moved to stand behind him, hands on his shoulders. The position triggered some reflexes of Warrick's own. "What do you think about it?" Toreth asked.

Under Toreth's hands, Warrick's skin tingled, sensitized by the current of danger in Toreth's voice. "I think...that she's very beautiful. One of the most beautiful things I've ever seen." In the thick glass he caught Toreth's reflection from over his shoulder, but couldn't read his expression.

"You feel sorry for it, don't you?" Toreth asked.

"Yes."

"More fool you. I'll tell you something—if you went in there with it, I bet it'd stop stereotyping pretty fucking sharpish." His hands slid up, circling Warrick's neck loosely. "It'd tear your fucking throat out."

Warrick forced his shoulders to relax. "Yes, I expect it would."

"That'd teach you not to feel sorry for things that don't fucking need it."

"Briefly, yes. Not a lesson you could really learn from, though."

Toreth didn't laugh. "No, it wouldn't be."

"You called her a poor fucking thing," Warrick said after a moment.

"So I was wrong. There you go—I don't say that very often, so enjoy it."

The hands released him, and the reflection dimmed as Toreth stepped back. He thought that was it, but Toreth spoke again. "You brought me here because you wanted a comparison, didn't you? To see us next to each other?"

The question caught Warrick as much by surprise as Dillian's had. Even though Toreth had obviously guessed, Warrick had never imagined that he'd say anything directly about it. "Yes," he admitted.

"Well? What's the conclusion?" Shadows moved in the glass as Toreth pointed to the enclosure. "That thing—is that what you see, when you look at me?"

Warrick hesitated as the panther passed him once more, trapped in the strange comfort of her invisible cage. He considered lying, but that would be more dangerous than the truth if Toreth had the slightest doubt. He turned to look at Toreth, meeting his expectant gaze. "Occasionally, yes."

Toreth smiled, as predatory as anything they'd seen during the day, but without the reassurance of a barrier between them. He reached out slowly, giving Warrick plenty of time to react, pulled him forwards, and kissed him hard. One hand pressed between Warrick's shoulders, the other slid up his chest to rest lightly, casually, around his throat. Fear sharpened the arousal until he was panting into Toreth's mouth. He heard female voices coming up the path towards them but for once he didn't care that they were doing this in public.

A sudden silence followed by a nervous giggle indicated that they'd been seen.

Toreth held the kiss for a few more seconds, slowly tightening his grip around Warrick's throat, then released him and stepped back. "Then more fool you, again." Toreth ducked smoothly under the tape and walked away without another word, back towards the flamingos.

Ignoring the women, Warrick went to sit on one of the benches scooped out the artificial rock at the back of the viewing area. He waited until his heart had stopped pounding—not until some time after the group had moved on—and then took the exit path away from the panther. It felt as if something had changed, or ought to have changed, but when he glanced back he saw the panther pacing away from him as if nothing had happened. Which, for her, was true.

To his surprise, Toreth had stopped at the flamingo pool to wait for him; he was sitting on the wall and watching the birds. When Warrick came up, he glanced around and smiled briefly, the aura of danger gone.

Warrick sat on the wall beside him and said, "I'm sorry." Open-ended enough that Toreth could accept it or ignore it, as he chose.

"It doesn't matter." Toreth shrugged. "If you're going to drag me all the way here to compare me to some bloody animal, at least it was something flattering. Better than a fucking tapir."

"Actually, I like the tapirs."

"How about the flamingos?" Toreth asked, then carried on without waiting for an answer, his voice distant and dispassionate. "We went on holiday once. Somewhere sunny. It was...okay, actually, as far as I remember. Or at least it wasn't unbearably fucking awful. I usually counted down the days until we went home, because at least there it wasn't like being trapped in a fucking cage with them twenty-four hours a day." He rubbed the back of his neck. "Anyway, the hotel had flamingos in the grounds. Only time I'd seen any. I liked them—I got up early every morning to go have a look at them. I suppose it's the kind of thing you do when you're however old I was." Toreth gestured vaguely at the birds. "I thought they were bigger than that, but then I thought: you always do, don't you?"

Warrick stared at him, stuck for a reply. A several-sentence reference to Toreth's family was quite unprecedented. The only responses that came to mind were flippant or sympathetic, neither of which would be well received.

Toreth looked at him briefly, reading his reaction, then stood up and turned away. "Come on. Let's go—I'm bored."

Unaccustomed As I Am…

❖

Toreth leaned back in the low seat and sipped his drink, looking around the club with a proprietorial air. So far, things were going very well. He'd organized Sara's ten-year service party personally, as per section tradition, so it had *better* go well. Or rather, he'd overseen the organization. In consultation with the General Criminal admins, he'd decided on the entertainment for later and then he'd delegated the venue, the food, and all the other dull parts of the evening to Chevril's admin, Kel.

Tillotson had, very sportingly, come up with a donation from some budget somewhere and Kel had managed to book the club for the evening at a discount. The reputation attached to the I&I name could come in handy. Consequently, the tickets had been cheap and there was a gratifyingly large crowd. The majority of people from their section had turned out, and quite a few from elsewhere. Sara, naturally, was having the time of her life. Her only complaint, repeated several times, was how *old* it made her feel.

She had a point. The idea that she'd been working for him for ten years made Toreth feel pretty fucking old, too. He remembered her arriving…well, no, actually he didn't. But he remembered that he'd had a completely useless admin, and then suddenly a very good one. Junior paras, when they had them at all, were generally given the most junior admins, but even fresh out of training she'd been ten times better than whatever-his-name-was had been. Plenty of people had tried to poach her over the years, and he was very glad that she'd stayed. His job would be hell without her.

Ten years. That meant he'd been twenty-five at the time. Four years before he'd become a senior, and seven years before he'd met Warrick. Measured out like that, it seemed to have gone past frighteningly quickly.

He finished his drink and shook the glass, rattling the ice. Had he really known Warrick for three years? God, now that made him feel old. Not to mention disconcertingly like…half of something. It was still strange, reading an invitation

125

and knowing that there was an "and guest." There hadn't been an invitation for this, of course, so he hadn't thought of it before now. No big deal, anyway.

Thinking about Warrick, he automatically checked to see where he was. There were very few occasions on which Warrick could be persuaded to have anything at all to do with I&I. However, this time he'd agreed with only a token show of reluctance. He'd even bought Sara a present. Toreth hadn't seen it yet, but an inordinate amount of giggling had accompanied her opening it, so Warrick's sense of humor had obviously had an outing.

Despite Warrick's ready agreement, Toreth had a lingering feeling of unease. Partly it was the fact that Warrick had spent a fair proportion of the evening looking as if there was a faint but unpleasant smell in the vicinity, which at any moment would turn out to be something nasty stuck to his shoe. Partly it was the effort of keeping an eye on who was talking to Warrick and, more importantly, what they were saying to him.

At the moment he had been cornered by Chevril, who fell under the heading of "dull but safe." He talked primarily about money, not work, and he wasn't going to start any fishing expeditions into their sex life. Toreth wasn't sure how many of the fuck stories he'd passed on to Sara had made it any further but, with one thing and another, he did know there were various versions floating around the section. It was only to be expected when Warrick was a) rich, b) attractive, and c) interestingly kinked.

Warrick, however, wouldn't see it like that. If he heard anything, he would have—using Dillian's phrase—fifteen different kinds of fits. Not in public, obviously, but the moment they left and probably for a tediously long time afterwards.

Earlier Toreth had spent an agonizing half hour while, at Sara's instigation, Warrick had outlined the sim to a group of curious admins. Most of the questions had revolved around sex, in one way or another, although that was fine as long as it didn't get personal. There had been a couple of nasty moments when the conversation had veered towards I&I applications for the sim. To his surprise, Warrick had merely deflected the inquires with polite (and as far as Toreth knew, untruthful) claims of commercial confidentiality.

He must have looked nervous at the time, because after the group had split up (with an assortment of optimistic requests for sim time), Warrick had smiled serenely at him and said, "Some of us do know how to behave in public."

At the moment, judging by the snippets he could overhear—and Warrick's glazed expression—Chevril was well into his favorite theme of "why my life would be perfect if I only had a job with a rich corporation." It would be less annoying if the man would actually go out and *find* another job, but he preferred to complain about it instead. Still, he was a good para. Takes all sorts.

If it looked as if Warrick was about to start chewing his own arm off to get out of the trap, he'd rescue him.

Anyway, it was getting close to the time to make the presentation to Sara and give his speech, to which he was looking forward tremendously. Sara had spent the entire week trying to wheedle out of him exactly what he was going to say, and looking increasingly panic-stricken by the whole idea. As well she might. He'd had a word with her multitude of friends in the division and reaped a variety of entertaining anecdotes, including some he'd forgotten and a few he hadn't even known about. Everyone had been very helpful. He'd mentioned that to Sara, once or twice.

In fact, he'd transferred the notes for the speech onto paper, just for the pleasure of watching her face as he took them out of his jacket pocket and paged through them a couple of times during the evening.

He checked the notes one more time. Looking up, he discovered that Warrick had made his escape from Chevril. Hell, where was he? Nowhere to be seen. Toreth told himself he was worrying unnecessarily. What could go wrong, really?

The music had quietened, so while he kept scanning the room, he tuned into Chevril's conversation. He'd turned his attention to Sedanioni, one of his investigation team and therefore obliged to give her boss a minimum level of courteous attention. "Fraser from level six left last year. I saw him a few weeks ago. Do you have any idea what he's earning now? Go on, guess. All right, I'll tell you..."

"Drink?" Warrick's voice, right behind him, startled him.

"What? Oh, thanks."

Warrick passed him a glass over his shoulder. Toreth leaned back and looked up at him. "Having fun?" he asked, without much hope of getting a positive reply.

To his surprise, Warrick smiled. "I'm having a tolerable evening, yes. I'm keen to hear your speech, at least."

"Oh, good." Toreth grinned and tucked the papers away again. "Sara isn't."

"I know. I saw her at the bar and she said that if—"

"The problem, of course," Sedanioni said to Chevril, pointedly and slightly too loudly, "is that *some* people don't know what they really want."

Chevril, naturally, failed to notice the hint. Or he noticed it and ignored it, because he carried on as if she hadn't spoken.

Warrick crouched down and rested his arms on the back of Toreth's seat. "I know what *I* want," he murmured, his voice low and amused. "I want you."

"Yeah, I've noticed." Toreth kept his reply equally soft.

Warrick stroked the back of Toreth's neck with a discreet finger. "I want you to fuck me," he continued. "I want you to chain me up with your lovely presents. I want you to hurt me. I want your mouth against my ear, promising me things I can hardly bear to hear because I want them so very badly."

The light caress was firing every nerve in his body. Warrick slipped his arm over Toreth's shoulder, not an overly intimate gesture to an observer, but his touch burned across Toreth's chest even through the layers of cloth. His voice whispered on, while around them everyone else continued their conversations, oblivious.

127

"I want to give myself up completely and let you take control. I want to kneel for you, bound and blindfolded, while you fuck my mouth. I want your hand in my hair, forcing me down. I want to taste your come. I want your fingers inside me. I want your cock inside me. I want you to hold me, to hold me down, so that all I can feel is you, all I can hear is my voice begging for you, for more, for everything. I want to lose myself so totally that when you finally let me come, I don't even hear myself scream." Brief pause. "That's what I want."

He stood up and moved away. Toreth sat frozen in shock, dry-mouthed and nearly shaking with lust. It took him a whole minute to realize that it was time for him to make his speech, and that Warrick had lifted his notes.

Helen

❖

The indoor section of the café was almost deserted. Everyone sat outside at the plaza tables, enjoying the unexpectedly warm October Saturday. When Warrick emerged from the café carrying the tray, he saw Toreth waving from a small table in the center. As he worked his way across the closely packed space, he hoped Toreth had simply been lucky to find a vacant table. He wasn't above using his I&I ID to clear seats when he felt like it.

He sat down beside Toreth and emptied the tray. "So, what do you think of open-air theater?"

While he watched Toreth pretending to consider the answer, Warrick tasted a teaspoonful of the nutmeg-dusted froth on his coffee. Bitter, but a pleasant combination.

"Not bad," Toreth said finally. "It's been a long week, I needed some extra sleep."

"You didn't enjoy it?"

"Well..." Toreth broke a corner off his cheese scone and ate it. "This is nothing like as good as yours."

"Thank you." Warrick waited, then prompted, "Well?"

"'A History of the Reconstruction of New London in Drama and Song'? They could've picked something more exciting. Like anything. And bits of it were complete bollocks, anyway—I've read some of the old files."

"You can hardly blame them for sticking to publicly available information for a public performance."

"Yeah, fair point." Toreth licked his thumb and finger. "I suppose it was okay, if you want to find out how many things rhyme with debris."

So he'd been at least that awake. "They're a talented group. Dillian was at university with one of the founders—they both read engineering."

"Yeah? Figures." His eyes crinkled, half smile, half reaction to the sun emerging from behind a cloud. "You could've told me we were only there to help make up the numbers. I'd have brought a blanket."

129

Warrick decided to up the game. "Don't worry, I shall know not to ask you next time."

Cornered, Toreth shrugged. "I've had worse afternoons. Didn't you say they do evening performances in bars? That wouldn't be so bad. Something to drink..." His hand dropped below the table and Warrick felt a touch on his knee, then fingertips walking slowly up his thigh. "Nice dark seats at the back."

About to protest, Warrick stopped, his attention caught by a woman emerging from the constant flow of pedestrians on the broad path that ran across the center of the park. Her clothes were respectable, if not new—appropriate for middle age but carelessly worn, the colors mismatched, the cardigan misbuttoned. Striding towards the outdoor café, apparently looking directly towards them, she seemed out of place amidst the drifting afternoon crowd.

Did he know her?

Toreth's hand stopped moving. "What?"

"That woman, over there."

As she reached the edge of the plaza, Warrick decided he didn't recognize her. At the same moment, however, the contact on Warrick's leg vanished and Toreth muttered, "Of all the fucking people..."

She pushed past a crowded table, ignoring an angry protest as a drink spilled. Halfway across the obstacle course, though, her approach faltered. She ground to a halt a couple of meters from the table and hesitated, darting glances at Warrick before her gaze settled on Toreth.

"I didn't..." Her voice was soft, breathy, and almost childish. "I—Did you lose my number, Val?"

"Helen, go away." Deliberate boredom, a tone Warrick recognized well.

She smiled rapturously. "Of course you did. I knew you had. Look. Val, please look."

She rolled back the soft beige wool sleeves. The neatly patched elbows caught Warrick attention for a moment, then he simply stared, horrified. Her bare arms were crossed with scars, dozens of them, new over old, cuts and burns; she must have taken some trouble to ensure the injuries healed leaving such visible marks.

No chance of his reaction upsetting her—all her attention was on Toreth. She edged closer. "I didn't forget. I hurt myself for you, Val. See?"

After a few seconds Warrick looked at him too, his eyes unwilling to leave the awful mutilation. Toreth appeared profoundly unimpressed, and annoyed.

"Helen, be a good girl and fuck off, or I'm calling Justice." Then, to Warrick, he added, "Don't worry; she's not dangerous. She's just a pain in the neck because she won't fucking—" he turned back to her, "—go away."

Cringing, the woman held her ground, her arms still extended like a security pass, hands clasped, knuckles white. "Don't be angry, Val," she whispered. "I looked for you, I promise."

130

"You're breaching the banning order, remember? Do you remember?" Toreth asked the question without any apparent expectation of an answer, because he was already pulling out his comm earpiece.

"Banning order?" Warrick asked.

"Yeah. There's a permanent antinuisance injunction that's supposed to keep the demented bitch away from me." Out of the corner of his eye Warrick saw her flinch again at the words. "And much as I hate to give Justice the satisfaction of asking for their help..."

"Val, why are you angry with me? I don't understand. Tell me what I did wrong."

The soft, miserable voice and the sight of the woman, so obviously disturbed, stirred pity. Warrick touched Toreth's wrist. "What happens then?"

Toreth jerked his hand away, frowning irritably. "Detention. With any luck they'll lock her up and lose the fucking code this time."

"Isn't there anyone else you can call?"

"What, you want me to find her a bloody psychiatrist?" Toreth hesitated, then shrugged quickly. "Maybe. There used to be a husband. Helen, are you still married?"

She frowned thoughtfully, then brought her hands up in front of her face, spreading her fingers. Thin scars netted the backs of her hands, and a wide gold band encircled her ring finger. "Yes. I'm sorry, Val."

"No, that's fine." He tapped a shortcut and waited. "Sara? Yes, me. Sorry to bother you at the weekend. No, I'm still in the park with Warrick. Yeah, but we stopped for coffee and cake afterwards. I know, I know, no need to take the piss. Listen, you've got three guesses who just turned up. No. No. No—Psycho Helen."

As he said the name he glanced towards Helen, who made a soft sound of longing. Toreth snorted and looked away. "Madder, if anything. Do me a favor, would you—link in to I&I, check the file and get in touch with her husband. Tell him that she's here with me and if he doesn't come and take her somewhere else in the next five minutes, I'm contacting Justice and calling in the banning order. Plaza Café. No, I'll wait."

Toreth sat in silence, watching his fingers tapping the edge of the table. Helen stood fixed to the spot, her whole body yearning towards him. Warrick looked between them, wondering.

Eventually Toreth's head lifted slightly. "He is? Thank God. Great, thanks. Yeah, see you Monday."

He turned to Warrick. "Her husband's in the park somewhere. He's on his way. And remember—you wanted me to call him. It wasn't my idea."

Silence again, until curiosity won out. "Toreth, who is she?"

Toreth sighed. "I interrogated her, a long time ago. You really don't want to hear the details."

"Why doesn't he?" a male voice asked from behind him.

Warrick turned around to see a man, about the same age as Helen, looking between them. He wore the same kind of clothes—a little out-of-date, a little dilapidated—but without Helen's distracted air.

"Why don't you tell him what you did to her?" he demanded, his voice harsh with anger.

"I did my job." Toreth tapped his watch. "Three minutes to get her the fuck out of here, or I call Justice." His hard, flat voice wasn't quite the game voice, but it was close enough to be unsettling.

The man's eyes narrowed. "That's it? That's all you've got to say?"

"My interest in you, and her, finished . . . what? Ten years ago?"

"Twelve," the man said. "It was twelve years in August. The seventeenth."

"Really? Time flies. If you don't want me to start taking an interest again, I suggest you get on with leaving." Toreth cocked his head towards Helen. "Or shall I take her off your hands? Take her in to I&I? With your history and the order I've got forty-eight hours before I even need to talk to a Justice rep and after that I can hand her straight over to them without you ever seeing her."

"You—" The man nodded sharply. "Come on, Helen. Time to go home. Helen—it's me. Helen? Can you hear me? We have to go home now."

Finally the woman turned towards him. "Michael?" She frowned, then shook her head. "I have to stay with Val," she said, sounding surprised that there was any doubt.

"He doesn't want to see you."

"Yes he *does*." Helen spun back to Toreth. "Tell him, Val. Don't be angry with me."

Toreth pushed his chair back, catching the table with his thigh as he stood. Cups rattled, coffee spilling onto the table. "Shut up and fuck off. How can I make it any clearer?"

He turned and Helen wailed, recognizing the planned departure before Warrick did. Before Toreth could walk away, she seized his arm. He spun back and struck her hand away, the blow audible over the noise of the park. "Don't fucking touch me!"

She whimpered, pressing her hand to her mouth. At precisely the same moment, Warrick stood and Michael stepped forwards, both stopping when Toreth held his hand up. "The banning order entitles me to use reasonable physical force to protect myself," he said to Michael. "You do know that, don't you?"

Michael's lips tightened.

"If she tries that again, I'll break her arm. Sound reasonable to you?"

"If you dare, *I'll* break—"

"No!" Helen stepped between them, facing her husband. "Don't hurt him!"

"Don't—?" Michael groaned with frustration. "Helen, *please*. Come away. Leave him."

"No!" She lunged for Toreth again, evading her husband's desperate hands, and Toreth hit her in the face. A single blow with a calculated placement and force that left a sour taste in Warrick's mouth.

Helen went down screaming, her hands to her face, blood already seeping between her fingers. Café patrons rose, then hesitated as Toreth pulled his I&I ID from his jacket and held it up. Michael, swearing loudly, seemed momentarily torn between going to his wife's aid and attacking her assailant.

Toreth looked around at the chaos, shook his head, and simply walked away.

By the time he'd reached the edge of the café, Michael was already on his knees beside his wife. "Shh. It's going to be all right."

"It's your fault," she sobbed. "You made him angry with me. You made him go."

"Yes. It's my fault. I know. Shh, now."

Warrick stayed where he was, frozen by the contrast between the man's soft, patient voice and the pain and despair on his face.

Slowly Helen calmed, letting Michael gather her against him, then finally help her to her feet and into a chair—not the one Toreth had sat in, although it was the closest. He picked up a handful of paper napkins and held them to her face. The blood from her nose had already stained her chest, clotting in the fabric of her cardigan.

Michael looked up, apparently only then seeing Warrick again. "Still here?" he asked Warrick.

He wanted to go, but ingrained politeness forced him to ask, "Is there anything I can do?"

For a moment he thought the man might lash out, then he mastered himself. "I need something to clean her up with, and a glass of water."

The café management provided both, and thankfully listened to Warrick's assurances that everything was under control and there was no need to call Justice.

Back at the table, he set the bowl and glass down. While he was away, Helen's sleeves had been rolled down again, hiding the scars. She sat in the chair, arms wrapped around her, staring down at the floor, rocking. Warrick caught a low murmur of words, but couldn't make them out. He didn't try very hard.

Without even a glance at Warrick, Michael picked up the glass and offered it to his wife along with two white capsules. "Take them, sweetheart. Please?"

She accepted the tablets, although her hands shook and he had to help her with the water. Some of it spilled anyway, adding to the mess. Then Michael picked the cloth out of the bowl, wrung it out, and handed it to her. "Do you think you can manage, or do you want me to do it?"

"I'll do it." She took the cloth, holding her head up. "I'm not a child, Michael."

"Of course you aren't." He pulled the bowl to the edge of the table nearest her. "I'm sorry."

Nevertheless, he waited until she began the task before he came over to where Warrick watched. "Thanks," Michael said. Then, after a pause he added, "I wouldn't have asked except that if I'd left her alone she'd only have gone after the bastard and got herself arrested or lost."

"Don't mention it."

"I'm only surprised he didn't call Justice right away. Or——" Michael looked at him. "Was that your idea?"

Caught out, Warrick nodded before he could stop himself.

"Figures." He looked Warrick up and down and asked, "You don't work for I&I, then?"

"No. I'm a friend." The word sounded odd, and as unsuitable as most other descriptions of their relationship.

"A friend?" Michael laughed, brief and bitter. "I'd never have imagined he'd have one."

At the table, Helen was busily cleaning the blood from her face, using a vanity mirror from her handbag.

"It's plastic," Michael said. "The mirror. Unbreakable. We can't let her have anything sharp. Her arms aren't the worst of it. That's what I was worried about when she disappeared—that she'd find something she could hurt herself with. I didn't think for a moment it would be him."

Warrick looked around, but Toreth was long out of sight. "I really have to go."

"Helen thinks he raped her," Michael said with no change in his tone.

Had he heard right? "Thinks?"

He nodded. "And the irony is, he didn't. All he did—*all* he did—was order the guards to do it. And stand and watch. And make sure that I saw it all. I remember what he said when it started. 'It's up to you. This goes on for as long as you allow it.' When they stopped...they didn't stop until I'd convinced him I'd told him everything I knew."

Michael looked around the café, a quick glance over the nearby tables. When he spoke again, his voice was quieter. "She couldn't tell them herself, because she didn't know anything. I always made sure she never heard anything, never saw anything dangerous. I thought that would be enough to keep her safe."

Apparently oblivious to the conversation, Helen rinsed out the cloth and started sponging her blood-soaked cardigan.

"I let a few friends use a room, that's all," Michael continued, words spilling out like they'd been trapped for too long. "I only went to one or two of the meetings. I didn't even know all their names, but I gave him every one I did know. I sold them out, and now they're dead, or they were sent for re-education and God only knows what happened to them. I did it to save *her*, and I didn't even manage to do that." His voice roughened. "Most of the time, she's all right. No. She's never all right, but most of the time she copes. Then she sees someone—someone who looks like him. Or she hears a voice in the street, or on the screen, or sometimes in her fuck-ing *head,* and she loses it all over again."

What could he say? Michael looked away, across the café, and Warrick saw the hastily averted faces.

"Not that I'm saying there's anything *wrong* with what they did to her." Warrick couldn't help staring himself at the words, and Michael nodded, his face set grimly. "I&I did what was necessary for the protection of the Administration from criminals and resisters. Exactly like they say in citizenship classes. I'm a good citizen now. Re-formed character. You can tell your friend that if he asks. Not that he will—he doesn't care." His voice cracked. "How could he do that to her when he didn't even *care?*"

Without waiting for a response, Michael went to crouch beside his wife.

An incipient hole in the sole of his right shoe caught Warrick's eye, drawing his attention back to the general shabbiness of the couple's clothes. Nothing sur-prising there, now. A conviction for political crimes would automatically disqualify an applicant from finding work with even semirespectable corporations. SimTech wouldn't even send a rejection note. It was the only sensible thing to do—any kind of association with a convicted resister was an invitation to trouble.

Michael took the cloth from Helen and dropped it into the bloody water. The worst of the blood was gone, but the whole café was watching and they would at-tract plenty more stares on the way out of the park. Perhaps Helen wouldn't even notice, but Warrick could barely imagine how Michael must feel. He dismissed a brief impulse to offer to pay for a taxi home for them—no doubt Michael would only feel insulted.

And any kind of association...

"Come on, love," Michael said. "Time to go home."

"Can't I wait?" she asked wistfully. "Please?"

"He won't come back. Tell her," he added without looking around.

"He's right. Toreth won't come back." That was certainly true.

Helen checked her reflection again before she slowly slid the mirror into her bag. She stood and turned towards Warrick, blinking vaguely, then smiled at him. "It was very nice to meet you. Will you see him again? Soon?"

Warrick glanced at Michael, who merely shrugged. Perhaps there was no right thing to say. "I don't know."

She nodded gravely. "If you do, give him my love."

Warrick had visited six bars on the route between the café and Toreth's flat be-fore he realized he was approaching the problem from the wrong angle. Toreth was avoiding him, and he'd probably also guess that Warrick knew that. Therefore he'd take care to be in the least likely place.

Warrick rang the comm at the entrance to Toreth's block of flats for two minutes, getting no response, then let himself into the building. Upstairs, he knocked on the door of the flat half a dozen times with the same result. Well, Toreth had given him the code, so there was no reason not to use it.

Inside he found Toreth sitting on the sofa with a glass in his hand and an open bottle of whiskey on the table in front of him.

"Oh, hello," Toreth said, just as if Warrick hadn't touched the comm or door. He downed the contents of his glass and poured another. "Didn't think I'd be seeing you around for a while. If ever. Nice chat with Michael?"

The bottle was more than two-thirds empty, and Warrick wondered if it had been full when Toreth started. "Toreth—"

"If you've come to tell me how much you hate I&I, or interrogations, or me, you can save your breath and fuck off right now because I don't give a shit what you think about any of those or anything else."

"Will you—"

"She was on a level eight waiver, so was he. The resister group was breaking up, they were the only link in we could lay our hands on." The defensiveness in his voice surprised Warrick. "I just picked the quickest thing to get the information out of them. If the psych profiles had fit, I'd have had them do him. Before they started on her, I explained what a section N interrogation clearance meant. I could probably find the recording somewhere if you'd like to see it."

He drank again, only a mouthful this time. "What else would you like me to say? I have nightmares about it? I'm sorry I did it? Well, I don't and I'm not. That's just the way it is. All inside the waiver, per the P&P. My first big case as a junior para—I got a commendation for the result."

This time Warrick stood and waited.

"I haven't run a lot of section Ns. It's not a very reliable technique. I'll tell you what's different with Helen, though. I fucked her." He looked up and grinned. "The funny thing is, her idiot husband thinks she's making it up, but she isn't. I really fucked her. Not in the interrogation—afterwards. After the trial. Christ, I was stupid. Anyone who's been through any kind of high-level waiver, never mind a section N, and wants to fuck their interrogator afterwards is guaranteed cracked."

Finally Warrick managed to get out a whole sentence. "May I sit down?"

"Do whatever the fuck you like." Toreth glanced over as he sat, then shook his head. "I fucked her once, dumped her, and spent months trying to get the deranged bitch to leave me the fuck alone. Everyone knew what I'd done, so it was a case of 'serves you right.' She couldn't get onto Int-Sec grounds, so she waited outside my flat every bloody day. I had to get taxis everywhere. I moved flats twice, and she found me again; I'm sure one of the bastards at work gave her my address."

He drained his glass and topped it up again although, to Warrick's relief, to only a third full. "Worst part was, I couldn't do a thing about it. Michael was away learning how to be a good boy. Level one re-education—reduced sentence because he cooperated in the end. Spineless tosser. Anyway, there was no one to keep her on a leash. If I'd laid a finger on her, Justice would've had me nailed. Para, ex-Justice interrogator. They'd have loved it. Jesus, it was a nightmare. So fucking embarrassing."

"What happened?"

"When her husband got out he had her locked up, thank God. She came back once or twice. The last time was..." He frowned. "Fuck. *That* must be eight, nine years ago. Not long after Sara started working for me, anyway. I know 'cause she eventually dragged a banning order out of Justice—pestered them until it was easier for them to do it than put up with her calling every day. I sent the order to 'em and moved flats again. And there you have it." He raised his glass. "The story of Psycho Helen. Fuck her, and her fucking idealist traitor husband, because I don't give a fuck about either of them."

"Then why did you run off?" Despite Toreth's numerous retreats, subtle and otherwise, it wasn't a question Warrick often asked.

Toreth blinked at him, then shrugged, whiskey sloshing dangerously. "Dunno. Getting my retaliation in first?"

"So what made you think I'd run?"

Anger flared up. "I'm pissed, not stupid—I know how you feel about I&I. It's gutless fucking corporates like you who make..." Toreth trailed off, then ran his hand through his hair and sighed. "Look, do you want a drink?"

"Thanks."

By the time Toreth had retrieved a glass, examined it, taken it into the kitchen and cleaned it and returned, some of the tension had dissipated. Warrick took the generously filled glass and settled back. Toreth sat beside him.

"Carnac asked me once how I could bear knowing what you did for a living," Warrick said.

"Yeah?" Toreth waited, then asked, "And? There is an 'and,' right?"

"And I said I didn't think about it. Which is true. However, I know what your job entails—I have enough self-respect not to delude myself entirely. I've read parts of your security file, and some of the Procedures and Protocols as well. I know what happens at I&I. I won't deny that meeting a—" no point sugarcoating things, "—a victim doesn't improve my weekend, but it's hardly earthshattering."

"Victim?" Toreth frowned. "He was a fucking resister, and she knew it. Sanctimonious prick."

Warrick wasn't sure which of them he meant. "Does it often happen?"

"Being stalked or running into people I've interrogated?" His voice had begun to slur. "Helen's the only fruitcake I've picked up, luckily. Some of the psych specialists have packs of the fuckers—Augins reckons his have a rota. Generally, yeah, it happens from time to time. Bound to."

137

"It doesn't bother you, does it?"

"'Course not. Shouldn't have done whatever the fuck they did."

"And the ones who hadn't done anything? The ones who were innocent?" Something he'd always wanted to ask, although he was sure of Toreth's opinion.

"Life's a bitch and shit happens." He grinned suddenly. "Sometimes it's me. That's what keeps all the little corporates safe in their beds. Or whoever's bed. D'you want to fuck?"

The all-purpose makeup and apology. How ever would they manage without it? "Do you think you're up to it, to coin a phrase?"

Toreth peered thoughtfully at the bottle, then shook his head. "Not a fucking chance. I feel like shit. Don't—don't go, though."

To produce a request like that the bottle must have been full to begin with. "I didn't plan to."

"Good. Thanks. I—" Toreth finished the glassful, then leaned back, abruptly pale. "Oh, Christ. Room's spinning. Shouldn't have drunk so much, so fast. Why don't I ever fucking learn? How old'm I? Sara asks me that, you know. She says—"

Warrick stood up and offered his hand. "Go get rid of it. You'll feel a lot better—it can't all be in your bloodstream yet."

"Yeah." Toreth let Warrick pull him up off the sofa. "Right as usual." He headed for the door, then stopped and held his hand up as Warrick started to follow. "I c'n manage."

"Very well."

Resisting the temptation to follow, Warrick tidied up—which in Toreth's flat was more a matter of rearranging the mess into more aesthetically pleasing piles—and listened to the faint sounds of retching from the bathroom.

After five minutes, Toreth reappeared, looking brighter but also visibly unsteady on his feet. "Jesus, my gag reflex isn't what it used to be." He swayed and put his hand out, connecting with the door then looking somewhat surprised by the success. "'Spect it's all that time with your cock down my throat."

"Why don't we go to bed?" Warrick suggested. It was early, but he'd rather get Toreth there while he could still walk.

Toreth leaned on the door frame, apparently requiring the support of both hands while he considered the question. It took rather longer than usual. "Yeah," he said at length. "Yeah, why not? Be better in the morning, huh?"

Something woke Warrick—a noise. He lifted his head and recognized it. Snoring.

Snorting breaths, catching in a throat relaxed by alcohol. Or possibly by the accumulated effects of too much fellatio. Warrick smiled and ran his hand slowly

138

down Toreth's chest, over his stomach and hip, molding his fingers over the lines of bone and muscle. Back up again, lightening his touch to a tickle. Toreth murmured an incoherent semiprotest and turned away onto his side.

Well, that solved the snoring problem.

Warrick slid up behind him, fitting himself against Toreth, trying for the maximum skin contact. No protest this time, although there certainly would have been if Toreth had been awake.

This broke their carefully delimited rules of touching, which seemed so ridiculous when he considered all that they'd done together. After all this time, sex was encouraged, foreplay was permitted, but too close an approach to a simple display of affection still triggered something between anger and panic.

Would it ever be different? Warrick smiled wryly, feeling Toreth's hair against his lips. The shock of a sober Toreth turning over and saying anything like 'hold me' would probably kill him.

He did wonder what lay behind the fear. Sometimes he wondered enough to consider the merits of a more careful study of Toreth's psych file. He'd looked at it just the once, not long after Marian Tanit's death, wanting to know that Toreth was a safe choice for a longer-term liaison. Or rather, just dangerous enough but in control of himself. He'd read no further than the summary, mindful of the risks of knowing too much. If he'd ever let something slip which proved that he'd read the file, Toreth would be furious. Perhaps furious enough to do serious damage and under those circumstances Warrick wouldn't blame him.

The psych file remained a temptation, but one he could resist when he considered the possible backlash. Besides, it was an unfair advantage to hold over Toreth, who was already at such a disadvantage emotionally. And that line of thought was taking him somewhere he didn't want to go, but knew he should. Better to get it over with.

Deliberately, he called Helen to mind—her halting, broken speech, the awful scars, her husband's despair. Toreth's earlier defensiveness hadn't been regret for what he'd done to them. Embarrassment over his professional lapse as a new para-investigator, an inarticulate fear of the practical, personal consequences—that Warrick might be driven away—and nothing more than that.

He tortures people, Warrick thought, forcing himself to focus on the words. Real people, guilty and innocent. Perhaps some people who've said no more against the Administration than I have occasionally, and certainly no more than Tarin has.

He orders rapes, he stands and watches, and he doesn't care. He kills whenever the Administration decides a death would be convenient. He killed when *we* decided it would be convenient. Politics, justice, individual pain: none of it matters to him, just as Marian said. None of it touches him. I know all that, and *I* don't care about it enough to give him up. Just enough not to want to hear about it and to blame him for what I feel when he mentions I&I.

Still, somehow, not real enough to banish the warmth of the bed. Not as real as the body against him. Marian's death had sickened him and then, only an hour later, he'd welcomed Toreth's aggressive passion in the office.

He pressed his face against Toreth's neck, touch and taste and scent, letting the warmth wash through him as it always did.

A couple of weeks ago they'd been at Sara's party and for most of the time it had seemed like any other office event. Warrick had spent half the evening anticipating his little trick with the notes, and the next half anticipating the consequences when they got home. He hadn't thought...and he'd rarely even had to try not to think. He was getting good at it.

I fuck Toreth, not his job, he thought. My defense. What does that make me?

Perhaps not very much more of a hypocrite than anyone else who deplores I&I and does nothing about it, or who pretends that what happens there doesn't happen because that's easier than facing up to what the Administration has become.

But still, a little more.

Shopping, No Fucking

The shop wasn't large, but its stock was comprehensive and for the most part expensive. As they entered, it occurred to Warrick that he really couldn't imagine a more unlikely setting in which to find Toreth.

Toreth apparently agreed, because he looked around and shook his head. "Sara once said I'd end up like this, you know."

"Really?"

"Yeah. Can't remember what we were talking about, but she said, 'You'll be buying curtains with him before long.' Or something like that. Mind you, that was a while ago now, and she probably only said it because she thought it would wind me up."

Warrick was willing to bet the windup had succeeded. He also took it as a sign of progress that Toreth sounded more amused than horrified by the memory. "She's a very perceptive woman," he said. "As I've mentioned before, I've always thought that she's wasted as an admin."

"I know. People keep telling her to take the investigator late-entry course, but, lucky for me, she won't. Mind you, the way she was whipping those fucking pool investigators into shape last week, she really ought to be a para."

He thought, very briefly, of Sara in an interrogation room. "I think she'd make a better investigator. And not, of course, that there's anything wrong with being an admin—it's a job that requires intelligence and dedication."

"Good breasts and a nice arse. God, I never thought there could be so many different kinds of crap for making curtains." Toreth looked around the shop and then at his watch.

Something of a record, even by his standards, but only to be expected. The surprise was that he'd come along at all. "Bored already? You didn't have to come."

"Yes, I did. It's got to be absolutely perfect. If it's not, you'd only have to get them done again. Besides, I'm the one who does all the standing around without a blindfold, so it's got to be something I like." He looked around the shop again, then squared his shoulders. "Let's get on with it."

141

They spent a while looking through swatches, then Toreth asked, "Why are there two prices on everything?"

"The top one is fabric alone, the lower is the price for made-up curtains. That includes the lining and so on. It's all in square meters."

"You live and learn. Jesus f—" Toreth stopped and lowered his voice. "Jesus fucking Christ, have you seen the price of *this* stuff?"

"Curtains are largely a decorative anachronism, so they lend themselves to expense." Warrick examined the tag. "Ah, no wonder it's pricey—it's natural cotton velvet. Beautiful. Feel it."

Toreth obediently ran his hands over the fabric, then smiled. "Mmm...not bad. Not bad at all. But I still think that's a fuck of a lot of euros for something you don't need."

"Nobody *needs* an antique wardrobe with chains, either, and you didn't object to spending what was no doubt a ridiculous amount of money on that."

"That's different." Toreth's voice lowered again, but in a quite different tone. "And it's also bollocks. You do need it—you know you do."

He saw the calculation in Toreth's eyes as he gauged the very deliberate effect of the words. Warrick kept his voice as even as he could. "That's wanting, not needing. Very like curtains, in fact."

"Really?" Toreth drew the word out. "Just wanting, is it? Shall we stop using it, then? Sell it?"

He shook his head, suddenly breathless. The cabinet was one of only two things in his life to which he'd ever felt in danger of becoming addicted. And, like the other thing, that only made it more dangerous and so more desirable.

The other thing smiled. "God, I can see you in it now. Could you get off like that without it? Without the chains?"

Without the absolute surrender. "No. And not without you. You more than any of it."

"Of course." The smile broadened. "And I'm free, if you don't count the dinners." He turned his attention back to the fabric. "Well, you're paying for it. This is nice. Green's wrong, though."

Warrick sucked in a quick breath, trying to drive the pictures from his brain. "They'll dye it to order—any color you want."

"Mm." Toreth stroked the velvet again. "How much do we need?"

Warrick took out his hand screen and paged down until he found the dimensions. "This is for completely enclosing the cabinet and enough floor space around it to—" He stopped, suddenly aware of where they were.

"Do whatever we want to do," Toreth said, unexpectedly tactful.

They'd spent a long time in Warrick's bedroom, measuring and discussing, and pausing halfway through to fuck because the subject of the discussion made it inevitable. Finally they'd settled on a space large enough to let them move freely,

142

but small enough to create the effect they both wanted: somewhere enclosed, confining. Constraining. A larger version of the cabinet. It would cut the space off from the rest of his bedroom and make it somewhere different. Somewhere special. Somewhere—

A touch on his back pulled him out of the reverie as Toreth looked over his shoulder at the proposed designs. "You know, if they're going to go against the wall, we could put some bolts behind them. They'll be hidden most of the time and then when you pull the curtains round they'll be exposed."

"Mm." He considered the idea, trying to think of it as a sim room design problem. Having Toreth standing right behind him, touching far too much and not enough, didn't help. "Not bad. But . . . "

"You don't like the idea of gear at the flat. I know. I could bring the chains round from my place when we need them. Or you could keep them in the cabinet."

"No."

Toreth had suggested that before and he'd refused before, but this time Toreth asked, "Why not?"

"The cabinet isn't somewhere to keep things. Not even chains. I appreciate it would make the game easier for you, but—"

"Forget it. Easy doesn't matter." Toreth slid his hands down his arms, circled his wrists, and squeezed gently. Then not quite so gently.

Warrick shivered—he couldn't help it. And this wasn't Fran's shop. "Please, don't," he said, which was rather like trying to put out a fire by pouring brandy over it.

"I thought you might need reminding that I don't need chains. Or anything."

He wished he knew what it was about Toreth's voice that could do this to him. It wasn't just the words, although they were exciting enough. It was something in the pitch, the timbre. Did it have the same effect on other people? With an effort, he said, "We came here to buy some curtains, so let's buy them."

Toreth let go at once. "Okay." The easy acquiescence made him suspicious, but there was nothing he could do about it.

They shopped for a while, or rather Warrick shopped and Toreth rejected his suggestions out of hand. Eventually, somewhat to Warrick's relief, Toreth wandered away somewhere on his own.

Warrick continued browsing, almost forgetting his missing companion, until he recognized footsteps behind him. "Yes?"

"I found something. Two somethings."

Something slipped over his shoulder and he put his hand up automatically to catch hold of it. It was a long curtain tie-back, real silk and a rich red, dark and bright at the same time, like sunlight through wine. "Lovely color," he said, turning it over in his hands and trying not to think of what else they could do with it.

"Yes." Toreth took back the length of silk, walked away a few paces, then stopped when Warrick failed to follow him. "Come on."

"Where?"

"To see the second thing."

All of the shop's walls were hung with curtains, in different styles and fabrics. Toreth walked along until he came to a heavy dark blue drape, then looked around. He lifted the curtain slightly and simply walked behind it, into what ought to have been solid wall. After a moment, his hand reappeared, extended palm up. Warrick look around too, but saw no one observing them. He took Toreth's hand and allowed him to draw him forwards.

The space behind was far too small to be considered a room. More of a cupboard, or a niche, housing ducts and piping running from the floor to the ceiling. It was barely large enough for two people, leaving a little space for maneuvering. The only light was what filtered through and around the thick concealing curtain.

Toreth still had hold of his hand. He turned them so that Warrick stood with his back to the pipes, then took his wrists and wrapped the silk rope around them. It felt quite different to leather or steel, or velvet manacle linings, or even ordinary rope. The soft length slid over his skin as Toreth carefully tied the knots, the tasseled ends stroking his palms. He closed his eyes—just for a moment—enjoying the feeling.

And then, before he could react, Toreth lifted his hands above his head and secured the ends of the rope around the largest pipe.

He tugged, not too hard because he didn't want to risk damaging the pipe. "Toreth!" he whispered.

"Yes?"

"What are—" On further consideration, the 'what' was fairly obvious. "Stop it."

"No. Not a chance." Toreth closed the few centimeters between them, hands on his body, mouth against his mouth, dizzying him. "I'm going to fuck you. Now. Right here. I know you want it."

No arguing with that. And even if he tried to deny it, his body was telling the truth. He closed his eyes again as Toreth's hand molded around his cock, rubbing through fabric. Almost as arousing, he could feel Toreth's erection, hard against his hip as he pressed against him. Wanting and being wanted and the silk cord around his wrists...

"Tell me you want it," Toreth whispered against his throat. "Tell me you need it."

His lips parted, silently shaping the words. Tempting as the idea was, though—and, God, *how* tempting—he couldn't do it. "Plastic duck."

Toreth stepped back at once. "Really?"

"Really."

Toreth sighed, reaching to untie the ropes. "Spoilsport. You're no fucking fun at all." Not entirely joking—Toreth hated to be thwarted, even as he always respected a serious no.

144

Once his hands were free, Warrick used them to pull Toreth close while he kissed him. "Don't sulk. Let's buy the curtains, go to your flat, and you can tie me to anything you like, for as long as you like. And do whatever you like to me."

Toreth laughed, keeping his voice low. "How *very* generous. I bet you'll hate every minute of it."

Warrick checked around the edge of the curtain to ensure that the coast was clear, and they slipped out, back into the shop.

"To return to the matter in hand," Warrick said, "the question is, what color? And what fabric?"

"Velvet. The stuff we were looking at first. And this color." Toreth held up the silk tie-back. "Looks good against your skin."

"Are you sure?"

"Very."

"I'll go order them."

Toreth handed the silk rope to him. "Buy this, while you're at it. And another three to go with it."

As he turned away, Toreth stopped him, lifting his hand to touch his throat where he'd kissed it only a couple of minutes earlier. "Better make it another four."

Losing It

❖

The SimTech security guard let Toreth go up in the lift unaccompanied, which didn't always happen. Maybe, Toreth thought, his dinner jacket and glossy evening-dress shoes had added a veneer of respectability. As well as the dinner jacket he was wearing, he had another with him, picked up from Warrick's flat on his way here. Warrick had been caught in the office, working out some life-or-death technical problem, making it impossible for him to get home.

As he stepped out of the lift, Toreth checked his watch. Ten minutes early—not bad. Should put Warrick in a good mood for the evening.

The office door was ajar, so Toreth simply pushed it open. Warrick sat at his desk, intent on the left-hand screen. He didn't react to the intrusion. "How's it going?" Toreth asked.

Warrick looked up, frowning slightly as though he'd been expecting someone else. "Fine." Then his expression cleared. "Ah, you remembered the suit. Thanks."

"Sara left me a memo." He laid it over the desk, and the shoes in the attached bag thunked against the wood. A solid, heavy, and robust desk, and there had been a few times in the past when Toreth had been grateful for Warrick's taste in furniture.

"I hadn't realized it was so late." Warrick hesitated, then stood up and un-zipped the front of the suit protector. "Look, I still have a couple of calls I have to make. I can do it while I change. Would you mind waiting outside?"

Toreth grinned. "Sure."

The admins were long gone, so Toreth sat in one of their chairs and put his feet up on the desk, still smiling. Maybe Warrick had calls, maybe he didn't. Either way, what Warrick had really meant was that if Toreth stayed in the room while he stripped then they'd probably end up being late. Ten minutes early wasn't *that* early.

He'd been waiting for only a couple of minutes when a woman he didn't recognize came into the office. He didn't think that he'd seen her at SimTech before. She was dark-skinned—beautiful Indian coloring, with skin like dusted chocolate—and petite. Nice, actually. Probably expecting Warrick's admin, she stopped when she saw him there instead, so Toreth continued his inspection. Her clothes were hard to place on a brief glance—smart and not cheap, but a little too casual for general corporate standards. Maybe a SimTech programmer after all.

After a few seconds of silence they both spoke together.

"Have you—"

"Can I—"

She laughed, and he gestured graciously. "Go on, after you."

"Have you seen Dr. Warrick?" Her voice was surprisingly low for her tiny frame.

Toreth pointed over his shoulder with his thumb. "In his office."

He waited until she was level with his chair before he added, "Changing into his dinner jacket, so you might want to wait."

She stopped and, as he'd hoped, leaned her hip against the edge of the desk. Up close, he guessed her to be in her midthirties. He also noticed that she was wearing a visitor's badge like his own. Good. Fucking SimTech staff required a tediously high level of discretion these days.

Toreth uncrossed his ankles, swung his feet off the desk, and sat up in the chair. Was that a flicker of appraisal in her expression? Maybe even appreciation. "You don't work here, then?" he asked.

"No. I work for a corporation called P-Leisure. Minority-market product development." She rotated her shoulders, her neck and spine popping. "Ouch. I've been in the sim with Dr. Warrick all afternoon. He was putting the sim through its paces for me, showing me some new applications."

P-Leisure. He ran his eye over her again, this time with a view not to how attractive he found her—still very, but less than ten seconds ago—but how Warrick might see her. Was this who Warrick had been expecting when Toreth opened his office door?

"Did you want to speak to him, or are you just saying goodbye?" Toreth asked.

"Actually, I've already done that. I was on my way out, but the lift won't respond to my pass." She looked at her watch. "Damn it."

"I'll call security, shall I? Get someone to escort you out."

"That would be very kind, thanks."

Toreth pressed a button on the admin's comm. They waited in silence, because Toreth couldn't think of anything more to say to her. Or rather, he could think of plenty. Did you fuck him in there? What did you do? Did he enjoy it? Have you done it before? Will you do it again? Do you want him, outside the sim? Is that why you're here?

Pathetic, pathetic, pathetic. It didn't matter what the woman looked like, or what she'd been doing at SimTech, because Warrick was so married to his precious corporation that he'd never do anything so unprofessional as letting sim-fucking bleed over into the real world.

Just like he didn't that first time, going from a guided tour of the sim to an evening with a stranger at the Renaissance Center.

That was a stupid comparison, Toreth told himself firmly, the admonition doing nothing to quell the unease.

It didn't take the guard long to arrive. Lucky, because however pathetic it was, the urge to ask the first question was becoming unbearable. *Did you fuck him?* He had bite his lip to stop himself blurting it out.

As the woman left, thanking him again, Toreth lifted his left hand in farewell. His right was clenched under the edge of the desk, tight enough that his nails dug into his palm. The bitch waved cheerfully back. "I'll tell Warrick you were here," Toreth called.

He wouldn't, of course.

As the car started off, Warrick yawned, obviously catching himself by surprise. "Hard day?" Toreth asked.

Still yawning, Warrick shook his head. "A long day," he said when he could. "And rather tiring, but not especially hard."

"Oh?"

"No. I spent most of the afternoon in the sim, which is always enjoyable, even if most of what I was doing was a demonstration."

Of fuck tech? "Anything interesting?"

Warrick shrugged. "An overview of the system for a new sponsor liaison. Nothing that you haven't seen, I don't think."

Not very reassuring, given what Toreth and Warrick had done together in there. He didn't like the word 'liaison,' either. It reminded him of Carnac.

Warrick settled back into the comfortably upholstered seat, tilted his head back on the headrest, and closed his eyes. Toreth watched him narrowly, unable to stop himself wondering.

He was putting the sim through its paces for me, showing me some new applications.

He fucks in the sim all the time, Toreth told himself. It's work, that's all. It's just his fucking job. It doesn't mean anything. I handcuff people all day, but that doesn't make them regular fucks.

It didn't help much.

The car stopped to allow pedestrians to cross. A couple stood on the curb, ignoring the people jostling past them. Mother and teenaged daughter, he guessed. The younger woman—still a girl, really—was nearly in tears, gesturing furiously as she tried to make some point. Her mother looked to be close to losing her temper, shaking her head from time to time, offering a short phrase or two that only seemed to exacerbate the confrontation. Finally, the car moved away, leaving them behind. Toreth wondered, vaguely, what they'd been arguing about.

He leaned his elbow on the windowsill and watched the world slowly passing as the car crawled through the tangle of evening traffic. The streetlights were outcompeted here by festive decorations. They had moved out of the university area into one of the shopping districts, and pedestrians crowded the pavement. Most of them looked preoccupied and harassed. Shopping for New Year presents, maybe; there were certainly plenty of people burdened with multiple bags.

Toreth hadn't decided what to do for New Year, and there were only a couple of weeks left before he'd have to make up his mind. Warrick had hinted obliquely that he'd be welcome at Kate's—actually, he'd told Toreth that Tarin was planning to spend New Year with his semi-estranged wife. Toreth guessed that the unrequested information was the prelude to an invitation. He might even say yes. At least at Kate's there'd be no annoyingly fuckable random women for Warrick to take an interest in.

The real problem with the sim was lack of forensics. Warrick could've spent all afternoon screwing the Indian woman and there would be nothing to give it away—no lipstick, no stray hair, no scent on his skin. Toreth sometimes still came in the real world when fucking in the sim, but Warrick never did.

All Toreth had was the perfectly casual admission that Warrick had been in the sim today. Of course, there was no reason why it shouldn't be casual; Warrick didn't know that Toreth had met his visitor. As Warrick didn't consider what he did in the sim to be real sex, it probably wouldn't matter if Toreth had told him. There was no realistic way of assessing the threat—no concrete evidence that there was a threat at all.

Perhaps there *was* nothing to worry about, and Warrick had spent the afternoon showing the woman his new collection of clouds and other weather effects.

Still. P-Leisure.

Grimacing, Toreth turned his attention back to Warrick. He hadn't moved, his eyes still closed, and the dim, uneven, artificial lights through the car windows left his face shadowed and unreadable.

Normally, Warrick in a dinner jacket brightened any day. This evening, though, the immaculate suit, which Toreth had so carefully not creased on the journey to SimTech, made him look oddly remote—almost unreal, or at least suddenly very corporate. His crisp collar stood out against the black jacket, matching the crescents of white cuffs where his hands were folded in his lap.

Toreth moved seats, over to beside Warrick, who opened his eyes and smiled. The illusion of untouchability vanished, leaving Toreth with a ridiculous sense of relief. "I thought it was quiet in here," Warrick said.

149

"I was thinking."

"Oh?"

Toreth shook his head. "Work stuff. Nothing important." He cast around for a distraction, for something sufficiently detailed and requiring enough concentration to drive out the memory of the woman and speculations about the sim. "I thought you could tell me who's going to be there this evening, so I'll have a tiny chance of remembering who the fuck any of them are."

It always surprised Toreth that places this big could be found so close to the center of New London. It shouldn't—he'd seen satellite images and there were plenty of green splotches on them. Some were parks for the ordinary citizens, providing a breath of open air in the overcrowded city. Many were houses like this one, corporate retreats for people who could afford a level of privacy which mere mortals in compact blocks of flats could only dream about.

The impregnable gate and long driveway alone must have occupied a fortune in real estate. Conspicuous wealth at its most conspicuous, with plenty of lighting to show off the gardens and the monstrous house. Toreth wondered if the place was an original survivor from the old city, or if it had just been built in an old style. Yellow brick—ugly as hell in Toreth's opinion—and a white-balustraded roof. Most of the windows were brightly lit, although the scenes within were obscured by one-way scatter-filter security glass. It made the house look like a half-completed sim room, where the details hadn't yet been filled in.

The double front doors stood at the top of a flight of a dozen steps. As they approached, one door opened with a faint, eerie hiss. It might look like old-fashioned wood, but the door clearly concealed very modern security. Just inside, a woman waited to take their coats and very politely check their ID. Toreth judged her to be ten percent cloakroom attendant, ninety percent corporate muscle; it took him only a few seconds to find the lines of the holster under her jacket.

Corporate socializing at its finest. He was about to mention something to Warrick when he heard a familiar voice. "Dr. Warrick!"

Caprice Teffera obviously remembered Toreth from the SimTech investigation but, as he'd expected, she was immaculately polite and greeted both him and Warrick with every appearance of pleasure. She escorted them through to the main reception room.

Toreth tried his hardest not to stare, but he simply couldn't believe the ballroom could be part of a private house. Four normal stories high, the room had a balcony holding real live musicians. A single one of the vast chandeliers would've virtually filled Toreth's living room, and their light reflected from an intricately patterned wooden floor with a glasslike polish. What wall surface he could make

150

out under the swathes of New Year decoration seemed to be covered in printed silk.

Jesus. Places like this really emphasized that Warrick was a *minor* corporate. Would Warrick eventually own an equally stupendous house when the sim was in use across the Administration and beyond? Toreth couldn't imagine it. Or at least couldn't imagine being a part of it, or see himself walking into somewhere like this and feeling at home. He wished suddenly that he was spending the evening at his own shabby flat instead, with Warrick safely there with him. Chained to the bed, maybe. Toreth smiled at the image and tried to push aside the unease.

The room was already crowded, voices competing with the music. Caprice ushered them into the room, then paused to introduce Warrick to a couple of people he apparently didn't know, but whom Caprice seemed to think he would like to. Perfect hostess, and more helpful than she'd been in the middle of a murder investigation.

The first introduction of the evening always made Toreth uncomfortable. Not a major trauma, just an irritation. "And are you corporate?"

"No. I work for Int-Sec, at the Investigation and Interrogation Division."

He rarely got an original response, and tonight the tight-skinned, middle-aged woman who had asked the question followed up by saying, "Which part are you?"

He gave her his best fake-sincere corporate smile and said, "Both. I'm a senior para-investigator."

That generated a tiny hiccup of silence in the conversation, and Warrick stiffened very slightly, while Toreth thought, well, why the fuck did you ask me to come with you, then? Business as usual.

After that, Toreth found a drink and finished it, and then found another one. That blunted the edge of irritation. It wasn't Warrick's fault, after all, if I&I didn't enjoy a sparkling reputation in corporate circles. It wasn't I&I's fault, either. All the corporates had to do to avoid I&I's attention was stop killing each other and defrauding the Administration. And that would happen about the time Caprice and Marc Teffera opened their overgrown house to indigents.

They circulated from group to group. Some of the guests Toreth had met before. He found it hard to remember names—a combination of his innate dislike of corporates as a species and not really giving a fuck—but he recognized faces.

At SimTech events, he could usually pick out the major sponsors, and even remember one or two facts about them onto which he could pin a conversation. Here there were more total strangers. Half an irritation, because it meant paying attention to introductions, and half a good thing, because he didn't have to remember if he'd spoken to them during a previous event, or fucked them after one.

Eventually, Toreth relaxed sufficiently for boredom to set in. The initial conversations were usually the dullest part of these evenings, all business, with everyone jockeying for status and fishing for information. Later on, after the alcohol had been flowing for a few hours, even corporates would unbend into something almost human.

After a while, using the excuse of needing a piss, he left Warrick talking to a safely unattractive couple and went for a wander. It gave him a chance to scope out the layout of the house and spot likely dark corners and empty rooms. In the car on the way here, Warrick had said strictly no fucking this evening. Toreth took it as a challenge rather than an order.

Tonight, assuming he could get Warrick to break his resolution, there would be no problem finding a venue. The Tefferas' vast house was like an extension of the LiveCorp headquarters, although there was no hint of the mass-media porn on which the Teffera fortune rested. The rooms were different in detail, but identical in overall impression: tasteful décor with a smooth and bleakly impersonal blending of styles. Unobjectionable colors, tasteful art, unmarked rugs, unused-looking furniture—the place must keep an army of expensive consultants supplied with designer drugs and designer clothes. Toreth found it hard to believe anyone lived there at all.

A figure stepped out of a doorway on the periphery of Toreth's vision, and he turned a little too quickly, training readying him for trouble.

Another security officer, male this time, stood a few meters away, his hand hovering ready to drop to the concealed weapon. Toreth kept still, his own hands carefully in view. "Can I help you, sir?" the guard asked.

"Yes. I'm lost. Where's the nearest toilet?"

The guard relaxed, if not completely. "This way, sir. I'll take you there."

Which he did, then escorted Toreth back to the main event, and very discreetly made sure that he was a legitimate guest before he let Toreth out of his sight. Sharp and professional, Toreth thought as the man left. However, it left him with the feeling that he ought to be wearing a collar and nametag—something to identify his corporate owner.

When he returned to the high-ceilinged reception room, Toreth spotted Warrick at once. He was deep in conversation, not with the couple with whom Toreth had left him, but with a single man. They stood together by the cavernous fireplace, against a backdrop of New Year decorations.

Warrick was listening intently to the stranger, his head slightly tilted, nodding agreement from time to time. Whatever they were talking about, he looked thoroughly engrossed. In Toreth's experience, that tended to mean something technical, but even so the scene made the hair on Toreth's neck prickle and his stomach tighten.

Maybe it was that there was no one standing close by them, which meant they could be talking about *anything*. Maybe it was the fact that the man was, if not especially handsome, at least perfectly fuckable. Fit, certainly, blond and tall, and notably young for the party crowd.

152

Whatever it was, it kicked off the familiar twinge of unease—familiar enough that Toreth could often pretend it wasn't even there. Not tonight, though, not after the nasty shock at SimTech. It seemed to have primed his system, so that the slightest possibility of a sexual interest threw another log on the growing fire.

He took a deep breath and walked over to join them. Toreth was so absorbed in a closer examination of the man—better looking than he'd thought from across the room, with the crotch of his trousers outlining a respectably suggestive bulge—that he almost missed his name when Warrick introduced them. Gavin Tordoff.

Toreth smiled and filed the information away, just in case he felt a need to check into the bastard's background on Monday.

It turned out that he and Warrick were enmeshed in computer-speak about ultra-large-scale data processing; the conversation lost Toreth after thirty seconds. Despite the mundane topic, there was still something about the man that set off irrational alarm sirens in Toreth's mind. There was nothing that he could put his finger on: no obvious flirting, no unwelcoming glances directed towards Toreth. However, there was something, and it was dismantling his self-control faster than Sara could take apart an arrogant junior.

His fist was itching for solid contact when he caught sight of the reflection of the three of them in the mirror over the fireplace, and realized how alike he and Tordoff were. Not just in height and coloring, but in build, bearing, even the bone structure of their faces, although Toreth could confidently say he was the better looking of the two.

The realization took the edge off the anger. Was that all it was? That the man was so plausibly someone Warrick might find attractive? "Fuckable" was a sliding scale when it came to worrying—wondering—about Warrick's opinions of others. At the high end, the danger end, were the Gavin fucking Tordoffs. Toreth had good reason to think that Warrick liked tall, well-built blonds—the kind of solid evidence on which he'd submit an Investigation in Progress without any expectation of it setting Tillotson's nose twitching.

If that had been it, things wouldn't be so bad. However, Girardin had been neither tall, nor blond, nor especially muscular. To add to the problem, he'd had a beard, which was something Toreth found off-putting. Warrick clearly didn't, though. Girardin's existence meant that a whole other segment of the population stirred up feelings Toreth hated having as much as he hated admitting to them.

It was a bad, bad idea to start thinking about Girardin. Toreth downed half his drink, the champagne bubbles making his eyes water, and forced his attention back to the conversation, concentrating on following the computer-speak.

Five minutes later, the man excused himself to join another group. Once he was a few meters away, Toreth said in an undertone, "He was fit."

Warrick's eyebrows lifted. "Was he? I didn't really notice, I'm afraid—we were talking tech."

Next moment, of course, Warrick turned to look after Tordoff, and Toreth wanted to kick himself. When Warrick looked back, Toreth could see from his expression that he *knew,* and wanting to kick himself transmuted into a deeper need to kick someone else. But Warrick smiled disarmingly, and laid his hand briefly on Toreth's forearm. "Not bad," he said, "but I already have a better one."

Before Toreth could reply, he heard Marc Teffera calling Warrick's name. Warrick smiled again and walked off to answer the summons, leaving Toreth blinking after him.

Follow or not? Toreth wondered when the surprise had dissipated. In the end, Toreth let him go and went in search of food instead. He'd skipped lunch, and during the conversation with Tordoff the rumblings from his stomach had started to get noticeably loud.

In Toreth's view, buffets were one of the main perks of these bullshit corporate events. Most of the other guests were still at the schmoozing stage, so he had the room almost to himself. The huge table was covered with a blindingly white cloth and decorated with holly and unnaturally red orchids—a nice blend of festive and financial.

He buttered half a seed-encrusted roll—the nearest thing to proper white bread he could find—and ate it while he surveyed the spread. Not one of the dozens of dishes had a hint of reconstituted protein about it. Fresh fruit and vegetables, fresh meat and fish, all beautifully prepared to emphasize the natural ingredients.

By the salads, he spotted a thin-spouted bottle of olive oil, and he grinned, thinking about fucking Warrick over the buffet table at the SimTech celebration. No way would Warrick risk that sort of thing here.

He was depleting a seafood platter of its fabulously succulent prawns when he heard a female voice. "Excuse me?"

He turned, prawn in his hand, and found a woman standing behind him. She wore plain gold jewelry, an unremarkable black dress, and her blonde hair hung in a simple, short bob. However, if the packaging wasn't especially showy, the body underneath more than made up for it. Athletic, holding herself with easy confidence—this one was most definitely Warrick's type.

She was hesitating, looking him up and down, then her clear skin flushed pink. "Oh, I'm sorry. I thought you were, ah—"

"One of the waiters?" Toreth guessed. The blush was rather fetching, and as he expected, it deepened.

"Security, actually."

On a closer inspection, he spotted darker roots to her blonde hair. Not that it meant dye for certain, because he'd known other blondes with naturally dark roots. Still, there was only one way to tell for sure. Two, counting asking her, but where was the fun in that? "And why did you feel the need for security?" he asked. "Someone bothering you?"

"What? Oh, no." She laughed lightly. "Nothing like that. I handed my coat over when I arrived, and I need my hand screen—I left it in the pocket by mistake."

"I can have a look for you, if you like." He tried out a smile. "I think I remember which way they took my coat."

It must have been a touch too eager, because she tensed slightly, suddenly defensive. "Don't worry. I can manage, thank you."

"Okay." He watched her go—the back view was almost better than the front. Pity. Still, there were plenty more fish at the party. But first, he'd finish the fish in here.

In the end the abundance of fresh goodies proved too tempting and he ate too much. At least the good food and another couple of glasses of wine muted the last of the ridiculous worries from earlier.

Still, he couldn't help wondering where Warrick was. He'd half expected—half hoped—that Warrick would have come to find him. Probably too busy drumming up business for SimTech.

When he stepped into the main reception room, the sight stopped him cold. Whoever was following him into the room ran into him, jostling Toreth's arm and slopping champagne out of his glass. Toreth ignored the surprised exclamation from behind him, and the small puddle of champagne fizzing at his feet.

Across the room, directly opposite the door, the woman from SimTech sat in a window seat. She'd changed from her casual corporate clothes into casual evening wear: a floor-length dress in muted pink silks. Not as showy as some of the outfits on display, but respectably expensive.

Beside her sat Warrick. He was listening as closely as he'd listened to Tordoff earlier, but this time he was smiling, too. There was no sign of the reserve and slight tension that Toreth often noticed in him at these kinds of events. Not stress, but a firm control and an awareness of everyone and everything around him. Right now, though, he seemed oblivious to the rest of the room. Just the two of them in the deep-bayed window, looking very fucking cozy. As the surprise started to fade, a prickle of anger replaced it.

Moving across the room to where he could watch with less chance of being seen in return, Toreth joined the periphery of a group talking about the problems of importing restricted equipment from outside the Administration. Luckily, they didn't seem to know who he was; if they had done, Toreth suspected that the conversation would have screeched to an abrupt halt. Angling for a view out of the corner of his eye, he settled in to watch.

Advice for the chronically jealous, Toreth thought sourly: stay away from bisexuals. Having fifty percent of the planet stumble at Warrick's first hurdle would have made Toreth's life a hell of a lot less tense. Wasn't it bad enough that he had to worry about Girardin look-alikes and younger versions of himself?

At least the Indian woman wasn't Warrick's usual type, unlike the woman Toreth had met by the buffet. Warrick's four-year marriage to the well-toned Melissa suggested that blonde, athletically built women as well as men pushed his buttons. For that reason Cele also worried Toreth slightly, even though she was brunette. She was fit and Warrick had hinted—okay, said openly—that he thought she was attractive.

Despite that, he'd never really considered Warrick's friendship with Cele to be a serious risk. Warrick had known her for years and nothing had ever happened between them. New arrivals were an unknown quantity and so always more of a concern.

Surely Warrick's current companion was too dark, too slight, too prettily feminine to be dangerous? Beautiful hair, though, long and threaded through with silk ribbons. Her hair looked even longer because she was so short—shorter than Sara. A bit too short for Toreth's taste, because it hit a point when relative height limited the available positions, unless you wanted to fuck and stare at the pillow at the same time. But he wouldn't throw her out of bed, and she'd be perfect for a woman-on-top fuck, where light and lithe were advantages.

Toreth finished his drink and picked another off a passing tray. All he'd managed, he finally conceded, was to talk himself into acknowledging that she was perfectly fuckable and there was no reason on earth Warrick would turn her down.

Anyway, her physique wasn't conclusive proof she was safe. Just because she looked like this here didn't mean she'd looked the same in the sim earlier. Had Warrick been showing her the possibilities for playing in (and with) other people's bodies? Toreth shook his head sharply, trying to dislodge the images. It drew a couple of curious glances from the group next to him; he ignored them.

Warrick *didn't* fuck around, Toreth told himself firmly. (Outside work, an unhelpful inner voice pointed out.) Or rather, Warrick had done it exactly once, and there had been reasons, if not very reasonable ones, for that. Now they'd reached a compromise and everything was back on an even keel and working fine.

Toreth ran through the usual reassurances, as familiar as the fear that triggered them. He knew his intermittent obsession over Warrick's aberration with Girardin was pathetic, but if he let himself dwell on it for too long it left him so angry he could barely breathe.

So *stop* fucking thinking about it. The resolution lasted about ten seconds, after which he found himself gripping his glass stem hard enough that he made a conscious effort to relax. Otherwise he'd make a spectacle of himself by severing a few tendons and spraying blood all over the parquet floor.

The Indian woman edged a little closer to Warrick, who pointed across the room, approximately towards Toreth. Toreth turned hastily away, wondering if he'd been spotted. However, no summons followed, so he allowed himself to look back. Fuck it, Warrick and the woman were *still* talking.

If Warrick was planning another revenge fuck, then surely Toreth would've noticed something wrong?

Just like he'd noticed the first one in advance.

But Warrick seemed happy with things recently, didn't he? There'd been a limited number of screaming rows recently. The last big one—the only serious one for months—had been over that bloody cabinet, nothing to do with Toreth straying outside the limits of their IIP. Don't ask, don't tell, and if Warrick had a problem with that he hadn't said anything.

Warrick certainly looked perfectly happy *now*, talking to the scheming bitch. As Toreth watched, the woman leaned closer and whispered something, and Warrick just fucking *glowed*.

What were they saying? What the *fuck* were they talking about?

Should he go across? There was no reason not to, except that he couldn't help wondering how long they were going to keep talking. He wished he knew how long they'd been there already. Groups might be quite stable at these events, but five or ten minutes was a decent length for a one-on-one conversation. Much longer than that meant people making a deal, or business partners, or another kind of partner...

Ten minutes had passed before Warrick stood up. The woman stood too, and Warrick bent down and kissed her—cheek only, Toreth thought, although he couldn't be certain from this angle. Even after that there was another minute of conversation before Warrick left her there. Too long. Far too fucking long. Toreth put his drink down and set a course to intercept Warrick.

"Hello," Toreth said. "Been looking for me?"

Warrick looked around—not a trace of guilt, for all that meant—and smiled. "No. I saw you talking, so I didn't like to interrupt."

"Going to try the buffet? The prawns are great, and I think I left a few."

"Actually, I'm just on my way to the toilet."

"I found that earlier—I'll show you."

"No need. I've visited the house before, a number of times."

Toreth shrugged and fell into step beside him, wondering why the hell Warrick didn't want him along. Assignation with someone else? With the Indian woman? No, he told himself firmly. There was probably nothing in it, and after his fuckup with the blond guy—Gavin Tordoff, he repeated to himself, making sure he didn't forget the name—the last thing he wanted was Warrick realizing he was twitchy over someone else as well.

I'll look pathetic.

Toreth managed to keep that thought in mind as they walked down the corridors—was Warrick looking nervous? preoccupied?—and while they waited outside the toilet for the previous occupant to finish.

157

Then Warrick went in, and Toreth was on his own. Not for long, but long enough to remember every detail of the conversation he'd witnessed. And to move from there on to entirely imaginary pictures of what Warrick might have done in the sim earlier.

He was putting the sim through its paces for me, showing me some new applications.

It's his job. It's just his job. Even if he spent all afternoon in there fucking her senseless it didn't mean anything because it was his *job*. Fair enough—SimTech was Warrick's job. Not this other thing tonight. Not a cozy little tête-à-tête in a window seat.

Adrenaline was already speeding Toreth's heart when the lock clicked, surprising him out of the reverie. When Warrick opened the door, Toreth pushed him back inside, followed him in and locked the door again.

Even the toilets in this place were huge. There was plenty of space for Warrick to step away and put his back to the pale green wall. "Toreth?" Warrick sounded wary, but more amused than angry. "I thought I said no—"

"What were you talking about?"

Warrick looked at him blankly. "When?"

"You were talking to that woman just now. The woman from SimTech."

His expression cleared. "Tavi? She mentioned she'd seen you earlier in the office. We were talking business, primarily."

Right. Which is why you looked like she had her hand down your fucking trousers. "What kind of business?"

"Well, I don't really recall, offhand. Corporate liaison with P-Leisure, product development ideas." He shrugged. "Nothing that would interest you, I'm sure."

The casual dismissal wound the spring another turn tighter. "Why wouldn't it?"

Now Warrick was looking at him as if he'd sprouted an extra head. "Because you've rarely showed any interest in the commercial side of the sim in the past?"

You were fucking her in the sim. I know you were, so don't try to deny it.

He couldn't bring himself to say it, because Warrick would probably raise his eyebrow and say, "Well, yes, I was," in that infuriatingly patient voice he used when he thought Toreth was being unreasonable. And then...then didn't bear thinking about.

He wanted to hit something—the wall, the fashionably asymmetric mirror. Warrick. "You know, sometimes I feel like some piece of rough trade you drag along to these fucking places to freak people out."

Warrick laughed. The bastard actually fucking *laughed.* "You're hardly that. I&I might not be universally loved but it's perfectly respectable. I very much doubt my social standing would be improved if I were here instead with that young programmer you were admiring earlier. Or even with Tavi."

158

And he seemed to find *that* idea even funnier. Was Warrick winding him up deliberately, or was he just too fucking absorbed in his corporate evening to notice anything was wrong? Toreth suddenly found he couldn't tell and didn't care anyway.

"It wasn't just work, was it? What the *fuck* were you talking about?" The pent-up anger exploded and he made a grab for Warrick, getting a firm grip on his dinner jacket, barely hearing Warrick's exclamation of surprise.

A thin thread of sanity and self-control held him back from punching Warrick in the face and instead he forced him down into a crouch, trapped between the wall and Toreth's legs. Warrick tried to rise but Toreth slammed him back, pinning him there with his knee. The tiled floor was smooth, but it gave him enough purchase to hold Warrick.

If he couldn't find the words, then he would damn well *show* him. He fumbled with his zip, cutting off Warrick's protest by twisting his other hand on Warrick's collar.

"Open your mouth," he snarled, fighting to keep his voice low. "Open your fucking *mouth*."

"Toreth—" Warrick choked out.

Toreth shook him by the collar, relishing the controlled violence. "Do it. Or I'll—"

Fortunately, he didn't need to decide what he'd do, because Warrick obeyed. Toreth struggled one-handed to free his cock, tangled in inconvenient underwear he wished now that he hadn't bothered wearing. God, he was hard, anger and arousal swirling together and feeding off each other.

He gripped Warrick's chin, tipping his head back a little as he drove in, not giving him a chance to get used to the brutal invasion.

You're mine. I can take you when I want, where I want, because you're fucking *mine*. You're here on your knees because you need it from *me*.

It felt so good, so perfect. Warrick's tongue moved against him, and he couldn't tell if it was participation or protest. He shifted his hands, twisting his fingers in the hair at the back of Warrick's head, holding him as he took him.

Toreth flung his head back and gasped, relishing every stroke. He could hear Warrick's hands scrabbling at the wall, but he didn't want to look down. As long as he didn't see Warrick's hands then he could honestly say that he hadn't ignored a signal to stop. Riding a fine line between the game and something awful, adrenaline firing him higher. He heard Warrick choking, felt his head jerking, the movements meaning nothing compared to the muscles spasming deliciously around his cock.

If he's telling me to stop, and I don't...

He crushed the thought ruthlessly, keeping the rhythm, hard and deep, in time to the litany in his mind.

Mine. You're mine. You're mine. You're mine.

Now he couldn't resist looking. He saw his own hands, fisted in Warrick's hair, holding him prisoner. He saw his own cock, thrusting fast and deep between the wet lips. He saw Warrick's dark eyes, open wide, but Toreth couldn't read them, couldn't tell if Warrick wanted this or if he had finally, once and forever, fucked things up irrevocably. Then he didn't even care because it was too much—all too much, and he was coming hard, his grip tightening in Warrick's hair, crushing Warrick against him.

Mine, mine, mine, and he wasn't sure if he was saying it out loud or not. *Mine.*

Then it was over, and Warrick coughed, pushing weakly at his hips. Toreth let him go and pulled back, wincing at a hint of teeth over his tender cock. "Fuck," Toreth breathed, jealousy and anger surrendering—temporarily at least—to the postorgasmic buzz. "Ah, *fuck.*"

Warrick shoved him away sharply, and Toreth almost stumbled. He caught himself with a hand on the wall, touching the cool glass of the mirror with his fingertips. Blinking, he attempted to bring the world back into focus.

Warrick sat with his back against the wall, breathing hard. Not looking happy. Toreth didn't know whether to crouch down and kiss him, or start trying to pull together some half-convincing apology. In the end, he simply held out his hand.

Warrick stared at it for a long moment, then shook his head slightly and accepted the offered help.

He pulled Warrick up, then forward, wrapping one arm around Warrick's shoulders and dropping the other hand to the front of his trousers, because it was the easiest way to answer the question. Warrick hissed as Toreth touched him, but he pressed towards him, not away. And thank fucking God, Warrick was hard. If it was a fuckup, then it wasn't a bad one; not so bad that Warrick still didn't want him, anyway. Maybe there'd be an argument about it after the party, but that would be no worse than the usual not-in-public crap.

He rubbed the heel of his hand hard against Warrick's cock, drawing out a gasp. "Let me," Toreth whispered. "Let me."

They stood for a moment, then Warrick stepped firmly away. "Later, I think," he said. He straightened his collar, where Toreth had held it, then smoothed down his jacket front. "How do I look?"

Relief loosened his tongue. "Fucking fantastic."

"I meant, am I fit to return to civilized company?" He ran his hands through his hair, then wiped the corners of his mouth.

"More or less. Hang on a moment." He flicked the stray bits of Warrick's hair back into place, and brushed his thumb over his lips, just to feel the slightly swollen softness.

"I think we should go back, before we're missed." Warrick glanced down significantly. "When we're both respectable."

160

"Yeah." Toreth reached to fasten up his own zip, feeling the last knot of anger in his chest finally untie. "Security was a bit keen earlier about tracking down straying guests. I'm surprised they aren't hammering on the door." Then he had to laugh at Warrick's expression of alarm. "Joke."

Warrick shook his head. "Not funny."

Fortunately, there was no one waiting outside, guest or security. They walked back in silence, but instead of returning to the main room or the buffet, Warrick turned left into a small room, full of floor-to-ceiling shelving holding paper books.

Toreth spotted them at once—the Indian woman Warrick had been speaking to and, oddly, the blonde woman he'd met by the buffet. From the inside of the house, the security glass in the windows seemed clear; the women stood together by one of the long picture windows, looking out at the floodlit garden. The blonde had her arm across the other woman's shoulders, pale against her thick curtain of hair. In return, the shorter woman had her arm around the blonde's waist.

Easy, unobtrusive, with the comfortable intimacy of long familiarity, and it made Toreth's heart sink. Shit. He stopped dead. "Warrick—"

"There's someone I'd like you to meet," Warrick said evenly, and it was only because Toreth knew him so well that he caught the gleam of steel in Warrick's voice.

"I didn't know," Toreth said in an undertone. "How the fuck could I have known?"

Now the steel was plainer. "You could have asked me."

"Look, Warrick, I'm s—" Then he gasped at the sharp pain as Warrick dug his fingers into Toreth's arm just above the elbow, hitting a nerve on the first pinch.

"It won't take long," Warrick said, tightening his grip until Toreth's hand began to go numb and Toreth surrendered and started walking.

"Tavi—Suzanne," Warrick called as they neared the couple.

They disengaged and turned, and at the same moment Warrick released Toreth's arm. The nerve tingled at the release from pressure, the semipain a welcome distraction from the growing embarrassment.

"This is Val Toreth," Warrick said.

The blonde woman—Suzanne, presumably—smiled. "And not a waiter after all."

Warrick raised an eyebrow, then continued when neither of them explained further. "Toreth, this is Suzanne and Tavi Lennox-Phull."

Shared surname, even.

"A couple of my oldest friends," Warrick said. "Even though we don't get together as often as we ought to do. We were all at university together. Suzanne and I went to the same college—did the same course, even. Now she's deserted the technical world and illustrates children's books. Tavi I think you met earlier. She started working for P-Leisure a couple of months ago, handling partnerships with smaller corporations."

"It was quite a surprise when I found myself at SimTech," Tavi said.

"It's a small world," Warrick said. "Full of coincidences. Although a surprising number have logical explanations if you can be bothered to look for them."

Toreth nodded, trying not to look at Warrick. This was the worst part of the insane, stupid fucking jealousy—when he let Warrick see it, and Warrick didn't pretend not to see. Sometimes he was annoyed, sometimes he was patient, sometimes he held it up and pointed it out and generally made Toreth feel as pathetic as he was. Still, on the plus side, it had been a great fuck. Toreth smiled at the women. "Nice to meet you both."

"Tavi," Warrick said, "Toreth was wondering what you said to me earlier in the ballroom—when I pointed him out to you. But I didn't think he'd believe me if I told him."

Tavi laughed. "Another coincidence—I was just telling Suze about it before you came in." She looked up at Toreth. "I told Keir that if I hadn't been a lesbian all my life, I might envy him."

"We need to talk," Warrick said as the door to his flat closed.

"You talk if you want to. I'm going for a shower." Toreth started walking down the corridor, away from the imminent row. "You can send me a memo in the morning, let me know what you decided."

To his surprise, Warrick didn't follow him.

In the bathroom, he stripped, feeling a dim shadow of the earlier anger. He should have expected a demand for a bloody conversation. Why the hell couldn't Warrick leave it alone? So he'd said no fucking in public. Big deal. The door had been locked. And if he mentioned Tavi and Suzanne...

Wadding up his dinner jacket and trousers, he threw them onto the towel hamper. He shouldn't have come back here, Toreth decided. The rest of the party had been okay. A bit strained, but Warrick had seemed to feel his ace up the sleeve over his long platonic friendship with Tavi-the-fucking-lesbian had balanced out the scene in the toilet. On the way back to the flat, though, Warrick hadn't said a word. The silence had grown in the car until it felt too dangerous to break. How the hell had Toreth been supposed to know that Tavi didn't fuck men?

You could have asked me.

Yes, he could have. He could have, and he hadn't, so he'd made an idiot of himself. He could live with that. What he didn't want was a postmortem of the whole sorry mess.

Once in the shower, he turned up the temperature and pressure, trying to wash away the irritation. After a couple of minutes the bathroom door opened and closed. Toreth rinsed shampoo out of his hair, wanting to be ready to tell Warrick to fuck off.

After a minute of silence, Warrick opened the shower door and stepped in. Naked, of course, which was instantly disarming. "Toreth—"

"Fine," Toreth said. "Talk, if you have to." He'd let Warrick have his say, and hope that he could then come up with some apology that would be enough to shut Warrick up.

"What happened in the toilet at the Tefferas'—" Warrick began.

Somehow, he couldn't keep quiet. "You wanted it," Toreth interrupted. "It turned you on, don't fucking deny it."

"Toreth, that isn't the point."

Toreth turned to face him, crowding him a little, enjoying the height difference, watching as Warrick's gaze swept down and up. "What is the point, then?"

"It was—" Warrick gasped as Toreth took his cock in his hand.

"What was it?" Toreth pressed closer, lowering his head to breathe the words into Warrick's ear. "Tell me what you were thinking about."

"Stop that." But Warrick's hands were stroking his back and sides, eager and restless, and he was hardening quickly in Toreth's hand. "I can't—I can't very well explain if you're doing that."

I know. Toreth ignored the protest, and Warrick took a deep, shivering breath and closed his eyes.

"All right, if you insist," Warrick said. Toreth slid his free hand up, resting his thumb under Warrick's ribcage, feeling his voice resonate. "You're right that— that it turned me on. But I can't keep risking that sort of thing in public. We'll get caught in the end, and while it might be very funny for you, it certainly won't be for me and—and—"

Toreth smiled, speeding the rhythm. "You loved it. You loved it when I was raping your fucking throat."

"I—Oh, God."

"And you love hearing about it now. Do you want me to tell you how good it felt, taking you like that?"

When Warrick spoke again, his voice was firmer. "Toreth, it was too close to the edge. It was too damn real."

The words set his heart hammering. Determinedly, he kept pumping. "You wanted it like that."

"Yes, I did. A great deal—far too much to stop it. And that's why it was too close. Dilly made me—" He moaned softly as Toreth released his cock.

Toreth felt as though Dillian's name had switched the shower from hot to cold. He stepped back, letting the water make a curtain between them. "What the fuck does she have to do with anything?"

163

"Dillian asked if what I do with you is safe, and I promised her that it was." Warrick opened his eyes and reached up to angle the showerhead down, clearing the air. "I've broken that promise once already, with the cabinet. I can't break it again. I won't."

Now he might as well have been standing under a snowmelt waterfall. "The cabinet's not a problem."

"Not now. But it was for a while, and it could have been a disaster, except that you prevented me from turning it into one. For which I'm extremely grateful." Warrick was looking straight at him, and his gaze pinned Toreth's helplessly. "I can't control it, not all the time. When it's happening, I can't see what's safe. Or even sane. That's—" He brushed the back of his hand across Toreth's ribs. "That's part of what makes it so good, of course. I trust you to take control, you know that. But if I'm not in control, and you're not either..." He shrugged.

Now he felt sick. "Warrick, I'm sorry."

"I'm not asking for an apology. What I need to know is whether or not you were still in control tonight. Whether you could have stopped."

"Of course I—"

"No. Not 'of course.'" Now he had his palm against Toreth's chest, pressing slightly for emphasis. "Whatever the answer is, this isn't goodbye, or never again, or anything melodramatic. I just need to be clear about it. And if there is a problem, then we can find a way to work round it." He smiled faintly. "I'm an engineer—I like solving problems. Think about it, please."

He pretended to consider it for a few moments, then wondered why the hell he was only pretending. Why was he worried? Although it wasn't easy to reach back into the maelstrom of anger and lust, Warrick had had his hands free all the time; he'd had his teeth around Toreth's *cock*, for Christ's sake. If he'd used either of those options with serious intent, Toreth sure as hell would've stopped.

And if something else had happened? If he'd twisted the collar too tight, or if Warrick had really choked...?

So he thought about it, staring down at the water running over Warrick's fingers, until he was sure of the answer and he let the tension out in a long breath.

"Toreth?"

He looked up. "Yeah, I think so. I sure as hell didn't want to stop, but if you'd really fought me, or if something had gone wrong...yeah. Then I could've."

"You only think?"

"It's the best I can do. I mean, you didn't fight, did you? Nothing did go wrong. But I think it would've been okay." He didn't let his gaze waver—Warrick had to believe this. The consequences if he didn't were too sickening to think about. "Yes, I was angry, but I hadn't lost it. I was still in control."

Warrick smiled warmly. "That's all I needed to know." He gestured around the shower. "Are you done in here?"

"Sure."

"Then let's go to bed, shall we?"

He hadn't lost it tonight, Toreth reassured himself as he toweled himself dry. He knew exactly what that felt like. Losing it was white light and noise, and not knowing what the hell he was doing until he saw the blood. Losing it was Jonny Kemp calling Sara a whore. Losing it was seeing the broken cane in his hands and Gee Evans on the floor moaning and clutching his jaw, and not having the faintest fucking clue how either of them had got like that. Tonight he might have been somewhere near that line, but he hadn't crossed it.

And with Warrick, please, Christ, he hoped that he never would.

Coming from America

❖

The Para and I were standing at Sara's desk, both of us leaning over her shoulder while we tried to make sense of the figures that Corporate Fraud had sent us, when someone called the Para's name.

"Senior Para-investigator Toreth?"

We both straightened up. Only senior management or outsiders put both the "senior" and the "investigator" in a para's title like that. I guessed the man approaching was most probably corporate, judging purely from the cut of his suit. He had a flawless complexion too, black skin so smooth it looked polished, and perfectly cut hair to match. Not one detail out of place, and that takes money and attention. He even smelled expensive; as he stepped right up to the desk, I caught a whiff of rich, subtle cologne, the kind my mother buys me for New Year where a tiny splash will stay in place all day.

"That's me," the Para said.

The man held out his hand. "My name is Edwards. I'm an official at the Bureau of Administrative Departments."

Well, that was another, less likely, explanation for the suit. Even at I&I, the bureau name gets instant respect. I can't imagine there's anywhere in Europe it doesn't, even though nominally all the bureau does is allow the heads of department to coordinate the smooth functioning of Administration bureaucracy.

The Para shook Edwards's hand, looking understandably a little wary. I moved back a pace, taking myself out of the conversation. Sara, of course, was watching the screen as if she couldn't even see the two of them. I knew she'd be listening to every word.

"And?" the Para asked.

The man's eyebrows lifted. "I've come to escort you to your meeting."

"My what?"

"Meeting, at eleven?" When the Para shook his head, Edwards sighed, as though he'd expected it. "That's always the problem with trying to be both discreet and quick. Just come along with me. Everything will be explained when we get there."

I had a quick glance down at the screen, as did the Para. Sara was already in touch with the reception desk systems, looking at the record of Edwards's arrival. If the man had made it inside the building, his identity must have checked out.

"Are we going to Strasbourg?" Toreth asked.

"Oh, no. Just to our New London office." Edwards smiled reassuringly. "Not far at all."

The Para hesitated. Then he glanced briefly at me and said, "Can I bring my senior investigator with me?"

The man nodded. "I don't see why not. I can't guarantee that he'll be allowed into the actual meeting, though. I can send his name ahead for clearance before we arrive."

"Senior Investigator Ainsley Barret-Connor," I said.

"What should I tell Tillotson?" Sara asked. "He's expecting team leader case-load reports today."

"Leave a message with Jenny," the Para said. "Tell her that if he asks—only if he asks—I've been called away."

Edwards nodded slightly, probably approving the Para's discretion, and I wondered if the senior management over at the Bureau of Administrative Departments was as bad as Tillotson. I found it odd that our section head hadn't been included in the summons, though. Interdepartmental etiquette dictates that even the bureau ought to put in a request, for form's sake, before helping itself to another department's officers.

It wasn't until we'd actually arrived at the bureau and been escorted up several floors to a reception area to wait in rather comfortable leather chairs, that I realized why the Para had asked to bring me along. Not because he'd suddenly decided he couldn't do without my penetrating insights, but because he'd wanted to know if whatever they had planned for him would be at all inconvenienced by the presence of a witness.

Actually, I don't think either of us was terribly worried, because the Bureau of Administrative Departments doesn't have that sort of reputation. It has plenty of other people—whole departments of them—to do its dirty work, and the orders would've come from so far up the system that you'd probably never know why whatever nasty thing that happened to you had happened. It was still a somewhat unnerving feeling, though, to be sitting somewhere as expensively decorated as any corporate HQ, knowing we were at one of the hearts of Administration power.

The bureau is an odd place, if you've never been to one of their offices. Not many people have, so I'll try to describe it. For one thing, the New London branch is in an old building, or it looks like one. I don't know if it's genuinely old and was missed by the bombs, or if the contamination was cleaned up at some horrific expense, or if it's a very beautiful rebuild. The furnishings are to match, although judging from their condition they have to be reproduction. Overall, it gives the place a very timeless feel. I can't imagine the bureau, as a lot of the younger corporations do, regularly redecorating to keep up with the latest trends. They're like the old guard; they don't need to be seen to be spending money to earn respect.

No other department I've visited is like it. The corridors felt a little too quiet, the carpeting killing sound very efficiently, and the few people we had seen as we came through the building barely glanced at us, which isn't the reaction I've come to expect from our uniforms. Yet, somehow, I felt the presence of power there, in the way one can when standing near a heavy-duty electrical transformer. Or maybe it was all in my head; subjective impressions can be very dangerous.

The reception area seemed to serve a small suite of offices, none of which had names on the doors. There were inset screens, which presumably could display identification if required, but all the ones I could see were blank. I suppose that anyone up there knows where they're going, or has an escort. Edwards had left us alone under the watchful eye of the equally smart woman seated at the desk. She reminded me of Mistry, same color skin and same serious expression, except that instead of a practical plait she had her long hair intricately pinned up. I was idly wondering what a senior administrative assistant made at the bureau, and whether it was more or less than a senior investigator at I&I, when Edwards reappeared.

"This way, please."

"Do I at least get to know who I'm talking to before I go in there?" the Para asked. Edwards had refused to answer a single question from the Para on the drive over, almost as though he'd been expecting a call at any moment to say that the meeting was canceled.

"Catherine Turnbull." Edwards flashed us a sudden smile. "Principal secretary to the bureau."

I don't know about the Para, but I was still trying to think of a reply when Edwards stopped and opened a door. "In here."

Before that day, I'd seen Secretary Turnbull only once in person, when she visited I&I. On that first occasion, I hadn't recognized her, although I knew I must have seen her on news items. The principal secretary of the Bureau of Administrative Departments is the kind of official who rarely speaks in public, rather sticking to the background while the current face of the Administration stands to the fore. The idea of being simply summoned into a meeting with her was so far outside my experience, I had no idea of the right reaction.

Luckily, I wasn't required to have a reaction. I assumed she'd been told about the unexpected addition to the party, but she only glanced briefly at me before

168

she turned to the Para. And that was interesting in itself, because we're not unalike and it told me either she'd studied his picture recently, or she could differentiate our uniforms at a glance.

To my surprise—and, I think, the Para's, too—she came out from behind her desk and offered her hand.

"Thank you for coming, Para-investigator. I apologize for interrupting your work like this."

"I&I is always willing to cooperate with the bureau in any way we can," Toreth said.

It's an awful cliché, but if you do remember seeing Secretary Turnbull on the screen, I bet you'd expect her to be taller in real life. She's very short, shorter by far than Sara. I wouldn't say that she's attractive—if she ever was beautiful, it hasn't carried over into middle age—but she has a quiet, absolute confidence that is utterly compelling. If a stranger had walked into that office, knowing nothing about who was waiting for them, of everyone there I bet they'd still end up with their eyes on Turnbull.

Actually, the only other people in the room weren't very attention-grabbing anyway—a man and woman in sober civilian suits with no departmental insignia, sitting side by side at a conference table at the other end of the room from Turnbull's desk. They had their hands folded on the table in front of them, stiff and uncomfortable. I realized why Turnbull had risen to greet us when she led us over to join them.

"I expect you're curious about why you're here, Para-investigator," Turnbull said as we all sat down.

"I only want to know what you want to tell me," the Para said.

Turnbull looked at him sharply, then laughed. "See," she said, addressing the silent pair already seated at the table, "I told you he came well recommended."

They didn't say anything. The woman was superficially rather attractive—just my type, too: blonde and fine-featured, with lovely long legs I wouldn't get to see until later—but there was something about her which canceled all that out, cold and hard-edged. She reminded me a little of an interrogator, and I wondered if that was what she was, maybe for one of the more hush-hush Int-Sec or Ex-Sec divisions. If so, I also wondered why they were out of uniform.

The man was quite the opposite. His dark olive complexion made an obvious contrast to hers—he might easily have come from the Iberian region of the Administration—but there was nothing striking about him at all. One of those infuriating people of whom, when they're a suspect in a case, everyone says, "Oh, yes, I saw him," and then entirely fails to produce a useful description. Unlike his companion, he wasn't making eye contact, although I have to say I rather preferred it to her icy inspection.

"We have a delicate matter which requires the attention of a professional investigator," Turnbull said when we'd all taken our seats. "Your name was suggested to me by Councilor Theodora Selman—I believe she in turn had the recommendation from her son. She told me that you were instrumental in finally closing her granddaughter's kidnapping, and you handled the case with exemplary tact and discretion."

I doubt when the Para famously closed the Selman case—a case I missed out on, so I'm afraid I can't supply much in the way of juicy details—he could ever have foreseen this consequence.

"I always try to keep the wider needs of the Administration in mind when I'm running an investigation," the Para said, and I expect he was as glad as I was that Sara wasn't around for anyone to see her face.

"Someone is missing," Turnbull said. A picture of a young man flashed up on the wall screen, and I looked at it obediently. He appeared to be in his late teens or maybe a young early twenties. He had dark hair and a pleasant, happy expression on his tanned, slightly plump face, eyes a little squinted as he looked into the sun; the glimpses of toys scattered on the grass in the background suggested it was an informal photo, maybe from a friend or relative. "His name is James Smith," Turnbull continued. "I need him found quickly, and absolutely discreetly. In return, you will receive a fulsomely worded commendation from the bureau for your file. Files," she corrected herself, including me suddenly in the conversation.

"What, exactly, has he done?" the Para asked.

"Entered the Administration under a false identity."

The Para looked at the other two at the table, and so did I. Now we had a possible explanation as to why they weren't in uniform: they were from outside Europe.

"And where did he come from?" the Para asked.

"America," the blonde woman said.

The Para's eyebrows went up. So, I suspect, did mine. Official diplomatic contact between the European Administration and the North American government has been limited at best. Mutual trade is too valuable for it ever to have shut down completely, at least after the first few years, but obviously there's no love lost. Certainly, no one like Secretary Turnbull would be involved unless there was something big—more than one random illegal immigrant.

"And our interest is?" Toreth asked Turnbull.

Turnbull smiled at the blunt question. "A figure of some political importance in Washington contacted people at the council and at the bureau directly to ask for our help. He wants this boy found and returned alive. Obviously, we cannot allow the official agents of any foreign power to carry out a search in a European city. Particularly in these circumstances, it would damage the public image of the Administration. However—" Turnbull nodded to the strangers. "In a spirit of reconciliation, we're willing to allow observers to follow the progress of our own investigation."

I knew what the Para was thinking as he looked the two Americans up and down—how he could ditch them as fast and as painlessly as possible. I have to say, I agreed with him. Being trailed by two even very unofficial representatives of the American government would not be conducive to discreet work. Half the office would be there by coffee time to have what my paternal grandmother would call a good gawp.

It looked like I wasn't the only one reading trouble on the Para's face. "We don't want to cause any problems for you," the woman said. "We just want Smith back, as quickly and quietly as possible."

"Secretary," the Para said, ignoring her, "the General Criminal section is a busy place. We get visitors from all over I&I—and from outside the division, too. I can't just put two strangers in an office and expect that no one will ask questions. Particularly not these strangers. It will cause chaos."

The woman shifted in her seat. "I was told when I flew over here that we'd be given whatever assistance we required. It we don't get it, we'll have to take this matter up ourselves."

"Agent Cardine, you have full diplomatic status as a representative of your government, and we respect that. But as I'm sure Agent Ruiz will have explained to you, your permission to leave the embassy grounds is a courtesy extended by us." Secretary Turnbull wasn't even looking in my direction, and I felt a chill.

"And we really appreciate that courtesy," Ruiz said. He had a surprisingly soft voice. "But our mission is important to us—to our government."

Not just a personal favor between two higher-ups, then.

"Would it help if we wore some kind of local uniform?" Cardine asked.

"Not very much," the Para said bluntly. "Because the moment you open your mouths, you might as well be waving a flag."

I have to admit, I glanced a little nervously at Secretary Turnbull, but she had an absolutely neutral expression. I suppose that she was quite happy to let the Para raise the objections she'd otherwise have to make herself.

The Para turned back to the secretary. "You said you wanted a professional investigation, Secretary. I can do that, no problem. I don't guarantee I'll find this boy, but I can guarantee no one else at I&I would be able to do better. But if I can't run the investigation to the best of my professional judgment, then I won't run it at all."

I would never have dared lay the situation out so plainly, but apparently Secretary Turnbull appreciated clarity, because she nodded. "Thank you for your honesty. Well?"

The question was directed to the Americans. After a moment, Ruiz nodded. "We'll need to be kept up to date on progress at all times."

"Excellent." Turnbull nodded to the Para. "Then if you're satisfied, I'll inform your section head of the situation."

So round one went to the Para, and shortly after that we were walking back down the plush corridor, as the Americans, looking sour, were escorted a different way. I wondered how many people in the bureau knew they were here.

"Recommended by a council member, Para," I said, just to make conversation, as we went back down in the lift.

He was obviously thinking about something else, because it took him a couple of seconds to focus on me. "What?"

"I was just saying, Para, probably not many seniors get recommended by name by a council member to the secretary of the Bureau of Administrative Departments."

"Which just goes to show you that most seniors know better than to do a favor for Liz bloody Carey. Americans." He snorted. "What next? Working with resisters?"

It was interesting that Secretary Turnbull had mentioned reconciliation.

Like everyone in the European Administration, I grew up with the images of beautiful historical cities in ruins, dying radiation victims, starving refugees. The history of the fundamentalist dirty nukes, and the aftermath during which the modern Administration was formed to save Europe from collapse and chaos, is taught to every child, but it a way it isn't necessary. With Europe being such a cosmopolitan place, I should think that in any decent-sized gathering of people you'd find someone in the room whose family suffered in one of the bombings.

The bombs changed Europe, not just by ripping out the hearts of our old cities. Without that day of horror and chaos, there'd be no modern departmental structure within the Administration—no Bureau of Administrative Departments, even, which was formed to oversee and coordinate efforts first to save lives and then to rebuild. There would be no Unification Day, marking the end of the nation states, and so there'd ultimately be no unified external and internal security forces—no Ext-Sec, no Int-Sec. No I&I. And the social changes go even deeper than that.

I suppose you could call it one of history's great ironies. The bombers were trying to strike at the principles of secular, socially liberal government which had always been a fundamental of European politics. Zealots of one religion committed an unbelievable act of barbarity that they tried to blame on zealots of another, were caught out, and in consequence, religion itself became something of a dirty word in Europe.

And so it was obvious even to me that any question of reconciliation with the North American government was a fantastically delicate one. Something as minor as our investigation could have repercussions way beyond I&I or even Int-Sec. Public opinion, which had been shaped over a long time by the Administration, would need to be carefully reshaped if the powers that be at the bureau and other places wanted an openly better relationship.

Frankly, I couldn't imagine that they did, but maybe that was my own years of citizenship classes talking.

Of course, you can't blame individual citizens for atrocities other citizens of their country committed decades previously. Not even when the citizens who carried out those atrocities happened to be secretly aided and abetted by parts of their government. Still, I was glad that we didn't have to take the Americans back to I&I. The Para was right when he said it would cause chaos.

We were in the middle of January, and the weather had been cold for several days, windy and with occasional showers of sleet and freezing rain. As we went back to the car the ground was slippery underfoot; it seemed like a good metaphor for a potentially tricky case.

"Where do we start?" I asked as we climbed back into the car. "James Smith? Do you think that's his real name?"

"Probably not. Or if it is, then the odds of finding him aren't exactly on our side."

"No. At least it's one step up from John Smith, I suppose. But either way, it's going to be a hell of a job."

The Para nodded slowly. "I'll have to think about it."

The Para isn't someone who's often baffled. He doesn't like to sit still on a case, and even when the leads he sends the rest of us chasing seem pointless, it's surprising how often they take us somewhere. But in this case, I could understand why he was at something of a loss.

For the whole of the drive back to I&I, the Para was immersed in his screen, and I guessed he was reading the files to which I wasn't yet privy. I stared out of the window, watching the traffic moving in smooth, well-ordered lines. I noticed something I hadn't on the way there: we made the journey quicker than we would've done in an I&I car. The traffic systems gave the bureau car priority over everything else.

The car stopped at the front entrance to I&I (not being programmed for any of the more discreet doors) and the Para climbed out. He didn't go in, though, just stretched and stood looking first at the people going in and out, and then at the statue of Blindfold Justice. A few small icicles hung from the scales, and I watched them drip as I waited patiently.

"Something's wrong," he said finally.

I glanced around once more, but everything looked to be as I'd expect, so I guessed he meant the case. "What, Para?"

"I don't know. If I did, I'd be a lot happier."

"I suppose there's a lot they aren't telling us."

"I'm sure. But even with what they have told us, there's something not right. I don't know what it is, or how I know, but..."

"Instinct?" I suggested, and he gave me a look that I'm surprised didn't wither the grass behind me.

"I should've taken Sara along," was all he said before he went inside.

Ask who really controls the European Administration, and you'd probably get more answers than you'd know what to do with. Optimists would tell you it's the Parliament of the Regions. After all, they're the ones that everyone votes into office every five years. Political realists would choose the Council of the European Administration, as being partly elected, partly administrative, and partly corporate. Braver cynics would probably split their opinions between the corporations and the Bureau of Administrative Departments. A few knowledgeable people with a taste for conspiracy might name specific entities, like Int-Sec (I only wish we were that well organized) or Socioanalysis.

Doctor Warrick once told me that the people who really hold the power in the Administration are the Data Division. I laughed and he laughed, and I don't even remember the context, but it made me think. It's the DD that handles most of the ordinary data for the Administration, the vast bulk of the information which is required to maintain daily organization and good government. And where it doesn't control data directly itself, it still controls the means of distribution. All the main routes of data transfer are maintained by the DD, and corporations that run their own secure networks need DD authorization and oversight. The Public Media Division at the Department of Financial and Corporate Affairs issues content provider licenses, but the DD does the hard technical work of monitoring compliance.

The Data Division isn't officially part of any one department. At a casual glance it looks like a bit of an orphan, a dull, donkey-work division nobody wanted. However, it reports, through some mechanism I've never needed to understand, directly to the Bureau of Administrative Departments. That alone ought to tell you how important the bureau thinks the DD is.

Because of the DD, finding someone in the Administration should be easy—there are housing records, movement notification, credit and purchase checks, ID monitoring. Even when someone is trying to stay out of sight, there are the accumulated years of information on their old habits, and it's amazing how often people slip up. The hardest people to find are corporate sabs, because they're professionals and they have corporate resources backing them up, but even then I&I keeps tabs on a surprising number of them.

And without any DD information in this case, we were at sea without a navigation system. So, who knows, maybe Doctor Warrick was right. Maybe data is everything.

When we got back to the section, the Para called Sara into his office with us as we passed her. I don't think he even considered whether or not to tell her everything about the case. The case was technically challenging enough as it was without crippling the nexus of the team.

"Americans?" she said incredulously when he reached that part of the story. "Inside the bureau offices?"

He grinned at her total astonishment, which isn't an expression one often sees on Sara's face. "That's what I thought. Wait until you hear the rest."

The Para outlined the case to Sara, while I chimed in from time to time with the occasional point he missed.

"All right," he said finally. "I'm still not convinced that someone somewhere isn't going to pressure Turnbull into having those two potential pains in our arses kitted out in bureau gear and sent over. So we need to get moving. The moment they show up here, everything will get fifty times harder."

"Give me a list of questions, I'll start finding places to look for answers," Sara said.

How she could possibly do that I had no idea, but I didn't say anything. I know better than to impugn Sara's investigative powers. I was surprised, though, when the Para didn't have any ready suggestions. I wondered, judging from his slightly pained expression, whether he was still trying to pin down the something which felt wrong about the case.

"Why he's here in the first place?" Sara asked after a moment.

"Smith? I don't know," the Para said. "Although... it wasn't in the files they gave us, so it must be something interesting."

"I assumed it was something political, Para," I said.

"So did I. But, actually, we don't know that either, for sure. But that's really two questions, isn't it?" he said, looking at Sara.

"I didn't mean it to be," she said.

"There's why has he run, and then there's why has he run *here*. There have to be easier places in the world to get to than Europe. And easier places to keep out of sight, once you're there. The borders are secure, internal movement is monitored—so why take the risk?"

"Perhaps he thought that the Administration would never cooperate to send him back?" Sara suggested.

He snorted. "Then he's a moron, and it ought to be a piece of piss to find him."

I was still thinking about what he'd said. "Even in the Administration, Para,

175

there are easier places to reach than New London. Security is tighter here than a lot of other cities."

Not just because we're one of the largest cities. The presence of the Int-Sec headquarters here makes us more of a target for resisters than other places.

"True," the Para said. "And I doubt he rowed the Atlantic. Come to think about it, how are they so sure he's in the city at all, if they can't give us any information about where he might be?"

"Maybe he was here already?" Sara suggested, reaching for her screen. "Officially, I mean. If he was, then the entry record might be in the immigration database."

"Image match him," Toreth said.

"Already checking. Just give me a minute."

The Para pulled over a scrap of paper and started making a list, with items under two columns. I've seen him do it before—it's some kind of concept organization system. I've never asked him about the details, but I have noticed that when one column is a lot longer than the other, we're in trouble. In this case, the right-hand column only managed two entries before he sighed and crumpled the paper up. He leaned back in his chair and stared contemplatively at the far wall. I knew better than to interrupt without having anything useful to say.

"Here's something interesting," Sara said. "I found the agents, at least. Carl Ruiz and Sarah Ruth Cardine. Ruiz has been at the embassy for six months. Cardine only arrived this morning. Direct flight from Washington." Her eyes flicked over the screen, picking out information. "And—oh. She's on a temporary assignment. And she isn't using her real title, either—she's a doctor. A psychiatrist."

The Para's eyebrows went up. "Interesting choice for a political criminal."

"Maybe she's from their equivalent of Psychoprogramming," I suggested.

"Oh, wonderful. Just what we need." The Para grimaced. "American mind-fuckers. And I don't see how it gets us any closer to finding Smith, anyway."

Sara took the hint, closing the agents' files and starting a new search.

"If we can get any kind of a fix on where Smith might be, we can trawl informants," I suggested.

The Para nodded. "Not a fast approach, though. Fast would be good. And as you say, we do need somewhere to start."

"Well, it's up to them, isn't it?" I said. The Para frowned at me. "These Americans, I mean. Either they want him found, or they don't. We can explain to them that if they want him that badly, they'll have to give us more to go on."

"And you're volunteering to be the one to go tell Secretary Turnbull we can't do what she asked, right? Want to go now and save us a wasted afternoon?"

I shifted a little on the chair. The Para is perfectly capable of carrying a threat like that through, although I didn't think he'd want to take the hit in prestige so soon. "Uh, no, Para, thanks all the same."

176

He didn't smile. "Well, you'd better come up with something better than that, or I'll be calling you a car."

"I've found him," Sara said, saving my rather crispy bacon with beautiful timing.

"That was fast," the Para said.

"Yes. If you narrow the search pool to Americans only, it's a quick match. Hmm...or maybe not." Over Sara's shoulder I saw her call up the picture we'd been given, and a more official-looking one. "No, that's definitely him, but it isn't the same name. This a security file for Luke Elliot, from the embassy itself. He's here on an internship."

"So that's how they know he's in New London," the Para said. "They paid for his flight."

"I didn't even know that foreign diplomatic staff had security files," I said.

"You'd be surprised what you can find if you know how to ask." Sara spared long enough from the screen to smile at me smugly. "According to the file, he arrived on a diplomatic visa six months ago, with a dispensation to attend some university course under restrictive movement notification. Seems like the visa went through smoothly. No notes to say otherwise on the application file, anyway. Except..." She whistled quietly. "Oh, yes. Oh, wow. This is *good*. Are you ready for a surprise?"

The Para just shook his head at her, clearly not in the mood.

"He's a real VIP," Sara said promptly. "Luke Elliot Junior's father is Luke Elliot Senior, head of Homeland Security."

The departmental name seemed naggingly familiar, but I couldn't recall any detail. "What's that?"

"It's a combination of Int-Sec and Ext-Sec, I think," the Para said. "With some parts of the army thrown in—like the old Department of Security. Interestingly enough, Ruiz works for them, too. Want to put any money on that being a coincidence?"

"Not really, Para." And I was beginning to rethink my ruefulness over missing out on the Selman case. Sticky high-power politics are never fun when you're in the middle of them. "No wonder they want him found fast, and Secretary Turnbull's willing to help."

The Para nodded. "If he's gone political over here, that won't look good for anyone."

"Or I suppose someone could've kidnapped him," Sara said.

"Not a chance. If they had, the American Embassy would be screaming blue bloody murder about it, with his real name." The Para sat up. "So who is this James Smith? If he's anyone."

"Hmm..." Sara scanned pages, opened another document. There aren't many people who can pick out information faster than Sara. "I saw a note somewhere about...ah! Smith is the name he was registered under with the university. And

177

that ID's security file doesn't say anything about whose son he is, or where he's from."

"And no doubt Ruiz and Cardine were hoping we'd somehow hit on the right James Smith in the whole Administration from a photo alone, and hand him over without asking any more questions." The Para snorted. "Genius."

"But on the bright side," Sara said, "now we can make ourselves look *really* good. If James Smith was an official alias, the ID should show up all over the databases after all."

Something had been bothering me since Sara told us the boy's real identity. "Para, if he's this important, don't you think the secretary ought to be told who—'

"No. We find him first. If the Americans catch wind that we know his real name, they'll be stamping all over here whatever Turnbull says. And I'll be surprised if she doesn't know already, anyway."

"Do you really think so?"

The Para shrugged. "The bureau can run pattern matches, too. Probably with even better codes than Sara." He turned back to her. "I'm going to find Nagra and make sure she can keep on top of things until we're done. You two get to work. Check to see if Elliot had the private use of any transport, from the embassy or anywhere else. And when you c&p him, start with the university itself—they're always good places to look for stupid idealists."

Technically, as an admin, Sara isn't supposed to take an active investigatory role in cases. In practice, she does an awful lot of the same work that Mistry or I do, except for visiting scenes and interviewing suspects.

Everyone on the team has told her at one time or another that she's wasted as an admin. She says she likes the job, though, and in lots of ways it's perfect for her: organizing, talking to people, producing information, keeping everything straight and on schedule so that when any of us need anything it's already there. She's definitely the best admin in the section, and probably one of the best in the division.

Lots of people—especially investigators and paras—assume that because she's an admin she isn't as bright as they are. Big, big mistake. Treat Sara like that and she'll eat you for breakfast without even blinking. She might giggle and gossip, but she's sharper than a scalpel.

The paras are all intelligent, too, of course. Perhaps some of the senior investigators are a bit brighter, but that's because there's a wider pool to choose us from. We don't have to have what the paras have: the skill and the stomach for interrogation. That's what makes the difference.

I could never be a para. I've done the introductory interrogation courses, the ones that qualify you for level one and two verbal interrogations, although I got abysmal marks at level two. I've done the interrogation habituation course, and chucked up along with everyone else, and been called a gutless wimp by the instructors. I've sat through a few high-level interrogations, and seen recordings and transcripts. I don't like it, at all, but that's not my job. *My* job is to find the suspects and put them into the interrogation room with enough solid facts to get the waiver the Para or the interrogator in there with them needs to do *their* job.

We're a team.

The trace didn't take long at all, in the end. If Luke Elliot had become mixed up with resisters, he was about to prove a terrible liability to them. As far as I could tell, looking at the credit and purchase records Sara produced, he'd gone about his business like any other law-abiding citizen who doesn't worry that his spending habits will ever be processed as evidence by the Justice systems. He attended his lectures, studied in the library, and went back to the embassy, with detours to sample some highly respectable entertainment complexes. The shopping trips were even preregistered with the movement notification system, as the embassy's terms of operation required. There were no unexplained gaps or unusual patterns; the system could've used him as a pattern for a boring diplomat.

Then, five days before we were called to the bureau, Luke Elliot simply vanished. He arrived at the usual university building, he bought a cup of coffee and a slice of cake midmorning, and then all c&p activity stopped. Dead.

"Do you think he could be dead?" I asked the Para.

"They always could be. And if he isn't, he certainly isn't out on a bender. Not unless he's even better at getting free drinks out of people than Chevril."

"Analysis system's suggestions for regular associates," Sara said, bringing up a new list. "The good news is that there aren't very many. I suppose it must have been a small student group. The bad news is that the course has a high-level rating for corporate security, and the name which pops up on the top of the list as his closest associate, by a long way, is Emile Durant."

The name didn't mean anything to me, but there was one very obvious source of potential trouble. "Important corporate scion?" I guessed.

"Very." Sara waved her hand at the screen. "I opened his movement notification file. He's staying at the New London family house while he studies law here for a year. Before that, he was in the family house in Paris, and before *that,* six months in Lisbon which wasn't in a family house, just some two-level flat they bought for him to use and then sold for more than either of us will make in a lifetime. If you get the picture."

I definitely got it. "If we arrest him we'll be up to our necks in corporate lawyers by morning."

"But we still have to bring him in," the Para said. "Otherwise we're going to look like prize idiots if the whole thing turns out to be political after all."

And the analysis system was fairly clear that Durant was the likeliest candidate to lead us to Elliot's hiding place. Since a few weeks after the start of term, Durant had been taking once- or twice-weekly trips out to an area of New London in which no corporate heir would ordinarily been seen dead. Or rather, might quite likely be seen dead, especially if he had no security with him. Not a good place for a politically important American, either.

Elliot was invariably recorded as being in the university library during these periods, which tend not to be the most difficult buildings from which to make an unobserved exit. Most conclusively, since Elliot's disappearance Durant's trips had become daily, and longer. "Are we going to search the area?" I asked.

"No. It would involve too many people, and the stupid little bastard might run. God knows what would happen to him out there." The Para frowned at the screen for a moment, as though he were hoping it would spontaneously offer some alternative course of action. "Well, at least we don't have to justify it all to Tillotson in advance, this time. We'll monitor Durant's movements, and then, when he takes us back to wherever he's been hiding, we can arrest him and this American, and hopefully anyone they're mixed up with."

Then, somewhat to my surprise, the Para called Secretary Turnbull. I could see the sense behind it, though, on reflection. I watched the screen over his shoulder while he outlined what we'd found. Throughout, she seem entirely unsurprised by the narrative, as though the Para were merely confirming things of which she was already largely confident. I expect that most departmental principal secretaries would make marvelous poker players.

"Do you want us to handle this ourselves and deliver him to the embassy?" the Para asked finally.

"No. I'm going to send Cardine and Ruiz to you—wait until Edwards brings them over before you make any arrests. I want them to go along as witnesses . . . just in case anything goes wrong. Mistakes can happen." She smiled very slightly. "And if one does, please do your best to make sure it doesn't happen to them, too."

In defense of I&I, I can say that although people are sometimes killed whilst resisting arrest, it's very rarely due to a mistake on our part.

"Assuming we find Elliot, what do we do with him?" the Para asked.

"If he hasn't broken any serious laws, and if they want him back right away, then hand him over. If for any reason they don't, then tell them there's a legal process which must be adhered to, and give them the forty-eight-hour time limit as though you'd arrested him during any other investigation."

In other words, get him out of Administration hands sharpish. I was interested to notice that she was aware of the processes we follow. I doubt that the head of Int-Sec itself could've told you off the cuff like that.

"Is there any likely reason they wouldn't want him back?" the Para said.

Secretary Turnbull shrugged very slightly. "I prefer to be clear about these things. It saves time and confusion."

The Para nodded. "The evidence analysis system thinks it's very unlikely he's involved with resisters."

"Do you think he's broken any other laws?"

"I have no idea. Certainly nothing probable we can point to right now."

"Good. Then let's try to wrap this up quickly."

Suddenly, we had the Americans coming to I&I, and one thing which hadn't changed was the Para's prediction that if we tried to put them in an office in General Criminal the place would turn into a three-ring circus. Potentially, an ugly one.

Luckily, there are a lot of side doors and minor access points to I&I. For one thing, there are underground connections to various buildings in the Int-Sec complex, and there are a few other covered walkways at various levels connecting us to nearby buildings. I don't know where half the ways in are, and I've worked here for years.

Getting our guests in without causing too much of a fuss was one thing. Keeping them quiet was something else. Of course, it turned out that the Para had planned ahead and asked Sara to reserve one of the level C lockdown security suites used for unusually dangerous or exceptionally politically sensitive prisoners. Basically, they consist of a small number of cells and interrogation rooms, plus medical facilities, in a self-contained unit. Most of them even have an office or two, so that whichever team is working there has somewhere to meet. All I&I units across Europe have at least one, but in New London we have more than most. The most important prisoners are usually moved here from across the Administration as we have the best-quality interrogators.

We installed the Americans in one of the smaller suites, with only two cells and an interview room in addition to their office. (Any interrogation of the prisoner would be their problem, presumably taking place somewhere else.) Best of all, Sara had found a route down from the closest ground-level access door giving us only minimal risk of them running into anyone on the way there.

So of course, fifteen minutes later, while we were still running through the plan of arrest with Ruiz and Cardine, someone knocked on the door then opened it right away, even though I could've sworn that the Para had locked it behind him.

The moment of panic subsided immediately when I saw who had interrupted us. Probably the only person who could open absolutely any door in the building at will—the head of security.

I'm not exaggerating when I say that HoS Bevan knows everything that happens at I&I. Or at least, I've never heard of him being caught out by something he doesn't know. His compilation of amusing I&I security recordings, shown every year at the New Year party, are a legend even beyond I&I. Nothing legendary was required here, though. No one just sneaks into I&I, and certainly not down here on the interrogation levels; the Americans must have been given some official cover for being in the place. Whatever it was had obviously tweaked Bevan's curiosity.

"Toreth," Bevan said, and glanced around the room. Long-faced, with thinning dark hair that somehow always manages to be in need of a trim, Bevan never looks to be in anything other than a bad temper, and looks don't very often deceive with him. He spotted me, gave me a disparaging once-over, and dismissed me. Then he looked more closely at the Americans. They were still in their suits, with the IDs issued by the bureau on display, but unfortunately there was still something indefinable about them which said "not from around here."

"Bev?" The Para raised his eyebrows. "Did someone double-book the lockdown?"

"Oh, I'm sorry. I didn't know there were visitors in here." Ignoring the Para, Bevan held out his hand to Ruiz. "Nice to meet you. I'm Head of I&I Security Bev Bevan."

Automatically, Ruiz stood up. "Agent Carl Ruiz. From the, er—" He shook Bevan's hand without finishing the sentence.

Bevan looked between the agents. "Are you American, too?" he asked Cardine.

She nodded, and then caught herself too late. Bevan almost smiled—at least, the lines on his face briefly lifted into something less sour.

"Fuck me. I knew it had to be something good, with a bureau car suddenly showing up here, but I wasn't expecting that."

"I need this kept quiet," the Para said. "I'm serious, Bev."

Bevan merely waited.

"I'll owe you a favor. A large favor."

"Which means that whatever *you're* getting out of it must be bloody good," Bevan said.

The Para shrugged. "Commendation from the bureau. I hope."

"Huh." Bevan's expression soured even more, which I wouldn't have believed possible. "I should've been told. This is taking the piss—I'm supposed to be head of security. How is having *them* here not a security issue?"

"I don't even have an investigation in progress," the Para said. "It's a favor job, off the books. You remember the Selman case? I only got tapped for this because someone on the council knows I can keep my mouth shut when I ought to."

"Of course," Bevan said. "The bureau *and* the council. That's just like you, you jammy bastard. You could fall in shit and come up smelling of fucking roses."

I honestly thought that Agent Cardine was going to have a seizure. However their Department of Homeland Security operated, vivid language from senior management didn't appear to be a feature.

"Come on, Bev," the Para said. "Do you really want to spend the next couple of days chasing people out of places they shouldn't be just because they're trying to find out what's going on down here?"

I wondered, suddenly, if the Para had foreseen this and that was why he'd chosen the high-security suite.

"I suppose not."

"Good," the Para said, like that was settled, and the HoS didn't protest. "Anyway, I'm glad you're here. I wanted to talk to you about something."

The Para had Bevan handpick us a group of security guards he considered trustworthy and discreet. The first quality could only be tested by time, but they were certainly discreet enough not to try to talk to the Americans, although in the transport from I&I I caught them making covert examinations more than once.

The building we eventually arrived at looked like exactly the kind of place you'd find someone who was hiding from the movement notification laws: run down to the point of being virtually derelict if there hadn't been signs of occupation, and in a part of town so shabby that surveillance was thin. They were old houses, prereconstruction, an odd collection of very small two-level houses in a long line with adjoining walls. The effect, I suppose, is something like a block of flats, only side by side rather than piled up. "Terraces," the style is called, and these days they're only found in very old parts of the city, or new places where people want to show off that they can afford to waste the land.

Old, dirty brown paper had been taped over the inside of the windows in lieu of curtains, but the scanners had no problem reading through the thin walls that the only two bodies in the place were upstairs.

When we opened the building's back door, I felt even more confident we had the right address. Despite the overall shabbiness, the kitchen wasn't filthy. There were plenty of touches which suggested someone with money had been staying here: a small, gleaming portable stove on the side, two glasses on the table, one of which held wine and the other something clear, and the remains of a takeaway Indo-French meal which smelled rather appetizing. The bag it had come in was made of thick, very white paper, with a string handle and the name of the restaurant embossed in silver on the side.

The stairs had been strengthened with some amateurish carpentry, and we progressed carefully upstairs. There were guards waiting on both sides of the building, and a helicopter on standby to track the boys if they tried to run, but everything that risked attracting more attention was something we wanted to avoid.

As it turned out, we'd drastically overprepared. We found them in the first room we tried.

They were lying on the bed together and, well, they weren't sleeping, but I wasn't surprised they hadn't heard us arrive. I recognized the Durant boy right away. He was lying on his back, and he had his face turned towards us—a coincidence, I think, since when the door first opened he had his eyes closed and his mouth open as he moaned very enthusiastically. The boy with him had his head down at Durant's crotch, and his hair hanging down obscuring his face; I didn't get a clear look at him right away, but he fitted Elliot's general description.

It didn't last long, of course, not with us crashing in through the door. One of them screamed, from surprise I think.

They tried to run, but that's never a good idea when you're seminaked and off-balance, and the house is full of trained I&I security. Elliot made it about five steps from the bed. Because the officers were concentrating on the big prize, the other boy dodged past us and out onto the landing before someone knocked him to the ground.

It wasn't until the crashing stopped that I remembered to check on our American allies. I'd expected them to look pleased, but instead they couldn't have looked more horrified if they'd found their wayward student chopped up in pieces on the floor. Cardine picked up a pair of trousers from the clothes scattered on the floor, and all but threw them at Elliot. His face was bright red, but he let them drop to the ground.

"Cover yourself up," she snapped, even though he was still wearing his underwear.

"I'm not gonna go back to the embassy," Elliot said.

"If you would please cooperate, Luke," Ruiz said, "the car will be outside by now. Otherwise, we'll have to ask these gentlemen to restrain you."

"I told you, I'm not gonna go back." He was still flushed, his eyes wide. "Never."

Ruiz looked to be about to say something else, but Cardine stepped up close to him and whispered something in his ear which made him close his mouth again.

"Secretary Turnbull suggested Luke could be taken to I&I," Cardine said to the Para. "We'd like to exercise that option, if we may."

Ruiz nodded, uncertainly at first, then more firmly. "That sounds like a real good idea."

"Don't say anything to them, Luke." Two guards were dragging Durant back into the room, but when he heard Elliot's voice he stopped resisting and practically pulled them in with him. "Remember what we talked about. Everything will be okay."

"Cuff them both," the Para said to the nearest guard. He looked at the pair, still trouserless, then shook his head. "Get them dressed, first." As he turned away, I heard him mutter, "Bloody students."

184

The Para doesn't have the highest opinion of academia. I suppose that, statistically, universities do have a greater incidence of idealism and borderline re-sister-types than strict random chance would suggest, but on the other hand, I've heard it argued—quietly—that it's simply a part of their historical traditions. You won't find many senior paras willing to see it like that, though. If you took a poll at I&I, they'd probably vote to close them all down, at the very least. Those of us at I&I who actually attended university don't mention it too often in the coffee rooms.

I suppose that when I was hanging around in the student union, I heard some rather questionable statements made. And one or two of our professors probably only kept their jobs, and maybe more than that, by virtue of having the kind of so-cial standing which makes arrest complicated. A lot of old corporate money has ties to the better sorts of university, and they don't like their alma mater to be made to look bad.

Incidentally, of those expressing their risky opinions, I know of several who now have jobs inside the Administration and have probably forgotten all about the things they said back them. Luckily, I suppose, no one else remembers either, or they don't care to make it into anything official. Everyone is young and stupid once, and left alone most of us grow out of it. Of course, it's the minority who don't who cause all the trouble for the majority of good, loyal citizens. And that, as my mother would say, is why we sometimes can't have nice things.

We separated the prisoners in the cars on the way back to I&I, sticking to the standard procedures. The Americans took Luke Elliot, and Durant went back with us. He looked older than the nineteen his file claimed, a combination of very adult calm and a slightly receding hairline. He didn't cry (which happens more often than not, in my experience) or raise his voice, or try to threaten us with his family, which spoiled corporate kids sometimes do before they realize how much trouble they're in. The only thing he said on the journey was to claim his corporate status, and ask to see a warrant. He read it carefully; I hoped he hadn't been too thor-oughly trained by his family security because, in actuality, we had no grounds for a formal arrest.

Back at I&I, I took Durant down to processing while the Para went off, pre-sumably to make his report to Secretary Turnbull. Other divisions at I&I seemed to be busy with real cases, because it took me almost half an hour to get the process finished and Durant installed in his cell. Elliot was already secure in the lockdown suite, having bypassed processing entirely.

185

Then I went for a cup of coffee and a snack. I'd missed my lunch and the case seemed to be wrapping up nicely, so I felt I deserved it. Since it wasn't my regular break time, I ran into a group of investigators from my training year whom I don't see often, so I might've spent a little longer than usual in there. I finished my second cup of coffee quickly, though, when I got an irritated call from the Para, wanting to know where the hell I was.

When I walked into the Para's office, I could tell something had gone wrong. "Who was out there watching this bloody kid?" the Para was demanding as I arrived. "Didn't we have anyone looking for surveillance when we picked him up?"

"He probably had a panic link," Sara said. "Or he missed sending in a safety check."

"Don't any corporates let their kids take a fucking piss without needing a report?"

"Think how many more kidnappings we'd end up with if they didn't," Sara said placatingly. Which was a valid point—everyone here hates kidnappings, because they're so tricky to close successfully and so messy when things go wrong. "Anyway," she added, "*my* mum and dad would've had me calling in on a schedule, too, if they could've made me do it."

Most kids of rich corporates live rather proscribed lives. I think it's why so many of them go somewhat crazy when they finally make it to university. "Emile Durant's lawyers are firing up?" I guessed.

"Fired," the Para said. "The first batch of files already arrived."

"They're demanding immediate access to their client," Sara said.

Technically, I&I always has twenty-four hours before we have to let anyone other than a Justice rep talk to any suspect or witness we arrest. However, with a corporate-status citizen and no actual IIP, we were on a rather sticky wicket.

"Surely we can charge him with something?" I said.

"Like what?" the Para asked. "Screwing an American? I suppose the lawyers might choke to death laughing, which would buy us a few hours. Did you have a screen done for illegal pharmaceuticals when they processed him in?"

"Yes," I said. "Nothing there, Para, sorry."

"He must be the only student in the Administration it wouldn't pick up." The Para drained his coffee. "But then, according to his lawyers, he has some kind of medical condition which means he's teetotal and strictly vegetarian. They want a list of everything he's been offered to eat and drink since he arrived, and another list of anything we're proposing to feed him. All ingredients." He replaced the empty mug on the desk rather hard. "Bloody corporates and their bloody lawyers. And their bloody kids, too."

Or not so bloody, in this case. The only good news was that whatever protein shows up in the prisoners' meals down on the detention levels can very rarely be related to any identifiable animal species, probably even with a DNA screen.

"What do we do with him, though?" Sara asked, ever practical. "The senior security officer wants to know about Justice rep access."

The Para pondered for a while, finger tapping silently on the edge of his desk. Then he looked up at me. "B-C? What do you think?"

He wasn't trying to shift responsibility for the decision; that always rests with the lead investigator on a case, and whatever the Para's other faults, I've never known him try to blame anyone else for a mistake in judgment he's made. I think sometimes he just likes to check that we're awake and keeping up with the case.

I weighed it up for a few seconds; the Para watched me, willing to wait.

"We still don't know for certain what they were doing there, but there was nothing that suggested resister activity to me. Durant doesn't have any even low-level associations. Odds are, the American boy is bored with the embassy, and he just wanted some fun while he was over here. So there's no point antagonizing any corporates over it. I'd say hand Durant over to his lawyers."

"I agree," the Para said. Something flashed on his screen, and he glanced at it and grimaced. "Hopefully before they kill the systems with paperwork."

Letting Durant go was one of those decisions which is difficult because there's a conflict between the optimal choice for the case in hand and one of the many other pressures we work under at I&I. If it turned out that there was some political background to the American boy's disappearing act, then we were probably losing our best lead and giving Durant time to warn anyone else involved of the danger. It's hard to recover a case from a setback like that. But a lot of the skill in running investigations at I&I, even in a section like General Criminal, is knowing when to give ground gracefully.

People sometimes talk as though it were possible to get rid of the corporates, which is insane, of course. It's not just political criminals, either, although many of them have a grievance against what they call "corporate privilege." They might be surprised to find how many I&I employees feel the same.

Anyone can own a business, but official corporate status is granted to a company by the Administration. It has to be applied for through the right departments, and earned. Or, so people will tell you, bought. It's a routine formality for the large European corporations, and the European branches of the multinationals, less so for smaller and starting corporations. However, that's all more a Corporate Fraud area than General Criminal.

Corporate status buys standing in the business community, tax breaks of all kinds, access to Administration contracts—you name it, it starts with incorporation. There's also some payback, because corporations provide a lot of basic social benefits for unfortunate citizens. It's a system based on what's best for Europe and the people of Europe. At least that's the theory.

Once granted incorporation itself, the corporation can decide how many of its employees it deems worthy of benefiting from that privilege. Corporate-graded jobs are generally better paid, with better benefits and more security, and more social status. It makes a difference in a lot of areas—applying for a reproduction license is a classic one. In fact, rumor would have it that noncorporates have no chance, which is patently ridiculous if you look at the birthrate. It is true, though, that a lot of the nicer housing complexes will only take tenants with a corporate grading on their ID.

Incidentally, that's not something I've ever had to worry about—I've worked for the Administration all my life, and they pay for my housing, my medical insurance, and all the rest of it. As part of Int-Sec, we at I&I generally get better gradings than a lot of other departments—the governmental equivalent of corporate privilege, and probably just as badly resented by others.

Corporate status also grants better legal protection than is enjoyed by the mass of citizens, and not just in employment law. That's where a lot of the I&I ill will against corporations comes from. A note of corporate status in a suspect's security file means that we can expect independent legal reps showing up to make our lives harder. There are differences in criminal charges and sentencing, too. A lot of nonviolent, nonpolitical crimes are downgraded to a lower category for corporate-status criminals—they're contributing to the prosperity of Europe, after all, so expensive re-education or restrictive detention makes no sense when they could be fined or given social service requirements instead.

As I&I's raison d'être is dealing with politically important crimes, a large percentage of the witnesses and suspects we handle can claim corporate status. Sometimes we can work around that—corporations are often willing to dump an employee who is about to cause them embarrassment. Sometimes we can remove corporate status outright, which is automatic for serious political crimes or provable obstruction of investigations. Rarely, the Administration will strip a whole corporation of corporate rights, but I mean *rarely*. The corporations don't take kindly to it, and they administer their own version of the law, the corporate accords.

And, however resented corporate privilege is at I&I, and however much the Para and others mutter about it, the ultimate truth is that we have to respect the corporations. They're part of Europe, just as we are.

At that point, I thought the investigation was more or less over. We'd produced the Americans' straying sheep, and rather promptly, too, which ought to win us some golden opinions. In any case, we didn't have much left to do while we waited for the Americans to talk to Luke Elliot and determine what had happened to him during his absence.

The Para went off somewhere, to deal with some business that wasn't any of my business. He's never been very interested in the psych specialists at I&I, and he always says that with specialists, results matter more than processes. I was curious about what had really happened to the boy, though. When I asked Sara for the code to the lockdown feed, she handed it over without comment, although I suspect she knew I was just being nosy.

I watched it upstairs, in my office. I didn't know if the Americans knew we could see what they were doing. If *I* were interrogating a prisoner somewhere like I&I, I'd assume everything I did was open to scrutiny, but I suppose it depends on their own working practices.

I'm no interrogation expert, but I've seen my share. By the time I started watching the feed, it was obvious they'd been at it for a while. Luke Elliot didn't look especially scared—less scared than most I&I prisoners, certainly—but he did look miserable and somewhat pouty. It's a look I've seen on a lot of corporate kids. I don't know much about how the American departmental system functions, but his security file seemed to indicate that Luke Elliot Senior's family had substantial funds and he was rather more of a corporate figure than one would expect to find as an Administration top-level bureaucrat.

"But you do know what you did was wrong, Luke, don't you?" Cardine said.

Elliot looked down at the table, refusing to meet her gaze.

"I can see that you do. And you know, too, that God still loves you, even if you've done these terrible things. It was your choice to turn your back on Him, and you can choose to come back to Him." She put her hand on his shoulder. From the perspective of the camera, I could see the grimace on her face when she touched him. "He will forgive you. And then, after that, we can start to get you well, again."

"There's nothing wrong with me," he said, low. "I don't have cancer, or something. I'm just attracted to men, that's all."

"Luke—"

"The only thing that's wrong is that I *do* feel like it's wrong, and yeah, okay, sure I do, but that isn't my fault."

"Of course not," she said. "There are temptations we all have to struggle against. Tests of faith. But you're still sick, Luke."

"No, I'm *not*." His head moved, like he'd almost lifted it, but he kept staring down. "If you'd heard all your life that wanting guys was an abomination, you'd hate being that way, too, but I promise you, it still wouldn't make you want girls. And I don't have to let people like you make it worse, not anymore."

Cardine took a couple of steps back, and I could see her thinking, reassessing her approach in the face of his intransigence. I've heard some of the paras say that level one and two interrogations—questioning only, and verbal intimidation—actually require more skill than the higher levels where interrogators have more tools available.

"Don't you want to be able to go home?" Cardine asked him. "We've been getting calls from your mom and dad every day. They were so happy when we said we'd found you. They just want you back."

"Like this? Really? I don't exactly see my dad rolling out a red carpet. I'd rather stay here." Finally, he looked up at her. "With Emile."

"And do you honestly never want to see them again? Because that's what staying here means. How about your grandparents? And Mary-Ann? She's only four— how are they gonna explain that her big brother doesn't want to be there for her?"

"Like even if I went home, they'd ever let me near Mary again."

"Maybe not, no, not right away. You can fix that, though, if you just accept that you need to change, and let us help you."

"I don't want your *help*. And I'm fine the way I am. What I *want* is for you all to leave me the fuck alone. Where's Emile?"

"They're letting him go. He's leaving right now."

"No." For the first time, his gaze flickered around the room, as though he were looking for hidden cameras. Maybe he thought Emile was watching. "He wouldn' leave me here." He sat up a little straighter. "He loves me."

This time I don't think she even tried to hide the disgust on her face. "Luke, seriously? You can't believe a word people like that tell you. His whole life is built on lies and deception."

"It isn't. Not over here. We ate lunch together every day and—and he put his hand on my leg, sometimes, and kissed me, and no one even *cared*. He says his mom and dad want to meet me, despite where I'm from."

Her eyebrows went up. "I'm sure he *said* that. But…don't you think you're taking kind of a rosy view of life in Europe?" Cardine looked deliberately around the room.

Elliot stood up. "If you take me back, I'll tell everyone what I did. All about Emile."

"Luke, you can't—"

"I'll talk to the news, I'll put it all over the 'net. And if you try to stop me, i Dad has me locked up someplace for *therapy*, I'll still find someone who'll do it for me. You know there's gonna be enough money in it for them."

"Don't be ridiculous," she said. "You know what would happen to you."

"I don't care. Or, okay, maybe I do, but I care a lot less than my dad will. Go on, ask him if he wants his disgusting pervert son telling everyone how good it feels to—"

"Luke!"

He laughed at her. "See? He has way more to lose than I do. You go off back to the embassy and you tell him that. I'm done talking to you."

Not entirely to my surprise, it wasn't long after the interview finished that the Americans called us down. Having watched the interview I had some idea of what to expect, but it took the Para, and probably Sara, a while to entirely grasp their problems.

"Let me see if I understand this." The Para rubbed his forehead, like he had a headache. "What they were doing is illegal in America. Criminal."

Ruiz nodded. "Sodomy is a felony."

"They weren't—" the Para started, then apparently thought better of it. "It's perfectly legal here," he said instead.

"That might've been a defense in the past, but according to the current law it doesn't make any difference whether it happens at home or on foreign soil. And there could be serious political repercussions if this became public knowledge."

"I won't tell anyone if you won't," the Para said. I think he was still annoyed that our record-breaking location hadn't been enough, and the case hadn't magically vanished once we'd brought the boy back to I&I, leaving nothing but a warm glow of commendations on all our files. Since there was absolutely zero evidence of any resister connection, the case was otherwise a dud for us.

Ruiz did not look amused.

"But Luke will tell," Cardine said. "In fact, he's adamant that he won't keep quiet, despite the penalties."

"Penalties?" I asked.

"Prison," Ruiz said. "Since Luke is young, and this is a first offense, and his father can afford the best attorneys, and they may be able to persuade a judge that he was led astray by foreigners—" Ruiz cleared his throat. "Well, I guess it might be as little as five years or so."

"This guy he was with, he's French, right?" Agent Cardine asked.

"His family comes from the French region," Sara said from the sidelines, always ready with a helpful fact. "Strasbourg."

One of the cities rather notoriously devastated in the bombings, happening as they did during the large Christmas market that used to be held there, but the Americans probably didn't know that. Cardine merely made a satisfied "hm" noise, as though Durant's geographic origins somehow strengthened the scenario Ruiz had outlined.

"Still, none of that changes the political effects," Ruiz said. "Elliot Senior is the best director we've ever had, but there's an election coming up next year, and no one with that kind of deviancy in his family stands a chance in hell of keeping a sensitive appointment."

I looked between him and the Para. Clearly, Ruiz had no idea whatsoever about the Para's personal life. I suddenly felt very glad that the two Americans had been kept away from the General Criminal coffee room, where half the division would no doubt have taken great delight in enlightening them and watching their reactions. Someone would probably have sold tickets.

191

The Para, of course, didn't even blink. "Can't you just have the story killed in advance?"

To, I think, all our surprises, the agents seemed as shocked by that as by anything. "America has a free press," Cardine said. "Once a story has gotten out, there's no stopping it. And Luke seems very determined that will happen."

"So change his mind," the Para said. "I thought you were supposed to be a psychiatrist? If you need any drugs, I'm sure the pharmacy can help."

"Modern psychiatric practice is rooted in faith," she said. "No one can have a whole mind unless he accepts Jesus Christ as his savior."

The Para's mouth moved, as though he were heading for a word starting with "W," and then he clearly thought better of it. He looked as baffled as I felt.

"And in the condition he's in now..." Cardine actually shuddered. "It's only to be expected in a place which outlaws God," she added, her voice suddenly savage.

It took me a moment to work out what she meant. "It isn't illegal to be religious," I said. "Who told you that?"

"No one observes the Christian holidays, I know that much."

"Well, no. The Administration government is secular, so the official holidays are secular, too."

"And everyone at the embassy says the same thing—mention prayer over here, and everyone will look at you like you grew an extra head."

"Well, yes. Praying." Even though we were in a secure suite at I&I, I found myself looking around to see who might be nearby. Honestly, I couldn't help it, and for the first time the reaction struck me as odd. I suppose it's like questioning any other social assumption with which one has grown up. "Most people would know better than to, I don't know—talk in the coffee room about whatever their private beliefs might be, or something like that. It would make the people they were with uncomfortable, at least. And it wouldn't do much for your chances of a promotion."

"So it might as well be outlawed," she said.

"No, not at all. Just try doing something which *is* illegal, you'll soon see the difference. Religion is...well. The closest equivalent is probably speaking anything other than English as your first language at home. People will think it's unusual." I shrugged. "Some might even consider it a somewhat political activity. And some wouldn't, of course. But it's usually mentioned in security files."

And I suppose that tells you something. It certainly seemed to confirm Cardine's opinions.

"The embassy will be holding the university responsible for what happened to that boy there," she said. "He was supposed to be educated, not *defiled.*"

"Well, to be blunt, that isn't an I&I problem," the Para said. "Or it won't be once the paperwork is done. Do you want him transferred right away?"

"We can't take him." Ruiz looked horrified. "As soon as he's back in the em-

192

bassy building there's a chance the story will leak out. He has to stay isolated here until we figure out what to do with him. His family needs to be consulted—and others."

"And Secretary Turnbull was quite emphatic that we hold him for as long as an initial investigative arrest allows, and no longer." The Para paused. "That's the day after tomorrow, by the way, unless you want us to charge him. I'm sure we can find something if we look hard enough."

"Of course we don't want him charged!" Cardine said. "We want him kept safe. He's a vulnerable young man—clearly he is, or he would never have been led astray like this. His reputation, and his father's reputation, have to be protected until this...business can be resolved."

To be honest, that isn't the usual sort of reason we have people at I&I. The Administration justice system does have options to apply to people the powers that be don't want to have making public statements in the future, but they tend to be rather more final than I imagined the Americans wanted.

We all stared at one another, with the mutual incomprehension of people from alien cultures. Clearly, the Americans wanted us to find some miracle solution to their wayward problem child. Just as clearly, we couldn't. I felt quite sure that Secretary Turnbull would have no intention of letting them leverage the bureau's apparent desire to unthaw transatlantic relationships into something which could come back to embarrass the Administration in the future.

We were still at an impasse when someone knocked on the door. I wondered about Bevan, again, but when the Para opened it, it was someone else. He seemed vaguely familiar, and when he spoke I realized it was one of the admins from prisoner processing.

"Something's come up with your prisoner, Para." He glanced at the two Americans.

"Tell me here," the Para said.

"It's Emile Durant. He, uh. He won't leave," the admin said.

"Won't what?"

I understood the Para's bemusement. In all my years here, I don't think I've heard of a single prisoner refusing to walk out on a free release.

"I thought he had lawyers crawling all over the place?" the Para said.

"No question about that, Para, and they're telling him the same thing we are. They've signed all the forms. But he won't budge from processing. He wants to see Luke Elliot first."

I didn't need to look over my shoulder to know how the Americans reacted. Two chairs scraped across the floor, and Ruiz said, "Oh, hell, no. Not a chance. Listen to me, you keep that sick—"

The Para turned around sharply and pointed at them. "This isn't your division, and you don't give orders. Wait here. I'll sort this."

He strode out, pushing the admin ahead of him. Sara scurried after him as smartly as me. Maybe she'd also guessed what he was planning to do. Once outside, he closed the office door and locked it. All doors in a lockdown suite have external security locks; that's why they're called lockdowns.

I just hoped we'd be back before either of the Americans thought to try the door.

Durant was as calm in the small side room in the processing area as he had been in the car, and during the half an hour I'd spent with him before. But now, with a top-class corporate lawyer backing him up, he was a lot more talkative.

"Luke doesn't have anyone else to look after his interests," Durant said.

"Mr. Elliot's interests are being represented by officers from the American Embassy," the Para said.

Durant snorted. "As if. Our family lawyers will be acting as his representatives from now on."

The lawyer, a rather unnervingly pleasant man who'd introduced himself as Linden, nodded. "My office has put in official applications on behalf of our new client."

"You have no legal authority to act for him," the Para said.

"And you have no legal grounds to hold him," Durant said. "Luke hasn't done anything wrong. He hasn't even been anywhere except the university and the squat. I'm staying here until we get to see him."

I suddenly remembered something that Sara had said at the first case meeting. Taking a few steps away, I opened my hand screen and hunted through the case files. Not only does Sara have an almost supernatural talent for finding facts, but she organizes them beautifully, too.

"Listen to me," the Para said to Linden. "You're free to send as many applications as you like—from your offices. But if Mr. Durant isn't gone from here in ten minutes, I'm going to charge him with impeding an investigation and I'll strip his corporate standing from him. You can see him again after the re-education."

Linden smoothed down his hair; pale blond and very fine, it seemed prone to drift out of alignment in the slightest draft. "Under the circumstances, since you've been unwilling to provide a formal investigation in progress, an adequate warrant, or even a charge, that would seem to be a rather irregular application of the regulations."

"Try me," the Para said.

I think he was bluffing, although one of the Para's rules is never make a threat you won't carry through. In any case, I stepped forwards before Linden could test his resolve.

"Elliot left the embassy under restrictive movement notification," I said. "Traveling anywhere beyond the designated locations, even within New London, falls outside the terms under which it was granted."

"That's a level one—"

"*Restrictive* notification," I emphasized.

"Level two, then." Being interrupted seemed to make him snappy. "Is that really an I&I matter?"

"Whether it is or not, it's still a charge," the Para said. "In the next forty-eight hours he gets access to a Justice rep. Maybe. We'll have to see what Justice makes of us charging an American citizen, and whether they want to touch it. And right now, you're all leaving."

The Para walked to the door and opened it, calling over the guards waiting outside. "Get these people out of here. Cuff them, if you have to. In fact, I don't give a shit if you put them in full body restraints and drag them all the way to the Int-Sec front gates, but they leave."

Durant folded his arms. "You wouldn't dare."

This time, though, I was quite sure the Para wasn't bluffing. Linden apparently believed the same; he put his hand on his client's shoulder.

"They know someone's paying attention, now, Emile. He isn't alone. Let's get you home."

The Para watched them go, his face still grim. Then he turned to me and smiled warmly. "Nice job, B-C—well done. Good thinking, there."

"Thank you, Para."

I'm taller than the Para. Not many people realize that. It's not much, just a few centimeters, but if you asked the other staff in the section, my guess is that half of them would say he was taller, and most of the rest simply wouldn't know. Perhaps the rest of the team would get it right, but I'm not sure even with them.

Not that he's short. Not tremendously tall, but on the high side of average. He's broader than I am, more heavily muscled, but the real difference is attitude. I'm quiet—too quiet sometimes, but that's why we have diversity in the team. I'm excellent with detail, and I can observe without attracting too much attention.

The Para, in contrast, is one of the most physically confident people I know, and I think that's what gives the illusion of height. He has incredible presence. Charisma, if you like. You'd think it would be normal amongst the senior paras, given that they're team leaders and they have to talk to the ordinary citizens so much, but it's not as common as you might think. They can all do at least one thing very well—scare people, say, or argue their way through opposition, or sweet-talk to get what they want—but not all of them have such a broad repertoire.

When the Para fires up the charm it's amazing to watch, for those of us who know what he's really like. He can exude a real interest in whatever people are telling him, too. It's all a performance. He can do the opposite just as readily—turn all the warmth into intimidation. There's a lot less acting involved in that, I think

He's frightened me on occasion. I think he's frightened all of us at some time even Sara: when he's focused on a case, when some corporate higher-up has made him- or herself untouchable, or when internal politics prevents him from doing his job. I don't think I've ever seen him genuinely lose control of his temper though. I know I wouldn't want to, even if it was directed well away from me.

When Emile Durant had been taken away by his lawyer, still protesting, and the Americans had left to go back to their embassy for the night under Edwards's escort, still grumbling, the three of us retreated to the Para's office. As we crossed the section's general office, I glanced at everyone we passed, waiting for whispers or other signs of unusual interest. I didn't spot anything, but after the kerfuffle at prisoner processing it was probably only a matter of time before the whole building knew something odd was going on.

With the door closed, we put together a quick report and sent it off to Secretary Turnbull. We were into the evening by now, but she didn't seem like the kind of civil servant who kept strict office hours.

The most optimistic piece of news for a fast and painless resolution to the situation was that Durant's lawyers had no legal mechanism for getting to their new client before the deadline came for his hand-over back to the Americans. But—

"What if Ruiz and Cardine refuse to take Elliot back when the deadline expires, Para?" I asked when he'd sent off the file.

"Then I'll have *him* put in full body restraints and thrown through the embassy doors. Even if they don't open them."

It's often hard to tell with the Para whether he's joking or not.

"Unless they manage to talk Secretary Turnbull into ordering us to keep him here longer," Sara said. "They're bound to try it, and from what they said she'd be doing them a pretty big favor."

Which seemed like exactly the kind of thing the secretary might want. Passing unwanted or difficult prisoners around between divisions or sections is sometimes called prisoner ping-pong. Justice plays it very enthusiastically. I couldn't say I was looking forward to being in the middle of a game of state-level prisoner ping-pong, especially now that we had a corporate player muscling in, too. When your metaphorical game has four sides, it can't end well.

Sara was still frowning at her screen. "I should probably talk to them about extending that lockdown booking, just in case."

196

"The problem is," I said, "the restrictive notification charge has given the embassy an excuse to leave Elliot here. I should've thought of that before I suggested it."

"That isn't the problem. I haven't even put the charge through, yet." The Para stretched, then pushed himself to his feet. "The problem *is*, they're all fucking mad."

Sara and I looked at one another, agreeing silently.

"Right. The important thing is, we did what Turnbull asked. We found him. Good job, both of you." The Para pulled his heavy coat on over his jacket, and patted the pockets, looking for gloves. "And now I'm going to go find a bar and get drunk, and then I plan to spend the rest of the evening making myself a criminal in the eyes of the American law. Maybe in the morning, this will all look less insane."

I thought it sounded like an excellent plan—at least minus the sodomy, which isn't really my cup of tea.

Actually, I have had sex with a man, just the once. That's not quite the non sequitur it seems. I bring it up because, indirectly, it proved to be the key to solving the whole problem. I never told Agents Cardine or Ruiz that, though. I don't think they would've found it very funny.

I'd been qualified for about six months when it happened. The occasion was an I&I party, around at somebody's flat. I won't say whose. I'm not a big partygoer, but it had been a good night. I'd risked taking my then-girlfriend along—Vanessa, her first name was—because it was mostly junior staff without many paras of any rank. No interrogators. At one point we had a visit from building security asking us to break it up, but the hostess invited the guard in. The last I saw of him, he was accepting a shot glass from Daedra Kincaidy, which is never a good idea unless you have a substance testing system with you.

There was no real decision for everyone to stay; it was more that people gradually fell asleep where they were, conversations growing quieter and quieter until they faded out completely. For a while after I dozed off, I was woken by people still talking and laughing in the bedroom, but in the end even that stopped. Come to think of it, that might have had something to do with Daedra, too—I remember a faint smell in the air like burned sugar, and she always likes to experiment with a big crowd.

After a couple of hours' sleep, the discomfort woke me up. I was completely dressed from the waist down, but I'd taken all the top layers off to use as a pillow. The room was heated by all the bodies there, and Vanessa was keeping one side of me warm, but not having a duvet to burrow under felt odd. We'd spread our coats out underneath us and there was a carpet, but the floor was still hard. My shoulder blades felt like they were trying to drill a hole through into the flat below.

There was a sofa, and the man who'd grabbed that had taken possession of a blanket as well, which was unfair. As I thought about that, I automatically turned my head to look at him. I could see him quite clearly. The hall light was on, because people kept getting up to stumble to the toilet, and even with the light, they always left a trail of curses as they stepped on sleeping bodies.

The occupant of the sofa was awake. He had one arm behind his head and one knee up against the back of the sofa. He'd kicked the blanket off, and I could see the muscles in his thigh picked out in the light from the door. They were tensing and relaxing, pressing against the sofa, and it took me a couple more seconds to notice his arm moving. Then it took me another moment to believe that he really was masturbating right there in a room full of people he knew. It seems strange now that I was surprised but, as I said, I'd only been qualified for six months.

And then, when I'd processed it and started to look at him more carefully...

I don't find men attractive. I'm not revolted by the idea of sex with a man, the idea just leaves me completely cold. It's like suggesting getting intimate with a chair or a table. However, there was something about the voyeuristic aspect, the invasion of someone else's privacy, especially someone I knew, that did turn me on. As I've said, I'm a good observer. I like to watch and notice things.

It didn't take me long to see variations in the rhythm he was using. Because of our relative heights, I couldn't actually see his hand or his cock, and maybe that was a contributing factor to not being put off, because that is the one thing that makes it really difficult to forget that you're looking at a man. He didn't seem to be in any hurry, and he must have been aware of the possibility of people waking up and seeing him. I decided he just didn't care, and that eased away the couple of twinges of guilt I had as I watched. He had his mouth open slightly and his lips were moving, although I couldn't catch a single word.

Finally, his head went back, the dim light picking out the cords in his neck, and he breathed out on a long, near-silent sigh, little shudders running through him. From the floor, I couldn't see anything that would get an adult viewing classification, but there wasn't any doubt that he'd come.

I was still holding my breath when he relaxed back into the sofa, and then lifted his hand up to his mouth and licked his thumb. For absolutely no reason I could give you that was so erotic that I must have made a sound, or moved, because his head snapped around and he was staring right at me before I could pretend to be asleep. I can see it incredibly clearly even now: his hand still poised over his head, thumb down, his eyes intent on me with just a hint of their blueness in the dim light.

In the long, long moment of silence, I was suddenly aware of all the sleep noises around me, and especially of Vanessa, breathing against my neck. Then he

198

smiled and stood up off the sofa. In the light from the hall I could see the whitish streak on his stomach before he picked up a crumpled napkin from the table and wiped himself off.

He was wearing white underpants and a rucked-up T-shirt, and nothing else. He pulled the T-shirt down and strolled over, somehow managing to make it casual even though he had to step over and around people. When he reached me he didn't ask, he didn't hesitate to give me a chance to say no, he just knelt down in the tiny space by my legs, and unzipped my trousers.

I squeaked and he lifted his head, then his eyebrow, and pointed to Vanessa. I stilled, although not because it was a real threat—if I'd pushed him away, Vanessa would have woken up and in the confusion I could have got everything sorted out and fastened up with no one the wiser. But he was offering me an excuse, and I took it. Even now I can't really tell you why, other than the general male reason that it *is* difficult to turn down sex when it's free and right there, and you're already revved up.

And, further in my defense, I still maintain Daedra had done *something*.

He folded the front of my trousers out of the way, and untangled me from my underwear with equal efficiency—he must have had a lot of practice. It wasn't easy because I was hard and even the surprise of having him see me and walk over hadn't taken much of the edge off. For a moment he just held me lightly, then he glanced up at me; it was an odd relief to see him smiling slightly.

Then he bent down and took me in his mouth.

I watched for a few seconds, but it was far too unsettling so I closed my eyes and concentrated on keeping very still and very quiet. If anyone had woken up and seen us, my life at work would've been hell for the next few weeks. Worse than hell, and it would *never* have been forgotten—never. There was Vanessa, too, still squashed up between me and the wall. She moved a couple of times, and that managed to be stomach-crampingly terrifying and a turn-on at the same time. The human nervous system can be a funny thing. I could smell her, and feel her warmth and softness, and in a way it wasn't that hard to forget whose mouth was down there.

Who am I kidding? I never forgot for a second, because it felt so damn dangerous. Not that I actually imagined he'd hurt me, but the simple fact of him being that close while I was so vulnerable was, to choose a word that probably isn't strong enough, unnerving.

The only practical difference from normal was that his mouth was bigger than a woman's and occasionally I could feel the rasp of stubble against my skin. Other than that, it was a really good blowjob. I've not been with many women who could take me all the way down—I'm not boasting about size, I'm just saying it must be even harder than it looks, speaking as someone who's never tried it—and he did it easily. He didn't touch me anywhere else with his hands, which I appreciated.

199

Nor did he mess around or try to drag it out, which was reasonable enough because, as I said, there were people waking up pretty regularly. I doubt that he particularly wanted to get caught either.

You know how when you're desperate for time to pass it crawls, and when you want something to last it rushes past in an eyeblink? Well, the four or five minutes he was kneeling over me felt like an hour. Coming seemed to last forever, because I was concentrating so hard on not moving—every time I thought it was done and started to relax there was another kick of feeling. I'm sure that in reality it was the same length as any other orgasm, but it seemed like five minutes of squeezing my eyes shut and clenching my teeth and fists.

And then it was all over and I opened my eyes. Without a word, he stood up, grinned, and made his way back to the sofa. I managed to get zipped up again without waking Vanessa. It took a while one-handed, and by the time I'd finished he'd fallen asleep. It took me rather longer, mostly because I was thinking about the consequences and worrying about . . . well, various things, the main one being, would I still have a job on Monday morning? Because it had been, technically, sex, and the Para—I assume by now you've guessed who it was—doesn't have sex with people on his team unless he's planning to sack them. We all know that, and although I couldn't think of anything I'd done that would piss him off that badly, it wasn't a nice feeling.

Then I was vaguely concerned that if he didn't want to sack me he might want to do it again. I have no idea why I thought that, because one of the things I do know about his sex life is that repetition isn't a big feature, or it didn't used to be. Maybe back then I didn't know that. In any case, I didn't like the idea of turning him down, although I would have done, no question.

I worried about it off and on all weekend, with Vanessa asking what was wrong and me not being able to tell her, which I remember upset her a lot. We'd been to-gether about three months by then, and it's a tricky time. Then on Monday I walked into the main office, with feet like lead, and there he was, sitting on Sara's desk. They both looked up as I went over, and I wondered if he'd told her.

"Enjoy the party?" he asked, deadpan.

"Yes, it was very good. Thanks." If the punctuation came out a bit odd, Sara didn't seem to notice. "You?"

He smiled. "Fantastic, I thought. One of your best," he added, talking to Sara although he didn't look at her. "Funny, wasn't it, with everyone crashing out like that?"

"I think Daedra put something in the air," Sara said. "Or the punch."

"Probably both," he said, still watching me. "Once in a lifetime thing, anyway."

The relief didn't last long—not wanting to repeat it didn't mean he planned to keep me on the team. His phrasing suddenly sounded ominous. "Can I have a word with you, Para?"

"Of course." He pushed himself off the desk. "After you."

In his office, I waited by the desk while he hung up his jacket and sat down. The senior para badge on the jacket shoulder suddenly looked very obvious. I badly didn't want to mess up my career at that point—it takes time to get over an abrupt dismissal from a team, especially when you've won yourself a good place right out of training.

"Well?" he asked.

"I—have I done something wrong, Para? Because if I have, I'd like to ask for a chance to put it right, whatever it is, before you..."

I stopped. He was looking at me absolutely blankly, and I already felt like an idiot before his face cleared and he grinned. "Have a seat."

"I don't think—"

"Sit," he said, and it wasn't a request.

I did what I was told, wondering if I'd really pissed him off now. Happily, he didn't look annoyed—he pushed his chair back a little and stretched his legs out.

"B-C, do you know why I have a rule about not fucking inside the team?"

I had, and still have, a few suspicions. "Not really, Para."

"It's because it makes my life complicated, and I hate that. I don't want people chasing me around because they refuse to understand that one fuck is one fuck and nothing more. Now, men who are ninety-nine-point-nine-nine percent straight aren't going to start demanding my personal comm, are they?"

It took me a couple of seconds to realize it wasn't a rhetorical question. "*God, no*, Para."

It came out more fervent that I'd intended, and his lips twitched with amusement, which was odd for a moment, thinking that he'd had my cock in his mouth, that I'd come in there. All that stuff about who puts what where and penetration and power dynamics? Complete rubbish.

"So there we are. I happened to hit you on your point-oh-one percent night—no big deal. And I'm certainly not planning to waste a mindfuck application having you permanently unstraightened." He tipped his head back a little, eying me assessingly. "Although if it really was that traumatic, maybe you should ask if they can make you forget it ever happened."

Honestly, what could you say to something like that? At least I spotted that there was no safe answer, and just squirmed where I sat until finally he laughed.

"Don't worry, B-C. Your job's safe, and I won't mention it again." He smiled, not very nicely. "And if you're lucky, I might not even tell Sara."

I could feel myself paling. "Please, Para."

He chuckled, again. "I won't tell her, because I don't want to lose a good investigator to fatal embarrassment. Now, clear off and get back to work."

He never did mention it again, and since I never heard rumors coming back from anyone else later either, I presume he didn't tell Sara or he threatened her with God knows what to keep her quiet.

201

On his part I think it really was just a sudden impulse that he'd followed because he's like that. Intuition, although he'd deny it with his last breath. And once it was done, it was done, for him. He's better at putting things behind him than am. I worried about it on and off for a while, and had a mild sexual identity crisis that must have been very trying for Vanessa because we split up not long afterwards. And then I slowly forgot about it, too.

But, after the day we'd had with our Americans, you can understand why might end up thinking over that particular incident in my life. And why it was or my mind the next day.

The Para had been wrong the evening before. Things got even livelier, and crazier, the next morning.

Durant's lawyers turned up promptly, while I was still taking my coat off in the office I shared with Mistry. They were early enough that Sara hadn't yet arrived The Para had had them directed up to his General Criminal office, and luckily spotted them through the open doorway, and intercepted them before any of the admins could. I think the way I shot out of the place rather startled Mistry, but she didn't comment; she knew we had a case involving a favor for the Bureau of Ad ministrative Departments, and being a sensible person she hadn't asked for any more details.

This time Linden had brought two sharp-suited juniors with him; he and they all looked exhausted but satisfied, and I surmised they'd been working all nigh on something they thought we wouldn't like.

"If you'd called, I could've saved you a journey," the Para said after I showed them in to his office. He didn't offer them a seat. "Noncorporate prisoners have no right to external contact for at least forty-eight hours."

Linden held out his screen. "Here is confirmation of the granting of corporate status to Luke Elliot. Nothing in the accords requires that status to be in place a the time of arrest."

I wondered what the corporate accords had to say about giving corporate status to citizens of other countries, particularly Americans. Knowing the length of the accords, probably enough to choke a horse. If Linden was willing to make that ploy, though, I guessed there would be at least enough doubt to require a forma ruling from the Confederation of European Corporations.

The Para didn't take the screen. "Send it to us, and I'll have one of our specialists go through it and tell me how valid it is."

Linden's good humor didn't slip. "Of course—I expected as much, which is why I'm providing advance notice. But in the interim, I expect full access to my client when we reach the twenty-four-hour mark. Although, I understand that Mr

Elliot still hasn't yet been formally charged with any crime, merely detained here at the request of his own government?"

"We're discussing the best course of action with the American Embassy, yes. It's still possible he'll be released without any charge being made, at least unless we're forced to take a different position."

The threat didn't seem to impress Linden. "And if he isn't charged?"

"He'll be taken directly back to the embassy, as per the movement notification terms of his visa."

"Those terms are, or soon will be, void. Mr. Elliot plans to claim Administration citizenship, and associated rights to protection and immediate asylum, under the relevant immigration articles." Again, Linden offered his screen.

It's one of the few times I've ever seen the Para look entirely nonplussed. I couldn't blame him, because that was pretty much my reaction, too. Partly it was Linden's breezy delivery of the bombshell, and partly because I'd never even heard of such a thing being possible, still less actually happening. All I could think was that if Linden was serious, the Americans were going to blow their fuses so hard the lights would go out in Washington.

The Para rallied faster than I did. "Come back when you can talk to Elliot," he said. "Until then, you're wasting everyone's time."

"Hardly. And we have solid evidence of intent to pursue this course of action. Mr. Elliot discussed it extensively with Mr. Durant in recent weeks." Linden was still holding out the hand screen. When the Para still didn't touch it, he laid it down on the desk very precisely. All our heads turned towards it, as though it were a live weapon. "Copies of these files will be sent to all interested parties. I came in person because I didn't want there to be any doubt as to whether or not I&I had received the information. I'll see you again, later, Para-investigator."

Now I knew why the assistants were there—witnesses.

"What do we do now, Para?" I asked when the lawyers had swept triumphantly away across the general office. On the far side, I saw Sara just arriving, stopping to stare after them as they headed past her towards the lifts.

"We call Turnbull," the Para said.

Edwards arrived at I&I an hour later, looking as polished as ever but with a distinctive whiff of concern competing with his expensive cologne.

"You're serious—they can actually do this?" the Para said when we'd settled down in the office.

"Oh, yes," Edwards said. "Or they can try. The legal instrument they're using has an interesting history. It was passed by one of the smaller pre-Unification countries, and allowed any US citizen to claim asylum and be granted immediate citizenship. Primarily it seems to have been a symbolic protest over some international incident. Certainly, there's little if any case law—and what there is falls under historical access restrictions—but there's no doubt it existed. When the national statute books were combined into Administration law, it somehow made it through the process, and there it is."

"Well, fuck," the Para said. I thought that summed the situation up quite nicely. "Can't the bureau do anything about it?"

"The legislature can be petitioned to change the law, of course, and certainly will be, but it can't be completed by tomorrow. Not without attracting a degree of attention to this case which the bureau cannot tolerate."

"What about the Durant family? Do they know what this bloody Emile boy is doing in their name?"

"Secretary Turnbull has spoken to his father, of course. Unfortunately, Thierry Durant is a very influential figure in the Confederation of European Corporations and, along with various others there, he's of the opinion that the Administration has been encroaching too hard on corporate privilege recently. He isn't known for his willingness to do favors for us."

The Para grunted unhappily. "So he won't rein the idiot in, and she can't make him?"

"That sums the situation up accurately, yes." Edwards sighed. "Our best approach might be persuasion. Perhaps the American boy could be influenced to consider the ramifications of the situation. The best solution is that he simply returns voluntarily whence he came, embarrassing nobody."

"Cardine said he seemed quite adamant about not keeping his mouth shut," the Para said.

And that was when I had my idea.

"There is one thing," I said tentatively. Everyone turned to look at me, which I admit tends to fluster me. "It's probably a long shot, odds are it wouldn't work, but you have contacts over in Psychoprogramming, don't you, Para? You could—"

"No fucking way," he said, with definite emphasis.

Now, to this day I don't know any concrete reason why the suggestion to approach Psychoprogramming should have made the Para react so strongly, beyond the reasons any sensible person would have for staying away from them. Normally, I wouldn't argue with a rejection like that. But that time I decided to stick to my guns.

"They don't want Elliot back because he's threatening to tell everyone he's had a relationship with Durant, right? Well, suppose there was nothing to tell? Suppose he'd forgotten the whole affair completely?"

Memory alteration has been a feature of one or two of our cases, most notably the one involving the immersive virtual reality corporation SimTech, where it was used to provide an alibi for a murderer. And, of course, Psychoprogramming has

204

techniques to treat the more recalcitrant and recidivist resisters. So it was possible Elliot could be made to forget, although I didn't know exactly how possible.

Edwards certainly looked interested in the suggestion. "The Americans would have to agree to it, of course," he said. "But otherwise...I don't see why we couldn't pursue it."

"It's the quickest way, Para," I said. "Maybe the only way, in the time we have. At least we could see if it's feasible."

He didn't look any happier, but after a moment he nodded. "All right. We can do that."

Unusually, he didn't ask Sara to make the call for him. The first number he tried was busy. After a few seconds, he muttered something I didn't catch, and tried another one.

A stocky, dark-haired man I didn't recognize answered right away. "Hello?" he said. I couldn't tell from his voice or his expression whether he was just surprised to see the Para, couldn't remember his name, or didn't know who the hell he was.

"Hello, Seiden. It's—"

"I know who it is. From I&I—Senior Para-investigator...Toreth, right? Which is originally a Welsh word, you know. Means 'abundance.' As in, I smell an abundance of bullshit approaching."

"Welsh? Why the hell do you know that?" the Para asked.

"Didn't anyone ever tell you we know everything over here?" Seiden grinned, showing some startlingly uneven teeth. "No, not really. We had some deep scanning passed over to us not long back, resisters using Welsh to communicate amongst themselves. Not something we have references for, so it was a hell of a job. Soon as I saw the word in the linguistic mapping buildup, I thought of you. And your girl with the memory implants—someone did nice work on her, I remember that. Did you ever find out who it was?"

"Yes. One of your lot, ex-employee gone freelance."

"Really? I never heard. Still, not surprising it didn't get back down to us, I suppose." He smiled again. "So. You must want something."

The Para grinned back. He always prefers it when people get to the point. "How much can you make someone forget, and how quickly?"

Seiden snorted. "Don't try and make a mystery out of it. I don't do this for love, you know. Just tell me what results you're after."

"I want a prisoner to forget a relationship ever happened. Someone he's known personally for several months."

"Personally and intimately," I added over the Para's shoulder.

"And I need it done by...tomorrow afternoon. By this afternoon, ideally."

Seiden shook his head immediately. "It'll be quicker and more fun for everyone if you take 'em out round the back of I&I and shoot 'em in the head. Because

205

what you'd get out of the other end here would be about as lively. Or he'd remember it all in a week flat."

Edwards, offscreen for Seiden, raised his eyebrows and the Para nodded. "But he would forget it for that week?" the Para asked.

"Maybe, give or take." Seiden shrugged. "That sort of crude blocking isn't very predictable."

We perked up collectively, all presumably thinking the same thing. As long as it *did* last a week, that would be enough for us to ping-pong Elliot out of our hands, and hopefully out of the Administration. There's nothing like a few thousand miles of water to put the stamp on a problem being someone else's.

The Para leaned forwards. "Listen, Seiden. Is there any chance you could do me a big favor? I need—"

"Sorry, no can do."

"I didn't even—"

"No, and you didn't need to. Any outside work has to come through the proper channels. After the trouble we had with Ext-Sec last year, they clamped down big time. Either genuine consent—*genuine*—or a waiver. And not one someone scribbled on the back of a napkin, either. From Justice, marked for PP."

"I'll get a waiver," the Para said with absolute confidence.

"Ange?" Seiden smirked, like he knew a lot more than the Para. "Good luck, there. She hasn't been singing your praises for a while."

"I don't need Ange for this. Save me a space."

"Hah! I wish I had one. You wouldn't believe the number of resisters coming through here in the last few months. If the stingy bastards upstairs would pay, we'd all be on double overtime."

"So," the Para said to Edwards when Seiden's image disappeared. "Do you want to risk it?"

"We'll need to float the idea with the secretary and our Americans colleagues, first," Edwards said. "I'll talk to her—I'm sure she'll agree, if the Americans do, too. See if you can persuade them it's our best shot. But I want you to be honest about the possible consequences to the boy."

The American Embassy put us through to Cardine and Ruiz right away; I imagined they'd been waiting rather impatiently for news. Somewhat to my surprise, Cardine at least seemed moderately familiar with Psychoprogramming's techniques.

"You have the same thing over there?" the Para asked.

"Similar. It isn't approved for general psychiatric practice—true mental healthfulness has to come from sincere repentance and the will to change, without any shortcuts. But...there are cases where there's a problem that can usefully be addressed first by a specialist. Deep-seated reorientation of disordered thinking, to provide clarity of thought."

"Then you know there are risks, but it can be extremely effective."

"I'd certainly like to talk to your own specialists about it. Luke's safety is very important."

"Of course," I said. "We understand that. It's our priority, too."

"But...there are other factors to be accounted for, and some of them could be considered almost equally important."

There was a brief, whispered offscreen discussion with someone I presumed to be Ruiz, then Cardine reappeared.

"Subject to be allowed to speak with the technicians carrying out the procedure, we agree to try it. Do you want me to certify that he needs the treatment?"

"That wouldn't hurt," the Para said. He sounded pleased by the idea, although I knew it wouldn't be enough for Psychoprogramming without a real waiver. Maybe it could help with Justice. "Send it over, and I'll let you know when we're ready to proceed."

Shortly afterwards, Edwards returned from my office, where he'd gone to call his boss, and confirmed that the plan had Secretary Turnbull's blessing.

"I have to go back to the bureau, to speak to some people in person. But unless you hear otherwise, assume everything is okay."

I'd half expected the Para to leave the exact arrangements to the bureau, but instead he called Psychoprogramming back himself. When you're doing a favor for someone, the more they have to help you with it, the less they owe at the end of the day.

A woman answered, on voice comms only. They can be a secretive lot over at Psychoprogramming.

"Hello, Ange," the Para said.

"Toreth? Well, well. I haven't seen you over here for a long while."

"You know how it is. Keeping busy."

"We're all that. I don't suppose you're calling to ask me out for lunch again, at last, are you?"

It was only then, rather stupidly, that I made the connection between this Ange at Psychoprogramming, and the name of someone with whom the Para had had the occasional lunch assignation. Everyone in the team, at least those of us who'd been around a while, knew about her. It wasn't all that surprising I hadn't made the link—as far as I knew, he hadn't seen her for three or four years. I wondered if that was why he'd been reluctant to get Psychoprogramming involved, although to be honest, the idea of him caring that much about it seemed out of character.

"'Fraid not," the Para said. "I need someone to do a quick mindfuck for me. Today. It's very important."

"Sorry," she said, not sounding it in the least. "There's no chance. And before you say anything else, do you have any idea how many times a day someone tells us that their case is the most critical one ever in the whole history of the Administration?"

The Para sighed. "Pity. Secretary Turnbull is going to be very disappointed. But I'm sure the bureau will understand."

"The—" I wished I could see her face. After a couple of seconds, she said, "Well, if it's for the *bureau.* Come on, be serious. Why can't you just put in a proper application, like everyone else?"

"I am being serious. This is a favor for the Bureau of Administrative Departments."

This time her voice sharpened. "You'd better be able to back that up, Toreth. I always said, I can tell when you're lying—your lips move."

"We'll have a waiver from Justice, with a bureau request ID on it."

"Don't think I won't check that," Ange said.

"Feel free. But do it when we're there. We don't have much time."

"I—let me check the schedules." Seconds passed, then she said, "Harrier can probably squeeze it in. I'll tell him to expect you ASAP. But, so help me, if this isn't on the level..."

"Can we sedate the prisoner to bring him over?" the Para asked.

"I'll ask Harrier to send over the prep drugs, including the sedatives. But don't mess with anything on the list, or the dosages. And if you delay bringing your prisoner over here, some of them can't be redosed quickly."

She sounded like she'd said that to a lot of people. I have to admit, beyond convicted resisters, I had little idea where Psychoprogramming found its subjects. They do some interrogations for us, and Seiden had mentioned Ext-Sec. I dare say there are other divisions, probably including ones I've never heard of, which need their specialist services.

"Don't worry," the Para said. "We'll be there. And thanks, Ange. You're a real diamond."

"Hm," she said, and cut the connection.

That left us just one problem.

"It could be a hell of a job getting a waiver from Justice," the Para said. "Bureau or not. They hate anything where they can't just slap a name on the standard form and send it back. I should've told Edwards to get on it as soon as the bureau gives him the final okay."

That day, I got a demonstration of what the Bureau of Administrative Departments really can do. The waiver arrived while we were still deciding the best way to go about getting it. I don't think we've had a level three waiver for the least complicated case you can imagine returned so promptly. Not even returned, in this case, since we hadn't asked for it, yet. Secretary Turnbull clearly had an eye on Psychoprogramming procedures, too.

208

"You can take him over there, B-C," the Para said once he'd read through the waiver. "No need to bring him back here afterwards. If Mindfuck bollocks it up, the embassy can glue the pieces back together." He nodded at his screen. "The woman you want to talk to is the admin to the head of division, Angela Morris. I'll send her a quick note to let her know you're coming."

Now it was my turn to balk at the Psychoprogramming name. "Me, Para? On my own?"

"Why not? You need to make a few useful contacts if you're going to get on around here, right?" Shifting the visit to me was apparently improving his mood no end. "And you'll like her—blonde, and she has great legs. Just your type. Got a vacancy at the moment?"

"Not right now, I'm afraid, Para."

As anyone in the General Criminal coffee room would tell you, I have a reputation for serially dating a lot of pretty women. Interchangeable leggy blondes, as Sara calls them, which I suppose I have to admit is true enough. I'm hardly going to deny that I can attract beautiful women, am I? The less appealing part is the "serially." I've never had much trouble getting into relationships, but staying in them seems to be harder.

The truth is, I care about my job more than I care about keeping a long-term relationship. I've broken up with several girlfriends simply because of the hours I work, not helped by the unexpected interruptions and calls. And one who said I did nothing but talk about work, and whose parting suggestion was I should be dating the Para, not her. That may well have been true—the former part, not the latter.

The job is hard on all of us, in terms of outside relationships. If there's work to be done, we have to do it, whether it's convenient or not. Even amongst the investigators, it's pretty common for people to end up pairing off inside the division. The paras, too, for those who have partners. I don't think I know of many interrogators with steady relationships.

People inside the division understand. There's a lot of misconceptions about the things that go on here, and after a while it gets tedious sorting them out with outsiders. I make an effort to keep up with friends from university and meet people away from here, but that's what it is—an effort.

Nowadays, I rarely even think about the fact that when I walk into a roomful of ordinary people, there's a moment of silence. My family approves of what I do—it's a respectable career—but even with them there's an edge of reserve around me that they didn't have before I started wearing the uniform.

I can understand it, I suppose, if I think about my own instinctive reaction to even a joking suggestion that I might date someone from Psychoprogramming. It's hard to imagine coming home and kissing someone popularly known as a mind-fucker, and asking how their day went. But who knows, perhaps there are people working there who think exactly the same thing about I&I.

Even at I&I—or at one of Daedra's parties—I don't think I've ever seen anyone as drugged out of his mind as Luke Elliot. Not and still be able to stand, which he could, albeit rather unsteadily.

"Try not to talk to him too much, hm?" the psychoprogrammer Ms. Morris had found for us instructed over the comm. "Or around him. They're very suggestible like that, and it's easy to implant something you don't want in their little heads."

So, more or less in silence, Cardine and I loaded Elliot onto a prisoner transport trolley and took him over to Psychoprogramming via one of the discreet undercover routes.

Security is tighter there than at I&I. Ordinary citizens have no access at all, so there's no symbolic statue out at the front of the building (I wonder what they'd choose if there were?) and no large reception area. Angela Morris met us at the entrance. She hustled us all past the guards and over to a lift with barely time for a hello. Incidentally, the Para was right—she does have very nice legs. With Agent Cardine there, too, this was rather the day for it.

When the lift stopped, someone was waiting for us in a dark blue outfit like a combination of a para's uniform and a doctor's scrubs. Something that was different from I&I was that instead of an anonymous rank badge, he wore a photo ID which identified him as Dr. James Harrier. I suppose Psychoprogramming doesn't worry so much about employees being recognized by former guests.

The treatment rooms at Psychoprogramming were nothing like I&I interrogation rooms. Down in the I&I psych specialist section they have a range of neural scanners, but nothing to touch the impressively large, shiny pieces of equipment and attached monitoring and analysis room that Harrier took us to.

Harrier had the callous briskness of someone who generally deals with people drugged into near or total unconsciousness. With a nod, he indicated the flat bed of a scanner, with a serious array of restraint straps on it.

"You can put him there."

The three of us moved him together. Normally, Harrier informed us, they have orderly-guards, but we'd asked to keep the number of witnesses to a minimum. With Harrier there, we didn't need the help, anyway. Tall, heavily built, and gray-haired, he looked more like a retired rugby player than either a doctor or my pre-conceptions of a mindfucker.

"I'll be as quick as I can," Harrier said. "But afterwards, it's important that you don't get him too close to any triggers. New memories are fragile, hm? Normally we'd run reinforcing sessions over a week, maybe more, but it's possible to do some of that follow-up without the kit. I'll give you the protocol. But keep away from the old memories, and let the new ones settle in, and they might even stick."

"Before we start," Cardine said as we finished securing the straps, "I need to talk with you. I have some questions about the process, and a couple suggestions. I don't know how feasible they are—I haven't dealt with any equipment quite this sophisticated."

Seiden might not be working in the place for love, but Harrier practically glowed at the compliment to his department. "We try to keep ourselves on the leading edge of the technology. Come this way and I'll show you the control suite. We can talk there."

That left me alone to watch the prisoner. Not a very challenging task, as he was now restrained as well as doped. I wandered around a little, inspecting the equipment but being very careful not to touch. I have only the vaguest ideas of the capabilities of Psychoprogramming. I&I doesn't hold open days on the interrogation levels, but another Int-Sec department would have no trouble getting hold of a copy of the *Procedures and Protocols for Interrogation.* Psychoprogramming, on the other hand, keeps everything tightly internal. I think that's one reason some I&I interrogators see them as a threat to us—we can't accurately judge what they *can* do.

I was checking over the medical monitors—one thing I did recognize—when out of the corner of my eye I saw Luke Elliot move. His head flopped one way, then the other, and then his eyes opened. They rolled, unfocused and not tracking together, until finally he seemed to register my presence.

Elliot blinked, very slowly. "Where'm I?"

"This is—" I hesitated, debating. Very likely he'd never heard of the place, but Psychoprogramming is hardly a reassuring name. "It's a hospital."

"Oh." Long pause. "I'm sick?"

"Yes." I took a few steps closer. "Just relax and try to sleep. They're going to make you better."

Which was even true, in a way. Certainly, if the plan worked out, then he'd have a far healthier future ahead of him than an inevitable prison sentence was likely to bring. That seemed a ludicrous punishment for stubbornness and a doomed holiday romance.

He licked his lips. "Sometimes...I feel sick. Emile said it didn't matter. Wasn't true. But. If I'm here I guess they must be right."

His eyelids closed again. I stood watching him, in case he woke again. A minute later, Harrier and Cardine came out of the monitoring room together.

"It's well within the level of manipulation covered in the waiver," Harrier was saying. "And a lot safer. I don't see any problems with it."

"You go ahead, then."

"Okay—with the proviso that I still can't guarantee it'll stick, long-term."

"You let us worry about that." Cardine had the kind of patronizingly reassuring smile that I'm sure is part of the curriculum for psychiatrists. "I can handle the fol-low-up, don't worry."

I raised my eyebrows at them.

"New approach to the program," Harrier said. He turned to Cardine again. "That's the kind of lateral thinking we like. Pity you don't work for us—you'd fit in perfectly here."

Her expression frosted over right away. "I don't think so."

Ruiz arrived at Psychoprogramming while the boy was still in the scanner. He joined Cardine and me where we were sitting and observing. Psychoprogramming in progress is possibly the most boring thing I've even seen. There are no visible effects at all, barring a lot of wavy lines on screens. I can't say that I like watching interrogations, but at least something happens.

"Everything working out okay?" Ruiz asked. "We're still counting down to this deadline for the lawyer."

"Almost done," Harrier said. "I'm just running the final checks, and easing him up. Believe me, the very last thing you want to do at this point is wake someone up too fast. One good sleep cycle is worth hours of artificial reinforcement, hm?"

Ruiz nodded. "Just as long as it's pretty soon. The embassy needs to know if this kid is going to be claiming his Administration citizenship, or not."

I wondered what would happen if he did. Not much over here, presumably— the Bureau of Administrative Departments would press very hard to keep news of it out of the media, and while theoretically Durant's father might have the clout to oppose them, he had equally as much incentive to keep it quiet. Even if he were willing to support his son's plan, he had no reason to trumpet an association with Americans, even one who wanted to defect.

Fifteen minutes later, Luke Elliot was sitting up on the scanning bed of the ma-chine that had just played copy and paste with his memories, feet dangling. He still looked very dazed, like everything that passed through his brain managed to get lost and take a few unnecessary detours on the way to his conscious mind.

"Do you understand what I'm saying to you?" Cardine asked. "Luke?"

He stared at Cardine for a few seconds, then said, "That's my name, ma'am."

Ruiz turned to Harrier. "Is this normal?"

"It's a common side effect of the accelerated reconditioning program," Harrier said. "Nothing we could do to avoid it, not inside the time constraints you set us, I'm afraid. Not much we can do to fix it, either. We could try; odds are we'll just make it worse, though."

"And will he recover?" Ruiz asked.

"Oh, a lot of them do. With luck, a few hours should make a big difference. Might take a few days to clear completely, might take a few weeks, hm? If it isn't gone in a month or two, whatever's residual is probably permanent." Harrier shrugged a little. "I did warn your colleague."

Ruiz and Cardine conferred in low voices. "Take him back to I&I, until we're sure?" Cardine suggested.

Ruiz nodded. "And if necessary, we can maybe invent some kinda accident? Head injury—that would explain the confusion."

"It's sympathetic." Cardine nodded. "And hard to prove it isn't true. Traumatic amnesia can cover a lot of issues."

Elliot was looking around the room, not with any particular curiosity, but as though it were a reflex movement of his head and eyes. When he spotted me, he smiled.

I'll admit, I felt a little twinge at that point. Cardine's model of mental health might have called what happened at Psychoprogramming a type of emergency medical treatment, but mine certainly didn't. Despite the technical breach of his movement notification restrictions, the boy wasn't really a criminal. Certainly not a corporate sab, or a major fraudster, or a resister working to bring down the Administration. Yet the Administration and the American Embassy, between them, were using the justice system to do something that was outside the strict definition of enforcing the law.

My personal squeamishness was just that, though—mine. I know full well that sometimes the safety and prosperity of the Administration requires us to take action on the margins of legality. Not as vigilantes, or without supervision, of course. But we have to trust that the politically focused parts of the Administration, like the Bureau of Administrative Departments, have the best interests of Europe and all its citizens at heart, and that sometimes things have to be done which, however distasteful we might find them as individuals, are for the greater good.

It's what will keep the Administration safe. It's what will stop anyone from ever again being able to repeat the atrocities which devastated Europe once before.

The I&I main prisoner processing area is fairly large, but it's sparsely laid out, to allow free line of sight for the cameras and the guards, and to avoid giving prisoners who might try to make a break for it awkward places to hide or easy weapons to hand. So, as we were halfway across the space, I had no trouble spotting Emile Durant and Linden as the doors to the main reception access lift opened.

They had an I&I guard escorting them, but of course I remembered right away what Harrier had said about not damaging the memory blocks by stimulating the real, hidden memories. Raising my voice would've attracted attention, so I moved to block Durant's view of Elliot.

"Trouble," I whispered to Ruiz, and tried with a quick, subtle jerk of my head to indicate the newcomers. He cottoned on fast, and put his hand on Elliot's arm, steering him away.

"We gotta go back out a moment," he said. "We've forgotten something important."

"Okay, Mr. Ruiz."

We almost got away with it, then I heard him from across the room.

"Luke!" Ignoring a warning hand on his shoulder from Linden, Durant hurried across the processing area. I saw the guards by the entrances suddenly paying closer attention. "Are you okay?"

There was no question that, despite the confusion, Elliot recognized him. For a moment, I was sure that the plan had failed. But when Durant got up close, Elliot actually cringed away. "Don't touch me!"

"I—" Durant stopped, bewildered. "Luke? Luke, what's wrong?"

"What's wrong?" Elliot's eyebrows rose. No one else had pulled such a strong reaction from him, and I still expected the Psychoprogramming treatment to break down at any moment. "How can you even ask that, after what you did to me? Just looking at you—what are you doing here?"

"Waiting for your twenty-four hours to be up. I tried to see you before, but it's the rules in this damn place. We were doing everything we could to get to you, promise. I'm sorry. But you can come with us, now."

"Come *with* you? Are you crazy? Why?"

"We talked about it, Luke." He took a step forwards, stopping when Luke backed up. "Don't you remember? About the immigration law I found, and claiming Administration citizenship?"

"Claiming—" For a moment, a small frown broke through Elliot's set expression. "I don't...why would I want..."

Cardine stepped forwards. "We're finished here, Mr. Durant. Tell him, Luke. You *know* what you want. You have faith, and a clear mind, and someone to watch over you. Now you want—what?"

"I want to go home, to my mom and dad. And...I don't ever want to see him again. You again." Elliot nodded, sounding surer. "You're—you need help, Emile.

214

What we did... it makes me sick to my stomach, but I know you tried to be a friend and—and I'll pray for you."

Durant spun around. "What the hell have you done to him?" He looked between us, from me to the two Americans. "What have you *done*?"

"We talked with Luke," Cardine said. "That's all."

"I don't believe you. Luke, did they give you anything?" Elliot looked away, refusing to meet his gaze, and Durant turned to Linden instead. "What can we do? There has to be something!"

It was with a certain degree of relief that I saw the lift doors open and the Para step out. I had no idea how he knew we were back, or that there was trouble in progress. I doubted it was just a lucky coincidence, though, because he started walking towards our little group without a break in his stride.

"Is there a problem, here?" he said when he came up. He was looking at Linden and his client, but I could feel the question aimed at me.

"No problem at all, Para," I said. "Everything's fine."

"Then he'll be ready to go back to the embassy, right?" the Para asked.

It didn't sound like much of a question, and the Americans clearly noticed that, too. They exchanged glances, then Cardine shrugged. "I guess so."

Without breaking eye contact with the lawyer, the Para beckoned over the nearest guards. "Mr. Linden, Luke Elliot is being processed out of I&I custody and back into the capable hands of his national embassy. There's been no charge, and so he has no need for a lawyer. And you have no excuse to be here."

The guards had arrived, looking expectantly at the Para. The threat the Para had made the day before was still hanging in the air, and he didn't need to repeat it.

"Luke," Durant said. He craned his neck, trying to catch Elliot's eye. "Luke, *please*. Listen to me. Whatever they've done to you—I know this isn't what you really want. Don't you remember how unhappy you were?"

Ruiz and Cardine were shepherding Elliot away. When Durant tried to follow them, the Para stepped in front of him and put his hand on his chest. Durant looked down, almost comically surprised. Anger quickly chased it away, though.

"Don't you dare touch me!"

"Mr. Durant. I know who you are. We both know who your father is. But you're not at corporate headquarters now—you're in the processing area of the Investigation and Interrogation Division." The Para leaned forwards a little, his next words soft and very deliberate. "Give me just one more reason, and I'll show you what that fucking means."

There's a power to the division's name when it's spelled out in full, and in this case it broke through Durant's determination. He swallowed, and glanced around. "Linden?"

"I think we should go, Emile."

215

"Good choice," the Para said, although he was still looking into Durant's face, refusing to relax the tension until Durant took a few steps backwards. Then he nodded to the guards. "Show them the way out."

A definite crowd was gathering down in the processing area as Durant and Linden were escorted away. We'd kept the existence of our unusual visitors quiet for longer than I'd believed would be possible, but the confrontation in the processing area, with Ruiz, Cardine, and Elliot in plain sight, was too public to go without notice. *There are Americans in the building* would be flying around the gossip networks and already people were finding an excuse to pass through processing and try to catch a glimpse.

Rather than stand around like a waxwork display, we went back to the lockdown suite to wait for a car to take them back to the American Embassy. We put Elliot in one of the cells, to let him settle down again.

"Thanks for the rescue," Ruiz said to the Para. "You were quick off the mark."

"Bevan let me know you were back and Linden was in the building," the Para said. "Seemed like a bad combination."

"No harm done, fortunately," Cardine said.

On the monitor Elliot looked quite calm, sitting on the bed with his hands tucked under his thighs, just waiting.

"You're lucky that didn't mess up the blocks," the Para said.

"There aren't any blocks," Cardine said. "Some confusion over details, maybe, but not lost time or substitutions. I figured in the end it wasn't necessary for him to forget, so long as he recognized the sinfulness of his actions."

"That was your suggestion to Harrier?" I asked.

"Yes. Luke was brought up well, by good people. Maybe he strayed for a while, but in the long run it's still better for him to know he did wrong. All I asked Dr. Harrier was for that understanding to be strengthened, and to quiet down the lies he'd been told." She smiled. "To straighten up his moral compass, you could say."

The Para appeared reluctantly impressed. "Neat. And easier to put together than a damn great memory block, I should think. Psychoprogramming are going to be very pleased with themselves."

"I'll talk to Secretary Turnbull, for sure," Ruiz said. "Ask her to include Dr. Harrier in the commendations."

Sara arrived, eventually, bringing Edwards with her. I expect if anyone had asked she would've had a sound reason for not leaving it to security, but in reality

I'm sure she just wanted to know what was going on. She's incurably nosy, which is one of the reasons why she's such an excellent admin.

We all shook hands, saying goodbye.

"We really appreciate all your help," Cardine said to me, and clasped my hand warmly. It was all very transatlantic entente cordiale, and I hoped that Secretary Turnbull would be suitably pleased by the outcome.

Edwards took them away—escorted by a guard that Sara had thoughtfully brought with her so she could stay behind with the Para and me—and I don't suppose that I'm ever likely to meet them again.

"Well, they weren't too bad to work with, in the end, were they?" I said when the door closed behind them.

The Para turned towards me sharply. "Did you lose your bloody watch, B-C? Why the hell were they here with Elliot at the same time as that fucking lawyer?"

My mouth went dry, from the shock of his abrupt change of manner as much as anything. "They—I'm sorry, Para."

"I told you Elliot should go straight to the embassy. Didn't I tell you that?"

"Yes, but—" I hesitated, and undoubtedly I should've stopped right there, but sometimes the need to justify the unjustifiable is overwhelming. "There were some side effects from the procedure, and Agent Cardine suggested Elliot could recover in—"

"*Cardine* suggested? Jesus fucking Christ." His hands flexed, and I had to force myself not to take a step back. "Why the hell were you listening to that crazy bitch? You're supposed to be a senior investigator. When I put you in charge of something, I expect you to take charge of it and *keep* charge."

"Yes, Para, of course. I'm sorry."

"You're bloody lucky that Cardine is a mindfucker at heart. If there had been a load of fresh memory blocks for Durant to blow away right in front of that loud-mouth lawyer, then Turnbull would be looking to have someone's balls for it, and I'd be giving her yours."

"Yes, Para. And you'd be right to. It won't happen again, I promise."

He stared at me hard, his expression as cold as I'd ever seen it on a feed from an interrogation, until I felt myself start to sweat. There's something about being down in the underground levels at I&I that can be very unpleasant if you become acutely aware of it. The claustrophobic breathlessness had me firmly by the throat by the time the Para finally relented.

"Good." He nodded. "Well, since there wasn't any lasting damage done, I won't have to take it any further."

"Thank you, Para." My heart was thumping hard, with relief and leftover adrenaline. Like I said, I've never seen him really lose his temper, and I'm anxious to keep it that way.

"Clear the booking for this place," the Para said to Sara. "If it shows up on the

217

budget for an hour longer than it should, Tillotson is bound to spot it and try to bill the bloody bureau."

Sara had somehow melted invisibly into the background during the reprimand; it was an impressive camouflage trick in a small and simply furnished office.

"Right away. At least it's all over, now," she added.

The Para grunted, but I knew he wouldn't take out any residual bad temper on her. "It should've been over yesterday. Instead we get all this palaver, mindfuckers everywhere, and why? Because he was screwing someone with a cock?" The Para shook his head. "I'm not surprised you forgot how to tell your arse from your elbow, B-C. I said it before—they're all mad. Completely fucking mad."

And that was pretty much that.

We went back upstairs to pick up our regular cases without even an IIP to be finished off or a file to submit to Justice. The Durant family lawyers made a discreet fuss over the next few days, or so I heard via Sara, but there wasn't much they could do. Elliot was back in the embassy, and then very shortly after that on a plane home to America. I have no idea what happened to him there, but a few weeks later, the promised Bureau of Administrative Departments commendations appeared on our records, so Secretary Turnbull, at least, must have been pleased.

All in all, it was one of the oddest cases I've been involved with at I&I—no major crime, no arrest or conviction, and yet of great political importance and delivering immense kudos for us. Certainly, it beat all records for the amount of high-level unofficial investment in the outcome of a non-case, Administration, corporate, and foreign. Just one more example of how interesting, and strange, life at I&I can be.

Printed in the United States
216823BV00002B/17/P

9 781934 081112